Emma's Fury

By

Linda Rainier

Copyright

First paperback edition December 2018

Cover Photography & Design by Ken Irons

ISBN: 978-0-9600229-1-5 (Paperback)
ISBN: 978-0-9600229-0-8 (Hard Bound)
ISBN: 978-0-9600229-2-2 (EBook)

Acknowledgements

I never really thought that the whole book writing process would be simple. In fact, I knew that it would be a long drawn out progression. But I didn't realize at the beginning, the level to which I would find myself turning to those closest to me for help. So I feel the need to thanks those individuals who have been vital in seeing me through this adventure.

Of course, I must start with my loving and insanely understanding, husband, Maurice. You have offered a wealth of emotional support in the book writing process and in life as a whole. You have been at my side through the roughest of times and I am looking forward to many years of joy with you.

I wanted to thank my father, Steven Karels, for helping with the numerous rounds of rough drafts and troubleshooting. Much thanks goes out to Ken Irons and Dylan Walker, for their tireless work on the photography and the design of my cover. It is awe-inspiring to see an idea develop into fruition, becoming something that I am proud to call my own. Thank you to Brian Tedesco, who helped with the many rounds of editing as well as answering all of my questions.

Finally, I want to dedicate this book to my mother, Diane Karels. An amazing woman, she truly believed in me and thought that I was capable of accomplishing anything. Through thick and thin she loved fiercely. So it is only natural that my first and most prized book be dedicated to a wild, kooky, sometimes crazy woman, who gave incredible hugs. I will forever miss you mom.

Table of Contents

Prologue

In a desolate time before the Golden Age, the god
Uranus, god of the sky, ruled over the Heavens and the
Earth. He was a cruel and unjust god. The world in its
mere infancy was a place of dark calamity. Along with his
wife Gaia they birthed many offspring, and their children
became gods and goddesses of their domains: the oceans
and fresh waters, of remembrances and time, the heavenly
light and the bright blue light of day, as well as wisdom and
law. Uranus also fathered the Titans and giants. They were
wholly wild and monstrous beasts that preyed upon man.

The youngest of their children, Cronus, wished to
overthrow his father and take the universe for his own.
With the help of his mother, Cronus ambushes and
wounds Uranus deeply. As his blood seeped into the
ground, three maidens arose: Alecto, Megaera, and
Tisiphone. They were to be the avenging spirits of the
world and protectors of justice. All in existence, gods and
humans, grew to fear their names. They were as swift and
evenhanded in their judgment as they were unyielding in
their pursuit of offenders. Climbing up from the cavernous
depths of Erebus, they travel the world around in a
merciless hunt for their prey. The poor sinful souls, weak
and weary from fatigue, often would be driven to madness

until they were left with the only option of taking their own lives.

As time passed even the great god, Cronus, was toppled by his own son, Zeus. An epic battle was waged between the Primeval and the Olympian gods. As they were defeated, Cronus and the Titans were imprisoned in the depths of Tartarus, the lowest and most impenetrable level of the Underworld. There they languished and suffered, away from the Earth and the light of day. Their defeat and confinement left the world under the domain of the Olympian gods. The strife and anguish of man continued unabated, and the Fury hunted those found guilty of oath-breaking and of murdering one's own family members. Residing in the realm of Hades, they oversaw the penitence of the cursed souls.

But even the gods themselves were vulnerable to the petty squabbling and conflict that sickens the human race. Their pride, lust, and avarice helped shape the mortal world around them. They were initiators and contributors to much mortal loss and misery.

On a midsummer's day the Olympians flocked together for a great wedding feast. As was their nature, the wine flowed as they argued and ate. Eris, the goddess of discord, was not invited, as she was mischievous and apt to cause trouble. The goddess was offended and she slipped into the banquet, plotting her revenge. As the gods gathered around to observe the ceremony, she tossed a golden apple

2

into the crowd. On the apple she had inscribed *'To the most beautiful.'*

Three of the goddesses stepped forward to claim their prize. Aphrodite, Athena, and Hera bickered and quarreled as to which one it was meant for. Dissatisfied, the three goddesses brought their claims before Zeus to mediate. But He refused to become involved in their dispute and told them to go and be judged by Paris of Troy, who was known for his great fairness.

Each goddess promised Paris something in return for his vote. Victory and wisdom in battle was promised by Athena, Hera offered to make him a king of many great lands, and Aphrodite bribed him with the hand of the most beautiful woman. Upon seeing an image of Helen, Paris chose Aphrodite, infuriating the other two goddesses. His decision leads to the great Trojan War.

During the battle, Eris appeared before Athena, urging her to have her archers shoot and kill Aphrodite. She argued that Athena was the rightful owner of the golden apple. Athena, convinced by Eris, had her bowman unleash their arrows against the goddess Aphrodite, but they were so enthralled by her beauty that all of their shots fell short.

After the war had ended Eris appeared before Aphrodite telling her of Athena's attempt on her life. Enraged, Aphrodite struck the ground three times, summoning the Fury. She pled her case before the three sisters, demanding retribution against Athena, but the Fury, seeing through Eris's ruse, explained that as Aphrodite is an immortal she had nothing to fear from Athena or her men. After denying her petition, they returned to their home in Erebus.

Aphrodite fumed with rage against Athena and the Fury. She believed that because Athena had favored them, offering them homage within Athens itself, they were unfairly influence to her cause. Aphrodite devises a plan to seek vengeance on all of them. She cursed Alecto, causing her to fall in love with King Echetus. A vile and wicked king, he scorched his lands with destruction and murder. And as his people cried out for deliverance from their tormentor, the Fury were called upon to enact justice.

Tisiphone and Megaera chased Echetus through his kingdom and into the vast wilderness. As they cornered their prey, ready to strike, Alecto interceded, halting them. They argued fiercely with one another. Alecto wailed and cursed at her sisters for the sake of her lover, but they would not listen, they would not be swayed. Tisiphone unleashed three poisonous serpents from the layers of her hair. The quick vipers stalked the king, breathing green fumes of madness into his lungs. Driven insane, Echetus threw himself off of a high cliff, landing on the jagged rocks below.

A great melee ensued between the three sisters, and they battled ferociously as the ground quaked beneath their feet.

4

Through the country sides and valleys and mountains they crawled and ripped at their kin. The sisters plummeted into a great caldera and fell down to the Underworld where their raging war continued.

At the end, all three lay mortally wounded by the others. The sisters only weakness was another Fury. Hades heard their cries and found them in a state of near death. As the Fury were creatures of the Underworld, he endeavored to mend their wounds, but failed. He summoned Athena, knowing that they were revered by her, but she could not aid them either.

Finally, Hades offered them a way for the Fury line to continue, but they had to acquiesce to his terms. The Fury had been vital to the existence of man, as their mere presence often dissuaded those from committing crimes. New laws would bind the Fury, making them more malleable to the will of the gods. They would need to offer up half of their strength to the gods, and never again shall a Fury be subject to love, nor could they take on a lover. The Fury would continue to maintain the balance between humans and otherworldly creatures. If called upon by a human for aid, that human, him or herself, must be weighed to prove their worthiness.

Athena urged Hades to allow them some means of defense. Reluctantly he agreed and offered them the protection of the Centimanes, a Titan which had guarded the gates of Tartarus. The sisters begrudgingly agreed, as their lives were slipping away. As they died their bodies turned to dust, which Hades collected in a small ceramic pot. He summoned to him the youngest of the Centimanes, by the name of Gyges. Hades placed the lumbering giant in a deep sleep before touching several of Gyges's arms and transmuting them into stone. Under the great strain of their own weight, the appendages snapped and broke off. Hades collected the pieces of stone and carried them along with the remains of the Fury to the great forge of Hephaestus.

There he threw the ashes of the Fury into the furnace where they were smelted into copper dust. He ground down the stone from Gyges's appendages until it was but a fine powder. Into the deepest well he poured forth the dust from Gyges. If a fierce enough warrior fell in battle, then he could be reborn as a Gyges and protector. Hades followed with the copper dust made from the ashes of the Fury. When a woman lies dying from an unnatural and violent death, she may possess within her enough wrath to rise up and become Death's vengeance.

For much time after that, no Fury walked the earth, and man stopped believing in those gods. As time passed the gods and goddesses wasted away, slipping into the endless void of the forgotten. Then as a new moon rose a trickle of lost souls crawled their way back from the grave. They wandered aimlessly, stumbling about a new and treacherous world. Trapped, they were neither Fury nor human. Others emerged, finding that within them lay a long-forgotten knowledge, and they were heralded as Mothers.

A few tried to bridge the gap between themselves and their Fury nature with disastrous consequences. The black magic ritual pushed them further away from the source of the Fury power and closer to their human nature. Because of this, the survivors found that they could no longer judge humans, nor other Fury.

They developed rigid laws and order amongst themselves that defined one's purpose and place. To fall outside these structures led only to death and a culling of the weak and unruly.

Chapter 1

The thin material of Emma's hooded sweat jacket does little against the biting chill in the air as the harsh New England winter drives many scurrying indoors. The plaguing cold leeches one's heat, biting at the skin and freezing the eyes. The endless night engulfs all sounds in the deafening roar of silence. Shoving her hands deeper into her pockets, Emma shivers. She quickens her pace as she crosses the deserted streets. A remote siren screams in the distance as a long train of brake lights travel up Interstate 93, the thin layer of frost coating the potholed roads of Boston. Dim streetlights cascade barely enough light to illuminate the cracked fissures along the sidewalks. As the sirens dissipate, the immediate area is plunged back into stillness except for the echo of her and David's footfalls.

David's hulking frame is covered by his thick gray overcoat. Bundled tightly, David's appearance doesn't draw any unwanted attention though at nearly six feet in height he dwarfs Emma. His well-developed physique is toned muscle, his form is an efficient balance between agility and strength. His shoulder length, chocolate-colored hair whips as it is assailed by another strong gust of frigid wind. The faded blue jeans and dirty work boots complete the look of utter normalcy. Outwardly there would be nothing about him that stands out as unusual, yet his eyes hold a lethality found in only the most hardened predators. Eyes, the color of a rich chestnut, have born witness to acts of great brutality. A thin scar bisects his eyebrow, but is not a deterrent to his masculinity.

Crossing over a wide footbridge, they turn toward the factory mills. Here, a thick layer of black ice sheens the path, yet neither of them slows their pace as they make their way to the far side. The red brick is a sickly shade of gray under the straining pale lights. The particular building they head toward is barren and shrouded in darkness. Thick overgrowths of bushes and weeds have hemorrhaged through fissures in the asphalt. Inside, the large expansive area is desolate, holding nothing but a few toppled pieces of furniture and dust. A structure that at some point thrived but now has fallen into neglect. Traveling down a constricted alleyway, they stop in front of a narrow boarded-up entry. A graffiti-laden loading door stands rusted shut several yards away. Emma's hand steadies as she gently raps on the entrance. A small rectangular slot slides open, revealing the stern face of an immense man, his eyes and nose taking up the entire opening.

"What the fuck you want?" he croaks. Emma's head cocks slightly to the left as she paints on her friendliest smile.

"We are looking for an audience with the fine owner of this establishment," Emma announces. He scoffs at them in derision as his waxy eyes shift back and forth between them.

"This here ain't no establishment. I'm the owner, so unless you're giving me money, fuck off." As he starts to close the slide Emma grasps the frame of the small opening and watches him stoically. She pushes her will against his, trying to bend his mind into a more malleable state. Emma hates this method. It is like trying to bounce a marshmallow off of an ant either you succeed or crush it. If the subject is strong enough he or she will smash your efforts aside and try to kill you. Emma often got the latter option. But from what she can see of the man, his spirit appears weak, so her chances should be better for success. As if releasing a levee, Emma can sense her will sweeping through his mind. She inserts calming thoughts, influencing him to grant them access. After some tense moments of silence the iron deadbolt of the door slides and the entryway opens. Quietly, Emma and David enter, passing the dazed man. The mountain of a guard leans listlessly against the wall. They walk through a small reception area and down a dimly lit hallway. A camouflaging illusion of glamour hides the true inner workings of the old factory. Many in the supernatural world will use this kind of deception spell to remain hidden. By bending or redirecting light they can make an object or building appear as something else, or even cause it to appear to disappear.

Ahead, Emma can hear talking, general chatter and the occasional moan and grunt. The hallway opens to the large factory floor. Red satin curtains have been hung over each window, and an extended bar spans the length of the room to the right. Numerous torches dot the walls around the room, providing a dim atmosphere. In the center is a raised dais blanketed with pillows and several plush sofas. Encircling the dais are several seating rooms that can be curtained off from each other. Each area contains a sofa or chaise and a multitude of pillows. It is reminiscent of the opium dens on the West Coast over one hundred years ago. Yet, here they weren't pandering narcotics. A few of the partitioned areas were open to reveal several individuals, the twisted forms writhing around each other. Even under the dim lighting their bodies glow with sheen from sweat and blood.

A cold shudder races through Emma at the display. The predators appear oblivious to her presence as they slake their hunger. The human buried among the mass of forms stares blankly outward. The young girl's features are hard and aged. The unnatural hue of her dyed black hair reflects the red glow of the torch light. It seems inconceivable to Emma why one would eagerly agree to be fed upon. Emma doubts that every human here has volunteered, but as long as there are no additional dead at the end of the night, there is very little she can do. Most nights these little soirees end in either an all-out orgy or a bloodbath brawl. Quickly searching the young woman's mind, she senses that she has agreed to the bloodletting. Shaking herself from the image, Emma turns away.

Toward the back of the building Emma notes another dais. Sitting in an overstuffed sofa is Nikos Di Angelo, the owner. Silently she motions to David and follows him as he makes his way to the back. A few of the vampires try to approach Emma only to be halted by David. The lethality in which he carries himself sends a persuasive message to stand down. As they pass the center dais, David and Emma are stopped by a massive bodyguard. Though the man was about the same height as David, he weighs about twice as much. The thick muscles of his chest and arms strain under the material of his satin dress shirt. His thick cascade of golden hair flows to his mid back and frames a very square face and jaw. He's a walking, talking nightmare of muscle and violence. Holding up his hand, his low voice is gruff and thick.

"Mr. Di Angelo does not wish to be disturbed this evening. We will ask that you seek his counsel at a later date."

Emma notes the man's tone is a harsh contrast to his overbearing appearance. His ancient appearance belies an underlying intelligence.

"Counsel?" Emma mutters to herself as she steps up beside David. Both men stare each other down as their hostility crackles in the air. Folding his arms over his very large chest, the guard watches them fiercely.

"I think it would be in the best interest of all parties involved if Mr. Nikos Di Angelo sees us now," Emma states firmly.

Emma knows at this point they have the full attention of Mr. Di Angelo and his guests. Every person seated at the small platform watches the scene intensely. Calmly, Emma touches David's shoulder as she continues, "I'm sure that no one wants any trouble. But it is of the utmost importance that we speak with him. My friend here," Emma nods her head toward David and then leans closer to the giant, "he's not a patient man. You'd be wise to step aside."

The titan of a man scoffs and is instantly swinging a hook toward David, who smoothly steps back, blocking the hit with his forearm. Clutching the guard's wrist, David strikes the man's elbow with enough force to shatter the bones. Screaming wordlessly in pain, the guard drops his arm uselessly to his side before stepping forward, swinging with his other arm. Ducking low, David dodges the blow and strikes quickly upward, breaking the guard's nose. The wounded sentinel slumps to the ground as others move in cautiously to help him. David squares his shoulders and breathes deeply, annoyance flashing across his face as he motions for Emma to proceed. Emma can feel her lips twitching in mild amusement. Curtailing her smile, Emma walks unhurriedly over to the large sofa and Mr. Di Angelo.

Resting casually, Di Angelo watches their approach apathetically. He is dressed sharply, a designer suit in a shade closest to charcoal, his maroon necktie setting off his already naturally dark colors. His midnight black hair is pulled back tightly to the nape of his neck while steel gray eyes follow every movement throughout the room. He could have been considered an attractive man except for the underlining coldness of his gaze. His smile showcases an impressive set of fangs, but the grin does not touch his eyes.

Two busty consorts flank his sides, each one wearing a differing shade of sheer material which barely covers their bodies. The women are complete opposites in appearance. One woman has long, flowing flame-red hair and skin that is an unnatural hue of white. The second woman's hair is cropped short and dark as pitch. Her skin is darker too, and is a lustrous olive tone. Each vampire glares at Emma with obvious loathing.

A few of the security have mustered their courage and inch cautiously toward them. Never shifting his gaze from Emma, Di Angelo raises a hand and the men recede.

"Emma. It is most wondrous to you see this evening. And might I say you are looking as lovely as always. Ah, but I would be remiss if I did not introduce my new wives." Clasping the red-haired vampire's hand, he turns to each woman. "This is Michelle, and this is Tisa." He brushes a kiss on each woman's hand. Both women sneer in their direction, and the insidious gesture mars their lovely features. His voice is smooth, enveloping her. Chuckling as he runs his tongue over his sharp fang, he continues, "Can I offer you and your friend a drink?" He gestures with a graceful long-fingered hand toward a small, cushioned stool in front of him.

Emma remains standing as David shadows closely behind her.

"No. Thank you." Emma knows that simple courtesies from a vampire always come with a price. In their world, to accept a beverage could mean being indebted to them for an act of kindness. And vampires have extremely long memories. But to refuse such courtesies can be seen as an insult as well. Dealing with their kind can be a dangerous game.

Shifting in his seat, Di Angelo sighs as the short-haired vampire, Tisa, nuzzles against his neck. "As much as I always enjoy our little visits, you can see that I am hosting tonight. So maybe we can continue this at a later time." His gaze slowly sweeps over her. "Or if you prefer we can retire to my quarters to discuss this matter in a more private setting." A low growl rolls from Tisa's throat.

Emma squares her shoulders, never taking her gaze from the vampire lord. "Nikos, you know why I am here. I have come to collect Anthony Rosario."

With an almost imperceptible movement, Di Angelo tenses. "My dear Emma, as you are most aware, my clan and I have always endeavored to aid you and the Fury whenever possible. I am certain that for whatever reason you are seeking poor Anthony it is merely a misunderstanding. When I manage to locate him I will certainly advise that he seek you out directly. Now, if you please…." He motions to several guards. Tisa laughs deeply, slinking her hand between Di Angelo's legs, cupping him.

Emma stands unyielding as she pulls at the energy around her. The temperature of the massive area drops rapidly, and the wine glass in front of Nikos frosts over. "Di Angelo. I believe you fail to see the severity of the situation." Emma clasps her hands in front of her. "Perhaps if you spent more time leading those under your care and less time cuddling dim-witted, gap-toothed whores then we would not have this problem."

Emma's hope that this job would go smoothly is quickly disintegrating. Avoiding a confrontation seems very unlikely now. Calming her breath, Emma struggles to maintain a normal outward composure. Tisa turns, glaring at Emma, her eyes shifting to a blood red. Angrily, she hisses as she tries to rise, only to be pulled down again by Di Angelo.

Emma doesn't try to hide the arrogant smile curling her lips. Tisa's pale skin turns a particularly intense shade of red. "I will rip your throat out, bitch," Tisa seethes, her voice harsh and rasping. She struggles to stand as Di Angelo easily restrains her, gently smoothing her hair, telling her to calm down and remain silent. "She will not talk about me like that!" Tisa huffs impetuously.

It is clear to Emma that Tisa is hotheaded and overly emotional. And she is Nikos's biggest weakness. Emma stands statuesquely. "Di Angelo…" Emma's voice is firm. "You will bring me Rosario, now. Or if you prefer I'll just take your fat whore over there in his stead." Emma jerks her head toward Tisa.

With a shriek Tisa launches herself from the sofa at Emma. Di Angelo moves quickly to grab her, clutching at the thin fabric of her outfit. Tisa is halted several inches from Emma, but it is close enough. Reaching out, Emma grabs Tisa by the wrist. In an instant Tisa's eyes widen as the realization of her predicament settles in. Emma opens the pathways within her, permitting a mere trickle of energy into the other woman. As the stores of energy build, it quickly transforms into a scalding pain which brings Tisa to her knees. A frantic scream rips from the woman. Searching the creature's mind, Emma can see into to darkest crevasses of her being. Widening that expanse, all of her deepest fears and darkest deeds are known. Searing sweat dapples Tisa's brow.

Emma pulls on the memory of an abusive father, hard fists, blinding pain, broken glass, and terror. It's the terror

17

that Emma concentrates on, intensifying it and pulling it to the forefront of Tisa's mind.

Emma senses several of the men moving closer. "One more step and I will break her," Emma warns through clenched teeth.

The vampires stop their advance. All eyes are on Nikos. He sits uneasily as he feigns indifference, struggling for the stoicism that eludes him. Emma can see the minutest hint of fear and rage lurking behind his steely gray eyes. She can tell that he is extremely close, so close to the edge of his breaking point. Spilling more force into Tisa, Emma wrenches a howling bawl from her.

"Stop, enough!" Di Angelo shouts as he vaults to his feet.

"Rosario. Now." Emma strains to control her voice. The familiar rage is boiling just below the surface. If she can't control it, it will overcome her.

"He is my charge. I am honor-bound to protect all who are under my care," Di Angelo whispers softly, indecision streaming across his features.

Emma steps forward, though not releasing her grip on Tisa. "You know why I am here. You know what your charge has done," Emma spits. "He has taken more than his allotment, and he must answer for that. His transgressions are yours. You are his master, and you must atone for your failings to guide him. You will bring him to me now. If you refuse, not only will I cull your herd here, but I will destroy every vampire within one hundred miles. Should I start with this one?" Emma fiercely shakes Tisa, pulling her off her knees as the vampire whimpers.

Nikos' eyes flash to Tisa before quickly coming back to Emma. Di Angelo stares silently, yet his expression is filled with hesitation. His eyes drop. Lowering her head, Emma meets his gaze. "In all the years I have lived, do you want to know what I have learned about vampires?" Emma pauses briefly, burrowing her gaze into Di Angelo. His eyes flicker and glaze with moisture. "Many believe that they know the means to destroy a vampire. Holy water, sunlight, or a stake– these all will certainly kill you, but in order to truly destroy a bloodsucking leech, you give them life."

Emma focuses the energy, pinpointing the silent heart of Tisa. She can sense the muscle shudder and spring to life. Tisa's eyes widen with a growing panic. In the overwhelming silence of the warehouse, Emma knows they'll all be able to hear the woman's hammering heart.

"You stand there atop your mighty pedestal thinking you've won against the siege of death. But every vampire in existence strives to grasp that which is missing. You incessantly crave the blood of the living in order to feel. To feel love and lust, a beating heart in your cold, black empty chests. All is an endeavor to feel human again. So, how do you kill a vampire? You give just the tiniest amount of that life and then take it away."

Di Angelo wavers as a silent tear trickles down his cheek. Emma tightens her grip on Tisa's arm.

Inhaling deeply, she composes her ragged nerves. The emotional cost of these missions is starting to take their toll. For the first time tonight, Emma wonders if she'll break before he does. The struggle to keep her feelings of remorse or empathy at bay weighs heavily on her. While they are not human, she often fights with herself to believe that they are truly monsters. If they are so horrible, why did Emma feel as if she were the villain? The Fury maintains order through terror and violence. This is not her way, but her way is not who she is now. Before allowing the weakness to spread, she mentally steels herself, pushing it away. With a subtle nod from Di Angelo, two guards leave.

After a few moments of silence the two men return. Between them they drag Anthony Rosario, his long arms straining weakly against his captors as he voicelessly mutters to himself. Emma studies the young man being hauled to stand in front of her. He is sickly thin, denoting an emaciated appearance of one who hasn't fed for some time. Dirt and soot cake his light auburn hair. His features are handsome for his age. Emma's guess is that he was no more than twenty-two at the time of his transition. His eyes dart fretfully around the room, appealing for aid. No one returns his gaze.

Emma releases her hold of Tisa, and the woman scrambles across the floor. Nikos pulls her protectively into his arms. Softly he whispers, cooing in her ear, trying to soothe her. Tisa's eyes are starkly wide and her pallor is ashen. She looks haunted now, but after a day and a feeding she should be back to normal, Emma reminds herself. Though, hopefully she'll be a bit wiser.

Turning her attention back to Anthony, Emma closes the distance between them. Standing mere inches from him she can see tremors rake his form as his gaze remains firmly toward the ground. The smell of fear and blood oozes from him permeating the area directly near him. Emma tilts her head, continuing to study the boy. "Anthony, do you know who I am?" Keeping his eyes averted, Anthony scarcely nods his head. "Do you know why I am here?"

Anthony rigidly tenses, but his submissive demeanor remains constant. Emma silently curses him, mentally beseeching him to fight for his life. Though his fate has already been decided, it would be easier if she could kill him while defending herself. But the pathetic creature before her is broken. Unfortunately, there can be no pity for him, no reprieve. His sins are too great to warrant a second chance.

"Were you not made aware of the limits?" Emma strains to strip the emotion from her voice, keeping it level. Anthony bows his head, remaining silent. Moving quickly, Emma reaches out, clasping his jaw, forcing his head up to meet her gaze. "Answer. Me." His eyes are pleading and scared. *There can be no pity for him,* Emma repeats to herself. She watches his dry throat working roughly as he tries to clear his throat.

"Yes ma'am," he sheepishly rasps.

"How many are you allowed to take?" Emma's voice carries across the room. Mother Mei Li wanted an example made of him. Everyone would need to hear this.

"F... Four. But I..." Anthony squawked, trying to pull away, but Emma's grip tightens.

"Shush now. How many did you take?" Emma asks.

Panic flashes across Anthony's face. He stares directly at Di Angelo, who only looks on statuesquely.

"Master, please, I beg you." Di Angelo simply ignores Anthony's pleas, his gaze directed toward the front wall. His gaze implores Emma. "I was weak. I promise it'll never happen again. Please, I swear!" His voice hitches up in his desperation as he sobs breathlessly, beseeching for his life.

Emma shifts her hold on the young vampire, clutching his throat. Lowering her voice to a more soothing tone, she leans closer, whispering in his ear.

"How many did you take?"

"Six." Anthony sags at the confession. His shoulders slump as the understanding rolls through him.

Maintaining contact with him, Emma circles around Anthony, stopping at his back. Her hand slides over his heart in between his shoulder blades. Emma inhales deeply and pushes the force of her energy into him. Like a rupturing levee, images cascade before her. His victims are old and young alike. Emma can see several children and an elderly woman– they are frightened and crying, all of them dead. Emma can see his callous indifference. He is so drunk on pure blood lust that all thought and reason fades away. His powerbase and will are weak. He will always be a slave to his primal predatory urges, his impulse control nonexistent. Not only does he revel in the kill itself, but in the act of inciting fear.

Peering deeper still, Emma locates his heart, enveloping it with her energy. Sharply, Emma applies a surge of force to the lifeless muscle, causing it to burst. Anthony inhales sharply and collapses to the floor, his corpse powdering instantly. Emma's heart races as she breathes deeply, trying to keep the overwhelming frenzy at bay. As she regains her control she turns to Nikos again, tremors rushing through her as she breathes deeply.

"We thank you kindly for your cooperation. We hope that you all will take this unfortunate lesson to heart in the future." Emma turns, walking toward the exit. Abruptly she stops, and not turning around calls out to Di Angelo. "In two days mediators will arrive to discuss the disciplinary sanctions for your clan." Not waiting for a response, Emma leaves the warehouse, shadowed by David yet again.

Chapter 2

As they step outside the frigid night air clutches at them. David hunches against the bitter cold, pulling his jacket closer around himself. While he is not looking forward to the long walk, it is preferable to a warehouse full of vampires and some mystical crap he still doesn't quite understand.

Being assigned to Emma for the last six months, he has seen some disturbing shit. As Emma's guardian he has often come face-to-face with creatures too heinous to comprehend. They were nothing like the monsters his nana used to warn him about as a child. His nana was born in France, just outside Paris. In her early twenties she married an Irishman and moved to the States. She was a strong woman whose life was steeped in tradition and lore. When he was younger he thought she was just overly superstitious, but he realizes now that she knew a lot about the things that lurk in the darkness. Emma has tried to explain what she could about this new world to him, but she is often tight-lipped about it. Most everything dealing with the Fury and about the Fury is on a need-to-know basis.

As a Gyges, his job is to protect Emma— and that is it. It is not his place to question, only to do his job. But fighting magic with brute force is not an easy task. Emma is a

Fury, and he is her Gyges. It was just that simple. For almost seventy-five years he has been in training. In that time it was brutally impressed on him the importance of his duty to the Fury and to the Gyges. Their origins are closely intertwined.

When the first three Fury slaughtered each other, Hades cast their souls into a deep well. The seeds of their spirit took root within women. They lie there dormant until the female dies an unnatural and violent death. Then she may be restored to life as a Fury. The legend also states that Hades knew their half-human counterparts would be weaker, so he called forth the Centimanes, three monstrous brothers who guarded the gates of Tartarus, to protect them. Hades turned the arms of the Centimanes into fine sand and also poured their essence into the well. The youngest of the brothers was named Gyges, and that is after whom they are named. Men who carried the seed of the Gyges and died in battle are brought back and assigned as guardians of the Fury.

When he died, the last thing he expected was to be hauled off and told his afterlife was not his own. Seventy-five years is a long time to be convinced that his role and sacrifice is for the greater good. By the time he had finished his training he was well versed in almost every supernatural being's strengths and weaknesses.

He follows silently, watching Emma as they cross back over the footbridge. Studying her, he is often surprised by the potential force contained within her small form. She looks more the part of a demure school teacher than a deadly Fury. Her hair, the color of honey, is always pulled up in a loose bun. David finds himself wondering how long and soft it is. Her petite figure belies the strength of her character. A tiny English lady who could easily kill half a dozen men without batting an eye. Capable of a cold intensity that has often left him with a strangely disturbing sense of awe. He has also noticed the suggestion of endless loss in her eyes when she is at play with the young Fury, Sara. Too damned complex and confusing for David's taste. His existence has become a jumbled combination of intricate rules and unspoken edicts. But he admires her strength and poise. She reminds him of his nana.

Darting forward, David catches Emma as she stumbles. "You are tired. You need to eat," David grumbles as he helps her to stand, holding her firmly. The more energy she taps into, the greater the fatigue that follows. As far as David can tell, the Fury act as a type of conduit for their energy. Pulling it into themselves, they can redirect it in many different ways. The Fury will often use copper to control the flow of that power, as it is a highly conductive material.

Emma inhales deeply as she tries to steady herself. Her complexion is ashen and her piercing, brilliant hazel eyes are now dull with exhaustion. David holds her elbow,

27

letting her readjust, feeling the subtle vibrations as she shakes.

"David, I told you I do not require food. I'll be fine." Her voice wavers as she speaks, and he knows that she is struggling to mask the weakness she feels.

"Well you may not need food, but I do. Plus we need to get you someplace warm where you can rest." David gently leads her down several side streets. He easily supports her as he tries to use his body heat to keep her warm.

Rounding a corner they come across a small, unassuming diner. Bright iridescent lights flood the front of the street as large pane glass windows allow a broad view inside. A bright red neon sign flickers and pulses color across the packed snow banks.

"Come on. This place has been here forever. It's in a bad part of town, but they have the best coffee. I'll get you some fries." David pulls the massive glass door open, helping Emma in and into a small booth in the back.

The dining area is empty save for an elderly man sitting toward the front window. Rows of patent-leather red booths line one wall, and a large counter the other. The linoleum floor shines brightly as if freshly waxed. A distant muted clatter emanates from a hidden kitchen out back. The diner has been here since he was a small child. Of course, that was over ninety years ago. And for him that seems like such a long time.

Growing up in Boston in the 1920s was rough. His family was poor, just barely scraping by with three kids. His father worked hard every day of his life. A proud man, he was a Boston police officer, and his family was the most important thing to him. Though their lives were humble, David fondly remembered the early days of a loving home. His parents laughed and they loved him and his two brothers.

Then his older brother James died. Barely seventeen, he was struck by a train arriving at the station. Some young girl had jumped off of the platform, trying to kill herself. James got her out but could not save himself. After that his father mourned the loss with such intensity that he was never the same. They no longer laughed the same way again. It is almost unbearable to think how they survived the news of his own death a few years later.

Much has changed since then. Buildings and people have come and gone, but the coffee is still the best around. Though the building is aged, it is clean and well lit. One of the overhead fluorescent lights flicker as an older waitress approaches, a welcoming smile on her face.

"Hi, I'm Dottie. What can I get you to drink?" Dottie looks to be in her early fifties. She is a handsome woman with a thick mop of graying hair sitting loosely on her head. Her vibrant eyes and demeanor are jovial.

"We'd like two coffees, a cheeseburger, and two orders of fries." David raises two fingers at the older woman.

"Coming right up." She grins widely as she turns and departs.

"Do you think we will have to go back there?" David asks.

Emma heaves a sigh. "I'm not sure. Nikos will certainly watch his people a lot closer now. But it is hard to say."

Dottie returns, setting down two empty cups and filling them to the brim with coffee. "Your food will be up shortly. Do you want cream and sugar?" Dottie asks as she finishes filling the cups.

"No, thank you." David holds his cup in both hands, letting the warmth seep into his numb fingers. They wait in silence until Dottie is back behind the counter. "How long have the Fury been in charge of regulating the preternatural world?"

Emma takes a tentative sip of her coffee before answering. "Longer than I can remember. I guess our primary purpose has always been to protect humans and to punish the evil. The regulations allow for some leniency. Now we simply guard humanity against the supernatural."

"Why not just get rid of them? The supernatural beings, that is."

"I don't think we have the capacity to destroy them all. Plus, if all supernatural beings were destroyed, then the natural balance would be off. Balance is important." Emma leans forward slightly as she speaks.

"Why is balance so important to the Fury when there is none within your ranks?" David poses.

Emma pulls her legs up underneath her and leans back. "The only way imbalance can be overlooked is when there is enough structure to compensate. The Fury have a structure that helps us to function. You are either a Mother, or a Fury ranked one through three. It just depends on your abilities. It ensures that a Fury isn't assigned a task beyond her capabilities."

David understands that a Mother is the highest ranking and most honored position. Rank one Fury are the strongest, then rank two and so on. When a fledgling female is brought into the fold she is subjected to a series of horrific tests designed to gauge her skills and strength. If she passes the tests she is assigned a grade. If she doesn't pass she is destroyed. The Fury are a hard bunch, even within their own ranks. The code of conduct for the Fury is more rigidly enforced than that of the Gyges. He has witnessed a Fury beaten and thrown into Erebus for the slightest infractions. Erebus makes Alcatraz seem like a day spa.

No one ever talks about what happens down there. Punishment is swift and brutal. And he thought the Nazis were bad.

"And what special ability do you have to earn those nice armbands?" David asks with a nod and a rise of his brows at her. Instinctively, Emma's hands move to her arms. David has only caught glimpses of the bands. No other Fury wears them, and from Emma's reaction they aren't a source of pride for her. Each band is coiled around her upper arm, molded from copper and made to resemble a serpent biting into her flesh. Copper seemed to affect Fury in the same way as silver did werewolves. The metal constantly touching her skin must be agonizing.

Emma's features harden as she drops her hands back into her lap. "You get the armbands for not following orders," Emma states coldly, her tone devoid of any emotion.

David doesn't bother trying to hide his frown. "How long have you had them?"

"I got them shortly after I became a Fury. It's probably been about four-hundred-and-fifty years or so."

"What happened? I can't see you doing something to warrant that kind of punishment." Several seconds pass, and David starts to think she is not going to tell him.

"One of my first assignments I was sent to kill a gargoyle. I couldn't do it. He had a reasonably decent soul, and nothing he had done justified punishment. So I chose not to do it. The Mothers do not appreciate being disappointed, so I was sentenced to fifty years in Erebus and got the armbands as a reminder."

They remain silent as Dottie has returned with the food. After asking if they need anything else she leaves them alone once again.

"Didn't you tell them he was innocent?" David inquires after they are alone again.

"That didn't really matter. I disobeyed an order." Emma stares off as she nibbles at the French fries in front of her.

"Why do you eat so little?" David tilts his head toward her.

"Why do you ask so many questions?" Emma challenges back, her eyes flash with aggravation.

"I'm a curious person." David smirks.

"You know what they say about curiosity." Emma sighs as she stares down at her plate of fries. "There was a period of time when I wasn't able to eat. After a while you sort of stop thinking about it. You don't feel hungry, so you just don't eat."

"When you were in Erebus?" David inquires.

"No. And don't ask." David contemplates how far to push the issue. After taking a large bite of his burger he leans back in his seat, studying her for several seconds. He inhales deeply, getting irritated with her cryptic answers. Every time he starts asking about her she shuts him down.

"You do realize it is my job to protect you, right?" Emma shifts uncomfortably under his gaze. "I need to know that I can trust you and that you trust me. I've got your back and you have mine. There can't be any other way about it. I don't like surprises. I understand that you feel the need to keep everyone at an arm's length, I do, but help me out here. Give me something. I need to know that I'm not risking my life for a heartless machine." He couldn't keep the frustration from his voice. She treated most everyone as strangers, and she is guarded with everyone. Pangs of guilt nip at him as shame and hurt dance across her features.

Emma rolls her neck, not meeting his eyes as she tentatively squares her shoulders, apprehension flowing off of her.

"Alright. Ask your questions. But first know this, you as the Gyges selected me, not the other way around. If you feel as though you can't trust me, then you can request that the Mothers reassign you to another. You are not stuck with me." Her tone is formal, almost cold, but her eyes convey the emotional battle raging within.

For David, one of the few saving graces to being a Gyges is that they had the choice of whom they were assigned to. While Emma may not have been his first choice, Mother Mei Li had rather firmly suggested he pick her.

"Why do you hate vampires so much? I know they aren't always the most agreeable, but still, why?"

Her gaze shoots up to meet his, but quickly drops downward. Her mouth softly chews as he can see her mind working, her eyes shadowed as she studies her plate.

"One night a long time ago a vampire broke into my home. He butchered my two children, my husband, and drained me dry, leaving me to die in the snow." Emma's gaze is distant as she recalls the raw wounds of her past. The pain and loss is still vividly there. "I awoke a few hours later I guess. I didn't know if I was dead or what. Everything hurt and I could barely stand. He returned before I could get help." Agonizing emotion radiates from her as she seems to be reliving the moment. "I was weak and disoriented, and he took me away with him. I didn't know if I was a vampire or dead or alive. I just knew I wasn't human anymore. My time with him was hell. I was starved and only fed when on the verge of death. Again, you go long enough without food and you can convince your body that you don't need it. Eventually I managed to escape, and the Mothers found me and brought me to The Hallow."

Silence spanned between them for several seconds as David wages a war of the best way to respond.

"I'm sorry, but thank you." He felt like it was an unbefitting answer for such a revelation, but it was all he could muster.

Emma softly nods, seeming to not need anything more. Inhaling deeply, Emma pushes her plate away.

"Do you want any?" Emma asks, motioning to her French fries. "So how did you end up joining the Gyges? Saving orphans from a burning building?" she teases with a smirk.

David shakes his head. She is trying to either lighten the mood or pull the focus from herself. Probably both, he would wager. It has been a long time since he thought about the day he died. "I met death in the forests of the siege of Bastogne on December 21st, 1944. I was a company commander in the 101st Airborne Division. We were quickly encircled by enemy forces. Day and night we were shelled with mortar and artillery rounds. I would hop from one foxhole to another trying to check on the men. I was hit by artillery, and I don't remember much after that. Just the sounds of the battle waging on as the snow fell around me. Though from what I can gather we won." David chuckles and takes another bite of his burger.

Dottie returns, smiling as she leaves the check.

"You two have a great night." She smiles slyly as she grabs the empty plates.

After dropping some cash down on the table they stand and head back out into the cold. Emma is more surefooted as she walks. With some food in them the air seems even more arctic than before. Quickly they wind their way through the alleyways, the confined spaces offering little protection against the furious gales.

Emma walks with purpose, finding an area where the veil between worlds is the thinnest. Stopping short, Emma's hand grazes over the rough brick exterior. She closes her eyes and inhales deeply. An eight foot square section of the wall begins to shimmer. Undulating, the surface becomes a reflective black liquid, the fluid wall swirling into a dark vortex. Clasping David's hand, Emma walks with him through the darkness to the other side. The atmosphere in the portal is oppressive. The feeling of the unseen walls bearing down on you is eerie. With each step you can lose sight of yourself. In silence they hastily make their way to the other side.

Chapter 3

The murky passage opens into a small, dimly lit dingy room. The floor is bare and earthen, the walls and ceiling roughly carved from a solid white stone. The area is sparsely decorated with only an undressed cot located against the far wall. A set of clean white linens and a worn blanket sit neatly folded at the bottom of the tiny bed. Forged metal wall sconces flicker from an unseen breeze as macabre shadows dance frantically along the stone leading to the only door. The visceral odor of mold assails the senses, clinging to ones skin.

Emma and David exit the portal, taking a few deep breaths to settle their sense of balance. Using the gateways allows them to travel vast distances, as well as enter and exit The Hallow, domain to the Fury. The mechanics are similar to that of a wormhole folding space in on itself. The subtle side effects can manifest as an unnerving disorientation and nausea. They silently pull open the door, heading out into a corridor housing a multitude of other doors.

"I have always wondered what is behind these other doors?" David asks.

Emma scans the long hallway before answering. "Mostly storage, but some of them were used as private quarters and detention cells."

"Why so many?" he asks to himself more than anyone else. His stature is rigid and guarded, the muscle in his cheek twitching as his eyes darken, scanning the area. "Too many hiding places. I don't like it," he mutters.

Emma shrugs slightly.

"There used to be a lot more Fury. Plus at one point the Mothers felt it was important for all of us to live together. They believed it would make us a more cohesive unit." Emma's laughter is devoid of humor. "But many died over the centuries, and for some reason the numbers aren't replenishing. Others among us chose to live in the human realm. Some would rather live alone then be packed in with others." Turning slowly, Emma walks away.

"You live among humans?" David trots forward to walk abreast of her.

"Yes, I do." She cranes her neck to meet his gaze, waiting for his next question.

"Do you prefer living with humans or Fury?" His tone is measured.

Emma shrugs casually.

"Both, neither." This time she laughs genuinely. "It was Mother Mei Li who actually suggested that I live among humans. She said it would help with my interpersonal skills. I never really thought social skills were a requirement for this job. But apparently they are."

"Emma." The voice resounds from down an adjoining hallway. They turn to see Olivia running toward them. Olivia's shoulder-length platinum hair flows around her as she comes to a stop, her crystalline-blue gaze shifting between them. Frustration radiates from her. Of course they would send Olivia to get them. Always one to be punctual, and she hated when others were late. 'It shows a lack of respect for one's position and duty,' she had once stated.

"Where have you been? Everyone has been summoned to the main hall. There is a trial in process. Come quickly."

They all quicken their pace, following Olivia as she navigates the vast expansive maze of corridors. The last hallway opens into a massive seating room. Large stone pillars are scattered throughout the area, holding up the vastness of the room. Several rows of wooden pews mirror each other as they lead up to a raised platform. Atop the dais spans a dark oaken bench where the three Mothers are seated.

As matriarchs of the Fury, the Mothers are tasked with the preservation of their vast abundance of knowledge. While they cannot access the source of energy as well as a lower ranking Fury, their other gifts are said to be quite extraordinary. An unassuming visage contradicts their immense strength and power.

Mother Mei Li is by far the eldest. Her appearance is that of someone in her early forties. Her blue-black hair is snuggly wrapped in an intricate bun at the nape of her neck. Born in ancient mainland China, her features are classically beautiful with flawless skin. Of the three remaining Mothers, Mei Li incites the greatest fear and reverence. While not overtly cruel, those that disappoint her are met with a swift and demanding punishment.

Mother Tatiana's semblance could have been molded from a solid slab of granite. The harshness of her steely gaze penetrates with an unsettling intensity. Her appearance is that of a fairly young woman, yet her hair is the same tempered silver as her eyes. In a sharp contrast to the other two Mothers, Tatiana is coldly cruel with an almost giddy desire to debase all of those around her. Routinely, she is a hard woman who is not above the use of violence in order to educate those around her.

Mother Agnes is actually much younger than the other two, but her unnatural death came to her very late in her life. Peppered graying hair held in a handsome bun with several wiry strands haloing her face. Her emerald eyes shine, reflecting the ambient light. She is a jovial woman who laughs loudly and is known to imbibe herself into a stupor on occasion. Her physical age has not dulled her wit nor fogged her wisdom. A sage fountain of knowledge, she has always been willing to lend counsel.

The trial is already in progress as David and Emma quietly take a seat in the back. All eyes are riveted on the scene playing out before them. Emma vaguely recognizes the young woman being accused. Melanie has only been a Fury for a short period of time, and Emma can only remember seeing her in passing. Even at this distance Emma can see that she has been held in Erebus awaiting her trial. Her auburn hair hangs limply around her face, her cheeks are shallow, and her left eye is bruised and swollen. Her one open azure eye darts swiftly around the room, silently pleading for aid.

Her Gyges kneels abjectly by the far side of the bench, the exposed skin of his chest stained with blood and dirt. Several angry lash marks crisscross his torso. The wounds are swollen and are beginning to fester. Both of his hands are shackled behind his back. His hair, matted and soiled, falls forward, obscuring the view of his face. To either side of him he is flanked by a Gyges staring blankly forward.

The Mothers sit quietly, watching as the poor girl fidgets in her seat. Her skin is ashen under the direct interrogation of the prosecution.

Ambrose looms over her as he oozes with condescending superiority. Emma, as much as everyone else, knew very little about the man who is a seemly obscure enigma. The only thing she did know about his previous life is that he was a man of noble birth. A reasonably attractive man with warm, coffee-brown hair and startling dark, taupe-colored eyes. Living the life of a noble aristocrat, he viewed others as being beneath him. There is an unnerving coldness to him that puts one on edge when around him.

When he was enlisted by the Gyges he quickly rose through the ranks and earned the position of Warden of Erebus. He assembled around him some of the strongest among the guardians of the Gyges that have not selected a Fury to protect. The rumor mills ran rampant that one as impressive as Ambrose hadn't selected a Fury until recently. The pairing between Olivia and Ambrose logically makes the most sense, as Olivia is the strongest amongst the Fury.

Gyges are allowed to affiliate themselves with the Ebon Mortis and also watch over a particular Fury. The Ebon Mortis struck fear in the hearts of all that crossed their path, Fury and Gyges alike. Their brutality is only spoken about in veiled whispers. With a warped sense of Manifest Destiny, they rule Erebus with a bloody iron fist.

Emma shifts uncomfortably as the inquiry continues. It has to be over soon. *"Please God, let this be over soon,"* Emma silently prays. The judicial system for the Fury is vastly different from the U.S. legal system. Here there was no defense, only prosecution. You could be convicted without a trial, and punishments varied from a whipping to a death sentence. Emma leans into Olivia, keeping her voice as low as possible. "What happened?" she asks.

"The Mothers have discovered that she was sleeping with her Gyges. She's had multiple warnings and has been punished several times." Olivia's features are strained as she speaks. No one enjoys the trial and punishment process. Olivia whispers as she continues, "According to the sources, they were caught, so to speak, in the act." Emma's gaze quickly snaps to Olivia as she fails to hide her reaction. Olivia's face softens as sadness touches her eyes. They both turn to watch the scene in front of them. "It's a shame for the poor girl. They won't show her any mercy, you know that."

Melanie is struggling to maintain her stoicism, but her eyes give away her barely leashed fear. Her breaths come in heavy rasps as her hands clench fiercely in her lap, her knuckles a pale white. An overwhelming sympathetic pain constricts in Emma's chest as she studies Melanie.

"With an overwhelming hoard of evidence, do you deny the charges against you?" Ambrose's voice resonates through the space around them. Melanie looks up, her eyes glossy with bridled tears. She seems only to be able to manage a shake of her head. "You will answer the question." Ambrose crosses his arms over his chest, glaring maliciously down at the trembling woman. She appears to steady herself as she inhales deeply, slowly blowing the air out.

Melanie returns his stare with a serene determination. She is still shaking, but the hint of apprehension has left her. "I regret none of my choices. Our actions, while forbidden, came from a place of genuine love. We both chose to love. I will not apologize for it, nor will I retract my feelings for Andrew."

Emma cringes at her words. If only one of them had pursued the relationship then only one of them would be punished. If they went into this together, then both of them would receive punishment.

Ambrose seems apathetic to her words. With a smooth grace he turns to address the Mothers. "Love is noble and it is just," he says with a firm nod. "It is the reason we are here, is it not? To love and protect those in need. But selfish desires can taint our purpose. I ask you, is that love? And to show a blatant disregard for the mandates that have been put in place to secure that safety of all of us. Will you allow her the opportunity to destroy the Fury and all that they stand for, all that they have worked for?"

The three women stare unwaveringly at Ambrose.

After several moments Mother Tatiana stands and turns her attention to Melanie. Clearing her throat, she speaks loudly. Her gaze remains steadily on Melanie, yet her tone and words are directed for the benefit of the onlookers. "Melanie, we understand the isolation that our duties can leave us with. But while we understand, we cannot allow such a breach of our laws. Therefore it is our decision that you shall be sentenced to one hundred years in confinement in Erebus."

Emma detects a slight smirk in Tatiana's voice. The Mother's intense gaze settles on Melanie as a wash of emotions flood over the young Fury. A wave of shocked murmurs rustles over the crowded room. Most punishments spanned for less than fifty years. It was viewed as counterintuitive to keep a Fury locked away for much longer.

Tatiana lifts her hand for silence before she continues. "It is also our belief that you have allowed yourself to become compromised by your attachment to your Gyges." Both Mother Mei Li and Agnes's faces are drawn tighter. Mother Mei Li fingers a small pendent which hangs loosely from her neck, yet both of them remain silent. "After repeated warnings you have left us no choice. So it has also been determined that upon the commencement of your incarceration, the Gyges Andrew will be taken from this place and brought to a final location wherein he will be executed. Your name shall be removed from the options of Fury available for guardianship. I pray that the gods will be merciful to you both."

The room hovers in staggered silence as the two Gyges pull Andrew up to stand. Andrew makes no gesture as to move, his eyes remaining downcast as if his will to live has been burnt away. A howling screech tears from Melanie and the temperature in the room plummets. Chaos erupts and everyone stands. Emma is jostled by those around her, and only David's strong grasp keeps her standing. Amidst a mass of shoulders and heads Emma cranes her neck to locate Melanie and the Mothers. Melanie is surrounded by four Gyges, their copper blades drawn and glinting in the candle light. From behind the bench, all three Mothers are now standing. Emma presses to move forward but is halted by David and Olivia. '*No.*' Olivia silently mouths to her with a shake of her head.

Melanie's slight tremor has flared into a full-on body convulsion, her eyes starkly wide as the pain and panic assault her. The azure blue of her eyes is swept away as a sheen copper color bubbles to the surface. The men encircling her make no move to grab her.

"I won't let you hurt him!" Melanie grits out, her hold on the growing force becoming tenuously thin.

"Oh dear god, she's going to burn herself out." The unknown voice is laced with a rising hysteria as it cuts through the enclave. "Don't be stupid, child." Tatiana's hand is clenched tightly to her breast as her features harden and her eyes darken. "You are only going to make this worse for yourself. Your actions could warrant your own execution. Do not be a fool."

"Death is preferable. I will not go back there. I would rather die than be locked up with those monsters. How can you stand there and let them get away with it? It is wrong. Please, you can't take him from me, I love him. I have served the Mothers and the Fury faithfully all these years. I will not lose the only goodness that has come from my wretched existence." Melanie's gaze drifts over to Andrew. A soft sadness and adoration graces her expression. Emma's chest tightens painfully and she must look away. "We are leaving here… together." Melanie's voice cracks under her resolve as a small trickle of blood flows from her nose.

Very few have observed a Fury burn themselves out, but most know it a deadly process. Not only do they risk killing themselves, but they risk everyone around them as well. The air seems to thin as Melanie draws upon more and more energy, her lack of training and skill making it impossible for her to control the forces moving within her. Intensity pulses as the danger to everyone builds into the inevitable explosion. The misuse of power is the reason why there are only three Mothers now. A failed attempt at harnessing more strength ended with two Mothers killed, and weakened the rest of the Fury population. As a result the Fury lost the ability to judge humanity, and this left them with only the option to police supernatural beings. Restrictions are in place to ensure they are not weakened further. The danger is too high that one could lose control and harm others. Melanie may be willing to risk them all to save Andrew. Either she leaves with Andrew or no one does. Her desperation rises to a frenzied pitch.

"No, Child. You must stay." Mei Li's tone is whispered, and it barely reaches everyone. She moves silently with just a soft rustle of her robes, and between one blink and the next she is standing mere inches away from Melanie. "I know you are pained, Child, but this will help no one." Melanie arches back trying to avoid any physical contact with the Mother. She looks erratically around as she realizes her choices are limited. She is trapped between the Mother and the surrounding guards. "Our laws are designed to keep us whole and strong and safe. They allow us to protect those who cannot protect themselves. The lineage of the Fury must be guarded against the weaknesses that destroyed our predecessors. The original three permitted the weakness of misguided love to undermine their purpose. It fractured their resolve, leading to their own demise. We must relinquish the aspirations of a simple existence that our human sides so desperately long for."

Mei Li's tone is soothing, and Melanie's shoulders sag as the words seep in. The life of the Fury is no longer their own. They are but a tool to be used for the greater good. Emma is as aware of this painful truth, as is everyone in this room. Mei Li reaches out, grasping Melanie's hand, and as the contact is made a static buzz fills the room, followed by a sudden rush of heat. Mei Li's gift is one of the more terrifying of the Mothers. She can sever the link between a Fury and their source of energy, negating any strength they have. Mei Li had once informed them that it was a way of balancing the strength of the Fury.

Melanie collapses as the guards rush forward to roughly grab her. Her body shudders as she whimpers as they prepare to drag her from the room. Mei Li steps forward, gently touching the crown of Melanie's head. "Be brave, Child. Have faith, and all may be righted in the end."

An anxious silence hangs heavily over everyone.

"Please do not kill him." Melanie's voice is small and pleading.

"We will discuss this further." Mei Li smiles compassionately.

"Enough of this bullshit." Moss, one of the larger Gyges, steps forward from the crowd. Moving with a purpose, he approaches Andrew with a six inch blade in his hands. Grabbing a fistful of the man's hair, he yanks Andrew's head back and quickly draws the blade across his neck. A gurgling groan escapes the man as his life's blood rushes out of the wound. Melanie collapses as inconsolable sobs overtake her.

Mother Tatiana moves forward, clearing her throat and addressing the bewildered assembly. "You will all return to your rooms or required duties. Hopefully we will all heed this unfortunate demonstration. You are all excused."

A low murmur rustles over the crowd as they quietly shuffle out. Emma, Olivia, and David stay waiting for everyone to leave.

"Do you think they will kill her too? She broke a lot of rules today," Emma asks as her stomach continues to knot.

"I don't think so." Olivia exhales sharply as she rubs her forehead. "With fewer of us being created, I don't believe the Mothers will have her put to death."

Moss approaches them from across the room. Emma didn't know what his first name was, as she has only ever heard him called by his surname. A thick mane of shoulder-length hair is midnight black and mildly shimmers under the muted lights. His nearly black eyes and hulking muscular frame lends to his air of intimidation. The man is a stewing cauldron of malice and sadism. Emma by no means envied Celia for being attached to that Gyges.

"Emma, David. Mother Mei Li wants to see you." His dagger is already cleaned and sheathed at his waist. Without waiting for response he turns curtly and retreats. All three stare at each other with questioning looks. Emma stands with muscles screaming as the need for rest weighs heavily on her. Heading through the main doors, they travel toward the personal sleeping quarters of the Mothers.

"Why do you think she did it?" Olivia queries, her features solemn. "She will be punished, and he's dead. And for what?"

Emma ponders silently for several minutes. The three original Fury let the love of a mortal destroy them. They failed to resist the flaws that came with love, and they had the advantage of not being partially human. What hope do the later Fury have? Their humanity makes them susceptible to the trappings of their nature.

"I think she was probably just tired of the loneliness. In the end maybe she just wanted to feel normal." Normalcy was a luxury that none of the Fury could afford. They continue walking in silence, jumbled nerves stirring in anticipation of why Mei Li has summoned them.

Chapter 4

Mei Li's personal quarters are warm and inviting. Very few have ever been granted access to the Mothers' sanctuary. Most of the issues requiring the attention of the Mothers are addressed out in the main hall, so this is the first time David has ever entered this part of The Hallow.

The area is a subtle mixture of classic and contemporary décor with some understated hints of an Asian influence. Polished lattice work made of a deep mahogany wood graces the walls. Shelves of neatly trimmed bamboo stalks and a well maintained bonsai tree are arranged in the far corner. On the wall to the right sits a simple bookshelf, an old-fashioned record player, and a faux window. The backlit casement frame displays a picturesque scene from mainland China. The aura of the room instills a sense of calming, which is enhanced by the complimenting shades of maroon and gold.

As they enter, David sees that Mei Li and Tatiana are seated around a large, mounded fire pit. Both sit rigidly in cushioned backless chair, silently watching the dance of the small flames, lost in their own thoughts. From behind their small group Moss coughs abruptly, drawing the attention of the two Mothers.

In a gracefully sweeping motion the Mothers rise and approach them. "Thank you, Moss. You may leave now."

Tatiana dips her head toward the man as he turns and leaves. As soon as the door clicks shut Tatiana turns toward them. The black cotton material of her simple gown swishes eerily in the silence, echoing her movements.

"Quite a nasty bit of drama. The trial I mean." Her façade of sympathy doesn't touch her eyes. A stone-cold woman lingers just below the wrappings of this cultured and proper female. "Well, it is time that we moved forward. No sense dwelling on it any longer. We have enough unpleasantness around here without adding any more." Tatiana scowls as she shifts her gaze, settling it on Emma. Emma's face darkens in response, but she remains silent. David notes there is some underlying animosity between the two women, but he doesn't know where it stems from.

"Answer this, Fury. How faired your assignment? Did you do as you were asked, or did you fail again?" Harsh condemnation rolls from Tatiana, her eyebrows arching upwards.

Emma tenses slightly, but she continues to stare blankly ahead. She swallows fervently, clearing her throat before the words will come.

"I met with the vampires and determined the judgment for the fledgling. He will not be an issue." Emma's tone is devoid of emotion and unwavering, but David senses the pluming waves of apprehension tightly guarded within.

Tremors shake her hands as she clutches them tightly at her sides.

Tatiana cocks her head to the side, studying Emma. "And after this judgment what was your prescribed punishment?" She tightly folds her arms under her breasts, her mouth working as if chewing a foul taste, her tone mocking.

"I found his fortitude to be lacking. He would always be susceptible to his urges to kill in excess. The only suitable outcome available was to destroy him."

"So you killed him? How? How did you do it?" Arms still crossed, Tatiana steps closer to Emma, mere inches away. David bristles at the intrusion. Tatiana's breath pushes and pulls at Emma's hair. This wicked woman exudes a threatening presence, but getting involved will be of no help to anyone. He clenches his jaw hard enough to break his own teeth, while every muscle rages against the growing danger. His instincts scream for action, but he forces his feet to stay.

"I destroyed his heart," Emma responds after a brief pause.

"How droll." Tatiana laughs sharply, clapping her hands softly in front of her. A sinister grin spreads across her face. "What of the others? Did you encounter any obstacles? Did you make an impression on them?" Her features rapidly flutter from sadistic euphoria to a callous mask.

"No Mother, no obstacles. The others appeared to be amicable, and they seemed to appreciate the seriousness of your concerns." Emma's voice wavers slightly under the direct scrutiny.

"Very good, Emma." Mei Li attempts to assert herself but is quickly overrun by Tatiana.

"Yes, yes, very good. If you don't mind, Mei Li, I have just a few more questions." Tatiana smiles impetuously at the other Mother. This time it is Mei Li's features that show signs of uneasiness. Again Tatiana lasers her gaze onto Emma. "You will answer me truthfully, Fury. Did you feel as though you betrayed them?

"Mother? Betrayed whom?" Emma inquires. Her voice is small in the open space, her face creased in confusion.

"Why, your own kin of course." Tatiana's tone is incredulous as her eyes widen. "You killed one of your own. Do you not feel any sense of remorse?"

"No, Mother. They are not my kind. His destruction brought me no joy, but it was necessary." Emma's voice is no longer cold as it wobbles and breaks, and she inhales a deep breath.

Tatiana huffs loudly in exasperation. Reaching out, she suddenly strikes Emma, nearly buckling her knees, but she remains standing. "Why do you persist in lying to me? You are revolting, full of lies and wickedness." Rage seethes from beneath the Mother's eyes.

"Tatiana, stop this!" Mei Li's voice cuts through the stunned silence. Tatiana ignores her words, raising her fist to strike again. David strains as he watches Emma make no move to dodge or defend herself. Olivia stands rigidly but a fluid emotion flows from her. As Tatiana's arm moves forward it is seized and halted. David doesn't remember moving, only that he is now clutching the arm of a very angry Mother. Her gaze flits back and forth from her arm to David.

"How dare you interfere, Gyges! Release me, you ingrate." David almost laughs as Tatiana's face runs the gambit of colors from rage-filled red to ashen white then to an interesting shade of puce. She struggles briskly against his weak hold.

"That's enough." David allowed his tone to remain cold as he thrusts Tatiana's arm away from them.

"You are either a complete moron or suicidal. I will not be manhandled by the likes of you. Prepare yourself, as your atonement will be legendary," Tatiana spits.

"My duty is to defend my Fury, even if that means protecting her from a screeching foul-mouthed Harpy like you," David bites back. The two stand-off, waiting for the other to move.

"David, stand down," Emma calmly whispers.

Her gaze is pleading and warning at the same time. Emma's cheek is still red and starting to swell. David battles the conflict raging inside of him. He inhales, rolling his neck to each side. "Keep your hands to yourself," he states in a calm tone as he steps back.

Tatiana's lips twitch as the door behind them opens. In unison they all turn to see Ambrose sauntering in. "Oh good, you have arrived, Ambrose. You must be fatigued after such a grueling evening, so we shall endeavor to be curt." Tatiana gushes sweetly. She is visibly shaken but regains her composure while smoothing her gown. She glares at David with a centered gaze.

"I only live to serve the Fury in all things. If ever you are in need, I am ready as your most humble servant." Ambrose's gaze flickers about the room, settling on David. His posture hints at a subtle underlying uncertainty, and yet a challenging glint lights his eyes. David chews on and swallows the overwhelming urge to chop the two-faced jackass in the throat.

"A very significant undertaking has been requested of us. The four of you will see to its successful completion." Tatiana addresses them in her familiarly regal tone, her expression once again statuesque. "A satyr by the name of Aidan has been abducted and is being forced into servitude. His family has pled for his release, but to no avail. You will retrieve him and bring him back alive."

"What of those holding him? Who are they?" Olivia asks calmly.

"He is being held at the brothel called Paasa that caters to supernatural beings and humans. It is owned by an unscrupulous imp by the name of Calder. He is not to be underestimated, and is as calculating as he is malicious." Tatiana waves her finger at them as she speaks. "Olivia will take the lead on this. You will all obey her orders as you would ours."

"This situation will be handled with the highest level of discretion. We can't afford the publicity. So you will not just waltz in there and start taking hostages." Mei Li smirks, raising an eyebrow as she gazes toward Emma. She passes a four by five, black and white photograph to David. Studying the image, David tries to memorize the slightest details of the man pictured. In appearance a young man, maybe mid to late twenties, with jet-black hair and a well-maintained goatee. He looks to be an attractive man of medium build. Two thick, spiraled horns curl from above his temples to his ears. Although the use of illusionary magic will hide the horns from most humans, their party will still be able to see them.

"There is a high likelihood that there will be humans in attendance, so there should be no need to reiterate how crucial it is that the world of man remains unaware of our existence. Our comings and goings will continue to be held in secrecy," Mei Li continues as she reclaims the photograph from Emma.

"Do we know why they took him?" Emma asks, her cheek still slightly red.

"The imps claim he accosted one of their noblewomen. From their account, the young Fairy was swimming at a secluded basin when the satyr happened upon her and assaulted her. They feared the satyr would have kidnapped her or worse if some of her guards had not come along. They said they captured him before he could do more damage, so his enslavement is a portion of his atonement for his crime."

"Then why rescue him?" Olivia interrupts. Her features squish in confusion, but there is also a darker emotion there as well. "It would appear his punishment is fitting. If he is guilty of rape then he should spend the rest of eternity enduring the same violations he subjected another to." Hard shadows creep over Olivia's features as her shoulders tense.

"His family asserts that the coupling was mutually agreeable, and that in fact they have been involved with each other for some time now," Mei Li calmly replies as she gently clasps Olivia's shoulder.

"Who is telling the truth then? Has anyone talked to the woman?" David inquires.

"That is the question, and you will find the answer to it. We have been told that she is too traumatized to speak to anyone," Mei Li answers as her gaze sweeps across the room. "Tomorrow night you will find this satyr and determine the truth. If he is innocent bring him here and we will deal with the imps afterwards."

"And if he is guilty?" Ambrose asks, arching his eyebrow. David had almost forgotten about the other man still standing on the outskirts of the room.

"Use your best judgment for him. Someone is trying to deceive us, and we will root them out. But now we must defuse the situation before it becomes uncontrollable," Mei Li states coldly.

"With all due respect, Mother, why is the fate of this satyr so important? We all know that similar requests in the past have been outright denied. His family risks a lot in approaching the Fury. Plus there are more effective methods of securing his return than for his kin to ask the aid of the Fury," David declares, shaking his head.

Beseeching a Fury for help can come at a great cost, or even be life threatening depending on whom you ask. To ask for a judgment means you will be judged as well. If you are found to be lacking, you may forfeit your own life.

"His family clan is an ancient one, and highly esteemed," Tatiana interrupts tersely. "It is better to ask forgiveness from the Fae than to ignore this request. Furthermore, it is not for you to question our decisions. You will do as you are ordered. Is that clear enough for you?" Tatiana's words are sharp, and she brims with indignation as she moves toward him.

David struggles against the boiling in his blood, his own rage rolling through him. Through gritted teeth he forces out his reply. "Yes, of course, Mother."

Silently, Tatiana strides closer to him. Her aura exudes pure hatred and impending violence. David refuses to be cowed by this woman. Before Tatiana can move further, Mei Li clasps her shoulder.

"I will deal with the Gyges, Tatiana." Mei Li casts a disapproving glance toward David.

A smug grin creases Tatiana's face. "Very well, Mei Li. I will leave his discipline to you then." Sharply turning, Tatiana sweeps from the room.

"Is there anything else you require of us, Mother?"
Olivia's voice wavers slightly as she looks on in uncertainty.
She appears conflicted as to whether she should stay or go.

"No, Child. You and Ambrose are free to leave. Make
sure all preparations are made for tomorrow evening." Mei
Li addresses them but keeps her intense gaze locked on
David, holding him in place. He watches, his eyes
following them as they silently leave the room, shutting the
door behind them. Turning back forward, Mei Li still
glares at him. "What kind of stupidity was that? Are you
trying to get yourself killed?" she reproaches.

"Mother, I…" David stammers, clinging to the hope that
he can calm Mei Li down. Having the skin flayed from his
back is something he wants to avoid.

"Do not interrupt me." Mei Li's exasperation is an
incensed mass churning just beneath the surface. Holding
his tongue, David allows her to continue. "Do you have
any idea how hard it is to keep everything we have built
from falling apart? Order and peace must be kept. And
you go and kick a hornet's nest with Tatiana." Mei Li
throws her hands up. "She may be a shrew, but she is still
a Mother, and you will treat her as such." Mei Li fiercely
jabs David's chest as she speaks. "Your dedication to your
Fury is admirable, but there is a time and place for it. Our
ways may not be perfect, but it keeps us from destroying
everything. Now I must go placate her and try to smooth
out the insult of your indiscretion so she doesn't demand

63

your head. I warn you, Gyges, do not give her another reason to cause strife. Just remember that it is not just your skin on the line." Mei Li takes a quick glance toward Emma.

A severe tightness clutches David's chest.

"My sincerest apologies, Mother. It was not my intent to cause greater problems." As a silent agreement passes between them Mei Li visibly calms as she inhales a deep breath.

"I am glad we can come to an understanding. There is also another reason I chose to speak with both of you in private," Mei Li states calmly. Emma steps forward to stand abreast of David. They watch the Mother intently as she makes her way over to the record player. Silently she cranks the handle, winding the machine, and gingerly places the needle down. The room is filled with the soft hiss and crackle as the introduction to Beethoven's "Moonlight Sonata" begins. The ballad reminds David of a bygone time of happiness with his family. Evenings spent with his father reading his paper and Mother's love of music and her children. A brief period of time before everything changed and was broken. David shakes himself back to the present and to the conversation around him.

"After the task of tomorrow is completed I have another duty for you both. It is an undertaking that requires your utmost attention and secrecy. Even if you are questioned by the other Mothers, you are not to divulge any of this information, is that understood?" Mei Li pauses until they both agree, her hands clasped in front of her. "It has become evident that there have been several breaches in our security. Several tomes have been stolen from the archives, as well as items of great value and importance."

"What items, Mother?" Emma asks cautiously. An uneasy tension flows between the two women.

"For right now, what was taken is not as important as why they were taken." Mei Li wrings her hands as she walks over to a simple desk and she pulls out a slip of paper and turns back to face them, handing the note to Emma. "As soon as you finish with Olivia you are to travel to this location. You will contact the new pack leader for the werewolves by the name of Bray. He has just taken over as alpha since his father's death, and is expecting you."

"When did his father die?" Emma asks.

"He was murdered a week ago, and as far as we know he was not killed by a rival pack. He wanted to bring peace to his people and end the continuous feuding and bloodshed that runs rampant amongst the wolves. He argued that the only way to accomplish this would be to unify under one leader."

"Like a king?" Emma poses, her features darkening as she mentally digests the information.

"Yes, a king of the werewolves. This could have caused enough animosity that might lead someone to want him dead, but the reason for Jackson's death is still a mystery. There was something ritualistic behind his execution, but we do not know what it means as of yet. That is what we need you to discover."

"Ritualistic? How?" David interrupts, stepping closer to the two women.

Mei Li's gaze darts uncomfortably around the room. Calmly she makes her way over to an upholstered chair and eases herself down. After several seconds of silent debating on what to tell them, her eyes lift upward.

"His heart was carved out and they found the newborn baby's heart lodged in his mouth. Also, a large section of skin from his back was taken. Whatever is happening here is not as simple as power struggles or turf wars. Agnes's visions only lend more credence to this. We must know what is happening."

"What did she see, Mother?" Emma asks, trembling faintly.

"The specifics are not a priority right now. The visions are only possible outcomes, and different actions can cause changes to the outcome of the premonitions. But there is a chance that the two events may be connected somehow. You are to find out the details surrounding Jackson's death and report them back to me, and me alone. Now go home and rest. We will all need our strength in the following days."

David and Emma leave in silence. Neither one of them seem to want to discuss the events with Tatiana. By the time he reaches his apartment the bakery it sits above is preparing to open. The mouthwatering aroma of bread and pastries waft through the predawn air. As he approaches the side entrance stairway he is stopped by Alfonso, who owns the building and the bakery. "Late night?" Alfonso calls out to him. Even at this early hour his apron and massive forearms are covered thoroughly in flour. Alfonso is a thick-bodied man who probably played football in high school. His dark hair and mustache are highlighted with grey.

David moved in a few years ago. The apartment is small, but the rent is reasonable, and for the most part the neighbors keep to themselves. But not Alfonso, he pries a lot more than most. David assumed it was just because he wanted to ensure he didn't rent to some twisted sociopath with heads stashed in his refrigerator. And he respected that. Alfonso seems to care about his community, where he donates his time and food to people in need.

When David approached Alfonso about the room for rent he had to lie to him that he worked as an overnight security guard. David hoped that would limit any suspicions about his late night comings and goings.

"It's always a late night, Alfonso. But at least it was boring." David chuckles as Alfonso passes him a cardboard cup filled with steaming coffee and a waxy white paper bag. Even through the bag David can smell the sweet cinnamon pastry.

Once upstairs, David sits, mulling over the events of the night, his coffee cup soon emptied, and food consumed. What did the death of a werewolf have to do with the Fury? And if there was a breach in security, what new danger did that pose? Both Mei Li and Emma's reaction to the news was a little unsettling, and without more information he is stumbling in the dark. Hopefully he can decipher what is happening before someone gets killed. The morning rays seep into the room as exhaustion overtakes him and he falls into a listless sleep.

Chapter 5

Waiting outside in the bitter cold is not the best way to start the evening's mission. Fortunately, Olivia's rising irritation at the tardiness of the others helps to abate the chill that is seeping in. Ambrose quietly leans against the wall of an adjacent building, the collar of his black leather jacket pulled up around his ears and his hands crammed deeply into his pockets.

"I told them nine thirty. Where are they?" Olivia stews as her breath curls around her. A lack of punctuality shows a lack of control, and one must exert control in all things or become fodder to the predation of others.

"It is only nine twenty, we still have some time yet. You worry too much. The building has been scouted inside and out, so as soon as they arrive we will be ready," Ambrose explains in a sardonic tone.

Paasa is one of the oldest whorehouses in town. It has played host to many dignitaries, politicians, and even kings. A seven foot high wrought-iron fence encloses the compound's structure. The brothel is only accessible from the road by the main gatehouse. Minor glyphs of concealment are strategically placed around the perimeter, giving the building an appearance of an upscale nightclub. The two-story building has only four points of entry. Rooms for business transactions are upstairs. Their source had informed them the satyr is being held upstairs as well. Heavily guarded, this place will not be taken by force.

From down the street, Olivia spies Emma and David approaching. With an unhurried pace they reach their hiding place in the alley. "Cutting it awful close, aren't you," Olivia chides, looking at her watch.

"What? We are on time," Emma replies with an innocent shrug. "The glyphs make opening a portal difficult. And you may be able to open one practically anywhere, but I can't. We had to walk for awhile." Emma frowns deeply.

"If I could open a gateway anywhere we would pop into the room where he is being held. We wouldn't have to worry about this sneaking nonsense. The satyr is being held on the second floor. Ambrose and I will sneak upstairs, find the satyr, and get out. You will head in first and give us a few minutes to follow. You and David will help with the distraction," Olivia explains, looking about the group.

"Distraction?" David asks, arching an eyebrow with a smirk.

"Splitting up the group may not be the best option," Ambrose cautions as he steps in closer, clasping her upper arm firmly, nearly overwhelming her with his presence. "There are courses of action that have not been considered. We could seek a private audience with Calder and demand that the satyr be released to us. They are probably just as tentative as we are about a public display. Or, David and I can slip in and collect the satyr. There is no reason to risk two Fury for one satyr." Olivia glances down at where Ambrose holds her. With her hand she pries away his with a cold determination.

"Our goal is to rescue the satyr with no human involvement. My preference would be to avoid a confrontation with the imps, for now." Her gaze turns ice cold as she speaks.

"And when they discover us? What kind of scene will that cause? How do you propose to handle that?" he argues.

"If we are discovered it is better that it takes place in a more secluded location, like upstairs. But the distraction should hold the attention of the majority of the guards. Those that we encounter will be minimal. Additionally, Emma has never had an exchange with any of the Fae, so it is less likely that they will realize who she is." Ambrose opens his mouth to argue, but closes it quickly as Olivia glares up at him. "The Mothers have placed me in charge of this assignment for a reason. They trust my judgment will be for the best. I appreciate your input and concerns, but I have made my decision as to our course of action."

The night sky flashes with vibrant, blinding colors, making everyone tense. A loud boom shakes the sky a few seconds later. Whistling fireworks scream through the frigid night air. For a brief moment the night is filled with light and sounds. The stimulus is weighty and oppressive, assaulting the ears and eyes.

"What the hell is going on?" Ambrose mutters, scanning the area around them.

"The football game is over. It sounds like they've won," Olivia moans. With each concussive blast Olivia fights the urge to jump. She'll never understand how even in the winter time diehard New Englanders will shoot off fireworks in the numbing cold just because the Patriots win a game. Olivia scans the small group, trying to refocus on the task at hand. Emma and Ambrose are watching the street. Olivia glances towards David. Even under the weak lights she observes the color draining from his face. His eyes stare blankly forward as if he is somewhere far away. He shakes slightly as a thin coat of sweat sheens on his skin.

"David," Olivia calls out to him. "David." This time nearly shouting as David's eyes snap toward her. "Are you with us?" she asks. David inhales a ragged breath and numbly nods. "We need you to keep it together. Remember, the sooner we finish the sooner we're out of here." Her tone is firm and direct. Olivia has seen that far-off stare countless times before. The cold truth is that warriors will always carry a piece of the battle with them.

Without waiting for any more of a response, Olivia motions for Emma and David to leave. As they are walking toward the main gates Olivia catches Emma telling David to follow her lead.

Several minutes pass before Olivia strides up to the main entrance, trailed closely by Ambrose. Twin mountainous men stand silent sentry at the outer doorway both clad in black dress pants and button-down shirts that are nearly bursting at the seams. The one on the left holds up his hand to halt them.

"No weapons or drugs." His voice crackles with a raspy low quality. He motions for them to open their jackets for a search. Ambrose quickly steps forward and extends his arms. The silent guard to the right swiftly pats down his chest and legs. Once satisfied, both sentries turn their attention to Olivia.

"Do you seriously believe that she has a weapon?" Ambrose asks incredulously.

"It is club policy to search everyone who enters," retorts the larger of the two men. Ambrose meets her gaze stoically. Steeling her nerves, Olivia steps forward and extends her arms as well. As the guard reaches for her she stops him, saying, "Keep this on the up and up, ok. Any funny business and you'll end up choking on your own blood. Capeesh?"

Both men smirk at each other for a moment.

In part Olivia is relieved that they don't perceive her as a threat. If they make the mistake of underestimating her, then that can work to her advantage. Though that knowledge does little to quell the raising panic as the sentry advances toward her. Biting back the hysterical scream welling in her throat, she cements her feet as his hands roughly palm her arms, sides, legs, and waist. Her stomach sieges against ebbing waves of nausea washing through her. With the task completed he withdraws, resuming his stance adjacent to his partner. Both men chuckle as they motion for the two of them to pass. The psychological scars of her death have rendered her abhorrent to being touched. Even contact with those closest to her can spark a panic attack. But being thrown out of a ten-story window to your death can make one a little sensitive.

Upon entering the bordello they pass through a small, dimly lit reception space. A short hallway opens into a larger oval seating area, the lighting muted with only a handful of spotlights shining down onto the floor. An arching staircase follows the curve of the wall to the left side of the sizable room. A horseshoe bar sits just below the stairs, with backlit shelving illuminating the display of liquor bottles. After a quick survey she realizes that there are only three bouncers in the room. One stands at the bar, one near the dance floor, and the last at the top of the stairs.

A dance floor and small stage take up much of the area to the right. The remaining space is occupied with about two dozen wooden tables and chairs. The thrum of syncopated music pulses hypnotically and drifts through the air. The constant press of humans and supernatural is almost overpowering. The dance floor is teeming with the gyrating mass of arms and limbs as the smell of sweat and body lingers and settles on your skin. Interwoven among the multitude of patrons are several of the brothel's employees, who are designated by a telltale green and yellow armband they wear. If interest is shown, the worker will escort the client upstairs where they will negotiate prices. In a place like this there are no limits, and everything has a price.

Standing by the bar and the stairs, Olivia glimpses Emma, David is shadowing her from several feet away, near the farthest wall conversing with an unknown man. An attractive blonde young fellow, Olivia would guess he is barely old enough for college. She smiles brightly, laughs, and talks as she sips from a wide-mouthed martini glass. Pale blue liquid sloshes over the brim to the floor, but Emma seems oblivious to the messy drink. She laughs whole heartedly, and Olivia becomes aware of just how lovely Emma can be when she smiles.

David silently watches the dance floor and Emma. As the crowd jostles, the throng pushes outward, an unseen form nudging Emma from behind. Though the contact appeared light, Emma's reaction is slightly exaggerated, her blue cocktail slashing onto the lap of a large man seated there.

The hulking angry man shoots to his feet, an interesting bit of illusion hiding his true nature from the onlookers. Massively built, he has sinewy broad arms and legs and numerous tattoos cover his forearms and neck. His dirty blonde hair flows down his shoulders to his mid back. Beneath the façade lies a descendant of Typhon. Known as the "Father of all Monsters," his offspring are notorious for their foul and violent tempers. With kin like the Hydra, Chimera, and Cerberus, this one is bound to be a nasty bit of trouble.

After studying him for a few seconds, Olivia vaguely recalls meeting him before. Her last encounter with Haimon was a few years ago. The Fury's presence was requested to mediate a violent dispute. Haimon was accused of beating a man to death over a parking spot. The punishment passed down to him appears to have done nothing to improve his demeanor.

Brushing at his now wet pants, he towers ominously over Emma. Violence radiates from him as he strides toward her, his imposing form dwarfing hers. Emma's young, strapping companion seems to have vanished at the first sign of trouble. Raising her hands up as if to ward off the approaching menace, Emma attempts to pacify him.

Over the now hushed room, Olivia can hear Emma clearly. "Hey, easy now. I'm sorry about the drink. There's no need to get all worked up."

But his advance isn't halted. Grabbing her arm in a vise-like grip, he hauls Emma up onto her toes. "Fucking clumsy whore! You ruined my pants."

"Look. I said I was sorry. I'll pay for the pants. What else do you want?" Emma offers as she glances around the room, no one making an attempt to aid her. Even the bouncers, who watch closely, seem frozen in their place.

"Yeah, you're going to pay alright." As Haimon rears his hand back to strike her, Emma's features flash with annoyance. She opens her mouth, releasing an ear-piercing shriek. The loud sound seems to snap the audience from their stupor, and the guards rush forward, seizing both Emma and the brutish Haimon.

"That's enough of that. You two are gone," the closest bouncer says as he pulls them apart. As they roughly pull Emma and Haimon out of the bar, Olivia glimpses David following closely behind them. When the guards disappear Olivia sneaks up the stairs, flanked by Ambrose.

The top of the stairs lead to a long corridor with several doors on either side. Red tinted light bulbs provide a subtle level of illumination, the musty odor of incense and sweat heavily perfuming the air. The sounds of muffled grunting resonate from behind several of the closed doors as they cautiously make their way down the hall, stopping to listen at each door. By the fourth door Olivia is ill at ease with her surroundings.

"Do you know where they are holding him exactly?" Ambrose demands, appearing irked as he surveys the area.

"Not precisely. The best we could manage was that he is up here somewhere."

"We'll be here forever, checking each room. Now that might sound like loads of fun to you, but not me," he scoffs mockingly.

As they approach the next room the door swings open as a young woman exits. Fearing that she will shout to alarm the guards, Ambrose rushes forward as they push her back into the room.

"Hey, hey. What the hell?" She gasps as Ambrose clamps a hand over her mouth.

Olivia shushes her. The small bedroom is decorated in loud colors and a multitude of colorful scarves. The girl herself appears to be barely in her twenties. Her gaunt form is covered by a shimmering silk robe that falls to just her upper thigh, her deep auburn hair is heaped messily on top of her head.

"We are not going to hurt you. We just need to find someone. Can you help us?" Olivia whispers. The young girl nods her head. "We are looking for a fella working here. He has brown hair, brown eyes, and a goatee. Good-looking guy. He's probably only been here for a week or so. Have you seen anyone like that?" She pauses only briefly as the girl nods again. Leaning forward, Olivia speaks softly to Ambrose. "I think you should uncover her mouth so she can answer."

Ambrose raises an eyebrow as to show his reluctance to comply, but he does remove his hand from her mouth while maintaining a firm grasp on the girl's shoulders.

"Well if you're asking about the juicy tidbit I'm thinking of, they keep him all the way down the hall." The girl's voice trembles as she tries to speak, forcing out the words. "They keep someone outside his door unless he is with a client. If you don't mind, I gotta go back to work." She eyeballs them nervously as she struggles against Ambrose, but he continues to clutch her tightly.

"Ok. Ambrose, let her go," Olivia orders.

"How can we know that as soon as she is out of our sight that she won't call the guards on us?"

The girl winces and silently shakes her head as Ambrose's hold squeezes painfully on her arm. His words are clipped, his gaze never straying from Olivia.

"Ambrose, you would do well to mind yourself. Mei Li's orders were that this be done discreetly with no casualties," Olivia snaps.

"Mei Li said nothing about casualties, only that we be discrete and make no scenes." Ambrose's retort is loaded with venom.

"The Mother's also stated that I am the lead on this assignment. You will do as asked, or you will find yourself mucking out the latrines in Erebus for the next five hundred years. Are we clear?" An anxious energy burns through Olivia, giving her an eerie countenance.

With a sudden jerk Ambrose releases the girl. "Crystal," he replies.

Wordlessly, the girl scampers away, heading in the direction of the bar.

Silently they continue to work their way back down the long hallway and approach the last set of doors. The corridor is empty, and there is no one stationed outside. The door to the left opens and a woman walks out, adjusting her skirt. As they pass each other the woman leers at Ambrose suggestively. An unsuppressed vileness emanates from the woman, and there is a pitch-black darkness churning just below her bogus facade. The close proximity to her wretchedness causes Olivia's stomach to churn, and she fights to keep the bile down. Slowing their pace, they allow time for the woman to turn down the corridor.

The door isn't locked and opens with ease. Not really knowing what to expect inside, Olivia enters cautiously. The room's light level barely illuminates enough to navigate the area. A naked form lies on the small bed. He is completely bare aside from a thin sheet drawn up to his waist. Both of his wrists and ankles are shackled to the posts of the bed. His eyes are closed, and as Olivia approaches she tries to determine if he is asleep or unconscious. The rhythmic rise and fall of his chest lets her know that he is at least alive.

"I am supposed to get twenty minutes before they send in another harlot to rape me." His voice is detached and sounds of a deep-set exhaustion. The picture Mei Li had shown them pales in comparison to the man in person. Even in this state he seems to exude masculine potency.

"I'm not here for that," Olivia answers as her cheeks burn. Minutely, he opens his eyes and studies them both. Squinting, his focus is on Ambrose.

"Sorry, but I'm not into guys. Not my thing." His eyes close again, but his body hums with an underlying tension. The muscles of his arms tense and flex as he fights quietly against his bonds.

"Your family sent us." His gaze snaps up at Olivia's words. He tries and fails to sit up and ends up flailing around. The jarring movements cause the transparent sheet to shift lower. She takes in a calming breath and keeps her focus on his face. "But first we need to uncover what is really going on here." In a somewhat formal tone she continues, "Aidan, you will be judged, and depending on what we find you will either be released or left here." Olivia sits down on the edge of the bed as she speaks.

"Go ahead. You'll find out the truth and you will see that I am the one who has been wronged." His eyes widen as he strains against his handcuffs.

Placing a single hand on his chest, Olivia closes her eyes and opens the barriers between them. Visions flood her mind as a reverse passage of time. There are numerous women from the last week, all of them pawing, groping, and riding him. It is an endless procession of marring claws and biting teeth. A chilling cream is being applied to his member to numb it and keep it rigid. Their faces are grotesque jackal-like masks out of some nightmare. She can sense his sorrow of loss and dishonor. The vision floods in. Aidan is tied to a chair and is being beaten by Calder and his men, their knuckles are bloodied and bruised. Then a beautiful Fae is lying atop him, kissing his face and chest, her expressions of love brushing an intoxicating heat over his skin. The rich fountain of her crimson hair flows all round them as she whispers softly.

Olivia's heart constricts with the overwhelming feeling of devotion and adoration before she releases the link between them, coming back to the present.

"I'll unshackle you and you will come with us." Reaching out, she clasps one of his manacles and sends a quick pulse of energy through it, popping the lock.

"What about Jenissa? I have to find her," Aidan pleads as Olivia releases the remains of his bonds.

"For right now our goal is to get you to safety. Calder will be called to answer for his crimes and deceit. Once you are safe we will see about locating your woman." Olivia averts her gaze and finds a pair of jeans and hands them over to Aidan.

"We need to move. Someone is coming," Ambrose cautions as he presses his ear to the thin door. "Can you open a portal?"

"The flow of energy is muted here, but I can try." Olivia stands back from the men and walks to the nearest wall.

Gently touching the smoke-stained drywall, she envisions the grand hall at The Hallow. The surface turns to the familiar black churning waters but then flickers back to a solid plane. Perplexed, Olivia tries again, and again the fluid portal snaps closed before completely opening.

"What is happening?" Ambrose questions.

"There are magical barriers that are hampering my ability to open the gateway."

"So we have to sneak out of here?" Ambrose huffs in irritation. "Just great." His stature emits tension as he begins to pace the small room.

"I may be able to open it just outside of the brothel. If the destination is closer in proximity I should be able to maintain it." Olivia reins in her rising frustration, and blocking out everything else in the room she focuses on the one task at hand.

"Well hurry up. We're about to have company in here."

Ambrose, with the help of Aidan, begins to drag an oversized bureau in front of the door, blocking it from opening inward. Muffled voices can be heard outside the door as the handle twists. With a solid thud the door bangs into the dresser. Closing her eyes, Olivia envisions the alley-way across the street. This time the portal stays fluid.

"It's time to go," Olivia announces as she grabs Aidan by the arm and leads him through the portal, Ambrose following quickly behind.

Instantly traversing the distance, they step out into the frigid night air. Immediately, Aidan folds his arms across his chest to hold in his body heat as he shifts his feet to guard them against the cold earth. From the darkness of the alleyway Emma emerges, followed by David. His nose is bloodied and his cheek is swollen. It appears the issue with Haimon followed them outside, but there is no sign of him anywhere.

"Good, it's you." Emma sighs as she peers over Olivia's shoulder, momentarily studying Aidan. Olivia can detect a rising level of distress in Emma's demeanor. "We have to get out of here now. Mother Mei Li just contacted me. Mother Agnes has been murdered. Everyone is being summoned back to The Hallow," Emma explains.

Shock and confusion course through Olivia as she hastily opens another gateway and they all walk into it.

Chapter 6

Stepping through the gateway, they are greeted by several Fury and their Gyges. The general demeanor of everyone is somber. The air is thick with barely controlled apprehension as the Fury and Gyges crowd together with hunched shoulders, their faces are long. Mother Mei Li is also waiting for them. She is dressed in a traditional Hanfu, a flowing dress tied with a sash at the waist and billowing sleeves. White in color, it is a sharp contrast to her black hair which is pulled into a tight bun atop her head. She eyes them nervously, and Emma can sense the rising tension that hums throughout the group. Never before has the murder of a Mother occurred. A Mother is to be revered, to be respected, and never to be harmed.

Pushing their way through the crowd, they approach Mother Mei Li. Her exterior is tousled and weighed down with exhaustion. Aidan stands just slightly behind them, his arms crossed protectively over his chest. He stands stoically in rigid reservation. "Aidan, we welcome you." Mei Li addresses him in a formal tone.

"Have I traded one prison for another?" Aidan asks tersely as he studies his surroundings.

"You are our guest and are afforded our protection for as long as you choose to remain." Mei Li touches his shoulder softly as she speaks. Under the harsh lighting

Emma can make out the partly fading bruises around his face and torso. His physical scars will heal quickly, but the mental wrongs he has endured will take much longer. Mei Li guides him toward David and Ambrose. "Would you two mind taking Aidan to his room? Make sure he receives food and clean clothes." Both men nod as they turn quietly and leave. Aidan is ushered away to receive clothes and some much needed rest.

Turning to address the remaining crowd, Mei Li clears her throat. "I ask that all of you please be on your way. As soon as the curfew is lifted we will let you know. Until then stay in The Hallow. Also, additional quarters have been prepared for those of you that require it. If you have a need, come and find me." As everyone proceeds to exit, Mei Li halts Emma and Olivia with a raised hand. "You two stay. I need to speak with you privately." In silence they wait until all of the others are out of earshot.

"Olivia and Emma, I am pleased to hear that this latest mission was successful. It is good to know that the issue with Aidan has been initially resolved. I imagine the Fairies will have something to say about our involvement with Aidan, but we will address that when it comes. Unfortunately, the pleasantness from a successful mission has been tainted in light of the current events."

"What happened to Agnes, Mother?" Emma inquires. It seems unfathomable that someone would want to harm a Mother— especially one as well liked as Mother Agnes.

Mei Li's countenance reflects the torrent of anguish that currently washes through her. It has been common knowledge that of the three Mothers, Mei Li and Agnes were the closest of companions. They seemed to gain strength and solace from their kindred bond. The three of them turn to walk slowly down the hall as Mei Li recalls the events of last night.

"Mother Agnes retired early last night. Something seemed to be ailing her, though she refused to talk about it. I had my suspicions that her visions were becoming more and more troublesome for her. It was commonplace for her to lock herself away in her room, as if by limiting her exposure to others might diminish the severity of the visions."

"What was she seeing?" Olivia asks. Her gaze shifts nervously up and down the hall, the long corridor echoing back a barren emptiness in either direction.

"I do not know what her premonitions entailed. Like I've said she would rarely talk about them. I was aware that she had not been sleeping. Sometimes she'd be awake for several days at a time. So the hope was that a good night's rest would do her some good."

Mei Li wrings her hands as she studies the floor in front of them, her voice quivering with a subtle hint of guilt. Seeming lost in her thoughts, Mei Li's pace slows nearly to a stop. In her left hand she rubs half of a broken comb.

The broken comb is part of a Chinese ritual of mourning. One half is buried with the deceased while a family member keeps the other half.

"Close to midnight I went to check in on her. I knocked on the door but there was no answer. I contemplated leaving her alone, if on the off chance she was sleeping. But something just felt wrong, and I opened the door. Only the bedside lamp was lit, and at first I didn't see her. She was on the floor beside her bed and was covered in blood, dead. A copper dagger was stuck in her chest and her throat was cut." Mei Li's face turns an ashen shade of grey as tears well in her eyes.

"She was stabbed to death?" Olivia asks, horrified as her voice trembles. "Could you read anything off of her?" For a few minutes following a death, a residual echo of the person's last moments is retained within the flesh and can be recalled.

"No," Mei Li responds sadly. "By the time I found her she had been gone too long. Her room seemed untouched aside from some mild signs of the struggle. There was no indication of forced entry, which leads me to believe that she knew her murderer. At least well enough to grant them access." Again Mei Li scans the hall to ensure their privacy. "What really perplexes me is the fact that a lock of her hair was removed. I don't know if this was done during the altercation or afterward."

"I still don't understand why someone would want to harm her? She was always kind to everyone, even overly kind at times." Emma ponders as her mind races through the possible reasons. Agnes had no known enemies, and her death would not be an advantage to anyone, politically or otherwise.

"I can think of no reason why either. It is crucial that we determine who is responsible for this. The why can be addressed at a later date." Mei Li shakes her head softly. "No one is to be privy to any of the details surrounding Agnes's death. The Hallow has been locked down until tomorrow evening while we finish the investigation. Unless you have been assigned an undertaking I want everyone to stay close. Is that understood?"

"Yes, Mother," the two women reply in unison.

"Good. Now go about your ways, and if you see anything suspicious inform me right away. And please be careful." A look of genuine concern rolls over Mei Li.

"Allow me to escort you back to your quarters," Olivia utters as she motions down the hall. Mei Li simply nods in agreement and both women walk away, leaving Emma alone to watch them depart.

The early hour coupled with the turbulent events of the evening means that sleep will not come easily tonight. The peculiar aura of foreboding has set all of Emma's nerves on edge. After weighing her options, Emma turns toward the direction of David's room. Anxious energy is best directed into mindless training. With any luck he hasn't retired for the night.

She locates David's door and taps quietly. After hearing a sequence of muffled sounds, the door slowly opens. Emma is momentarily relieved as she realizes that she hasn't woken him. But a sudden flush of warmth blaze at her cheeks as she rapidly becomes aware of his partial state of undress. Clad only in his jeans, the warm light emanating from his quarters highlights the contours of his form. Emma forces her gaze to remain trained on his face.

"I hope I'm not disturbing you," she stammers, then clears her throat.

"No. Not really tired anyway. Is there something you need?" he asks as he leans against the doorframe in an irritatingly nonchalant manner, smirking, mildly amused.

"I didn't know if you maybe wanted to do some sparring?" Her view inadvertently travels back to his bare torso, and her eyes snap down to his naked feet. She wages a battle to school her expression, looking anywhere else but at him as another flood of heat burns at her skin. David chuckles softly, a comforting sound which rolls over her. Enveloped in its cozy warmth, its rich velvety tone sedates her tattered nerves.

"Sure. Let me get changed and I'll meet you there," he answers with a twitch of his lips. Emma manages a simple nod as he closes the door. Heading down the hall toward the exercise area, she is plagued by the image of Andrew's death.

For the most part the training area is rarely used at this time of night, but a small group of men are taking turns sparring with each other in the center of an open, matted area. The training arena is sizeable and is relatively well lit by long rows of hanging lights. Each saucer-shaped light fixture is encased by a metal cage to protect it against breakage. The majority of the floor is covered by canvas matting and Nautilus and exercise equipment are set up in the far back corner against the wall.

Trying not to watch any one person in particular, Emma observes that the men training are Gyges. Among them are Moss and Ambrose. Both men are covered in sweat and blood, their breaths coming in quick pants. Each man's hands are fisted in front of them as they circle around the other. The spectators watch silently, enraptured by the battle playing out in front of them.

Moss leaps forward on his toes, swinging wildly at Ambrose, who pushes the blow aside and counters with a solid shot to the other man's ribs and side. Moss stumbles backward, clutching his side as he grunts. A purely malevolent sneer spreads across his face as he leans and spits out blood-filled phlegm.

David walks up to stand beside Emma. Silently they continue to look on. Again, both competitors are measuring each other. The men equally are lunging in at the other, each landing blows or blocking them. Both competitors appear to be evenly matched. Although Moss looks to be stronger and outweighs Ambrose by about fifty pounds, he lacks the skill and finesse. In contrast, Ambrose's movements are elegantly fluid.

Ambrose lands several jabs consecutively, followed by a bone-jarring left hook which sends the larger man to the ground with a solid thud. Moss glares up, his face contorting in a murderous rage. Moving faster than Emma thought him capable of, he launches himself up and at Ambrose. Both are locked in a clinch, vying for a dominant position. As the seconds tick by, Moss finally hoists Ambrose up into the air, slamming him down. Ambrose, from his back, scrambles to control Moss's hands as the barrage of punches start raining down on him.

While absorbing several fierce blows, Ambrose manages to secure Moss's right arm. His hips twist and he pushes his legs up higher on Moss's torso. Locking his ankles, Ambrose traps Moss's arm and head between his legs. Moss pushes against his captor with his free arm, trying to release himself from the hold. By squeezing with his legs, Ambrose uses Moss's own arm to cut off the blood supply going to his brain. After only a few seconds Moss's movements slow until he blacks out.

The onlookers rush in, and it takes all of them to pull the unconscious Moss away from Ambrose. Four men lift Moss and carry him out. Ambrose looks exhausted, and his left cheek is beginning to swell. Two of the Gyges stay behind with Ambrose to check on him. Emma knows the two men accompanying Ambrose. Branson and Lee have been lackeys for Ambrose for the last one hundred years or so. Branson is thickly muscled and stocky. His fiery rust-colored hair matches his robust, surly demeanor. He has never seemed overtly dangerous, but he can be boorish and tactless to those around him. Lee, on the other hand, is one of very few words with a calculating iciness to him. His aqua-blue eyes shift listless around the room. He has a lean swimmer's physique and hair the shade of summer wheat.

Without the aid of the others, Ambrose pulls himself to his feet. From across the gymnasium, Emma sees him smirk and bow his head slightly toward them. The three men turn, their steps in unison as they make their way over to where Emma and David stand watching.

"That was a good match, Ambrose," David states with a nod.

"Much thanks, David." Ambrose tilts his head in reply. "It is always a good principle to keep one's mind and body well honed. Especially in such chaotic times as these." His dissecting gaze shifts to Emma. "Have you received any information about Mother Agnes?"

"No, Ambrose. We have learned nothing as of yet." Emma's throat nearly closes shut under the intensity of his stare. Ambrose nods thoughtfully at her response.

"I am pleased that the Mothers were able to find you a suitable Gyges. David has proven to be quite the able protector." Ambrose speaks in a formal tone.

"You mean they found someone stupid enough to partner with her," Branson taunts, chuckling at Ambrose's immediate frown. "What?" Branson shrugs in a feigned innocence. "You know what she did to her last Gyges?" he asks David. Emma's insides clench at the intrusion of the unwelcome memory. "All the others refused to be with her."

"That's enough, Branson," Ambrose barks. Branson stills instantly from Ambrose's glare.

"Please forgive his impoliteness. His thoughts are not shared. We will leave you to your own training." Ambrose bows slightly again and walks out, followed by the two others.

"What did he mean, your last Gyges?" David asks, rounding to face Emma.

"The first Gyges assigned to me was killed." Emma shifts nervously, her arms held taut at her sides. David waits patiently for her to continue, but she remains silent. "You're not going to say anything else?" he probes.

"Please, David, I don't think I can talk about it." Emma scans the room looking for some avenue of escape.

David sighs in frustration and nods. "Very well. But promise you will tell me eventually."

Relief floods through Emma as she dares to hope that he will let it go.

"I will try." Emma tries to smile back at him.

"Well at least the fight was entertaining," David states as he changes the subject. He glances at the door the others had left through.

"Yes, it was a well matched competition. Plus it's always nice to see Moss put in his place." Emma's voice shudders with nervous energy.

"Well he's a bully. If I had my way he wouldn't even be here." David slowly scans the now empty area. "So, what shall we work on tonight? Boxing, quarterstaff, grenade tossing, Mau Tai... What's your choice? My suggestion would be grappling, as we might learn some interesting techniques rolling around on the mat." He smiles wickedly, wiggling his eyebrows at her, causing Emma's cheeks to warm with a quickening pulse as she studies him.

"Swordplay. I need the practice." Smoothing her features, Emma inhales deeply as she walks over to a weapons rack mounted to the wall. While she could use more training in hand to hand combat, the idea of being that close to this man right now is strangely terrifying. "Try not to break my nose this time," she chides to him with a smile, trying to redirect her train of thought. He grimaces, recalling the incident.

"I've apologized for that about a thousand times now," he pleads, pulling a short sword off of the rack, weighing it in his hands.

"I know. But it's amusing to watch you ruffled by it." She grins wider. After a quick search she selects a well-used katana.

"Let me ask... Why do you only spar with me? I've shown you as much as I know, and the others could probably show you some different Fury styles of fighting."

Next he pulls a saber, again weighing it and slashing the air. The overhead lights reflect on the blade's surface.

"None of the others will practice with me." Her expression sobers. "Well, except for Olivia, but she can be a bit intense. The last time we trained she broke four of my ribs and fractured my arm. It took forever to heal." Emma walks to the center of an open area. Turning around, she waits as he joins her, though standing several feet away.

"I am surprised she will spar with anyone. She has more than an obvious aversion to being touched," David notes as he flexes his shoulders, which produces a loud cracking sound.

"She is a little better with the other Fury, but it probably has something to with her death. Shall we begin? Or are you going to sit there and talk me to death?" Emma arches her eyebrow at him.

"Ha ha," David barks with a toothy grin.

Both of them assume a beginning stance. Emma stands feet apart, the blade held with both hands low in front of her. David circles wide and to the right as Emma follows, turning as well. Darting in quickly, he slashes at her, causing her to shift quickly to parry. The clash of metal on metal resonates through the open space.

"Have we learned anything new about Agnes's death?" he inquires, breathing heavily.

"I can only tell you that they are investigating it. The Hallow is on lockdown until tomorrow night," Emma pants out.

"So it was someone among us?" Asking as he attacks again, David thrusts at her several times.

"More than likely." Emma blocks as she retreats from the oncoming assault.

"So why don't you just judge everyone here? Isn't that what Fury do? They can see a person's actions. That would seem to resolve everything rather quickly."

David parries as Emma comes forward, slashing at him.

"We do not possess enough strength to judge one another. It is a downside to being half human. Some say the explosion that killed the other Mothers actually weakened us all, pushing us all further away from the source of our power," Emma explains between pants.

After several minutes Emma's arms bare several cuts and her clothes are saturated with perspiration. David fakes to the right and spins quickly to bring his blade down in a sweeping overhead attack. She can barely react in time, and blocks the strike only inches from her face. David leans into her using his weight advantage to press the blade closer, Emma's arms burning from the exertion of the prolonged bout. David bows his head until his lips are only a breath away from her skin.

"Are we having fun yet?" he whispers softly. His presence is overwhelming as his heat envelops her. Steeling herself, she pushes fiercely against his blade, but he stands firm and unmoving.

"You would be wise not to anger an old woman," Emma grits out through clenched teeth.

"Maybe I like older women." David laughs quietly as Emma's legs finally give out, sending her to the mat. Standing over her, David presses the tip of his sword to her throat. "I win," he says with a wicked smile.

"That was an underhanded trick." Emma ignores his offered hand and climbs to her feet. "You are trying to distract me."

"Your opponents will never fight fair. You must always assume they lack honor and that they will use every weakness you have against you. Remember that." They both walk back to the weapons rack and begin to clean and oil their weapons.

"I am impressed. You have really improved," David admires as he takes her weapon to put it away.

"Yeah, I actually hit you once or twice." Emma points to his shoulder where a small cut still seeps.

"Oh that… I almost forgot about it. It's just a scratch." He smiles teasingly at her.

"Just a scratch? Really?" Emma reaches out quickly and flicks the wound. David instantly winces. They laugh at each other as they walk out. Fatigued and bloody, Emma needs a shower and bed. As they are about to part ways, David turns silently to face her, clutching the outside of her elbows.

"I really am quite impressed with you. If you keep up the hard work and training you may someday beat me. Even with my advantage you could best me." David's expression remains serious.

"And what advantage is that exactly?" Emma laughs cautiously.

"I will always have the advantage against you, because unlike your other foes, I know you." Without another word he turns, walking away down the receding corridor.

Chapter 7

After a fitful night's sleep, Emma wakes disoriented by the unfamiliar surroundings of her temporary quarters. The mild injuries she sustained during her sparring match with David have all healed, though a slight ache still lingers in her muscles. Following her second shower, she stands in front of a simple sink, wiping condensation from the fogged mirror. Showers and hot water are at the top of her list of modern conveniences that she truly enjoys. If you're cold you can warm yourself up, if you're dirty you can be clean.

For the first time in ages, Emma actually looks at her reflection. Her form is neither large nor thin, and she is not too tall nor short, beautiful nor unsightly. As the youngest of four daughters, her hand was not sought for land or an advance in social status. Her husband, James, was a poor farmer, and her dowry just a cow named Beth. She loved James, and he loved her. He was a simple man, they lived a simple life, and they were happy. After several failed attempts they were blessed with their two beautiful children. Anna and John were utterly perfect. They were tiny magnificent mirror images of their father. The best parts of their mother and father rolled into one. Both of the children had thick tufts of jet-black hair and James's warm green eyes. And in the singular moment of their birth they became her heart and her world. Emma's gaze drifts to the ragged scar on the right side of her neck. Though centuries old, the wound still pains her.

But none of that matters now. She scolds herself. She mentally thrusts the memory away. In her likeness her eyes are heavy with unshed tears. It is silly to remember a life that doesn't exist anymore, or in dreaming about a happiness that is now lost to her. Why should she care about something as pointless as appearance? *Stupid woman*, she chides. She is a killer, solely an instrument to be used against the wicked.

Thoroughly annoyed with herself, Emma quickly dresses. She roughly pulls on jeans and a plain white t-shirt. Leaving the room, she heads down into the catacombs to where the archive is hidden. Down a dusty flight of crumbling stairs she comes upon two vaulted doors. Etched into the wood spanning the width of the doors is the semblance of Cerberus, the three-headed dog that guards the gates of Hades. The latch to the door is located inside the gaping mouth of the whittled beast. Slipping her hand into the jaws, she clasps the long metal tongue, depressing it. In the blink of an eye the mouth snaps shut, piercing the skin of her hand. Her blood begins to flow, filling the deeply-etched grooves running throughout the carving. A warm rush of breath exhales from the monster's nostrils, followed by a subtle click.

The bloodied mouth releases her and the door swings open and away from her, a gust of stale air rushing out to meet her as muddled blackness engulfs the space across the threshold. The small trickle of blood runs the length of a waist-high groove etched into the wall. As it reaches a small wall sconce, a small amount of blood is leeched up into the wick, setting the torch ablaze. The line of blood continues on, lighting each lamp until the vast library is illuminated.

The high, arched ceiling is adorned with time-worn frescos. Ancient scenes of a pastoral bygone era are depicted. It is a rendition of an epic battle of winged seraph combating a menagerie of grotesque demons amidst a smoldering sky of fire. Large tapestries are woven, showing mythical woodland beings. The long wings of the library stretch left and right and are lined floor to ceiling with immense bookshelves. Each bookshelf contains hundreds of tomes and ancient texts collected over the millennia. Several small tables and chairs are nestled in small alcoves for reading. The distinct odor of old papyrus and mold is pungently overwhelming in the capacious area.

As she slowly makes her way down one of the rows of shelves, Emma scans the titles and selects several cumbersome volumes. She walks into a secluded alcove and approaches a desk as a lamp perched beside it burst into life and illuminates the area. The diminutive reading area is also lined with bookshelves. The table takes up a good deal of the room, leaving only a narrow path to walk around. The tomes are weighty and send up a plume of dust as Emma plops them on the surface. For a moment Emma stares blankly at the covers trying to organize her thoughts as to where to begin. All she has to go on is fragmented bits of information. Nothing about the two murders point in a clear direction.

Opening the first over-sized book, she scans through a regional listing of demons and paranormal beings with a penchant for body parts and skin. The Egyptians have the demon Ammut, who would eat the heart of those found to be impure. Upon death, one's heart is weighed by Anubis. If their heart is pure they can continue onto the afterlife. Tik-Tiks, Sigbins, and Wak Waks from the Philippines are all known for eating the hearts of their victims, but for the most part they seek the heart of a fetus or child. The Wak Wak will devour a human completely. Even werewolves are known for sometimes eating the hearts of their victims.

Or perhaps Jackson's heart wasn't taken to be eaten. The heart holds a strong significance in a multitude of rituals, and it is a weakness for many species.

If his heart was taken for some other reason, then why would someone place a child's heart in his mouth? Mei Li said they didn't believe this was the work of a rival clan. Though, could it be an act of revenge? The circumstances of his death appear to be personal in nature. The connection could lie in the child's heart or even his own being removed.

The three possible reasons for his execution might be because of Jackson as a person, or Jackson as a werewolf, or even his position within the packs as a leader. To remove him as leader would mean another alpha would take his place. His decision to unify the packs would certainly cause a serious disruption and would change the dynamic of the species' social structure. Even if he were to succeed, the hierarchy would mirror a monarch-type system. Others have tried to accomplish that in the past and failed.

The killer could potentially be his son or even another member within his pack vying for the leadership position. His death could have nothing to do with his push to become king of the werewolves. The meeting with his son, Bray, will have to be handled delicately. If this was a personal attack against Jackson, a sit down with the pack may answer a lot questions.

There is still the possibility that he was killed simply because he is a werewolf. Several years ago, the Fury had to address an issue with some vampires killing other species for trophies. That would explain the missing skin. Emma thumbs through the thick pages of another book. It is a detailed study of animal shifters. Some of the oldest legends describe a belief that a person's beast was physically there underneath the skin, and you could determine if someone was afflicted by slicing open their flesh. If they were a werewolf then you should be able to see the fur inside. Taking the hide of a prominent pack leader would be a significant trophy.

One of the faded prints catches Emma's attention. It is an ancient illustration of Lycaon, the King of Arcadia, and of him being transformed into a wolf. According to the Fury, it is the origin of the werewolves. In order to test the hospitality of humanity, Zeus traveled to Arcadia. Even dressed as a peasant the townsfolk recognized him and showed him great courtesies. But Lycaon doubted that it was truly Zeus and devised a test of his own. He ordered a young child slaughtered and roasted into a meal for his guest. If this visitor was truly Zeus then he would be omniscient and not eat the meal. Enraged by the attempted deceit, Zeus killed everyone within the palace and called upon the Fury to punish Lycaon. They transformed him into a wolf. He was driven mad with bloodlust, and for his remaining days he roamed the land in search of his next prey. The history of the Fury has always been closely interwoven with that of the werewolves.

Mother Agnes had always stressed the importance of maintaining our ancient ties. As she put it, 'In our world it is not a matter of us versus them. We are all intricate pieces of the same puzzle. It is only by cooperating that we can achieve our long term goals'. Agnes always strove for peace above anything else. Emma assumed her desire for tranquility had something to do with the visions she suffered from.

Although they were different ages physically, their human lives were lived roughly at the same time– within a few hundred years of each other. Agnes had befriended Emma and seemed to watch out for her, trying to keep her safe. On several occasions Agnes stood against the other Mothers on Emma's behalf. Her steadfastness stopped when Emma was sent to Erebus. From the rumors, Agnes had defended her with such fervor that she was sent there as well. Emma never asked for the specifics of what led to her being punished, but their relationship was different afterward. Agnes still remained friendly, but she seemed to distance herself.

She was a passionate, outspoken woman, and Emma couldn't believe that someone would want her dead. She grabs another book from a tall shelf. The fact that someone removed some of Agnes's hair seems a prominent point of interest. After scanning several texts, the only relevant information she can find is part of a funeral ritual in ancient Greece. A lock of hair is removed and given to Thanatos, the god of death. Downtrodden, Emma stares silently at the towering books around her.

A darkly oppressive aura fills the cramped space around her. As the heaviness of the air presses down, an itching sensation scratches its way along her spine. Looking up from the books, Emma scans the area, searching for any possible threat. The torches lining the archive flicker and begin to wane in unison. Emma wills the flames back to life. Pushing to her feet, she gathers her wits, intent on leaving immediately. In a breath all of the torches sputter out, enveloping Emma in a thick cloak of total darkness. Rising terror and claustrophobia claw at Emma's throat, and she must fight to hold back the scream welling within her. Scrambling to ebb the growing panic, she focuses on her breathing. Inhaling deeply, she holds her breath for several seconds and releases it slowly. The scuff of her shoes is a jarring sound against the bleak void of silence.

Minutely in the distance, a speck of light radiates. It is a muted green ember that shimmers with an eerily unnatural pulse. Emma's eyes must be playing tricks as her mind races to process what she is seeing. The light starts to slowly expand, growing larger and with more intensity. Within several seconds the space is illuminated with a sickly green hue, and the ember has morphed into a gaseous sphere. It blocks all avenues of escape with its mass and span. The orb pulsates with an overwhelming energy, and a rush of white noise floods her senses. As if immersed in a raging river, all other sound is muted. This continues on for what seems like an eternity until subtle clicks and sounds begin to break through. As the tones grow in force they take on the likeness of several voices whispering all at once.

Amidst the tidal wash of sound, Emma's feet feel as though they are cemented to the floor. The voices grow more pronounced as single words become audible. The surrounding rush of background sounds die as the whispers push forward.

"Child of Gaia, of light and death, of flesh and sky. Listen and heed." The disembodied voices speak in accord. A fluid movement swirls within the confines of the orb, giving way to a solid mass which walks out from within the green gas toward Emma, and she recognizes the visage is that of Mother Agnes. Startled, Emma steps back and bumps into the chair behind her. The spectral Agnes raises her hand in greeting.

"Be at ease, Emma. I must speak with you, and we have very little time." Although her form is semitransparent, she radiates the presence of her former self.

"Who are you?" Emma shakes her head as she finds her voice.

"It's me, Agnes. Have you been drinking?" the ghostly figure chides with a familiar smirk.

"What? No. I, I don't understand. What is happening?" Emma's mind careens.

"As I said, I don't have much time. So listen. The Fury and the human world are in grave danger. A great darkness is clawing its way up from the depths and could destroy the balance we fight to protect. Your trust and honor will be your undoing, and you must be wary of all." Agnes turns, gazing into the glowing mass behind her and responds to voices Emma cannot hear. "Yes. Yes. I know. Just a little while longer." Again her stare settles on Emma. There is a fierceness in her emerald-colored eyes as her back straightens rigidly. "I failed you in the past, but I can't change what has been done. I pass to you my essence, my gift. I pray to God that it will assist you."

"Wait. I don't understand. Who are you?" Emma pleads.

Ignoring the question, Agnes steps back and is reabsorbed into the mass. The humming vibrations strengthen as Emma is immersed in the green glow, the green vaporous fumes swirling around her, and then in a second it rushes into her body. Her senses are set ablaze as a hailstorm of energy courses through her. Searing agony causes Emma's knees to buckle, crushing her to the cold ground. A scorching white fire rages behind her eyes. Slowly the torturous assault begins to ebb and her senses return. The orb has vanished and the torches are relit. Breathing in deeply, Emma struggles to gather herself. Tremors run through her. Staggering to her feet, she has to clasp the back of her chair. The waves of nausea rise and fall as she struggles to tamp down the bitter taste of bile.

A flash of movement draws her attention back to the library. An indistinguishable phantom shape is shifting and moving, obscured in the depths of a shadowed area. As

111

the large form saunters casually in her direction, Emma squints to make it out better. Moss breaches the inky darkness moving toward her at a measured pace. A premeditated malice emanates from him, oppressing the air in the cramped space. His black eyes reflect the pale candlelight as over exaggerated shadows play across his face.

"What are you doing in here?" he asks gruffly, his tone cold as he crosses his arms over his expansive chest.

"I could ask the same thing. Gyges cannot enter the archives unattended." Emma masks her features in a serene façade. Internally she battles the urge to bolt from the room. *This man is dangerous,* she reminds herself.

"Celia asked me to get her some books," he responds blankly. With an arrogant confidence he stalks further into the room.

"What kind of books would she send you for?" Emma shifts to keep the table and chair between them.

"She wants books about the Fury." Turning from her, he skims his eyes over the shelf to his right. Insolently, he tips books out toward him and then slams them back into place.

"She is a Fury. One would think she has a fairly good knowledge on the subject." A boiling irritation starts to grow within Emma.

112

"Well, you know, I've found that the Fury seem to be a curious lot. Like cats." He chuckles softly to himself. His face snaps suddenly back into a blank unreadable mask. "Always wanting to know more, sticking their noses into where it shouldn't be. Unfortunately it is often a deadly trait to have." Taking another step forward, his massive frame blocks Emma between the table and bookshelves.

"What do you mean by that?" Emma calculates quickly. If he comes at her there is a limited chance that she could defeat him in a physical match. Against most opponents she'd be fairly confident, but Moss has great skill and is freakishly strong.

"Nothing, little cat." Glancing downward to the table, he robotically flips through the pages of an open book.

"Well I will leave you to do Celia's bidding." With a nod Emma steps forward, trying to skirt between Moss and the closest bookshelf. Moss's view remains locked on the open tome. Just as she is about to pass, Moss's arm juts out, resting against the bookshelf, effectively blocking her with a dangerous lack of space separating them.

"I am no one's fucking errand boy." His features harden with barely checked indignation.

"Of course not. It was not my intent to imply that." Emma schools her features, keeping her voice calm and fluid. *Exude an air of confident civility and maybe this won't turn ugly,* Emma assures herself.

"Perhaps you can help me find these stupid-ass books." While his annoyance has appeared to have washed away, he keeps his arm firmly planted.

"There are certain texts that I do not have access to. But what, in general, is she looking to find?" Emma fights the overwhelming desire to step away from him. She can't show any sign of fear or weakness. Not with this man.

"She wants to know how to kill a Fury." The sudden shock of the statement slams Emma in the stomach, twisting it into a mangled mass. Moss focuses his watch on her, scrutinizing her every response. The intensity of his meaningful stare makes her uneasy. A kind of wicked glee radiates from his eyes.

"Why would she want to know that?" A tightening sensation assails Emma's chest.

"Celia's got an unusual appetite. She wants things that others don't. She wants to know stuff that bothers the shit out of other people." With lightning speed, Moss reaches out, grabbing Emma by the throat. His huge hand spans her skin easily. "Though it makes you wonder how many times can you choke a Fury to death before they stop coming back? Will they survive having their pretty skin flayed from their bodies?" Moss's gaze surveys the length of Emma's body, inspecting her. His grip tightens as she struggles against his hold. There isn't enough room between them for her to gain any advantage.

While she would survive the strangulation, there was no way she was going down without a fight. Concentrating her efforts, she tries to dislodge his hold. The initial rise of panic is quickly traded for a seething rage. It is a growing anger at Moss and at herself for being caught off guard.

As the seconds tick by she can feel the pressure build as her trapped blood fights to get to her brain. The rush of blood is deafening, and the peripheral rim of her vision starts to blur and darken as Moss squeezes her neck more firmly. Pressing his weight into her, he is effectively pinning her against the bookshelf. His mouth hovers mere inches from her ear and she can hear him inhaling deeply, as if smelling her.

Darkness threatens to engulf her as she can hear someone calling her name. The muted voice lingers just on the peripherals of her earshot. Emma senses the sudden tautness overtake Moss's body as he reacts to the sound.

"See you around, little cat," he rasps in her ear.

The force of his hands around her neck vanishes, and she is helpless as she collapses to the floor. Coughing, she pulls in a lungful of air. She has no idea where Moss has fled to. Searching the archive, she can't see if he has run away or is in hiding somewhere. The sound of soft footsteps approach and Emma steels herself for the next attack.

Chapter 8

⁓ঔ⁓

Through the alcove doorway a small figure hops into the room. As soon as Emma recognizes the young girl the ominous foreboding and tension drains from her body. Sara's gaze settles on Emma, her eyes brighten, and a large, toothy smile spreads across her face. The tiny girl's shoes sparkle with various colored lights each time she takes a step. Dying at the tender age of six meant that Sara will forever remain as she is right now. As time progresses she will mature mentally and emotionally, but she will stay trapped within the physical form of a child. An untimely death has stolen a childhood from her. Even now, because she is a Fury, she will never be able to have one.

"Emma, where have you been? I've been looking all over for you," she gasps with a breathless excitement. Her tiny head cocks to the side and she frowns as she takes in Emma's disheveled state on the floor. "What happened? Did you fall down again?" Skipping forward, her delicately undersized form stops just in front of Emma. Her tiny eyebrows furrow and her lips skew to the side as she quizzically studies her friend.

"No. I didn't fall, I..." Emma, embarrassed, stops herself. She is not going to tell Sara about Moss or the green entity. "I thought I saw a mouse. I was looking for it when you came in."

"Ooh, a mouse. Where is it? Was it cute?" Sara's eyes grow large with glee. She eagerly searches the floor around Emma.

Emma's hind end starts to turn numb from the cold stone floor, and slowly she struggles to pull herself to her feet. "Wait. Let me help you." Sara places a small electrical device down on the table and reaches a hand out to Emma. Trying to hide her amusement, Emma clasps Sara's tiny hand and continues to stand. Fury or not, Sara's small frame means she still had the strength of a child– albeit a strong child. Though Emma stands on her own, Sara's face reddens as she labors dramatically to lift her friend. With shakiness still wracking her body Emma leans against the nearest bookshelf. Sara pats some imaginary dust from her hands and beams happily back at Emma with an amazing sense of accomplishment.

"There. Now, what do you say?" she asks sternly, her little hands fisted on her hips. But her childish features ruin her attempt at a reprimanding demeanor.

"Oh, of course." Emma straightens her back and gives a brief nod. In her most formal tone she addresses the small girl. "My dearest madame, I thank you ever so kindly for the valiant aid you have provided to me in my time of utmost need. For generations to come, they will sing most heartedly of your great and noble deeds." Sara giggles loudly as Emma curtseys. They both begin to laugh gleefully.

"You are welcome." Sara laughs and attempts a clumsy curtsey of her own. "My mom says it is important to thank someone when they help you."

"Seems like good advice." Sara walks back to the table to retrieve her device. Emma realizes it is a smart phone with a large touch-screen. A vibrantly colored game is playing on it. Emma doesn't know the name of it, but it is something with birds and a slingshot.

"Where did you get that?" Emma asks, motioning toward the phone. She is more than a little curious.

"David gave it to me." Sara smiles brightly. For such a young child she has quickly managed to steal the hearts of those around her. Most of the Fury tend to dote over her incessantly, bringing her dolls, toys, and candy. Last year, Emma overheard Mother Agnes asking if a gaming system could be set up down here. As children are a rarity in The Hallow, the Fury and Gyges are often enraptured by younglings. When children die they are still blessed and spirited away to reside in Elysium, a plane of existence where it is an endless summer and they are at peace with those they love.

Maneuvering herself into a chair, Emma sits heavily, admiring the beautiful child. "David is very fond of you, as we all are." Even though she is almost nine years old, she still looks exactly as she did the day she passed. Her plump cheeks are framed softly by rich waves of platinum-blonde curls, and her eyes are a vibrant blue that sparkle in the light. Her light pink top is decorated with sparkling colored rhinestones designed to look like a puppy.

"Well, I like David, he's always nice to me and he smells good," Sara declares as she plays with her phone.

"He smells good?" Emma asks with a laugh.

"Yeah. He smells like my daddy's soap. But I like most everyone here. I miss Mother Agnes. She was always pinching my cheeks, which hurt a little, and she was always giving me dolls like I'm a baby, which I'm not, but she was nice too." A deep frown creases her little brow as she recalls the deceased Mother. Sara pulls herself up into the large chair next to Emma, her legs swinging to and fro as she sits.

"I miss her too, sweetie." Emma drapes her arm around Sara's shoulders, hugging her tightly. "I miss her too."

"Do you think she's in heaven?" Sara cranes her neck, meeting Emma's gaze, her soft eyes questioning.

"I don't know." The sense of concern and trepidation are muted, but evident in the small child's eyes. "But I'd like to think so," Emma continues. "I'd like to think that one day when I pass I will get to see my children and hold them again."

"Your little boy and girl?" she asked, her voice a hushed whisper.

"Yes. My daughter, Anna, was about your age." Emma softly brushes the hair from Sara's eyes.

"Will I get to see my mom and dad too?" The girl's somber tone mirrors the poignant emotion resonating through her.

"Yes, sweetie, you'll see them again."

"But what if they don't want to see me? What if they think I'm bad? Is that why I died? Cause I was bad?" Agitation mounts rapidly in the small girl, advancing toward torrential hysteria.

"No. No, why would you think that?" Sara's gaze turns downward, thin trails of wetness streaking her cheeks. Gently wiping the tears from her face, Emma tilts Sara's chin up to meet her eyes. "Who told you that?"

"Celia said we are all here because we are bad. We are demons who live in Hell, and that when we die we will become nothing. We don't get to go to Heaven, and I'm tainted cause of how I died." Glossy tears flood Sara's eyes as she buries her head into Emma's chest.

"Listen to me. You are not bad or tainted. You are not responsible for anything about your death. And if any of us are going to Heaven, it's you." Sara's wracking bawl ebbs slightly to a low, mournful sob. "You can't listen to people like Celia. She's just a mean bully. Do you hear me?" Sara's doesn't look up, but nods her head. Emma kisses her head, softly humming to her as the young girl weeps. Emma recalls her first years as a Fury– she cried a lot too.

Celia knowing the details of Sara's death is more than a little distressing. As a general rule, no one ever speaks about their death. Only the Mothers are privy to the events that led up to your death and what sent you to The Hallow. Last year, Sara had finally confided to Emma the events surrounding her passing. Even after this long it still enrages Emma what was allowed to happen to this happy child. But unfortunately it seems more and more a common occurrence. A child is snatched within feet of their front door by a predator. They are tortured and killed. They die alone, terrified, and one can only hope that the body is found so the parents can have some closure. There is no such luck for Emma's parents. No remains are left to find when you become a Fury.

After several minutes, Sara stops crying and wipes her tears and a snotty nose on her sleeve. Her eyes are red and puffy, but the shimmer has returned to them.

"Better now?" Emma asks, sympathy rich in her tone.

"Yeah, a little bit," Sara replies nasally and glances up with a nod. Popping up off the chair, Sara heads over to the table and flips through the worn pages. "What are you looking up? Ooh, are you going to meet with the werewolves? I can't wait to meet a real life werewolf." Her demeanor instantly shifts into a wide-eyed, unbridled exuberance.

"Yes, and don't bother asking what it's about." Emma stands, her legs much steadier now. Walking over, she closes the books and begins replacing them on the shelves. Sara pouts petulantly, and for a moment seems ready to argue. But a stern look from Emma quells the desire.

"Okay, okay. But you know, when my interment period is up I'm going to go out all the time. Mother Mei Li says that I can be very useful, and I might even get my very own Gyges to take me places. Do you think David will take me to the mall?"

"When you are told that it's okay for you to leave I'm sure you can ask David and see if he will." Emma stretches on her toes to replace one of the books on the top shelf. When a fledgling Fury dies they are quarantined in The Hallow for seventy-five years. It is a callous form of torture that is sugar-coated in the guise of protection. The prospect of spending nearly a century in this underground hell, has driven some to take their own lives. But again, the Mothers justify this imprisonment as a way to safeguard the Fury while they are at their most vulnerable.

The Fury are stronger and faster than most humans, and they can more than hold their own against supernatural beings. They do however have one devastating frailty. Pitted against their Dolofonos, the one who killed them, the strength and speed of a Fury means nothing. To combat this, the assumption is that the recently deceased Fury will be stowed away until their Dolofonos dies. Within seventy-five years it is fairly likely that the killer will have passed on either naturally or otherwise.

Sara stares whimsically at her phone. The screen displays a rich green forest. Solid rays of sunlight slice through the canopy to the soft warmth of pine-covered ground. The young girl yawns widely as she rubs her eyes with the heel of her hand.

"You look tired. Are you not sleeping well?" Emma approaches, touching Sara's head lightly. The child's eyes do not waver from the screen as another outdoor scene flashes on the display. This time it is a cityscape illuminated at night. Sara wordlessly shakes her head.

"Bad dreams again? Have you talked to Mother Mei Li about them? She may be able to help," Emma offers quietly.

Sara turns her gaze upward. "I did talk to Mother Mei Li. I told her everything I've dreamed about, and it still doesn't help."

"What did she say?" Emma asks. With a soft hand she guides Sara toward the door.

"She said the dreams are proph...proph...prophetic." Sara struggles with the word. "Each night I say a prayer before I go to sleep, that the dreams wouldn't come. I wish I would dream about puppies and fun things, like when Mommy and Daddy took me to the beach." Sara leans in closer, lowering her voice. "But the bad dreams still come, and they scare me."

Emma kneels and turns Sara to face her. "What do you dream about? It's alright to tell me, sweetie," Emma says reassuringly, as she can see the hesitation on the young child's face.

Sara stares back down at her phone. Her expression is guarded and haunting. "It's black and cold and I'm outside. I'm shivering, but I'm all sweaty too. I go through this long tunnel, and all of a sudden there's a forest. It's real dark, but I can kind of see. I come to an opening in the woods and there is a baby deer being killed."

A pained look etches Sara's face as she recalls the vivid nightmare. "It is being attacked by a black bear and a huge snake. I'm afraid and I want to run but I can't. The little deer is screaming. It's this awful sound." She closes her eyes tightly as if to block out the image. "After the fawn is dead I can see that the bear and snake have collars around their necks. Their leashes stretch all the way into the darkest part of the woods. Something else is there. I can feel it,but I can't see it. It's bad and evil and it's not alone." Emma feels a tremor run through the petite child and pulls her closer, holding her gently. "What's worse is that I also keep dreaming about David." Her large eyes widen with sorrowful angst.

"What about David, sweetheart?" Emma feels a sudden upsurge of apprehension rising within her own body. The idea of some harm coming to David sets her teeth on edge and twists her insides into painful knots.

"I don't know, it's really hard to say." Sara's face crinkles and she tries to remember. "It's like he's hurt. He's surrounded by an awful green mist. I can't get to him and I can't help him." Pleadingly, she lifts her eyes to Emma. "Emma, promise me you'll keep David safe, promise you will."

"I promise," Emma manages with a weak smile. "No one is going to hurt him. Come on now, you need to get some rest." Emma continues to direct her out of the room.

"But what if I have more bad dreams?" Sara asks diminutively, her voice a breathy whisper.

"The dreams are a part of who you are now. They will be both a blessing and a curse to you. One day you will understand the purpose of these dreams, and they may be able to help you save someone's life. But first you need to rest. Being exhausted will do you no good."

"Oh, alright." She sighs as the fatigue settles throughout her. Exiting the library, Emma reseals the exit, the halves of Cerberus's mouth merging together with an imposing clunk.

Seeing Sara's heavily-laden footsteps, Emma is worried the poor child won't make it to her room. "Do you want me to carry you for a bit?"

"No, I can walk. I'm not a baby." The sentence is punctuated with a large mouthed yawn.

"Alright, just be careful walking. The ground can be uneven." Sara nods her head sleepily as Emma lays a hand on her back.

Making their way through the maze of corridors, they steadily ascend the several floors back to the common areas. From down the length of the hall a small group enters the passage, approaching them slowly.

Emma's stomach drops as she takes in the crowd. Celia is flanked by three Gyges that are not bound to her. In fact, they are not attached to any Fury at all. Emma has a suspicion that they have not opted for a Fury because they are biding their time, waiting for Moss to die. Upon Moss's death, Celia will be available to be selected by another Gyges as her guardian. These leeches flock around her with a fruitless abandon.

A cloying, sweet smile is artistically applied on Celia's exquisitely stunning features. A thick draping of smooth auburn hair flows softly to her mid back. Almond-shaped tawny eyes, the color of a summer doe's coat, shimmer under perfectly arched eyebrows. Her slender figure and ample bosom are the quintessential standard of beauty. Though truth be told, if Celia is the poster child for all that is loveliness and allure, then Emma would rather be considered ugly. The woman's outward facade seems to hide something truly menacing underneath. Somewhere within Celia is a dubiously toxic evil that is so deeply ingrained it is nearly impossible to detect. Emma has always believed in her uncanny ability to read the personalities of those around her. But Celia has always been a mystery. She is a dichotomy of flamboyant extrovert and shelled secrecy.

As the entourage approaches their voices fade into an awkward silence. Emma steps forward, shielding Sara with her body. "Emma," Celia purrs ostentatiously. "I'd like to say how wonderful it is to see you, but that would be a lie, wouldn't it?"

"And of course we all know that you are the pinnacle of honesty and candor," Emma retorts sarcastically as she battles to keep the utter revulsion for the woman from her voice.

"Whatever do you mean, Emma?" Her tone is sickly sweet, again radiating an overt show of innocence. "Oh, by the way…" She taps her full lips with a long, sculptured nail. "How is David doing? I've been meaning to have a little chat with him. Such a strong handsome man shouldn't have to endure his time here alone. And I imagine your tedious nature tends to wear on him ever so much."

"You know damn well what I mean. You and your toadies just need to stay away from us– all of us." Emma struggles to ignore the woman's incessant taunts. Celia's gaze flickers toward Sara.

"Oh, I can see she told you about our little chat." Her smiling face melts into a callous mask. "What would you have me do, Emma?" she spits out, punctuating each word sharply, adding a staccato quality to them. "Should I lie to her or fuss over her as you do?" Her eyebrow spikes up at the question.

"I want you to leave her alone, it's that simple. It is simple enough that I am certain that even you can understand it." Two of the men with Celia step forward, but she halts them with a motion of her hand.

"Emma, I agree with you. It is quite simple. It is a simple truth that you and this poor pathetic child just don't belong here. If there were truly any justice in this world, you would both be made to leave this place. Either that or put out of your misery. But we don't live in a just world, do we? So everyone else is forced to endure your insufferable presence."

"We are allowed to be here. We passed the tests just like you did," Sara squeaks angrily, still partially hidden behind Emma.

"Passing the tests isn't the only thing that makes you a Fury." Celia's hands are planted firmly on her hips. "What good will those tests do you? Will they help her to kill a minotaur? She will never be strong enough to survive out there." Celia roughly jabs her pointed fingernail toward Sara. "That little troll may have passed your precious tests, but the Mothers will never let her leave here. She'll stay down here forever, just taking up space, and we'll have to carry the load for her." Sara tenses and inhales sharply. Without glancing down, Emma can tell the words cut Sara deeply.

"Shut up, Celia, just shut up now." Emma steps forward, blocking Celia from Sara's view. Celia rounds her blistering glare toward Emma. The woman seethes with barely leashed ire.

"And you... What are you going to do? A half-breed freak. Let me ask you, did you cry when the Mother's ripped you from the arms of your undead lover? Do you still miss him?" An eerie smile creases Celia's face, making Emma's skin crawl. "Your only truly significant talent is that you have an uncanny ability to disturb people around you," Celia taunts with a raise of her eyebrow.

Before any conscious thought can form, Emma's arm flies outward on its own. The blow lands firmly on Celia's nose and is accompanied by the delightfully satisfying sound of cartilage snapping. The woman's eyes bulge widely for a second before she stumbles back into the arms of the Gyges.

"You bitch," Celia screeches, holding her now bloodied nose. One of the men supports Celia while the other two start to advance toward Emma, stalking her.

"Stop!" A sharp voice booms loudly as it instantly halts the men advancing. Tatiana eyes them sternly from an open doorway. "Stop this lunacy at once." Celia rushes forward, clutching at the Mother's arm.

"She struck me, Mother. Do you see?" Celia displays the already dried blood on her nose and hand.

"Yes I see," Tatiana replies coldly.

"I demand retribution. She must be punished, Mother. To raise a hand against another Fury is tantamount to…"

"Be silent," Tatiana interrupts. "I am well aware of what has happened here. And there is no excuse for such behavior. Both of you should be ashamed of yourselves." Utterly shocked, Celia stares at the Mother in disbelief.

"The Fury must coexist in relative harmony. There will be no violence toward each other." The Mother turns her attention to Celia, her expression that of formal indifference. "You may not care for one another, but Emma and Sara are in fact Fury, and as such you will show them the respect that they so rightly deserve. Do you understand?"

Completely cowed, Celia stares at the ground and nods simply in response.

"Emma, David was asking after you, and the child needs to rest. Go. The four of you stay here." She pins the others with her stare. "I will have a private talk with you." Without any further prompting, Emma ushers Sara down the hall.

Chapter 9

Thanatos sits in quiet meditation behind his brobdingnagian desk. His hands are steepled in front of his face as his elbows rest on the arms of his chair. The quiet ambience of his personal quarters has always had a soothing effect on him. While it is not as grandiose as some of his other residences, this one suits him just fine. The décor is gothic in style, yet elegantly done. His massive bed is the centerpiece of the living space. The desk and clothing chests are made from elaborately carved poplar wood. The muted color of the hung tapestries swallows up much of the open space, inspiring an intimate feeling. A small lamp sparsely illuminates the area around it.

He calmly watches the panel of monitors across the room. The grainy black and white images flash as they alternate between the different locations being observed. On occasion a figure scurries up and down the long hallways. Often they are alone, but at times they are accompanied by another Fury or Gyges.

For centuries he has kept a keen eye on the comings and goings of The Hallow. His reconnaissance was made easier when he covertly had the closed circuit surveillance system installed. Spending so much time studying his foe has allowed him a unique insight into their behaviors and weaknesses. It is a wicked deception, of course, but all is fair in love and war. His own personal war must be won through several significant victories. The key to a decisive victory lies in knowing one's enemy completely, as well as patience. As the god of death, he is nothing if not patient.

After all this time his plan is finally coming into fruition. For millennia he has waited and bided his time. The unassuming brook of his design has started to flow, and soon it will be transformed into a raging torrent that will wash aside everything that stands in his way. Collecting all the necessary elements has taken the longest time, and the risk of being discovered is a constant danger. Even he, at times, had his doubts that the final pieces would surface. But at last, the final Fury has been reincarnated. These three are the living embodiment of the original three sisters. Now that Olivia has blossomed into her utmost strength, the triune is complete. Olivia, Mei Li, and Tatiana have been hand selected by the Fates themselves to bring order back to this savage world. Each of them exhibit powers vastly superior to those around them. The mistaken view flourished that with fewer Fury being summoned back from the dead that their kind was dying out. But Thanatos realized many centuries ago that this was not so. As the weaker Fury died off their power pooled and congregated to the strongest among them.

Each of the three women possesses a different skill set that will aid him in remolding the world. Olivia's acumen for battle is unquestionable. Cool and calculating in the midst of battle, one would be hard-pressed to find her better. Tatiana is the callous, unmoving will of justice. Her ability to know one's past is a decided advantage. No one will be able to hide behind a veil of deceit. Mei Li is the heart that binds them together. She controls the ebb and flow of power accessible to them. She can keep them grounded or set them free. They will be the tools by which he will mete out his judgment.

With the power of the Fury under his control, all that has been taken from him will be returned. He, by rights, should be honored and respected. For eons he has been ridiculed and subjugated by the Olympian gods. They viewed him as a fool, a lesser god and a common errand boy. But no more. Older than the gods themselves, his claim to the domain of death is indisputable. There is not a being in existence that is immune to the decay of time. Death comes to everyone, even to the gods, trapped in their mountainous prison. They war against the crushing siege of time, mindlessly clinging to a world that no longer believes in them. They are but fanciful myths now, treasured ideologies that inspired an archaic people. And for this they waste away, dissolving into the putrid sacks of dust that they really are. Thanatos laughs quietly to himself.

The beauty of it all is that he will never share their fate, as everyone still to this day believes in and fears death. Death is a constant in a world that continues its metamorphosis. Very few aspects of this dying rock remain unchanged. The gift of a tranquil death is his to pass on to the human nations of the Earth, and no one else's.

From the door comes a solid knock. Glaring at the wooden portal, he fumes at the unexpected interruption. Unless one wanted to be flayed alive, his people knew never to disturb him during his isolated solace. Fortunately for them he is awaiting several communications. Breathing deeply, he reigns in his anger, not wanting to rage at the poor idiot on the other side of the door.

"Come," he commands with a gruff bark. Silently the door swings inward. A young man in his mid-twenties steps into the room. His dirty blonde hair is trimmed closely to his head in the current military style. The youth scans the room, examining the area for hidden dangers.

Thanatos ponders for a moment, trying to remember the lad's name. He has carefully cataloged and memorized the names and history of all of those around him. Kevin, yes, Kevin Wilson. He recalls that the boy died in Afghanistan six months ago. He left behind a young wife and baby boy in Atlanta, where he lived. He is a decent soldier, smart but not too smart. He seems more than competent in carrying out most tasks assigned to him.

"My apologies for the interruption, sir. You had requested that I let you know as soon as they left. Ten minutes ago they exited The Hallow. No one else accompanied them." Kevin's tone is composed and monotone. He stands rigidly at attention, hands clasped behind him and his feet apart, staring blankly forward.

"Thank you, Kevin. What is the status of the other tasks assigned to you?" Thanatos asks, remaining in his seat but leaning back and reclining slightly.

"The books you wanted have been removed from the library. They have been secured in your private vault. Also, sir, Celia is waiting to see you outside."

"She can continue to wait," Thanatos answers sharply, not taking his eyes from Kevin.

"She seems really upset, so I told her I would tell you she was here."

"I said she can wait," Thanatos growls sternly.

Kevin shifts uncertainly for a moment before quickly regaining his composure.

"And what of the Mother's body?" Thanatos inquires, but he already knows the answer. "Was it collected and disposed of as I had ordered?" He tamps down his brewing anger.

"The female's body was discovered before it could be collected." For the first time the man's voice wavers. The death of the Mother is an unfortunate necessity. Thanatos sincerely regrets the need to eliminate Mother Agnes. Her skills were quite impressive, as she had an impeccably rare talent of foresight. If she were more malleable she could have become a powerful addition to his cause. But the damn woman could not be reasoned with. She was starting to get too close and prying where she should not have. The loss of her strength is acceptable in comparison to the greater goals. "Orders, sir?" Kevin asks, interrupting Thanatos's thoughts.

"Follow the two of them, at a safe distance. Do nothing. When they arrive at their destination I want you to contact Desiree and tell her it is time. She will know what to do. Return and report to me with a status update."

"Yes, sir." Sharply, Kevin turns heading for the door.

"Kevin." The young man halts but does not turn around. "You may send Celia in now."

Within seconds of Kevin's departure Celia storms into the room. The woman fumes, her sometimes lovely features contorted into an unsightly mask of rage. Dried blood still outlines the rim of her delicate nose.

"Do you see what that freak bitch did to me?" She boils with rage, pointing at her face. "And you, making me wait outside like some commoner."

"I see your face, and it has already healed," Thanatos states impassively.

"Who the hell does she thinks she is? I want her dead. You have to do something about this." She points angrily at him. His shoulders square as he returns her stare with a deathly silence. Briefly he allows her to see the barely leashed rage brewing within him. She shifts nervously as he continues to pin her with his stare.

"You are not in a position to make demands," he states firmly, pointing at her. "That Fury will die when I deem it appropriate, not you. In order for us to achieve our goals you must do as you are told. And your little theatrics today could have very well cost us everything. You were brought into the fold for a very specific purpose, but I will have no qualms about cutting you loose should you endanger us again. What do you think they will do when they find out about your little hobby?" he mocks. Tilting his head to the side, he studies her, watching as her agitation grows. "Perhaps it is time to remind you of whom the master is and who the servant is." He keeps his voice low but hard as he casually leans back in his chair.

In a brief instance her fear is replaced by a heady excitement. Her head lowers as she submissively stares toward the floor. A smirk graces her soft lips while he gauges the measured tempo of her heartbeat as her breathing hitches up slightly. After so many years of existence, Thanatos has learned every exquisite method to motivate and control. For Celia it is a matter of pushing her thresholds. She excels at masking the depravity of her true nature– a master manipulator who strives to control everything around her. Thanatos's objective is to obliterate her delicately constructed façade. Pushing her and making her bend until she breaks. Through a painful submission she allows herself a respite from her relentless mental torment.

"Your clothes…take them off," he commands blankly.

Without uttering a word or lifting her gaze, Celia begins to disrobe. Her hands tremble slightly as she masterfully handles the garments. Obediently, she carefully folds each piece of clothing and places it on the floor next to her. Even under the low lights of his quarters, the pallor of her smooth skin is clearly visible. He notes that the scars from their last session have healed nicely. The swell of her full breast and curved waist would be irresistible for most men.

But for Thanatos, her physical beauty is irrevocably marred by her corrupted character. He cares very little for the woman herself. Her soul is saturated with despicable darkness. Upon meeting her he quickly realized that he could never have any real affection for Celia, nor has he any misconceptions that she is capable of such an emotion herself. For the time being she simply serves a purpose. She meets some of the requirements for his physical needs as they arise. And he will ensure her needs are met to keep her compliant. Right now his plan requires she do as she is

140

told and keep her mouth shut. So catering to her unusual tastes is a minor price for the realization of his long term objective.

Rising up, he rounds the front of his desk as he stands in front of her. Her gaze remains downward as he roughly grabs a handful of her thick hair, wrenching it back sharply, causing her gaze to meet his. With the tilt of her head, it exposes the long line of her neck. Inhaling sharply, he can detect the perfume of vileness that wafts from her delicate skin. Using her hair as a rein, he spins her around, facing her away from him. His teeth bite down hard on her supple skin and he notes the thunderous pounding of her heart against his tongue. Using his free hand he cups the fullness of her breasts, squeezing and kneading the flesh. Between two fingers he pinches and pulls at one of her bright red nipples. A throaty groan escapes her lips as she arches into his hands. Pressing his lips to her ear, he pulls her roughly into him, her back against his chest, and he is enveloped by the rich jasmine scent of her hair. He shushes to her as he squeezes the flesh painfully hard.

"Not a word. Such a wanton whore you are."

She stifles another moan as she watches the movement of his hands with lust. His touch skims down her stomach to the glistening patch of red hair between her legs. As his fingers push through the folds she bucks violently against his hand. His grasp is still entangled in her hair, and some of it pulls from the roots. Another low guttural moan

141

erupts from Celia. With his fingers still in her core, he yanks on her hair, grinding himself against her plump ass.

Picking her up with one arm, he pivots and places her down in front of the desk her knees pressed up against the cool wood. With a firm grasp on the nape of her neck, Thanatos pushes her head down until it is resting on the smooth and highly polished surface. "Stay there," he commands, "Don't move a muscle." He releases her and is pleased to see she makes no movement. Rounding the desk again, he opens a low drawer and comes back with several feet of thin copper chain. Thanatos tosses the fetters onto the desk with a jarring clatter, the restraints landing mere inches from her head. With widened eyes, she looks upon them with euphoric amazement. Running the chains through a series of eyelets he has installed, Thanatos is able the quickly restrain Celia, maintaining her in a position of supplication, bent over the desk. As he closes the clasps of the thin metal around her wrists the skin instantly reddens. Thanatos knows that by the time they are finished her wrists and ankles will be an angry mass of blisters and welts.

Once she is adequately secured he leisurely walks to a small chest by his bed. From it he retrieves two sets of flails and a riding crop. Returning to her side, he carefully lays out each item before her, ensuring that all three are clearly visible. The first flail is the more benign of the two. It is a traditional Roman flail with several long leather thongs that are dotted with pieces of sharp bone and pea-sized metal balls. The second flail is similar to the first with the exception of the bone and balls being replaced with shards of roughly cut copper. The riding crop is standard with no frills. It is simply a thin fiberglass shaft with a leather keeper at the end. He has always made it her choice which one of these he will use. Up to this point she has never opted for the riding crop. It was too mild for her. She has always needed the pain and blood to achieve her release.

His personal preferences are quite different. His needs seldom broached the realm of blood and violence. And he has always prided himself on being a skilled and masterful lover. His most impressive achievement was bringing his partner to climax simply through the art of tickling.

"Choose," he instructs firmly.

Her whole body shakes with a mild tremor. Her elegantly manicured fingernails claw into the desk, whittling channels of shredded wood. She grimaces, her features an odd mixture of distress and euphoria. With one finger, he gently strokes the wrapped handle of the first flail.

"This one?" he asks. After several seconds she shudders and shakes her head. "You must choose the one for your punishment," he instructs again.

She moans through clenched teeth, eyeing him lustfully. Firmly he slaps the meaty part of her rump, the skin instantly turning a bright shade of red. She gasps as her breathing is now a heated pant. He slaps again, harder, and she grunts in response as her back arches. He follows each spank by gently rubbing the area with his hand, soothing the skin. After a third slap he sinks two fingers deep inside of her. Violently, she pushes herself up from the desk and into his hand.

"Which one? This one?" he asks breathily in her ear, his fingers working in and out of her.

Staring at the second, rougher flail, she pleads. "Yes, please," she pants out, nearly choking on her words.

Again he pushes her head down. With one hand he securely presses her to the desk, with the other he grabs the flail adorned with the copper shards. With a gentle precision he drags the leather strands up and down against her back and behind. Minutely, the bits of metal start to snag and clip the skin. She desperately squirms and writhes against her restraints as she tries to move closer to the source of her torment. Rows of red lines stand out against the perfection of her white skin as she pleads for release.

"Please, please now," she whimpers.

With a flick of his wrist he brings all the leather thongs across her ass with a snap. Metal bites into the flesh as she shouts in pleasure and pain. Again he whips the leather thongs across her flesh, pulling from her another heightened scream. With each successive blow he can sense her building closer toward her release. He strikes one final time as her body tenses and the orgasm pulsates through her. A mixture of blood and fluid runs down her legs in salmon-colored rivulets. She gazes forward, her eyes half closed as her breathing begins to calm. She looks upward toward him, her eyes still filled with a burning desire. Licking her dried lips, she tries to form her words. "More please, Master." Her eyes glaze with an awed rapture. He rubs his palm over the torn and bloodied skin of her cheeks as she moans loudly. Even now the flesh is beginning to suture itself closed. As the blood smears, her skin takes on a rosy red hue.

Standing behind her, he focuses his attention again on the thick patch of slick auburn hair between her legs. As he touches and probes the still swollen flesh, she moans. He unbuckles his pants and slides them down, not wanting to stain his clothes with her blood. Pushing himself firmly against her wet core, he leans over her, whispering into her ear.

"Tell me how much you want this." He nearly growls at her. "If I believe you, then maybe I'll mount you like the dog you are. And if you are a good little whore, I'll let you clean me up with your mouth."

She responds by arching and pushing into him.

"Please, please, sir. Take it, please. My body is yours, use it," she whispers, her eyes half closed.

Grasping her splayed hips, he drives hard into her. Without pause he rapidly pumps into her, withdrawing then thrusting in again. His pace is fevered as he focuses on his own need. Her coming again is neither his problem nor his concern. By this time in their sessions he is usually sick of looking at her. As his own release approaches his mind drifts to another woman. One that he lost many centuries ago. A woman he would've destroyed the world for.

Chapter 10

The car jostles as it bounds down a country dirt road just outside of Baltimore. The sun has been set for several hours and the moon provides limited light to navigate by. The thick, inky blackness of the surrounding forest threatens from all sides. They haven't seen another car in thirty miles, and the small farmhouses are becoming sparser. There is an unnerving feeling of hostility in this area, as if something menacing lingers just beyond the reach of their headlights.

After six hours of driving David realizes that Emma must be as tired and sore as he. His back is in spasms and feels like he's been kicked by a mule. As they turn off to another dirt road David must slow down as the road becomes gnarled with dips and potholes. The car rocks to and fro as it bumps and dips down the rutted road. The two year old rental car got them here with some relative ease, but it won't stand up to much more abuse.

Emma's head bobs slightly as she stares out into the darkness. Aside from directing him to their destination and telling him what she discovered in the library, Emma has been pretty tight lipped. She can be fairly aloof at times, but the extreme quiet is bothersome.

"How much longer are we on this road?" he asks, glancing in her direction. Once again he attempts to distract himself from the silent void in the car and the painful ache in his lower back.

"It's about another half an hour. There will be a fork in the road, just stay to the right. Hopefully the road won't get much worse." As she speaks they hit a particularly deep rut in the road. Emma's head bounces to the side, banging with a thwack against the side window.

"Ouch." Emma rubs the painful egg already rising on her head.

"Why couldn't we just open a portal here?" he growls angrily.

"Mother Mei Li advised against it. The werewolves won't be especially cordial with strangers– not since their king has been killed. Mei Li believes that driving will be seen as a less aggressive move." Emma sighs as she studies the darkness.

"But we also don't want to appear weak in front of them either," David argues.

"True, but right now it is possible there is a void within this pack. A wolf pack without a strong leader can be susceptible to frenzied behavior. They can also become fodder to other stronger packs. We would do better to tread lightly. Plus, opening a portal may draw some unwanted attention."

"You would figure they'd be more hospitable seeing as we are here to help them," David complains as he massages the growing knot in his neck.

Emma sits quietly, watching him for several seconds before answering.

"I don't know how they will view us. Their king was just brutally murdered, and we are outsiders. It's not too farfetched to think they will be a little distrusting. But going in there guns blazing won't help us. We need them to feel that they can trust us. It's the only way we'll find the truth," she calmly explains.

"It feels like we are blindly walking into something. Perhaps the wolves will be able to shed some additional light for us." After some silence he continues. "A penny for your thoughts?"

"I'm afraid they aren't worth that much. It seems like all of this should be connected, but I just can't see it. The library wasn't all that useful."

At the mention of the library, David feels his blood begin to boil. He saw the red handprint shape that marred her neck. Before they left he dropped several hints and asked about the library, hoping she'd tell him what happened. They continue to drive in silence for several miles. As the distance ticks by he takes a few deep breaths to stem his rising irritation. By the time he slows the car to navigate the upcoming fork he is close to furious, an internal battle waging within him.

His rational side observes that she shouldn't have to tell him everything. She's an adult and should have her own life. But then there is the growing black pit that lives in the center of his stomach. It's from here that his emotions threaten to overwhelm him. He knows that someone hurt her. Someone dared to lay their damn hands on her. It is his duty to protect her, to keep her safe. He wants to rage and scream and rip someone's face off. And he wants to rage and scream at her for not telling him or letting him in.

"So are we going to talk about what actually happened in the library? Or are we going to sit here and keep pretending that I am blind as well as stupid." He exhales forcefully through his teeth, trying and failing to keep his voice light.

"Oh that…" Her hands flutter briefly to her neck then fall back down to her lap. "Well, first of all, I believe that you are neither blind nor stupid. Secondly, there is really not much to tell. It was just a slight altercation, and it's nothing to concern yourself about."

"It's nothing to concern myself about?" he spits. "Someone tried to crush your throat. I would think that would be a little disconcerting, don't you?" David pins her with his stare. If she's intimidated by his look, he can't tell. "From now on, you are not going anywhere without me. I can't believe you would've just sat there and said nothing about this. My job...."

Before he can finish, Emma blurts out, interrupting him.

"The turn, you're going to miss it." She gasps as he slams on the brakes. Emma lurches forward but is held in place by the seatbelt. Momentarily, they are both dazed. David steadies his breathing and takes stock of his surroundings. No one is hurt, nothing is broken.

Emma looks up from her lap. In the darkness her eyes are unreadable, but her voice is full of unexpected emotion.

"I'm sorry I didn't tell you. But what would you do if I had? You might've said that I was dumb for being down there on my own in the first place. Or you'd go on some insane rampage which, worst case, you end up dead, best case, we'd both get into trouble. I spent plenty of time in Erebus, and I don't want to go back. And I know what your job is. But I am not going to sit by and let you throw your life away for something silly or unimportant," she stammers in frustration as her hands are clenched tightly in her lap.

"Well you're important to me." The words flood out before he can stop them. The hub of his emotions pushes at the back of his throat, trying to escape. Emma meets his gaze as she fidgets slightly for a moment. And before saying anything she looks back down to her lap. An awkward silence extends between them as David starts driving again.

After several seconds Emma looks out the side window.

"This should be the driveway. Go in slowly. Also, we may not want to pull all the way up. I don't want to get blocked in." Her gaze flickers to him before returning to the outside. After navigating the first one hundred yards, David pulls over to the side of the driveway and shuts off the headlights.

They exit the vehicle and cautiously walk ahead. The wind gusts around them, sending little cyclones of leaves dancing across the road. As the cold wind wicks away their heat, Emma migrates closer to him. Now with her within arm's reach, he is very much aware of her intoxicating presence. He detects the subtle fragrance of honeysuckle on her, even over the turbulent winds whirling around them.

The spacious hunting lodge at the end of the driveway is barely lit by a single light over the front porch. Inside it appears that only a few lights are left on. The home looks to be several decades old, but it is well maintained. None of the paint is chipping, nor are there copious weeds growing around the property. David almost chuckles at the thought. Nothing worse than being butchered by messy homicidal werewolves. At least these wolves will be clean with their butchery. Emma stares at him quizzically.

"You know this is exactly how horror movies start out," he says in a loud whisper, leaning in closely.

Emma smiles even as her teeth chatter. Again another gust of wind howls and slams into them. Several heavy pine cones fall from the surrounding trees, landing with a pronounced thud on the ground. The steel jaws of a bear trap snap shut just as David pulls Emma closer to him. A falling pine cone had triggered the mechanism, causing it to deploy just feet from them. The trap was concealed under a heap of fallen leaves. As they continue to walk David scans the ground for more hidden dangers. "Yeah, this is not going to be fun," David grumbles loudly.

Mounting the stairs of the porch together, Emma reaches out, touching his arm. He can feel the warmth of her through his jacket. Tilting her head as if listening, she whispers, "There are several wolves inside." David strains to hear, but detects nothing. Warily, he raises his fist to knock on the wooden door. But prior to making contact it slowly swings open.

Standing before them is a young man, his warm, cocoa-colored skin glowing in the light of the fireplace from behind him. He radiates a kind of feral energy which is unmistakably werewolf. The energy within him culminates in his striking golden eyes. He scrutinizes them suspiciously before gruffly asking, "May I help you?"

"We are here to see Bray. Is he available?" Emma states softly. He again studies them, his nostrils flaring as he scents the air. The young, attractive man's eyes darken slightly as he realizes who and what they are. David mulls over their options should they not be granted admittance.

The man's head tilts faintly as if he is listening to something below their audible range. Whatever he hears doesn't please him, as his scowl deepens. The change in his expression casts his features in an ominous shadow. Suddenly, straightening his stance, he peers down his nose at them.

"Very well, follow me." He turns, walking away from them. David and Emma quickly cross the threshold and trail closely behind him. Once inside, their guide closes and locks the door. They are escorted into a large, open living room. The area is about fifty feet wide by roughly thirty feet deep. A staircase of thick polished pine connects the first and second floors. The equally polished wood walls display a plethora of animal mounts, from deer to bear to geese in flight. A stone fireplace casts a heavily shadowed light throughout the room.

David quickly takes stock of everyone in the area. A total of fifteen werewolves, male and female, are scattered throughout the space. Several observe them from a cluster of well-worn sofas by an immense fireplace. The remaining wolves dot the room, surrounding them as they either lean against walls or stand statuesquely and glare at them with obvious disdain. Their guide turns abruptly to face them and barks, "Stay here." Without further explanation he pivots and ascends the staircase, disappearing in the lurking darkness.

"This seems to be going splendidly." David shifts closer to Emma, his voice low. There's no point in whispering, as these beasts are capable of hearing their prey's heartbeat from a hundred yards out.

"Just stay calm," she says with a somewhat forced smile. While her tone may be soothing, David can sense the pent-up apprehension within her. Her stance is rigid as she surveys the room. David breathes in and out, focusing his thoughts and senses on all the individuals in the room. His awareness is heightened to the slightest action. Movement from the upper balcony draws everyone's attention. In unison, all eyes lift upward to the approaching figure.

The stranger standing before them exudes an almost feral dominant energy, his movements graceful as he seems to glide rather than walk. By his best guess, David estimates he is probably in his late twenties. But with wolves it is often impossible to determine their actual age, as their bodies age slower than a human's. Even without the aid of wolf-inspired animal magnetism, the man clearly has no issue attracting the ladies. His eyes are a blue green like the water of the Boston Harbor in the summer. But his larger pupils mark him as a wolf. His shoulder-length blonde hair falls in a disheveled manner, but there is no mistaking that he is the leader of this group. All of the wolves watch him with an awed sense of reverence. As he descends the stairs with a confident ease, David notes that the man's feet are bare.

"Isaac told me we had guests." He glances towards their guide. "I am Bray," he continues, his tone carrying a practiced formality to it. He arches an eyebrow as he inquires of them. "So what would bring a Fury and her pet to our door?" David clearly senses the attempt at goading him, but he will not allow himself to rush headlong into a mistake.

"Thank you for seeing us, Bray. May we speak with you in private?" Emma returns his formality in kind.

"Anything you have to say can be said in front of all of us." Bray gestures around the room with a smirk. Knowing that they are significantly outnumbered, Emma and David must proceed with care.

"As you wish." Emma remains rigid as the wolf meanders closer, standing within arm's reach of David. "It was requested that we come in regards to your father's murder."

"And you have come here to seek justice for him? Is that it?" A charged tension flares in the now seemly confined space. Bray's words are laced with the unspoken accusation. His eyes are aglow with churning anger that claws just beneath the surface of his skin. Emma glances at David, looking mildly confused and uncertain.

"I know very little about what happened to Jackson. We are here to determine what occurred." Emma weighs her response carefully. David sidesteps, impeding Bray's view and reach to Emma. Every cell in his being crackles as the man in front of him stares down at his Fury. Isaac walks slowly, taking up a sentry position at the door. His arms cross over his chest as he eyes them menacingly.

"And why would the Fury give a rat's ass about a pack of wolves and their dead leader?"

"We all know that your father wasn't just a pack leader. His intention was to unify the werewolves, putting him in an interesting position. His success would mean that the packs would no longer be scattered and isolated."

"Is that why you killed him?" A young girl's voice drips with venom as she stands shaking next to one of the large sofas. Her fists are clenched tightly by her side, her appearance very similar to Bray's. She appears several years younger but possesses the same vibrantly colored eyes. David ponders how many of these wolves are Jackson's biological children. "You had him killed to keep us weak," she spits at them.

David senses the fist driving toward him just a moment too late. He shifts his balance to dodge, but can't avoid the brunt of the blow. Bray's fist makes enough contact with David's throat to force the wind from his lungs. Gasping, David falters back a step or two before coughing as he attempts to regain his breath, but is crushed as a mountain of wolves rush in around him. Hands and claws dig into him, holding him in place. He kicks and punches, but soon his arms are pinned as he is held by numerous foes. A beefy arm snakes around his neck, stifling his access to much needed air. They pull and yank at him, but he stays on his feet.

Searching the room with his eyes, he locates Emma, and his gut clinches. Bray hoists her into the air by her throat and effortlessly holds her off the floor. Emma's eyes are wide as she struggles to remain calm. She clutches Bray's arm to stave off having her throat crushed. Even over all the ragged breathing in his ears he can clearly make out the low primal growl that emanates from Bray.

"Do you think you can come in here and lie to me after you killed my father?" Bray roars. His whole body is tight with murderous energy. "My father was a fool to trust the Fury. Understand this, I won't make that same mistake. I will end you before I let you harm my people."

"Bray, please listen to me. I didn't kill your father." Emma coughs, struggling to breathe as her feet dangle beneath her. "I can tell you have a clean soul. You don't want to do this. And I know you have no reason to believe me, but I swear to you that I don't know who killed him. I promise you I will find them." A red frenzied rage plumes across David's line of sight. Incensed, he continues to battle and screams against those holding him.

"Shut up. Shut your lying, stinking mouth." Bray's face reddens as he screams at her.

"Emma, just kill him," David screams, but his words are cut off as the savage blow hits him in the stomach. Being a Fury, Emma is capable of popping this wolf like a tick. Why is she not defending herself?

"No, David." Emma meets David's stare with her own steely intensity. "Please, trust me on this. More violence will not help the situation. No one is going to die tonight."

"That's where you are wrong, Fury," Bray sneers as he squeezes her neck, blocking her air flow completely. David struggles fruitlessly as she turns from scarlet to slightly blue.

The front door swings open with a loud crash, sending small fragments of broken wood skittering across the floor. Chilled air sweeps into the living room. All eyes shift to the gapping entryway door. From his angle, David can't see who is entering, but he hears the subtle click of shoes on the hardwood floor. He senses something growing in the darkness. At first there is a mild tingling of energy, so low that it is nearly imperceptible. It is as a hushed hum just below recognition. Then the murmur surges into a cacophony that pulses in waves over the room in sync with the pounding of his heart. No one moves as the sheer intensity of the force petrifies them in place. The scene around him stills as these real life mannequins are frozen and poised in the pantomime of a mock battle. Even David's arms and legs cease to obey him, refusing to move.

Through the doorway a woman glides into the room. She is a stunningly exotic beauty. White-blonde hair rolls down the length of her back, her striking blue eyes enrapturing everyone in the room. She radiates a raw sexuality. The skin-tight black leather pants and bustier showcases her ample bosom and tapered waist. The woman is built for all things lusty. Even the other females seem seduced by her allure.

"Oh my, I hope I'm interrupting," she purrs, her voice thick and rasping. Slinking forward, she runs a hand over the hard contours of Isaac's chest. "All this fun and excitement, and you started without me," she bemoans with a petulant frown. "My name is Desiree."

"What do you want?" Isaac questions as tiny tremors cause his muscles to twitch. He shakes with the effort to gain control of his rogue body.

"I come bearing gifts, lover– yearning and extinction." In a blink she drives her hand deep into the gut of Isaac. Her hand easily rips through skin and muscle to the organs beneath. Blood plumes around her wrist, pooling to the floor. Isaac's eyes bulge, but his body is still rigidly frozen under the effects of Desiree's power. Even as she removes her hand from the man, with a wet slopping sound, he remains standing. His blood washes to the floor and the life begins to drain from his face. Only his eyes dart frantically, pleading around the room.

Chapter 11

An orchestra of howls and snarls echoes through the room, as the onlookers watch in horror as their comrade bleeds out. The deafening sounds assault David's senses. All eyes are focused on the destructive intruder, and his arms are firmly held in place by his captors. His mind reels, and he tries to comprehend the staggering chaos. He measures his breath to shake off the fog that is beginning to cloud his thoughts. A clear focus is crucial for saving himself and Emma. Several of the wolves try to shift- it is their vain attempt to break free of their invisible bond but they are instead locked in various stages of transformation. Frozen mid-change, some have thickly jagged claws jutting from fingertips or elongated faces brandishing razor sharp rows of teeth. It is a terrifying menagerie of grotesque monsters as if from some nightmarish realm.

Desiree slinks toward them, her hand still dripping blood and meat. She stretches, rolling her shoulders and neck languidly, her movements exhibiting a feline grace. Half-lidded eyes gaze at them as a sensual smile touches her lips. David spies her long whip-like tail as it swishes behind her. The lengthy appendage is weighted by a spaded tip that is razor sharp. Her actions are an illustration in the art of seduction. Finally, David puzzles together what she is. There are too many telltale signs for her to be anything other than a succubus. But why would a succubus be here of all places? Succubi are not particularly known as violent creatures. Most certainly, they don't typically attack without reason or provocation.

Her ethereal gaze settles on him with an unnerving intensity. It is an overpowering look of hunger that causes his body to quake against his will. Sensually, she glides forward, her long legs effortlessly carrying her over to the large group. Every instinct within him bellows for retreat. But she is there, so close, invading his senses. The air is thickly perfumed with her power. With each ragged breath he inhales, he brings even more of the intoxicating aroma into his body, making rational thoughts all but impossible.

Somewhere in the deep corners of his mind he senses someone calling to him. It is a soft whisper playing on the fringes of his awareness. Concentrating on the sound only serves to make it seem more distant and less important. His attention is steadily pulled toward the alluring creature standing before him. Why hadn't he realized until now how exquisite she is. Her lush lips and bountiful bosom call to him as his body reacts to her. His hands ache to reach out to touch her, to feel the soft perfection of her skin. Silently, he curses his infuriating arms which are still held securely. The restriction to his movements makes his torment all the more excruciating. His body lurches forward as she skims her delicate hand up his stomach. She strokes the contours of his chest, meandering upward until she is cupping his face. Her thumb softly caresses his cheek as she snakes her other arm around his neck, pulling him down to meet her. His body bends, compliant to her demands.

Her lips claim his, and a sudden flush of heat fills his core. It is a lava flow cascading down his throat and setting fire to his gut. She explores the line of his mouth with her tongue and nibbles softly on his bottom lip. His entire being becomes focused on the feel of her mouth and breasts as she presses firmly against him, her hands entwining in his hair, pulling him into her. His body is set aflame as her soft stomach presses against his engorged cock. His pulse pounds in his ears, and he knows that the sensations battering him are deliciously destructive, yet he needs more.

In a heart-wrenching movement she pulls away from him. Yet she lingers there, hovering, her mouth mere inches from his. Breathlessly, she suckles his bottom lip, pulling it into her mouth. With a pop she releases it.

"Yummy," she coos, licking her lips as if to savor the taste of him. A wicked grin touches her lips as she studies him for several seconds. "Aww, how sweet. You have feelings for her," she mocks. Her laughter is a deep and throaty sound that crawls along his skin. "That's good. Unfortunately she'll be long dead before you can get a chance to tell her." With a stark snap the enthrallment is broken, leaving David feeling hollow and cold. A burning sensation in his chest threatens to knock him down, and for the first time he is grateful for the hands securing him.

Desiree lifts her hand, now brandishing a long dagger. In a smooth, graceful motion she plunges the blade into the heart of a wolf holding onto David. A thick splatter of blood coats his face and side as the man's lifeblood flows out. Desiree giggles gleefully. It is a bile-inducing sound now. She calmly wipes the blood from her hands onto David's shirt. "Watch this, lover," she purrs as she turns from him. She strides purposefully over to Emma, who is still dangling in the grasp of the petrified werewolf. Relief floods through David. Emma's head lists to the side— she is still alive.

"Are you ready to die, Fury?" Desiree asks coldly, her voice lacking all of the sexual potency it held before. A shrill laughter erupts from her lips as she stalks the captive Fury. She is seemingly oblivious to the plummeting temperature of the room. "Let's see. Should I have the wolf crush your throat?" She is nearly giddy as she asks. Her eyebrow cocks at the question. "Or maybe we'll have him shift and tear you to shreds." She looks up thoughtfully, as if mulling over her options. A devious smile creeps across her face as she leans in closely and whispers softly to Bray. "Show me your big bad wolf." David strains to hear her words. Bray's eyes shift, maintaining his color, but taking on an eerie canine quality. His form shakes as he fights the impending transition.

In a snap movement Emma's arm flies up, clutching Desiree by the throat. Her gleeful expression suddenly melts into a shocked, disbelieving stare. "How? You shouldn't be able to break the paralysis." She struggles against Emma's clenched grasp.

"It's your time to die, bitch." Emma's voice trembles as her eyes shift to solid copper pools. Releasing her pent-up energy, Emma sends Desiree flying across the room. The succubus collides with the wall with a harsh thud, the drywall crumbling around her. She lays motionless on the floor. Slowly, the thick veil of paralysis lifts and everyone in the room regains control of their bodies. The stabbed wolf that was holding David lies still on the floor. He didn't survive his injury, and as others rush to check on him they confirm his passing. David hurries over to Emma just as Bray is setting her down. Examining Emma's neck, he also checks the rest of her to ensure that she's relatively unharmed. Some of the pack members dash over to Isaac to tend to his wounds. Bray's gaze flutters around the room, taking stock through all of the chaos. Grabbing a nearby wolf, he barks out several orders. The perimeter is to be secured and all the injured are to be taken upstairs. Two men hoist up the dead succubus and bring her outside.

"What was that?" Bray asks as his mind fights the dense fog muddling it. He shakes his head several times as if to clear the cobwebs.

"That was a succubus. My guess is she was sent here to kill one, or all of us," David replies. "The paralysis is used so they can have sex with their victims, draining their life force. But with everyone frozen there is no reason to believe she couldn't have killed us all." One of the females hurries up to Bray, her complexion ashen, the concern visible in her eyes.

"Bray, it's Isaac. He is dying," she states breathlessly, urging him to follow her. Rounding the corner they find the young man lying on the floor. Another wolf struggles fruitlessly to stop the flow of blood– his hands are thickly coated as he holds pressure on the wound. Without help the man will be dead in minutes, though David is surprised he is still alive. A multitude of raw emotions wash over Bray's face. He kneels next to his second, touching his arm softly.

"I can save your man," Emma states carefully.

"Haven't you and your kind caused enough damage?" Bray snaps, his gaze never leaving his friend, his massive form radiating his inner rage.

"I can help Isaac, but you would let your pride kill him? Doing nothing will ensure his death. His wounds are too grievous to heal on their own. If you value his life you should at least allow me to try," Emma states with a soft but formidable confidence. Bray weighs her for several tense seconds before bowing his head in concession.

Emma kneels next to the fallen man, studying his wound. She addresses the werewolf compressing the open gash. "When I tell you, remove your hands. Do you understand?" The wolf nods silently, his stare never leaving her. Emma closes her eyes and breathes deeply as the temperature around drops. Without looking, she reaches out, laying her palms on either side of the compression. "Now," she whispers with a nod. Her hands replace those of the wolf. Though David cannot see what is happening beneath the make-shift bandages, he can feel the hum of Emma's power as it envelops the injured man.

As the minutes tick by the color starts to return to Isaac's face. As Emma withdraws her hands the wound has closed and the skin is unmarred. Bray clasps his man, helping him into a seated position. All of them stare in astonishment at her. It is amazing even to David. Each time he thinks he knows her, she surprises him yet again. Emma slouches, her arms hanging heavily at her sides. David moves over to her, holding her and letting her rest against him.

"Thank you. That was…" Bray struggles for the words. "I didn't think that was possible. I thought the Fury could only destroy with their powers."

"Our energy can be directed to create or destroy," Emma states numbly. David pulls her up, walking her over to sit on one of the large sofas. Bray follows at a close distance.

He looks around, surveying the area. "I need to attend to my people. Wait here. Once things are settled I will return and we can talk more." He watches them wordlessly for a couple of beats before turning to leave.

"Are you ok?" David asks once they are alone. Bray's claws had pierced the soft skin of Emma's neck, but the puncture marks are quickly closing. "I'm sorry, Emma," David says as he gently rubs her neck. "I should have…"

"Shh. No worries. I'm fine, and don't you dare blame yourself." She gazes at him sternly.

"I wasn't going to blame myself, I just was going to…" He fumbles momentarily for the correct words.

"You were going to blame yourself." Her eyes gleam delightfully at him. "You seem to forget, David, that I know you too." A small silence separates them. "Though truth be told I'm more worried about you. What did that succubus do to you?" The genuine concern etched on Emma's face makes something in his gut clench. The unsettling realization shudders within him. The last twenty minutes seems to be a vague blur that he can't really remember. It is like trying to remember events from the previous drunken night.

"I can't really recall. I don't know what happened," he says with a shrug and shake of his head. "How come you never told me you could heal like that?" Now it is Emma's turn to shrug. A timid smile graces her lips.

"I guess it has just never come up. Every Fury is bestowed with their own unique gift. And contrary to what Celia might say, mine is healing, not the ability to disturb everyone around me." Emma's lips turn upward into a broader smirk.

Bray returns a few minutes later, the main living room now empty. All the other inhabitants seem to have escaped upstairs or are outside searching the woods around them. Bray leans casually against the mantel of the fireplace. The intensity of his earlier anger has melted away, leaving him with a haggard and exhausted appearance. Battling the overwhelming frustration, he roughly runs a hand through his hair as he breathes deeply. Squarely, Bray meets their stare.

"I will not apologize for trying to protect my people," he states calmly. "As you can see, after current events it is difficult to discern the intent of others. But I may have misjudged you. For that I am sorry."

"All in all, we can understand the circumstances and position you are in." David shoots him a questioning stare. "Now, do you mind telling us what is going on here?"

"Well, there's not much to tell really." Bray shrugs his shoulders. "About a week ago a Fury and her lover show up here unannounced and storm in demanding to speak with my father. They say he's been harboring man-eaters. Which is total bullshit. We all know the rules about killing humans."

"Why do you think they were consorts?" Emma questions. "It is well known that the Fury are forbidden from taking on a lover. Are you certain she was a Fury?"

"For starters, she introduced herself as one. And they were intimate, as they both reeked of sex and blood," Bray explains. With a single finger he taps the side of his nose and smiles arrogantly. "Believe me, I know the smell."

"What do you mean by smell?" Emma asks, her indignation flaring.

"Every species has their own particular..." His head tilts as he mulls over his word choices. "Fragrance."

"Why don't we get back to the issue at hand?" David tries to steer the conversation back on course. An unexplainable sense of unrest is building within him the longer they remain here. "So an unknown woman shows up with her friend and wants to see your father. What then?" David asks pointedly.

"She says something about needing to judge him. I haven't met a lot of Fury, so who knows about their particular quirks. So she lays a hand on his shoulder. Problem is, I didn't feel anything," Bray states with a shrug.

"What do you mean?" David asks.

"With any paranormals, when they tap into their powers there is an aura that is emitted that we can detect," Bray states plainly. "It is a subtle hum that can be felt. Like just before you hit the succubus, I could feel it when you were drawing on that energy. But with this lady? Nothing, zilch."

"So she was what? Pretending to do something? For what purpose?" David asks as he folds his arms over his chest.

"My best guess is that they needed it to look like he was guilty," Bray asserts. "So she says he is responsible and they start to haul him out by force. Which is no small task considering who my father was." Seeing their obvious confusion, Bray sighs heavily and continues. "My family line is one of the oldest among werewolves. And there is a certain level of inherent strength that comes along with that. So strong-arming the man out of the house should have been more of a chore. We tried to stop them, but my father told us to wait, and that he would return." Trapped within the moment, a dark guilt washes over him. "By the morning he still hadn't come home and we knew something was very wrong. Searching the forest, we found him. I should have stopped them. If I had known what they were going to do I would have fought them."

"From what it sounds like, if you had crossed them you could have gotten the whole pack killed," Emma responds.

"What I don't understand is, if a Fury was sent after him, we should have been told about it. There would have been some kind of buzz going on." Looking at Bray she asks, "Can you describe them?"

"Not really. The whole scene gets hazy when I try to recall it. It's like I'm trying to grasp something that's not really there. They were fairly bundled up too. What I can remember, though is that she was fairly pretty... I guess. Maybe... reddish colored hair, she was thin and unpleasant. Her friend was a walking mountain and not any better. Mean as shit. Both of them threw off a really bad vibe," Bray answers with a shrug, again running a shaky hand through his hair. "I wish I could tell you more. I do know their scent. Faces can be masked, but not someone's smell. If they come anywhere near me, then I can pick them out blindfolded."

"I'll need to speak with the Mothers to see if they know why a Fury would be coming here," Emma muses to herself. A sudden flash of copper hue briefly overtakes the color of Emma's eyes. She rubs her temples, seemingly lost in her thoughts as David steps toward her. Her gaze flashes up to David. "We need to leave here." Her voice hitches as she speaks with an underlying urgency. Turning to Bray, "Whatever I find out I will let you know. Keep your people safe." Bray nods as he walks them to the door.

Stepping out onto the porch, they are greeted by the turbulent onslaught of wind. David scans the area, assessing any possible threats. As they make their way down the stairs their car explodes in an enormous fireball. The stifling wave of heat engulfs them as David pulls Emma under the porch roof, trying to shield her. Chunks of debris and glass rain down over them as parts of the car clunk against the roof and break some of the windows of the cabin. Within seconds the car is rendered to a meager metal skeleton as the fire guts the insides.

"We have to open a portal to return," Emma whispers, her voice trembling.

"Are you sure that's a good idea?" David cautiously asks, sensing her escalating unease.

"There is no time. We can't waste time driving back."

"Emma, what is happening?" Her tension seeps into David at an alarming rate.

"It's Sara, it's bad. We have to go." Descending the stairs, she practically runs to the nearby shed. Slapping the outer wall, a gateway quickly rips open. David is right behind her as they both step through.

Chapter 12

Emma races through the barren wormhole at a fevered pace. The area between realms is a frigid abyss of emptiness. Her heart hammers her chest, and she is only mildly aware of David following closely behind her, the solid beat of his footfalls keeping tempo with hers. The abrupt exit through the wash of energy renders her legs to jelly, but she presses on, steadying herself with a hand to the wall.

Moving through the familiar labyrinth, Emma enters the main assembly room, which is teeming with people and is abuzz with an uneasy energy. A busy chatter of conversation fills the area with a low but overwhelming audible noise. A massive sea of bodies blocks Emma's way as she scans the room. Quickly, she spots Mother Mei Li and Tatiana standing on the raised dais.

Mei Li's expression is haggard and forlorn as she watches the crowd dejectedly. Tatiana stands besides her, radiating her usual regal demeanor. Tatiana raps a wooden pocket gavel forcefully on the long bench as Emma pushes and squeezes forward through shoulders and arms as the trial is called to order. Olivia steps directly in front of Emma, blocking her path and view.

"Emma, you shouldn't be here," she whispers sternly. She grips Emma's shoulders, trying to turn her around, away from the scene ahead. Emma's gaze drifts downward, noting that Olivia's hands are trembling. Searching her eyes, Emma is caught by the heart-retching sympathy reflecting back. Choking fear claws at Emma's throat, the air seeming frozen in her lungs. Olivia's peculiar behavior amplifies the rush of distressed panic surging within her.

"What is going on?" Emma stares at her quizzically, her voice nearly lost as her chest tightens painfully. She tries to push past Olivia, yet she is held firmly by the other woman. A small gap opens in the press of the group, and Emma's insides seize and drop. A shocked gasp bursts from her lips. Sara sits on a secluded chair next to the dais, her hair and clothes disheveled. A thin chain of copper connects shackles on her tiny wrists and ankles. Frightened and pleading, her crystalline blue eyes scour the crowd of apathetic onlookers.

"Sara, no."

Emma wheezes as she struggles against their hold. Olivia presses her backward to the outskirts of the assembly. She talks in hushed tones, taking Emma's head between her hands. She speaks softly, trying to soothe her, but Emma can't hear. Every color falls away and the world blurs into a vague shadow-land that contrasts the pale blue gaze that beseeches her for help. The blue eyes of a young child that she promised to protect. A quick shake brings Emma's attention back to Olivia as the fog of horror instantly dissipates.

"Keep your voice down," Olivia hisses. "You doing something stupid will not help her," Olivia chides as she quickly glances over her shoulder. "We can get her out of this, but we have to do this the right way. Do you understand?" She shakes Emma again as if to wake her.

"What is this about? What happened?" Emma's voice is plaintive as it cracks. She licks her dry lips, pushing down the rising swell of terror that has nested in her stomach.

"They are saying that Sara tried to escape The Hallow. Allegedly, someone caught her sneaking out of the southern entrance. Although I highly doubt she was planning on swimming across the River Styx." A skeptical look graces Olivia's face.

"Escape? I don't understand. Sara was unhappy here, but she wouldn't just…" Emma's mind reels as the severity of the situation comes into focus. "I don't believe it. This is some kind of mistake." Her struggles renewed against the hands holding her.

"Stop," Olivia barks hoarsely. "We both know she wouldn't run off, but that's what they are saying." Olivia pauses, studying Emma. "Our best option is to let the trial run its course and work on both of the Mothers to get her released as soon as possible."

"We can't let them lock her away in Erebus. She'll never survive that place." Emma looks on with a pained expression. The fear in her belly is growing into a growling beast with sharp fangs to gnaw her insides. "Who accused her?" Her mind races as she watches the room of people. She measures her breathing, trying to remain calm and clear-headed.

"I don't know. They haven't been mentioned." Olivia sighs with a shrug.

"Wait. Don't they need all three Mothers present to conduct a trial?" Emma queries with an ember of hope sparking to life.

"One of the Mothers is dead, so we have what we have. Unless another Mother appears in the next five seconds we have to rely on the judgment of the two. Sorry," Olivia apologizes as Emma's hope flutters away.

Over Olivia's shoulder Emma watches horrified at the scene playing out in front of her. Sara's timid eyes are red-rimmed with tears as she sits quietly. Tatiana's voice booms over the assembly as she lists the charges placed against the small girl.

"The rules and edicts we have in place are here only to secure the safety for all of our sisters. We understand that they can be harsh and difficult to live with, but these laws must be upheld, regardless of whom the perpetrator is. It pains us all when our duty obligates us to perform unpleasant tasks such as these." Her tone is crisply sharp, her demeanor the armored shell of the unwavering aristocracy. Her gaze never turns to the young girl they are condemning.

"Mother Mei Li and I have reached an agreement for the appropriate sentence." She glances over her shoulder, gesturing as the second Mother slowly steps forward.

Mei Li's features are drawn with fatigue. Her thick black hair is wrapped tightly in a simple bun and dark circles are nestled under her eyes, which give her a shallow appearance. A look of pained anguish flashes across her face as she spots Emma in the crowd. Her gaze flickers nervously about the room. She clears her throat as all eyes settle on her.

"Taking into account that this is a first time offense, we believe it is best to show tempered lenience. Therefore, it has been determined that Sara will be incarcerated in Erebus for a six-month period. This is the least amount of time one can serve in Erebus." With a forlorn demeanor, Mei Li steps away from the dais and Tatiana sharply raps the gavel against the table to dismiss the crowd.

Pooling all of her strength, Emma ducks and quickly pushes past Olivia. Worming her way through the dispersing group, Emma calls out, trying to get the attention of the retreating Mothers. As she breaks through an opening, Emma collides with a wall made of flesh. With sharpened reflexes, Ambrose clasps her arms, holding her firmly, and effectively barring her way. For only a brief moment they meet each other's stare.

Emma leans, shouting around his obstructing frame. "Mothers, please, a moment of your time." Her voice is hoarse and coated with an underlying tremble that ripples throughout her entire body.

Realizing that Ambrose can detect her weakness should have been enough to force Emma to back down. But the near hysterical compulsion to protect Sara is overriding any need to hide her vulnerability.

"Mothers, please." Her voice cracks under the strain, but it halts the two women. Each of the Mothers turns slowly around, studying Emma. Olivia and David have moved up to flank Emma on either side. Even the two guards escorting Sara out have stopped.

"What is it that you need, Emma?" Mei Li asks, her expression warring with the forced coolness of her tone.

"I would implore you to reconsider your judgment in regards to Sara," Emma shouts, craning her neck to see around Ambrose, whose vise-like grip still holds her firmly. Shooting him a venomous glare, she makes no pretense about her current feelings toward him. "Do you mind?" she barks, trying to shake free of him. He studies her momentarily before releasing one of her arms, and while holding the other he turns to stand beside her.

"Six months is the least amount of time she can serve. Or are you asking for her sentence to be longer?" Tatiana asks snidely.

"No, Mother. I am asking that her punishment be something other than service in Erebus. As you have said this is her first misdeed," Emma pleads as her insides twist in knots. The two Mothers exchange glances. Just as Mei Li opens her mouth, Tatiana steps forward.

"We understand your desire to protect the child." Tatiana's tone is at first pacifying, then instantly cold. "But justice must be served, and the sentence will stand," she states blankly. Emma's mind races as an icy claw constricts her throat.

"And what happens in Erebus, does that constitute justice?" she snaps as her well-kept anger and pain surge forward and boil near the surface.

Olivia places a hand on Emma's free arm, attempting to silence her. "Emma, mind your words. It isn't wise to speak like this," she whispers.

"You've never been there, have you?" Emma rails at the other Fury, unshed tears burning at her eyes. "It is common knowledge that there is no justice in Erebus." Emma pins Ambrose with her stare. "If you are determined that penitence is required for the sake of justice then I will take her place." Olivia clutches Emma's arm fiercely, her whole form seething with anger.

"Are you stupid? What are you saying?" Olivia scolds.

"If I can save Sara, then I will do whatever is needed," Emma whispers with a cool intensity.

"There are other ways to do this," Olivia barks through clenched teeth as Ambrose's grip shifts on Emma's arm, causing her gaze to lift to his.

"Do not worry. The child will be well guarded and kept quite safe while she is in my care." His words, while meant to be soothing, do very little to calm Emma's nerves.

"Unfortunately there is no way that we can allow you to shoulder the punishment for the child." Tatiana's voice hangs ominously in the air. "Now, it is possible that in a month's time we could revisit the issue to see if more leniencies can be afforded. This, of course, is conditioned upon there being no further outbursts of raucous behavior." Emma opens her mouth to argue but is silenced by Tatiana's raised hand. "Your choices are simple, either you accept our generous ruling, or you can continue to dispute it and the child's punishment will be increased at a drastic rate." With that, Tatiana turns quickly and exits the room. The two escorts turn to lead Sara away. She shouts over her shoulder to Emma before she disappears.

"I'll be ok, Emma. Don't you worry about me," she squeaks with a half-hearted smile. Emma's heart shatters for this brave girl.

Mei Li approaches Emma apprehensively, and they both watch the other Mother's departure. Mei Li lifts her hand as if to touch Emma, but then drops it back to her side. "I will see what can be done for Sara." Mei Li's manner is formal and saddened. "Ambrose will ensure that Sara is cared for and kept safe," she adds. "David, please see to it that Emma makes it home safely. I will call upon you sometime tomorrow to discuss the outcome of your last assignment."

Stepping forward, David takes Emma's arm and gently guides her toward to the door. At the same time, Ambrose relinquishes his grip on Emma, and a quizzical look crosses his face as he studies her.

The vast tunnels of the underground shift by in a hazy blur for Emma, the journey playing out as a black and white movie. She floats through each choppy scene as it transforms. Through the numerous corridors and passageways, up and down stairwells, David remains silent as he leads her forward. The final passage is through a network of interlaced caves and subterranean springs which open out into a nearby forest by way of an old bear den. David zips up her sweat jacket to bar against the cold. Emma is only vaguely aware of the brutal chill surrounding them. A ten minute walk down a hiker's trail brings them to a secluded parking lot where many of the vehicles used by the Fury are stored. David ushers her into the passenger seat of one of the cars. With still a few hours until sunrise, the streets are empty as they make their way toward Emma's apartment. Parking outside, they climb the stairs and quietly enter the apartment. Though Emma spends most of her evenings here, the apartment is modestly decorated. Simple beige furniture and a small dining table grace the room. Turning on only a small desk lamp for light, Emma heads toward the kitchen.

"I'm making tea. Do you want some?" she asks blankly.

"You sit and I'll make the tea," David barks softly as he points toward the couch. She almost chuckles as a surprised look flashes across his features.

"I'm too tired to argue with you." Emma yawns as she sinks into the soft cushion of her loveseat. She listens for several minutes as David clumsily rampages through her kitchen. Resting her cheek on a propped-up hand, she watches the city outside glisten.

David enters the room carrying a steaming hot coffee cup. "I couldn't find your tea cups or a tray or any cream. I did find the sugar, so if you need some I'll get it."

"It's fine, thank you." She sips the beverage, letting it warm her chilled body. David grabs his own tea off the counter and plops down onto the couch adjacent from Emma.

"Do you think Tatiana can be swayed for anything less than a month?" he asks, blowing across the rim of his cup, trying to cool the scalding liquid.

"As a favor for me? No. But if we can come up with a reason as to why releasing Sara now would benefit either the Fury or herself, then maybe."

"Is it really that bad in there?" He crosses his leg over his knee as he leans back.

"Honestly? It's worse. I've never really talked to anyone about what happens there." She inhales the sweet fragrance of the brew, willing it to calm her ragged nerves. "Over the years I have probably spent as much time in Erebus as I have in The Hallow. Even within the solitude of that place you can be witness to the deplorable acts of depraved cruelty."

Placing both feet on the floor, David leans forward, his drink forgotten. With a quiet intensity he watches her and waits for her to continue.

"Erebus is basically Hell. But it's not Hell in a traditional sense. It's this cold, dark, barren hole that seems to swallow all the light. But the place is tolerable in small doses. It is the guards that make it a truly horrendous prison."

"The Ebon Mortis?" David asks cautiously, the hairs on his neck standing on edge.

Emma nods, never altering her gaze. "At a certain point you become quite literally numb to the beatings. Not willing to have their enjoyment ruined, the guards would find even more innovative ways to torture you. As you know, Fury are hard to kill, so they have a lot of options available to them. The guards are cruel because they can be. They are violent because they can be. You are sent to Erebus to be forgotten. It is an Oubliette that has no bottom. You seem to lose the sense of time passing. It's just this all-encompassing blackness that you are trapped in. One of the other Fury was raped every night. Every night for what could have been years. Every night. Her cries were the worst torture of all. All I could think about as I listened to her screams and wails is that I needed to help her. But how? Escaping was a near impossibility. In the end you ask yourself if it would be better to kill her tormentors or to mercifully take her life." Emma's voice trails off as she stares at the nothingness outside. "Shortly after that she killed herself," she states numbly, her tone alien even to her own ears.

"And what about you? Did they try to hurt you like that?" David shifts in his seat uneasily as he struggles with the wording.

"Oh, rape, no." She inhales deeply, rubbing her stiff shoulder. "The first time I was in Erebus one of the guards tried. But then another one came in and yelled at him in a language I didn't understand. He dragged him out. I was terrified every night that they would come back. But they never did." Emma yawns wide-mouthed and stretches sore muscles. "I need sleep," she says, stifling another yawn. Setting down her tea, she stands and heads toward the bedroom. After a quick search she locates an extra pillow and blanket and hands them to David. "Here you go. Hopefully the couch isn't too uncomfortable."

"Thanks. It will be fine, and if it isn't I'll come snuggle with you," David says with a grin as he pulls off his t-shirt. Trying not to ogle the man, Emma is thankful for the low lighting. It hides the red flush seeping into her cheeks. Quickly she retreats to her bedroom, closing the door behind her. In the darkened silence her heart races. Sleep is slow to come, but after tossing and turning exhaustion finally overtakes her.

Chapter 13

The reoccurring dream has become as familiar as a second skin to Emma. It is the same twisted replaying of bittersweet memories and agonizing horrors. In the dream, Emma is immersed in a perpetual mist. The fringes of her surroundings are blurred and lacking substance. The afternoon sun warms their skin and saturates the nearby fields in a soothing ginger glow. She and James would spend their time here in the summer months.

Their sanctuary is a secluded meadow that is carpeted in delicate bluebells and edged with majestic elms and alders. Her daughter, Anna, is playing close at hand, picking wildflowers to make wreaths for their hair. She is the perfect reflection of her father, beautiful almond eyes and coffee-colored hair. She sings the lullaby that Emma taught her as she gathers the vibrant blue buds. Robert is just a wee babe, sleeping blissfully on the wool blanket next to them. Even in the dream the sun dances across his subtle little features, pulling out the red highlights in his otherwise brown tuft of hair. His small mouth moves feverously as he slumbers. To sit and watch his miniature chest rise and fall is immensely soothing. James pulls her in close to him. He looks down on her, the adoration in his gaze warming her soul. Reaching up, she gently touches his cheek, feeling the coarse stubble. She inhales deeply the earthy scent of her husband.

Then with a sudden shift the sky blackens, deeply fierce storm clouds roll in, blotting out the sun, and the air around them freezes. Heavy unrelenting snowflakes start to fall, quickly blanketing the fields, crushing the newly bloomed wildflowers. Emma struggles to get to her feet, as she is held down by James's arm around her waist. Turning to him, horror clutches at her chest. James is a frozen corpse, his lifeless eyes staring back at her. Wrestling with the rigor-stricken limb, she finally frees herself. The frigid wind slashes at her exposed skin and the snowfall is a sightless blizzard.

Digging through the mounting snow drifts, Emma searches for her children. She screams their names in a whirling panic, but her voice is carried off and swallowed by the wind. As an unnatural night settles over her, Emma finds them buried in the deep snow. She claws at the hard, packed ice trying to free them, her hands soon becoming numb and slick with her own blood. Her husband and children are dead. Encased in an icy tomb, their bodies are cold, lifeless husks. Their features are a reflection of the terror that governed their final moments. Emma screams wordlessly, trapped in a moment of utter loss and despair.

A screeching howl rings out as a vast darkness blankets the ground, sweeping toward her. An overwhelming need to run pulses through her, and she pulls herself up, crawling across the snow and ice. Atop the ice sheet she forces her deadened legs forward. As she reaches the tree line, the malevolent shadow chases quickly at her heels. Branches and roots of the blackened trees clutch and tear at her with brittle fingers, her breath escaping in ragged puffs as she pushes herself onward. Harder and faster, her heart pounds against her ribs.

A flickering silhouette bounces toward her, darting from one tree to another within the vague darkness. Her senses are assailed at his approach. She feels his movements more than seeing them, his painfully familiar scent of wine and death floating around her. Within the distorted haze of the forest, corpses' cold hands reach out, grasping at her. Razor sharp claws rake at her neck and face as she is yanked into the cold abyss of his embrace. Petrified by fear and despair, Emma snaps her eyes shut against the image of him. Trembling and cold, she waits and prays for death. In the endless replay of this dream, her longed for death never comes.

Amid the oppressive anguish of the scene, a kernel of realization slowly creeps into Emma's mind. The hands holding her radiate a tantalizing warmth that seems so out of place in her current surroundings. Slowly her mind emerges from the thick fog of the dream. She becomes instantly aware of the hard body pressed against hers. A hot breath rolls over her neck as a tongue flicks just below her jaw line. Emma inhales sharply as a strong, calloused hand cups her breast, thumbing the nipple through the fabric of her shirt. Gooseflesh rises on her skin as her body reacts to David's distinct scent. His presence is nearly crushing and breathtaking in her befuddled state.

Her pulse quickens as his rogue tongue and mouth explore the contours of her neck and shoulder. A shuddered gasp escapes from her as she raises her hands to his chest, unsure if she should push him away or pull him closer. A shocked exhilaration rockets through her as her fingers graze the hard planes of his bare chest. His skin is a blazing contrast to the arctic setting of her moment's old nightmare. Emma's heart thunders as her mind processes his state of complete undress, her mind whirling at the notion that only her clothes separate their bodies. A throaty groan breaks free from her as she relishes the feel of him beneath her hands. Thick, corded muscles etch his chest with a soft patch of hair. Through her palm she senses his pounding heart. The heat of his mouth and hands rove over her skin. His lips close over her taunt nipple, sucking the delicate skin through the fabric.

In that moment her mind and body clash against each other. Each Fury will find a way to cope with the constant excruciating loneliness, yet it is always there. The physical needs can be managed, or ignored, but it is the emotional needs that are the hardest to overcome. It is the feeling of being wanted, desired, or even loved that Emma misses the most. To feel as if you are more than just an empty husk, to feel alive again. And that is what she wants– and has wanted it for so long. All this time she has hidden her desire for David. But being honest with herself, she longs for happiness…and for David.

Her intruding reason cautions that the dream about James and the children has emotionally compromised her. She needs to clear her mind and stop this before it's too late. If they are caught, then the Mothers will kill David. The image of Melanie and Andrew flash to her mind. The Fury was beaten and broken, and her Gyges lost his life. The Mothers would show them no mercy. That sobering thought along with David's hand slipping up underneath her shirt caressing her bare breast snaps Emma's thoughts back into place.

With an undeniable sense of disappointment, she pushes on his shoulders. "David, you need to stop. David."

With his considerable weight advantage, Emma only manages to shift him a few inches. It allows only a breath of space between them. Not enough to cease his roaming hands, but sufficient to lift his gaze toward her. Emma's stomach drops at the sight of his entranced eyes. Even in the dimly lit bedroom Emma can see that his eyes have become the solid black of an obsidian shard. The sclera and iris have been absorbed by the pitch blackness reflecting back at her. There is no indication of recognition either. His expression is dull and as lifeless as a puppet.

A tide of panic starts to swell within her. She struggles against his weight pinning her down. With a determined singular purpose, David brushes her hands aside. Securing her chest down with one arm, he tries to slide down her sweatpants with the other.

"David, stop. Wake up, David!" Emma screams in his face. Terror, anger, and frustration build within her, fueling her struggles to escape. Tears burn at her eyes as she manages to free an arm. Slapping a flat palm to his chest, she inhales deeply. *Be sure to miss the heart, just enough to stop him.* She repeats it as a mantra over and over. Focusing her thoughts, she pulls a layer of energy into the space between her hand and his chest. Pushing outward, the sudden surge lifts David and sends him up and arcing across the room. He lands with a solid thud, his naked form lying motionless in the corner of her room.

Emma scrambles to her feet, crossing the small bedroom to where David rests. Grabbing his head between her hands, she checks him for injuries. "Oh dear God, David, please wake up." Her voice is a strained whisper as she pleads with him, lightly slapping his cheeks, attempting to rouse him. With a groan his eyelids flutter open.

"Stop hitting me. I'm awake," he growls. But his expression turns to confusion as he takes in his surroundings. His eyes scan the darkened room, settling on her. "Emma? What the hell is going on?" he croaks, then winces. His chest is a bright red, and he gingerly touches it as he shifts to sit up. David stares down at himself, at once aware of his nudity, and covers himself with a nearby blanket. "Emma, I am so sorry. I thought at first maybe it was a dream, but then I couldn't wake up. I couldn't control my body." His whole demeanor reflects his internal war against the confusing fog of his mind.

Watching him, Emma again becomes painfully aware of his naked form. A light cascading through the window highlights the ridges and hard lines of his body. Emma's cheeks burn as she scurries to her feet, heading toward the kitchen. She is in desperate need of some fresh air and space away from him. "I'm going to make some tea," she calls over her shoulder.

By the time Emma has the pot on the stove she has managed to settle her nerves and calm her racing heart. She carefully listens to David moving around in the other room. From the sound of it he seems to be searching for his clothes. He emerges from the bedroom several minutes later, his hair wildly disheveled, but at least he is fully clothed. His gaze flickers about the room, landing on everything except for her.

Running a rough hand through his hair, he scratches the back of his head. "I'm sorry, Emma. You know that I would never try to hurt you. I don't know what happened. It's like one minute I'm lying there asleep, and the next my body is moving on its own." He expels an aggravated breath, the weight of his own guilt forcing him to look away.

"No worries," Emma replies, attempting a nonchalant tone.

"Stop saying that!" he roars, shattering the silence of the small kitchen. With a barely constrained anger he paces in the cramped space, his gaze leveling on her with a determined intensity. "My one job, my purpose, is to keep you safe…and I keep failing at it. In the last twenty-four hours how many times have you been hurt? And in there?" He jabs a finger toward the bedroom door. "Do you have any idea what it's like to be trapped in a body that you can't control? I could have injured you, Emma, or worse. I saw myself hurting you and I couldn't stop it."

"I am very well aware of what could have happened," Emma states calmly. "I am also well aware of the high potency of a succubus's power. Sometimes even the death of the succubus can't dispel their magic. Being a Fury and doing what I do means that I will be hurt, I will be banged up and bruised. It is just the nature of the world in which we live in, and I have accepted that. I don't enjoy the idea of pain, but the risk comes with the duty." With a huff she sits heavily in a kitchen chair. "Do you want tea or coffee?"

"Do you have a beer?" he asks, looking exhausted.

"You can check in the fridge." Emma nods her head toward the refrigerator. Crossing the room, he peers into the ice box.

Pulling out an old brown bottle, he scrutinizes the label. "How long have these been in here?" He twists off the top, sniffing it and taking a swig before she can answer. His face contorts at the apparent foul taste. He spits it in the sink and dumps the remaining bottle down the drain.

"Nope. Not good," he says, pouring himself a cup of coffee. It's cold, but probably tastes better than the beer.

"Don't know really. I think I bought it when I moved in." She chuckles with a shrug.

"How long have you lived here?" After microwaving the cup, David sits across the table from her.

"Oh jeez, I've been here maybe twelve years or so." She can't help the grin curling her lips.

"So I've been meaning to ask you something. And in light of this evening's events, I was thinking that maybe you'll give me a pass and answer it."

"Ok," she states dubiously.

"What happened with your first Gyges? The rumor mill says that you killed him, but I don't believe that's the case."

Emma studies David for several seconds, trying to decide if it is best to tell him. She hadn't talked about what happened with Alec to anyone. When he died everyone acted as though he never existed. She has always known that she would need to tell David about him sooner or later. With that being said, it doesn't make the conversation any easier.

"You are right, I didn't kill him, but in the end he still died because of me." Emma studies her now lukewarm tea. "Alec was my Gyges right after my period of quarantine ended. He was an older gentleman. Some people thought he was too old to properly defend anyone. He was coarse, rude, unapologetic, and as hard-hitting as they came. And he was like a father to me. He taught me how to fight with a sword."

David watches her silently, allowing her time to pause and continue as needed.

"He was killed by the same vampire that murdered me. He was butchered by a monster, and I was helpless to do anything about it." Emma laughs dryly to herself. "Maybe that's a perfect example of irony. The Fury are meant to avenge those taken by violence. I couldn't seek justice for myself, my children, or Alec."

"What are you talking about?" he asks, his eyes never leaving her.

"You know that when one becomes a Fury they are quarantined for a period of time. This is usually about seventy-five to one hundred years, all depending on the circumstances surrounding their death. This ensures that enough time has passed so their Dolofonos, their killer, has died."

She waits quietly until he nods in understanding. He sits stoically, watching her as if he were carved from granite.

"As it turns out, there is a loophole in the system. My Dolofonos is an undead, and won't die of natural causes. We were out one evening searching for some missing pixies. I don't know how he found me, but he attacked, and Alec tried to protect me."

Emma stands and walks over to refresh her stale tea. Steeping the tea, she rubs her lower back with a groan. Lack of restful sleep is making her joints sore and stiff.

"What I don't understand is why the Fury didn't just kill this vampire. It sounds like he probably deserved it, and I would think they would seek vengeance for you." David shifts in his seat, wrenching a whining protest from the wooden chair. "Plus, why would a vampire risk going up against the Fury for some food? For lack of a better word, no offense intended."

"I really don't know." Leaning against the counter, Emma rolls her neck from side to side. "As we both know, the motives of the Fury are not always clear. Maybe they had trouble finding him?" Emma said with a shrug. "After he killed my family he came back to collect me. I was his pet for nearly two hundred years. Fortunately, most Fury are found by the Mothers within days of their death. It took them a lot longer to come for me, and that was only after I managed to escape. They found me wandering through the woods. That may also be one of the reasons he came after me."

David leaves his seat and stands next to her, as if his presence could protect her from the past. Emma smiles weakly as the painful memories swell and course through her.

"Is it because you escaped?" he guesses, rinsing and putting his cup in the sink.

"Yes, it was partially because of that. I was a renewable food resource, and a Fury's blood is rather potent. He became stronger the more he fed from me. But more likely the reason he came after me is that I killed his whole clan." Her tone is so matter of fact that David simply stares at her for several seconds. "It was daylight and they were all asleep, so it was actually quite simple. I don't really remember too much about it. Maybe there is a part of me that doesn't want to remember it. I just remember being so terrified."

"Terrified of what?" he asks softly, his eyebrows furrowing together.

"Myself." Her body is wracked with tremors. She is thankful that the counter is there to help her stand. "I'm terrified of what I am, of what I could become." She inhales a deeply ragged breath.

David steps forward, pulling her toward him. Emma's heart skips in her chest as he hugs her, holding her closely. He is a solid strength and warmth that wraps around her. It is a simple embrace that has a powerful effect on Emma. As he continues to hold her, Emma feels her body slowly relaxing as an unacknowledged tension seeps away. Emma's cheeks are hot and wet as tears stream silently down her face. David says nothing, but holds her, rubbing her shoulders and head as she weeps. Emma is overwhelmed by the sense that this is the first time she is actually mourning for the loss of her children and mourning for herself.

David whispers softly to her soothing her as she weeps.

"Thank you for trusting me. You cannot know how much that means to me. Sometimes I am amazed by your strength."

"I'm not strong," she muses, finally meeting his gaze. "Most of the time I'm just wandering around feeling…broken." She swallows hard, forcing the tears back.

"You are much stronger then you think. I won't promise you that everything will be perfect and easy, but I'll do everything in my power to keep you safe. And maybe we can work together to make things right." He lightly kisses her temple, hugging her closely to him.

A loud crack of her front door splintering rips her back to the present. Fragments of her doorframe skid across the floor. David reacts, turning their bodies to shield her. Her small kitchen is flooded with several Gyges, followed by Moss. Each of the men eyes them with a dark disdain. Through the massive wall of men, Moss saunters over to them with a casual ease, his look of utterly arrogant delight sending shivers through Emma's body. David tries to tighten his hold at the other man's approach as Emma pushes away from David but gives him a calm, reassuring glance. She squeezes his arm subtly before turning to face the men.

"What do you want, Moss?" David's voice is cold yet speaks of an underlying threat of violence.

"I am here to take you both into custody." Moss's eyes gleam with a calculated malice.

"For what?" Emma's own tone is ripe with the growing hostility.

"Your secret is out. We know you've been doing David here." The man dismissively nods his head toward David. "And here we find you shacking up together. Though I don't know if I feel more sorry for you or David." His look turns to one of disgust as he looks her up and down.

"Why don't we step outside, then we'll see how sorry you feel, you lying sack of..." David advances toward Moss but is halted as Emma touches his arm. The smug Moss laughs as he crosses his arms over his chest.

"Unfortunately it is probably wiser to go with them." Emma tries to appear serene to hide the trepidation flooding her system. An unrelenting worry gnaws painfully at Emma's insides. Their options are extremely limited at this time. Even if they managed to escape these men, others would be sent to track them down. Two of the men step forward, roughly grabbing Emma by her arms.

"Come with us," one of them barks as they pull her roughly out the door.

Chapter 14

The dank cold of the small cell seeps into Emma's skin, rooting within her a fierce and uncontrollable shiver. Her t-shirt and pajama bottoms provide little protection against the frigid air circulating through the drafty prison. Sitting atop the shabby cot, she wraps the scratchy woolen blanket firmly around herself, willing the unpleasant chill to go away.

Leaning her head back against the ice-cold stone wall, Emma once again studies her morbid surroundings. The claustrophobic holding cell has few qualities that would make it appropriate for existence. Aside from the small bed there is a dingy porcelain sink and a bucket in the far corner. Emma mused to herself about being afforded running water but not a toilet. Although she is highly suspicious of what's coming out of the faucet– whatever it is, it isn't water. Water should lack a sickening sweet acrid smell, and it is not as viscous as what gurgles down her drain. The charcoal-black dirt floor and obsidian walls consume whatever paltry light is emanated from the wall torches.

One blessing from the cold temperature is that it distracts her attention from her physical wounds. By now there is only a hint of bruising on her upper arms and shoulders. The swelling in her right knee has gone down as well. All in all, she estimates that she faired the events reasonably well, even with being pushed down the last few steps of her stairwell. Her busted lip is mending itself as she runs her tongue along the wound. The bleeding has subsided and the broken skin is now just raw. In a few hours it will be completely healed.

She hadn't expected Moss's men to be gentle with her, nor were they. Pincer-like hands yanked and pushed her down the stairs. She missed the last steps, which sent her crashing down onto the landing. Securing her arms behind her, they lobbed her into the back of an awaiting van. Tossing her onto her side, her shoulder took the brunt of the hit against the cold steel. The interior of the van is un-upholstered with a long bench built into the side of the vehicle. The freezing metal of the floor saps away her body heat.

The travel route they opted for seems to be on the most pot-hole-ridden road, as she was bounced and bumped the whole ride with no means to brace herself. Several times when the van halted or turned sharply it would send her sliding across the floor. By the time they arrived Emma had a deep, bleeding gouge on her head, the blood trickling slowly down the nape of her neck. Just as they were shoving her into the cell, a wild sucker punch came from nowhere. Having no time to react, the strike landed squarely, her knees buckling as the blood filled her mouth. Rough hands drag her into the cell, and she is shoved with such force that she stumbles into the far wall. They laugh as they leave, and she spits a mouthful of blood into the sink. Silently, she curses them. Down the darkened hallway she hears the thick iron gates close with a resonating chime.

Finally left alone with her own thoughts, Emma tries to puzzle out the events that landed her here. Her options have all seemed to slip away. The Mothers are not known to be understanding in regards to romantic entanglements. Convincing them of her innocence will be a near impossible task. It is a seemingly fruitless endeavor. They will show her no leniency. If she is locked away in here, how can she hope to save Sara? What will they do to David? Emma's stomach lurches with a frantic sense of building terror.

Through the haze of mild hypothermia, Emma strains her ears, listening to the slightest scratching sound, the muted noise seeming to echo throughout the confined area. By the smallest of degrees the volume increases, morphing into a dull chorus of whispered voices. The words are impossible to discern. It is a language she is unfamiliar with, a garbled mass of syllables that are distinctly foreign, but they resonate deeply within her. Recalling her experience in the archive, Emma scans the room, watching for any sign of movement. Yet she sees nothing out of the ordinary. The lights remain illuminated, and there is no sudden appearance of the deceased Mother. The air cracks and all the sounds cease in an instant, leaving behind only the raging sound of quiet.

"With as much time as you spend down here they'll probably name a wing of it after you."

Startled from her thoughts, Emma looks up to see Olivia striding toward her cell door. Her short blonde hair takes on a fiery glow as it reflects the wavering torch light.

"Not really much of a vacation spot if you ask me. I can personally think of a lot better places to spend my time."

Folding her arms across her chest, Olivia eyes Emma. Scrutinizing her with an open look of disapproval, Olivia blows out an exasperated breath. Her eyes darken, turning nearly black under the dismal light.

"How could you be so stupid? Seriously, Emma you've been here long enough. You know what they can do to you. They could have you killed. It's only a matter of time before locking you up for years seems pointless," Olivia snaps, near boiling with frustration.

"My actions, or lack thereof, will have little bearing on whether or not they decide to execute me. Even if I toe the line from now until eternity, they will find a reason to destroy me eventually." Emma's tone is flat as she meets Olivia's gaze. "Where is David?" Emma asks cautiously.

"He had himself a downright conniption fit when he heard you were being held down here. It took five men to get him under control." As if sensing Emma's agitation rising, Olivia waves a hand dismissively. "Oh, he is alright. A little bruised up, but relatively unharmed. And he is being held in one of the cells upstairs. He is lucky they didn't just kill him." While the idea of David being locked up is disheartening, at least he is alive.

"We will need to convince the Mothers of your innocence," Olivia continues. "If they believe that David initiated the tryst, they may go easier on you both." Emma's mouth is agape with the audacity of the suggestion.

"I will not ask David to take on blame that is not his. Plus, my guilt or innocence was determined before the Gyges even entered my apartment. It is you who are the fool if you think otherwise. I am too tired to play along with their mockery of a trial."

A Gyges is not barred from taking a lover, as long as it is not a Fury. The only punishment handed down for the crime was death to the Gyges. Pushing down the cold tendrils of fear, Emma breathes deeply resolving herself.

"I'm guilty, so let's just move on."

"But why? Knowing what would happen, why?" Utterly baffled, Olivia shakes her head at Emma.

"I was lonely. He's a good-looking man. I offered myself to him and he rejected me." Emma allows all hint of feeling to seep out of her tone, leaving her voice cold and lifeless.

"I don't believe you." Olivia studies Emma dubiously, tilting her head to the side. "I think David came onto you, and for some stupid reason you are trying to protect him. You have never been able to lie to me."

Emma leans further forward. Leveling her gaze on Olivia, her tone icy and matter-of-fact. She may not be able to deceive this woman who was the closest thing she has to a friend, but she isn't going to back down either.

"Prove it."

"Don't be insane. You will be locked up and still lose David as your guardian. When an accusation of fraternization has been made, the Fury and Gyges are always at the very least separated. Lying for him won't help you." Olivia strides up to the cell bars, her frustration seamlessly morphing into anger.

"If they find me guilty, I'll lose time. If they find David guilty, they'll take his life. David was enthralled, a puppet under the control of a succubus's magic."

"I could go to the Mothers and tell them you are innocent. They'll believe me," Olivia offers.

"No. No they won't. If Tatiana has her way they will always believe the worst of me. And there is no way to prove that David was being manipulated."

Olivia's features soften as she reaches up to clasp one of the bars to the cell. "David is a good man, but don't risk your life for him. Don't let yourself fall for him. It will only hurt the both of you in the end."

Emma's heart drops at the statement. Is that what she felt for him? Love? It had been so long, that the emotion felt like a distant memory of someone else's life.

"Oh, God, you do love him." Olivia's face contorts in anguish. "Listen, you have to let that go. To love someone...nothing good comes from that, believe me." The hardness of Olivia's features melt, becoming poignant as her thoughts turn inward.

"What happened to you?" The words tumble out before Emma can stop them.

Olivia studies a section of the floor for several seconds before looking up again. Sighing deeply, her gaze retreats back to the floor as small lines form on her brow.

"Growing up, I was taught the importance of finding a good man, a hard working man, one with a good head on his shoulders and could go places. A stable guy who could provide for his wife and kids. And that's what I wanted, someone to love and a house full of children. So I waited for Mr. Right to come along. In the meantime I needed to work. But in the 1920's, even in Chicago, my options for a career were limited, so I found a job and worked as a secretary in one of the most prestigious high rises." A timid smile curls Olivia's lips as she recalls the memories. "One day when I was leaving work, I met Eugene in the elevator. We were both heading downstairs. He was a CPA whose office was down the hall from me."

Emma leans forward, listening intently. She is stuck by the impossible vision of Olivia as anything but the fierce Fury that she is.

After clearing her throat nervously, Olivia continues. "After a few weeks, we started dating and things were wonderful. Six months later he asked me to marry him, and I said yes. We planned the wedding together, and I was so unbelievably happy. As time went by his behavior started changing." Olivia gnaws fretfully on the corner of her mouth.

"How?" Emma's voice is a breath of a whisper, as if speaking loudly would frighten Olivia off. From the distant glaze in her eyes, she could tell Olivia's thoughts are focused on the past.

"We stopped going out anywhere. He was always at his office, and when he was at home he'd refuse to go out. He locked himself in at night and became paranoid, started drinking. He seemed so agitated, almost like he was afraid of something. I would ask him about it, but he refused to speak to me. Late one afternoon I found out what it was." Olivia lifts her gaze, meeting Emma's, her piercing blue eyes rimmed with unshed tears. "I stopped by his office one night to see if I could convince him to go out. That or at the very least to walk me home. I wasn't trying to eavesdrop, but I heard him talking on the phone." Wringing her hands, Olivia shifts listlessly on her feet. "He'd somehow gotten caught up with the mob and laundering money. I walked in and confronted him, told him we should go to the cops. He said he wouldn't, he couldn't. He said that they would kill both of us, and he was trying to protect us. I told him, 'If you don't go to the police, then I will.' He started crying and pleaded with me, and when that didn't work he became enraged. He started hitting me. He beat me nearly to death and threw me out his office window. One hundred stories down." Her voice rattles with the strain of controlling her emotions. "From what I gather he put a bullet in his brain later that night."

"I had no idea, I'm sorry." Emma's voice seems to thunder in the quiet cell. Her heart mourns for the seemingly resilient woman standing before her.

"You see, even a good guy can turn into a monster." Olivia briskly rubs her eyes, quickly trying to regain her composure. "Something is happening here that is dangerous and very wrong. I can feel it in my gut. And you being locked up for God knows how long won't help us. I know you care for David, but we need you here with us to fight whatever is coming."

"I will consider what you have said. But it is quite possible my cards have already been dealt."

From behind them there is a sound from the heavy iron doors. Thick tumblers are pushed loudly, opening the door. Through the doorway, Moss and several of the Gyges emerge, the massive column of men filling the hallway as they make their way toward Emma's cell. The bulky men shuffle into a single file behind Moss.

"Get up!" he barks to Emma, motioning to the door as another man steps forward to unlock the cell door. "They are ready for you."

Emma's insides clench as she stands slowly and throws the blanket onto the worn-out cot. She recognizes Branson and Lee immediately as they enter the cell. Each man steps to Emma's side and roughly grabs her by the arms. They both lift her as they drag her from the small holding area. Crossing the threshold, Branson pushes her, and the momentum sends Emma careening forward, slamming into the far wall. Her shoulder slaps the stone slab with a bone-jarring thud.

"Hey! What the hell are you doing?" Olivia yells, stepping toward the group. Moss holds up a meaty hand, blocking her, but careful not to touch her.

"This is none of your concern." His tone is bland and straightforward. Olivia's face darkens as she scowls at Moss. Branson leans slightly, hauling Emma away from the wall. Briskly, they usher her up the stairs, down several long corridors. Entering the main hall, Emma is shocked by the fact that the room is barren. Only three people occupy the area– Ambrose, Mei Li, and Tatiana. Shuffling her across the wide area, Emma is marched to stand before her three judges, each of them watching her silently as the group of men stands abreast, creating a line behind her. From somewhere behind her she hears the great wooden doors close and lock.

Just outside the wooden barrier Emma can hear Olivia's voice as she snaps at the sentries, arguing about not being admitted. Sounds reverberate around the vast area of the hall. Her escorts brusquely lead her to a straight-back chair, pushing her down to sit.

"Thank you, gentlemen." Tatiana motions for the guards.

"Do you know why you have been brought here?" Mei Li's voice is clipped as her countenance is vacant. Seconds of silence stretch between them.

"Yes. You believe I have committed a crime." Emma's insides clench violently. Fear and anxiety rage through her, though she refuses to show any signs to them.

"Do you deny the charges against you? You have been a participant in sexual acts with your guardian."

"I do not believe that any offences have been committed." Struggling to keep her tone smooth, Emma returns their gaze.

"The truth will be determined whether you confess or not." Tatiana strolls forward, exuding an aura of malice and indignation. "Either you will tell us or we will be forced to get a confession from David." Standing directly in front of Emma, Tatiana tilts her face downward, her sculpted eyebrows arching slightly. "How well do you think he will fair under such an inquisition?" The Mother purrs. "His mind and body will be broken, but we will have our answers. Of course he'll no longer be useful as a guardian, but I'm sure we can find some menial tasks for him here. Now, you can save a lot of pain, and possibly his life, by simply telling us what happened."

Emma's throat seizes up in an agonizing constriction.

"Child, just tell us what happened." Mei Li's voice floats softly across to Emma. "I am certain that leniency is the best course in this instance. But we need to know the truth."

Stepping forward, the second Mother stands abreast to her counterpart. Inhaling a ragged breath, Emma studies the two women looming over her. In that moment the sheer extent of hopelessness weighs heavily on her, threatening to crush her under its mass. With no apparent avenue for escape, Emma's thoughts turn to damage control.

"You are right. I have sinned." The words catch in her throat, but she forces them out. Mei Li's expression is a mixture of dubiousness and astonished disappointment. Tatiana remains stoic, unmoving.

"Tell us what happened." Tatiana's tone is bitterly cold, a steely grey gaze cutting straight through Emma.

"David escorted me back to my apartment. Later that night when he was sleeping…" Emma pulls in a sharp breath of air, tamping down the jitters and trying to calm her wriggling innards. "I snuck to where he lay sleeping and tried to seduce him."

"What did David do?" An elegant arch of her eyebrow signals that Tatiana is enthralled.

"He rejected me. I thought for a moment about destroying him, but decided against it." Unshed tears sting at her eyes. Emma can no longer meet their stares.

"We will discuss this matter and return with our decision." Tatiana turns to address Ambrose. "Please be sure that she stays here."

Ambrose curtly nods as both Mothers exit through a small door to the left. Several minutes stretch by in near silence.

The only sounds are that of scuffing boots and an occasional cough.

"Why did you lie for him?"

Emma looks up to see Ambrose studying her intensely. "I didn't lie…" Emma starts, but Ambrose cuts her off.

"I can always tell when someone is lying. What I want to know is why?" He steps forward, directly in front of her, forcing her to crane her neck to meet his stare. "Why risk your life for a Gyges?"

"Does it really matter?" she asks, keeping her voice smooth. She battles against herself to remain collected. Something about Ambrose sets her nerves on edge.

"Perhaps, perhaps not," he muses with an easy nonchalance. "Maybe it is of great importance. To understand why one is willing to gamble against life and death. They could impose a death sentence. I assume you are aware of that."

"Yes, they could." She tries to push back her seat, to provide space between them, but the damn chair is nailed to the floor. "But I will fight and die for what I think is right. If David were guilty then I would kill him myself, but he bears no responsibility in this. How can I claim integrity if I were to do nothing to protect him when he is innocent?"

"That is a noble ideology, but not very practical. Whether David lives or dies, it will not change the nature of our existence. One moment and one act will have no great effect on the whole. Evil will still run rampant, and justice unmet."

"I disagree. The whole of our lives are a collection of minute actions in the smallest of moments. Each act or decision we make causes a ripple effect moving out and away from us, touching all that surround us. And our duty as Fury is not only to punish the wicked, but to protect and nurture the innocence of this world." A smirk spreads across his lips as the far door opens again.

The Mothers emerge from their chamber, Tatiana striding with a determined purpose, and Mei Li, seemingly run-down, trails behind her. They halt, standing directly in front of Emma. Ambrose side steps but remains uncomfortably close.

"After much deliberation, Mother Mei Li will pronounce our verdict," Tatiana announces as she sweeps her hand toward Mei Li.

"It has been determined that Emma has been found guilty of the charges against her. The normal punishment for such an offence is one hundred years, but there have been petitions for leniency in this case. With that being said, we have also taken into account the many years of loyal service from Emma. So she will be sentenced to twenty-five years in Erebus, to start immediately."

Pivoting sharply, Mei Li and Tatiana exit the room without another word. Emma sits momentarily dazed in her seat. She is befuddled at such a short sentence, and also terrified to serve it.

Ambrose pulls her to her feet, clasping her arm firmly. "Come with me." His words seem muted in her confused state. In a blur of movement she is led from the now empty room.

Chapter 15

The fog of desolation slowly lifts as they make their way down the hallway leading back to the cells. Ambrose flanks Emma, who is walking in silence. The clipped echo of their footsteps is the only sound that accompanies them. Numbly, Emma rubs her palms together, trying to warm them against the sudden chill that weighs her down. She is resolute in the fact that she will not regret her decision. Ragged fingers of desperation curl in from all sides as she faces the prospect of her internment.

"I will make sure some warmer blankets are brought to you."

Startled from her thoughts, Emma looks up to see Ambrose watching her as they walk.

"There is no need to go to any trouble." The crippling sense of helplessness and despair that permeates this place starts to settle in around her, crushing her under its mass. Forcing air into her lungs, she battles to calm the racing tempo of her heart.

"It's no trouble really. I know it can be quite uncomfortable down here. Unfortunately, that has always been the point. If it was pleasant here it wouldn't be much of a deterrent. But I will try to offer you what little comforts I can while you are here."

They come to a stop just outside her cell door. Emma stares bleakly into the inky depths of her new residence. Ambrose unlocks the door with a thick iron skeleton key. Holding the door open, he turns, watching her with a forlorn look in his eyes.

"The events of today sadden me greatly." Ambrose sighs as his gaze remains unwavering. "As much as I have accomplished here, I've come to realize still how little is in my control."

"While I wish for a different outcome, I do not regret my decision." Emma studies the cracked stone floor. She is distinctly aware of his presence as his gaze dissects her.

"That's admirable. You have always possessed strength of character and determination, unlike many of your fellow sisters. It is important to fight for what you believe in. Even if it means giving up the things we want most in the world. We risk what could bring us joy to accomplish the greater goal."

"Thank you," Emma mutters, uncertain of what else to say to him. An eerie vibration of power pulses like an aura around them and throughout the room. She shivers as gooseflesh rises on her arms, and she briskly rubs them. Ambrose, moving silently, clasps her shoulders, turning her to face him. His eyes are dark and intense, with an almost mesmerizing quality. For the first time she sees the extent of his attractiveness. He is distinctly masculine, with the subtle scent of a campfire on a cold night.

"Aside from the Mothers, you are one of the eldest Fury in The Hallow. You may be unappreciated by the others, but your sacrifices do not go unnoticed." His thumbs softly caress the exposed skin of her arms. "Just remember, should you have need of anything, just call. My men will come and find me." Lifting his hand, he gently brushes loose hair away from her face.

Where his hands contact her, there is a crackle of underlying energy, a strange buzz that tickles along her skin. She knows that it is not coming from her. The back of his fingers gently brush against her cheek. His head lowers slightly toward hers. Believing that his intent is to kiss her, Emma pulls back in confusion. Ambrose's hands fall away from her.

"I thank you again for your kindness, but I will let you know now that if any of your men enter my quarters with the intent to do me harm, I will kill them." Walking through the iron archway, Emma turns to face him.

"I wouldn't expect anything less. Until we meet again." For an instant, a hint of a smile touches his lips, then vanishes just as quickly. His body shifts, becoming rigid as he squares his shoulders and studies her. "Just be careful. There have been some odd occurrences down here in Erebus. Should you hear anything out of the ordinary or strange noises, just remain in here. It is safer to stay where you are." He swiftly gestures toward her cell and curtly nods. Before she can ask what he meant he shuts the door and retreats.

Sitting in the frigid silence, Emma mulls over the oddity of Ambrose's behavior. Knowing virtually nothing about him, it is impossible to determine if he is at all trustworthy. She senses nothing about him, which may be what bothers her the most. Olivia trusts him, as do the Mothers. But there is an uneasy familiarity whenever she is near him. Then there is the unsettling thought that he was going to kiss her. While he has always been civil, he didn't seem the type to give in to his baser needs. She determines that perhaps she had misinterpreted his intent. That seems to make more sense.

From the formless darkness, the solid metal door scrapes open with a belligerent screech. Mei Li approaches Emma with an easy grace. Her black silken hair is pulled back in a tightly twisted bun, her skin glowing against the sharp contrast of her charcoal robe. She steps directly in front of the cell, analyzing Emma under the dim lighting. Her cool expression gives nothing away.

"I brought you a change of clothing." Carefully Mei Li squeezes the small bundle of clothes through the bars of Emma's cell. "I imagine you're cold and would like something a bit warmer." The chill of her stoic mood adds to the brewing guilt within Emma.

"Thank you, Mother." Emma clutches the clothes but can't bring herself to look up at Mei Li. "How is Sara? They won't let me see her. They won't even tell me how she is." Now Emma risks a slight glance toward Mei Li, her concern for Sara outweighing her fear of incurring Mei Li's wrath.

"I am not permitted to see her. Why would they allow you to do so if I cannot? Do you know how many lives I had to threaten just to be able to see you?" Mei Li huffs. She squints through the darkness, scanning the floor and all around her. "Why do they have no place to sit here?"

"I'm not sure, Mother. Maybe they don't expect you will have any visitors while here." Emma shrugs.

"Oh well. It's not important." The Mother waves the thought aside with a motion of her hand, then sternly folds her arms over her chest. "You do realize that your being locked up in here puts us in quite a predicament."

"I am sorry, Mother. I was lonely and weak."

"You can stop lying now. I know the truth. I spoke with David."

"David's just trying to protect me," Emma blurts out.

"I am well aware of what David and you are doing." Mei Li's brow lifts high. "I also know you both well enough to see the truth in his words. I'm not blind. I've known you long enough to recognize that you are a horrible liar."

With a sense of defeat, Emma plops down on the cot, clutching the ball of clothes close to her.

"He was enthralled by the succubus's magic, and I didn't want him to die. Is he alright?" Emma asks, staring down numbly at her trembling hands.

"We wouldn't have killed him. Even if Tatiana wants him punished, he is too much of an asset to lose. He is unharmed. I don't need to tell you that he is quite unhappy about your lie." Emma cringes, shifting her gaze to the grimy floor. "Livid would be a more accurate description. He explained what happened at your meeting with the wolves, and about the succubus. Why didn't you trust me with the truth?" Mei Li asks with a hurt expression.

"I thought it would be easier for you to think the worst of me. It is well known that Tatiana has little love for me."

"Tatiana can be gruff and at times intolerable. She makes no effort to hide her feelings, nor does she consider the feelings of others, but she is fair in her judgments. A sentencing should never be too harsh or too lenient. But needless to say, you should have been honest with me. You should have faith that I will see the truth…and your innocence."

"Would you really have stood against Tatiana on my behalf?" Emma fails to hide the bitterness in her voice. Past experiences in these matters have made it painfully clear who the Mothers will and won't stand up for. Agnes had defended Emma, and they turned on her. Mei Li's gaze darkens as a sad shadow crosses her face.

"I have always strived to find the truth. Dissention among the Mothers can be a dangerous path. We must be the mortar that holds everything together." Mei Li's voice chills with indignation. "Also, you confessed prior to me questioning you. How can I defend you when you have already admitted to committing the transgression? Sometimes you act too rashly."

"Sorry," Emma replies sheepishly. Shame once again spreads through her gut at her impulsive decision. Yet she keeps her gaze focused on Mei Li.

"Being sorry does little to help us now. A great darkness looms in the distance, biding its time until it can scatter us into the wind. We are all needed for whatever is ahead of us." Mei Li's eyes brighten as she spies a small stool in one of the darkened corners of the hallway. Gliding over, she sweeps it up and plants it squarely in front of Emma. She sits gingerly, as if wary of the condition of the chair. The wood creaks slightly but holds fast.

"Olivia and Celia are stronger fighters. With them at your side, my absence will be of little consequence. As a rank three, I highly doubt I would be able to add anything. I'll stay here, safe and out of the way."

Mei Li clicks her tongue at Emma's words.

"All of the Fury are valuable. You must be careful. Losing another Fury could prove to be devastating." Mei Li nervously gnaws at her lip. The underlying agitation coming from Mei Li sets Emma's own nerves on edge.

"I'm locked up in prison." Emma controls her features. Her tone is a forced calm as she motions to her dismal surroundings. "I'm reasonably safe from any outside forces while in here."

"Even still, you must be cautious. You mustn't risk yourself like this anymore. I don't think you understand." Mei Li pauses as her gaze falls to the floor. "How could you understand?" she mutters distantly to herself.

"Understand what?" Emotions swirl in Emma's stomach, dread and fear washing throughout her at a fevered pace. Mei Li's gaze flickers guardedly all around them. All of the adjacent cells are empty. They are alone in the vastly secluded space.

"You are much stronger than you can comprehend." Readjusting in her seat, Mei Li fidgets with the sleeve of her gown. In all of the years they'd known each other, Emma cannot recall Mei Li being this physically distressed. "Do you remember when you first came here to live with us?" With a clenching throat, Emma manages a slight nod. "There was a lot of uncertainty about what should be done with you. The complications surrounding your death were one that we had never encountered before. We were all at a loss as to how to keep you safe…how to keep all of us safe. Your Dolofonos would live a very long time and would always be an issue. We thought it would be best to shield you from the danger. The copper in your armbands would diminish your capacity to draw from the source, but it would also mute your presence, making it harder to track you. There would be less of a risk that he could locate you."

Emma numbly touches the metal serpent entwined around her arm.

"To placate suspicions, we told everyone that you barely passed the tests. A muffled presence is expected with lower skill and strength. But truth be told, you are just as strong and valuable as everyone else. That is why we need everyone to face what is coming. And now I have to try and fix this without raising any questions. How do we release you from Erebus without it appearing as partiality?" Mei Li questions.

"So you kept this from everyone? Why didn't you tell me?" Through the baffled shock, Mei Li's confession settles in. She was just the same as all the other Fury, she wasn't weak or inferior.

"It would just complicate the situation even more. If someone knew, then it could be used against you, against the Fury." Mei Li's voice cuts through.

"So you let me think that I was less than everyone else?" Anger skitters up Emma's spine as she battles to tamp it down.

"Unfortunately, in this instance, yes. Honestly, we thought it would be for the best. We have all lost so much being here. We are plucked from one life and tossed into another, losing our families, our friends, our homes. I understand the difficulties of adjusting to this new life. When I lived as a human, I too had a husband and a son whom I loved very much. There is much pain in knowing that they are still out there and I can never see them again. The water spirit that carried me into the lake had no care that I would miss my family. All the decisions we make are in an effort to lessen any additional suffering." Emma shifts her head as she listens.

"How can your husband and son still be living after all these years?" Emma asks cautiously. Mei Li's natural life ended thousands of years ago.

Mei Li brushes aside the question with an impatient movement of her slender hand.

"That's a long story, perhaps for another time. There is much more pressing news that we need to discuss before I leave." Mei Li's features morph into a stern mask that causes Emma's pulse to quicken and a cold sweat to sheen her arms. "Tatiana and I must leave The Hallow for a few days. It is very important that you stay safe while I'm away."

"Safe from what? Where are you going?" Emma stands and walks up to the cell door, clutching the icy metal with her hands.

"It is a diplomatic mission of sorts. A master vampire has had two attempts on his life in the past week. The reason for the attacks are, as of yet, unknown. We are heading there to see if we can learn the truth. David will be coming with us. He is good protection, and I think it will be best to get him away for awhile." Standing from the small wooden stool, Mei Li glides toward Emma. Her voice drops to a near whisper, and even in the desolation of the cell Emma must strain to hear her. "I want you to promise me that if something happens you will find Sara and leave this place. Go and find a vampire by the name of Bastian. He isn't particularly friendly to outsiders, but if you tell him I told you to ask for him, he'll offer you aid."

"Why would he help me? How can you be so sure?" Emma asks.

"He will help you because he owes me a very large favor," Mei Li answers calmly.

"A favor? For what?" Emma's whole body trembles in the chilled, stagnant air.

"I spared his life." Mei Li stares at her with a resolute coolness. "He had committed a great many sins, hurt a great many people, and his life was mine to take. He will help if you have need. Now I must go. They are waiting for me. Please be careful, keep Sara safe if you can." She reaches out, clutching Emma's hands over the bars.

"I will try, Mother," Emma solemnly replies, terrified that she may never see Mei Li again. Unshed tears gloss her eyes.

"Good." Mei Li nods and turns, receding back into the blackness to the hall.

Chapter 16

Sweat runs in rivulets down the small of Olivia's back. Her hair and t-shirt are soaked. Perspiration had soddened the material hours ago, but her pace doesn't slow. After running the gauntlet of every cardio machine, she is still filled with an unshakable nervous energy, as though millions of fire ants have wormed their way under her skin, crawling around. After an especially stressful night she often comes here to burn off excess tension. Mind-numbing, repetitive exercise that will quiet the voices of self-doubt and send her to bed exhausted. Yet even after several hours on a treadmill, stationary bike, elliptical machine, and several circuits of calisthenics, her mind still refuses to shut down. Her muscles scream and her limbs feel as though they're going to explode, but she is still on edge.

The well-worn, faded-blue punching bag sways slightly in front of her. Its hypnotic movement is usually quite soothing. But tonight nothing seems to be helping. In the past few days so much has changed within The Hallow, none of which is for the good. Changes can bring many unexpected dangers. After throwing several punches in succession, the fraying bag develops a small fissure, causing tiny grains of sand spill out of the small crack, running on to the mat floor. From the creases in the leather vinyl a crosshatched pattern of fabric peeks through.

Of course, none of this would be an issue if Emma hadn't been so stupid and proud. *Damn that woman*, Olivia fumes to herself. She has always respected honesty, as well as integrity. Emma did lie, but it seemed to be for a good reason. Who knows what punishment the Mothers would have opted for? Perhaps if she trusted anyone the way Emma trusts David she'd risk a lot for them as well. She'd always been hesitant to trust or rely on others. It is better to be alone and a whole person than to allow someone in who will rip you to shreds. She trusted once, so long ago and what had that gotten her? She had given Eugene every ounce of her being. Everything she was belonged to him. He destroyed that with his lies and betrayal and bloody fists. He smashed away everything in her that was whole and alive. Without a care he took from her and left her to turn to ash.

With Sara locked up, one Mother dead and the other two acting strange, who could one trust anyway? And if she were to be honest, not everything bad that had befallen them could be blamed on Emma. She made her decisions and they landed her in Erebus, locked away. All the other malarkey going on had nothing to do with her– not really.

Her eyes refocus on the now-still punching bag. The passage of time and the late hour wore her down. Her shoulders droop against the effort of holding them up. Past any reasonable point of exhaustion, Olivia walks slowly toward a line of benches to retrieve her things.

Hopefully a hot shower and some sleep will help to settle her mind. *Address the issues you can today, save the rest for another day*, she thinks to herself.

Through the open silence of the gymnasium an explosion from one of the upper levels rocks the ceiling above her. Olivia's senses rocket to attention as dust and fragments of debris shower down around her. Her belongings forgotten, she hurries to the nearest door, her heart thumping in her chest as if it were trying to claw its way out. Stepping into the hall, she is halted suddenly by three hulking men blocking her path.

Moss, Branson, and Lee fill the claustrophobically small hallway. The corridor is barely wide enough for two people to walk abreast. The two young men crowd around a flimsy table that is partially blocking the rest of the path. In the distance Olivia can discern the sounds of glass shattering and panicked screams. The overhead lights of the hall sporadically flicker, the ambient light level rising and falling around them. With their faces shadowed by the overhead lights, they silently stare.

"What is happening?" Olivia questions in a raspy breath.

"You are to come with us." Moss's tone is thick with an unwavering decisiveness. His head bent toward her, he stares at her intensely from under his thick eyebrows. Moss approaches her slowly, cautiously, but with a determination. He comes to a halt next to a small table as his gaze flickers momentarily to the polished surface. Reaching into his pocket, he pulls out a copper choker and tosses it onto the wood with a jarring clatter. "Put this on," he orders coldly, his dead eyes staring back at her. The copper leash is often used only in extreme cases to subdue the most unruly of Fury. Olivia's chin rises as she squarely meets Moss's gaze.

"No. I am not doing a damn thing until you tell me exactly what is going on. Where is Ambrose?" Olivia clenches her hands, studying the three men opposite to her. Her muscles tense, screaming at her in protest. The onset of adrenaline pumping through her aids to counteract the crippling fatigue.

"You will do as you are told. We have orders to keep you alive. Now we can do this the easy way or the hard way, your choice. Don't be dumb." Moss's stare is meant to be unnerving, but it is his words that cause Olivia's blood to run cold through her veins.

"As long as we get you there it don't matter how broken you are," Branson snickers sadistically at her.

"Go to hell. The first one of you dumb asses that touches me is going to die."

The men chuckle softly in response. The corners of Olivia's mouth perk up. *Good, underestimate me,* she states confidently to herself. Never would she have believed that she would one day confront a Gyges, let alone three. While the three possess impressive skills and strength, she has little doubt that she can defeat them.

Branson and Lee step forward to either side of Moss. In a swift movement, Branson lunges for her, reaching for her hands. His sudden attack is lightning fast. Sidestepping the assault, Olivia swings, landing a solid strike to Branson's upper abdomen. His breath gushes out, and as he struggles to inhale Olivia clasps the back of his head, fisting a handful of hair. Pushing his head downward, she smashes his skull into the small table, causing splinters of wood to fly all around them as the weak furniture cracks and shatters. Branson collapses, his blood pooling amid the debris.

Without pause she dashes backward, reentering the gym. Her mind quickly assesses all of her options– fight, flight, or surrender. Well, meekly giving up has never been her forte. Trying to outrun the men seems possible, but there is a limited chance for success. Even now as she races to the far end of the gym she can hear two of them gaining ground on her. The heavy plodding of their boots rings louder in her ears. Additional foes may prove costly if they are not the only ones searching for her. Taking them out while they are alone may be the best choice.

Planting her foot, Olivia stops abruptly and spins around. Her pursuer's momentum and weight propels him forward. Moss has no time to stop as Olivia shifts sideways, bringing her forearm up to meet his throat. Driving through with the strike, his legs buckle as he crashes to the ground. Moss writhes and gasps, wincing as he clutches his damaged neck.

Olivia looks up to see Lee bearing down on her quickly. Behind him Branson follows at a slower pace. His face is awash with blood that gushes from a cut on his forehead. She spares a brief glance back down to Moss, knowing that he will only be incapacitated for a few more seconds.

She screams to herself to move faster.

Sprinting toward the nearby equipment rack, she reaches it only seconds ahead of Lee. Just as her fingers graze the cold, cast-iron dumbbell, Lee is upon her. Swinging at her wildly, Lee's punch grazes her as she tries to dodge. Even the glancing blow is enough to push her off balance and into the equipment rack. Steel rods push painfully into her back. Kicking outward, her foot makes solid contact with his solar plexus. She is greeted with the sound of several ribs cracking and a whoosh of air escaping him as he slumps forward. When the briefest moment of opportunity appears, she strikes twice in rapid succession, the first blow hitting the artery in his throat and the second landing squarely on the jaw, below his ear. As he crumples to the ground Olivia grabs one of the ten-pound weights and crashes it down on his exposed head. Skull and skin fracture as blood, tissue, and brain matter stain the floor.

Her eyes lifts just as Branson's foot collides into the side of her head. The force sends her tumbling over the bloodied floor. As the room spins, Olivia staggers to her feet. Moss is also recovered and moves to stand next to Branson. Olivia, bruised and exhausted, lifts her fisted hands in front of her.

"Now you can either push your luck, probably ending up like your friend over there, or you can walk away. The choice is yours," Olivia throws back at Moss. She takes the opportunity to calm her ragged breathing.

"I'm going to kill you, bitch." Spittle flies from Branson's mouth as he screams. His face has shifted to a deep crimson red. As he steps forward, Moss halts him with a hand on his arm.

"What the fuck, man? She fucking killed Lee. I can take her." Branson struggles against the much larger man's hold.

"Maybe you can, maybe you can't. Why risk your life when we can let the big guns handle it?" Moss's voice is graveled, and he forces the words out.

A low clicking growl seems to skitter over the room. As it penetrates the air, the hairs on Olivia's neck stand on end. Steely talons scrape along the stone walls. It is a sound that she has only ever heard one other time, but will not likely forget. Even amongst the evils that reside in Erebus there is one being that will cause all others to quake in absolute horror. The Faceless are a sheer force of destruction. They were created by the original Mothers as a way to control rogue Fury. True monsters that are known for their stubborn determination and insatiable need for carnage. Many tales abound of the faceless hunting their prey all over the globe. Unrelenting, they would chase them for years.

Through a darkened doorway a twitching movement catches Olivia's eye. Seemingly the form absorbs the light directly around it. Tendrils of a vaporous mist wisp up and off of the blackened shape. Two other mirrored images follow the first into the room. Their slender bodies are black as midnight, lacking any discernible features. They have no hint of clothing or lips or eyes. They are just smooth expanses of malevolent darkness draped skin-tight over a human form, their bodies wrapped in a thick neoprene-like skin. Long, eight-inch fingers brandish razor-sharp claws, and the subtle smell of sulfur lingers in the air.

The beasts move in lurching steps, almost disappearing midstride. They flicker in and out of perception as they stalk toward her. Mouth less heads emit darkly disturbing sounds as deadly fingers slice back and forth, their bladed fingers cutting through the air. Olivia's throat clenches painfully in a visceral response. Her heart pounds frantically in her chest as a steady flow of sweat trickles down to the small of her back. The lights of the gymnasium begin to pulse, undulating in tandem with the movement of the beasts. Their chatter of clicks and hisses seems to grow steadily louder as the lights dim and fall.

Launching herself in one bound over the weight rack, Olivia dives toward a storage cache of weapons. This arsenal is intended for sparring only, but anything will be better than facing these things barehanded. Most of the blades are fairly well maintained. Pulling the scimitar from its scabbard, the thick, curved, sharpened edge glints under the lights. The blade is weighty in her hands, helping to center and steady her nerves.

Feeling a pulse of energy from behind her, Olivia spins around, the ominous figure standing directly in front of her, its entire core appearing to absorb any energy around it. Olivia feels a portion of her life-force being peeled away, eaten up by the unholy monstrosity. She tries to tap into her own flow of energy, and is alarmed to find it is muted. Usually her connection to the source is strong and vibrant. Now it is a feeble version of what it should be. The harder she pulls at it the further it withdraws from her. The startling realization sets in that her greatest strength would be of no use to her against these foes. Her insides nearly turn to liquid as she battles back the rising panic.

In a blink, jagged claws reach out to grab her, shredding the air in front of her. Ducking, she rolls out of the way and slashes at the creature's legs. Though the sword is honed to a razor-sharp edge, the blade harmlessly skims off of the monster. Their skin is akin to Kevlar mesh that is near impossible to penetrate.

It absorbs the hit blankly and continues with determined strides towards her, stalking her. Standing quickly, she levels the sword in front of her. From her peripheral vision she picks up the two others skulking up around, trying to flank her. Moss and Branson have yet to move from their position. Their arrogant scorn causes her blood to boil as they stand by eagerly waiting for her to be destroyed.

Launching herself at the thing directly in front of her, Olivia rapidly attacks with a barrage of slashes. For each strike the faceless parries, returning back to her the same in kind. Its long fingers slice through the air, narrowly missing her each time. Armed with only their claws, they block her strikes barehanded.

Movement catches her attention, and she sidesteps just as a second faceless attacks. The three now circle her patiently, throwing wild strikes toward her. She dodges and blocks as she can, but the speed of their attacks quickens to a blinding pace. Her muscles scream as her arms and legs tremble and quake against the exertion. A droplet of sweat seeps into her eye, momentarily blinding her.

A slashing claw clips her arm below the shoulder, causing pain to blast through the wound as the paralyzing venom begins to course through her. The tips of her fingers start to chill as they numb, her vision blurs, and movements become fractionally slower. Four more claws streak down the center of her back, cutting through skin and muscle. The searing pain causes her knees to give out, and she hits the ground, the scimitar clattering down next to her.

Olivia frantically tries to push herself up, but a solid black foot is planted on her back, driving her down, holding her there. Fruitlessly, she struggles against the weight, her sweat running into her wounds. The pain is excruciating, but it keeps her from passing out. The clawed foot securing her in place grinds against the slices in her skin. The scorching pain that floods through her wrings out a guttural scream.

A hand clutches Olivia's hair tightly, holding her head motionless, her cheek smashed into the textured canvas floor. She tastes the salty metallic mix of blood in her mouth. Large, meaty hands string and latch the copper choker around her neck, the cold metal burning into her skin as Branson's childish laughter sounds in her ears. Her energy wicks away from her as she slumps into the ground. With tunneling vision, the darkness threatens to overtake her.

Callously, two hands lift her off of the ground. The three Faceless pace anxiously about her as Moss holds her up. The beasts prance about like dogs, eager to be fed. Olivia ponders what her fate will be. To be torn to bits by these monsters seems a deplorable way to meet your end.

With pain and fatigue overpowering her, Olivia allows her head to fall forward. The sludge of the creature's poison muddles her mind as she tries to find some way out of this situation. They stand motionless for several moments before Olivia begins to sense that something is amiss. She is expecting that they will kill her, or at the very least drag her away. But instead they continue their silent vigil in the center of the gym.

In the distance, the sound of approaching footsteps helps to clear the encroaching fog of her mind. She has spent the majority of her existence only relying on herself, but right now she knows that she could really use some help.

Ambrose enters at a hurried pace. Olivia's spirits soar as her eyes catch sight of him. With a renewed vigor, she battles against her floppy limbs as there is a prospect of hope and rescue. Trotting across the vast room, Ambrose stops directly in front of the party.

"Help me, Ambrose," Olivia pleads. Her voice warbles as she tries to discern Ambrose's odd behavior. He glances at her briefly before turning his attention to the two men.

"Good. You waited for me. Make sure she is securely restrained and locked in one of the lower cells. There is no room for mistakes." Ambrose's voice booms throughout

the thinning air as his words rake over her. She trembles in
a cold sweat as Moss begins pulling her toward the exit.
She tries vainly to halt their movement, but her legs are
jelly, falling uselessly beneath her.

"What are you doing? Why are you doing this? You have
to help me, Ambrose," she grits through clenched teeth,
trying to pull away from Moss's grip. Ambrose raises a
hand, halting their recession. With an unsettling grace he
walks to stand before her.

"But I am helping you."

Olivia winces as he gently touches her shoulder.

"I am helping you reach your full potential. Together we
will unleash the true power of the Fury. I am here to set
you free, and together we will set things right again," he
reassures her.

"Ambrose, this is insane. You don't have to do this." Her
fuzzy mind whirls. Negotiations have always been her
strong suit, but at this moment her muddled mind and
rising panic are making it difficult to speak.

"Yes, I do have to do this. More than anything else in the
world, I have to do this."

"Thanatos. We need to leave." Branson's stare falls
directly on Ambrose.

"Why is he calling you that? Who are you?" she stammers. Her blood rushes, pounding in her ears.

"I am many things…and nothing. I am the end and the beginning. Every culture has a different name for me. But you, my dear, may call me Thanatos." With a smirk, he turns, exiting the room.

Olivia's insides twist as the true extent of his betrayal settles in. This whole time he has been lying. Lying about…everything. Moss yanks her painfully toward the door. With his arm around her waist he half drags her, half carries her. Collecting her remaining strength, she launches her elbow at his face. The strike misses his nose, but makes jarring contact with his chin. He drops her and she plops harshly on the ground.

Lying face down, she fights to stand, but her body refuses to obey. Weakly, she paws at the floor, attempting to lug herself along. Heavy boots plod up beside her, and a fierce kick to her temple sends her spiraling into a vast void of darkness.

Chapter 17

Emma glides effortlessly through the endless corridors of The Hallow. As if following a predetermined path, she twists and turns, sensing her way through the labyrinth of long halls and dead ends. The caverns are minimally lit by the torches dotting the walls, the gloom around her swallowing up any surrounding light. She is aware at least on some conscious level that this is a dream. The surreal aura of this place adds to the melancholy tone that is looming and settling all around. An ethereal mist swirls and flows about her ankles, masking the ground. The thick moisture clouding the air clings to her skin, raising gooseflesh on her arms. The solid thumping of her heartbeat drums as it resounds deafeningly in her ears. The crypt holds an odd familiarity, but this is a place that she has never been before.

Through the eerie silence skitters an unnatural sound. Raspy breathing echoes loudly as sharpened talons etch their way over cold stone. With each progressive step the twilight nears as darkness creeps in from all sides. Her breath quickens as a shadowed form shifts and ripples. The smoky figure breaches the darkness, gliding toward her, its shredded black robe flowing in an unseen current as it hovers above the ground. Burning green eyes peer back at her through the vacant shroud.

The dream state around her slows at its approach. Turning to flee, she is struck by uncontrolled terror as the ground beneath her transforms into a mushy sludge that engulfs her feet. She struggles but is sucked further into the mire. Trapped, she falls forward as her hands are also swallowed by the soft earth and liquid stone.

Her pursuer inches ever closer, and with the gap between them shortening, fright threatens to overwhelm her. Thick tendrils of growing terror slither across her skin, clamping her windpipe closed and stifling the rising scream, accelerating her heart rate as she fights desperately against her prison. Wrenching her arms free, she rolls onto her back. Emma claws at the mud caging her feet. Each handful of dirt that is removed is replaced twofold.

Long, skeletal fingers reach out, grasping her forearm in a steely vise-like grip. The chilled bone burns her skin as the fragrant smell of charring flesh assails her senses. Pulling at her arms, it lowers itself, hunching its form. The distorted feature of a pale skull peeks from within the hood. Waxy skin is pulled taut over its bony face, and jagged razor fangs distend from thin lips. Black blood oozes from the cracked mouth, its breath emitting a putrid smell of rotten meat. The mouth and jaw move feverously for several seconds before she realizes it is speaking. The Gaelic of her native tongue sounds out of place through its rigid lips. From around its bulky teeth the words are obscured and difficult to understand. Three words are continuously repeated: death, collects, souls. Her heart barrels in her chest as the wraith's fervor peaks, her own blood flowing from gashes on her arm as she tries to wrench herself free from its clutches. The sounds of anguished cries ring in her ears, a symphony of tortured voices filling the air around her. Panic wells inside of her as a scream pushes at the back of her throat.

The strangled screech continues to claw at her throat as Emma sits up, ripping herself from the nightmare. Glossy, chilled sweat glistens on her skin. Pulling her knees into her chest, Emma studies the open space around her. She fights to calm her manic breathing and slow the racing of her heart. The formidable misery that dominates the air settles into her bones, leaving her to drown in its solemn emptiness. Her stomach churns in a sea of nausea as she catches sight of the half-eaten bowl of stew brought to her by the guards. The harshness of her own breathing fills the enclosed area, cutting through the prevailing silence.

As her respiration settles she becomes keenly aware of the subtle rise in temperature. Her skin begins to flush as a warmer current of air flows into the room. Scanning the area, she searches for the source of the arid heat. The torches mounted on the wall outside her cell flicker wildly as they begin to take on an eerie green hue. The flames grow in intensity as the emerald light spreads, filling the gloom of her prison. The light entering the room thickens until it is a putrid haze. Emma attempts to push her legs off the bed but finds that they will not respond. They are deadened limbs that seem fastened into place. She struggles against the rigor that paralyzes her.

She is weary, and her dread begins to escalate as the green mist freely sweeps into the confined area. With no means of escape, she can only clutch her knees tightly. The dense miasma clogs the room as Emma battles for breath against the congested air, the alien vapor tickling at the back of her throat. The fog radiates its own light and pulses along her skin as pinpricks of electrical shocks dance over her flesh. From somewhere within the fog, the skittering of voices begins to build. Emma silently listens, wondering if these unknown strangers are here to release her or kill her. She prays that once again it is Mother Agnes that will appear and aid her in escaping this hellish place.

As with the previous encounter, the muted tone is barely audible. But it subtly builds, growing ever so slightly in volume and fervor. Within seconds the crass cacophony of sounds are speaking in such a disjointed and conflicting manner that Emma can barely distinguish one word or voice from the next. Tones and patterns are all merging together in a waterfall of white noise that barrages Emma with its sheer force.

Emma covers her ears, trying fruitlessly to block out the deafening noise. The steadfast iron beat of the chorus pulses, melding together to create a single repeated phrase.

The words hammer through her as if endeavoring to smash their way into her bones.

"Get out, get out." The rhythmic chant matches the frantic tempo of her heart. "Get out, get out." A ragged scream rips from Emma as the oppressive weight of the air threatens to crush her. Her lungs burn from the strain as white blotches of light assail her vision. The flashes grow as they encompass her sight completely. Icy tears stream down her scalding cheeks as the light and roar of sound claim her. Weightlessly, she is pulled into the vast openness.

For several seconds Emma seems to float amid the nothingness of pale light. For the briefest of moments she feels the peaceful serenity of Elysium. In this place devoid of sound, utter silence surrounds her, shielding her from the outside. Bit by bit her body becomes heavier, and she can sense the pain ravaging her body. Yet the discomfort seems isolated from her.

The fog and light around her fades slowly as she detects an angelic sound. The soft humming of a little child slices through the befuddled cloud. Disoriented and lost, Emma follows the tiny voice. The wall of haze that engulfs her is pushed back as it changes, transforming into the menacing grey of thunderclouds. As they darken they are sporadically clipped by a sudden lightning strike. Through a tunnel of ominous clouds, Emma sees the faintest glow of a lamp.

Pushing herself forward, Emma glides toward the welcoming voice and light. With each step, the illuminated haze around her starts to dim even further. At the end of the passage the light within the mist vanishes, leaving her in the midst of an undulating ebony fog. The single point of light that she has been following shines from within a barred window that has been set into a grey, bricked wall.

Approaching the opening, Emma peers in, searching the depths for the source of the melodious humming. For several seconds Emma can see nothing in the inky reaches of the cell. Then as her eyes adjust she spies a small girl sitting atop a cot as she sings to herself, combing a doll's silky hair. The doll's body and clothes are covered in dirt, yet its hair shines brightly under the lamp light. The tiny child's appearance resembles that of the doll– rumpled clothes, dirt-smeared face, and shining blonde hair. Emma's heart soars at the sight of Sara. As tears well up in her eyes she clasps the bars tightly and calls out to the young girl.

"Sara." But she doesn't respond, not even lifting her head. "Sara, it's me, Emma."

Sara remains seated as she silently whispers to the toy. Emma's voice is raw, its sound swallowed by the air between them. Her heart staggers, and she wonders if she is dreaming still, or even dead. *Why can't Sara hear her?* she questions. Reaching through the bars, Emma waves her arms trying to get Sara's attention.

The loud click of the cell door draws Emma's eyes. Celia, Branson, and Moss enter the cramped room. Sara finally looks up to see them enter as well. Celia's auburn hair flows wildly, swishing back and forth as she approaches the bed. Planting her hands on her snuggly corseted hips, Celia leans forward, speaking to Sara. Her supple lips are moving, but Emma can't hear the words.

Emma's heart pounds as she watches Sara clutch the doll closely to her. Anger and fear rages through her, boiling her blood as she glimpses Sara wilting in terror. She screams at them and fretfully slams her fists against the bars, trying to draw their eyes. The skin of her hands is instantly bruised from the force.

Screaming in frustration, Emma focuses as she watches both Sara and Celia's mouths engaged in their silent conversation. Straining her ears, she wills them to let her hear the unspoken words. Centering herself, Emma reaches outward with her power, attempting to pierce the hidden barrier.

"You lied." Emma jumps as the sound reaches her. The sound coming from the cell is distant and muffled, but she can hear it. Sara glares at the older woman, her large eyes glistening with unshed tears.

"I didn't lie. I told you I would take you outside, and I did." Celia's head tilts sideways as she folds her arms over her chest.

251

"Yeah, but you did it just to get me in trouble. I wouldn't have gone if I knew you were going to tell on me." Her small lips tremble, but her chin has a defiant set to it. Her gaze shifts from Celia to Moss and Branson.

"Well, you see…" Celia squats next to the bed, her hands grasping the rickety frame. "We had to. We needed to make sure we didn't raise any suspicions. Do you know what suspicions means?"

"Yes. I read. Raise suspicions about what?" Sara asks petulantly.

"We, the three of us, have been charged with a very important task. And you are the final element needed to complete that task. We needed you here so we could keep you safe." Her tone belies an underlying agitation about her. A long, sculptured nail taps on the wooden rail.

"What kind of task? Is it a mission from the Mothers?" Sara's voice hitches with mild curiosity.

"No, it is not a mission from the Mothers. Come with us and I will tell you." Celia twists, looking back at the two men.

Sara gnaws on her lower lip. Uncertainty flashes over her face as her gaze flitters over the three of them. "I don't know. I don't trust you." The last seeming to be directed at Moss as her stare settles on him. The large man, arms crossed over his chest, shifts his stance as his dark gaze drops to the floor.

Celia stands, her hands lifting back up to her hips.

"Sara, you will come with us now," she snaps curtly.

"No. Not until you tell me why," Sara responds stubbornly.

"Enough of this baby dawdle bullshit," Branson interrupts. "Sara. Come here," he commands, his words harsh and overbearing. Sara stands on the small cot, her chin lifted as she glares at him defiantly.

"No." As courageous as a mountain lion, she meets his gaze fearlessly.

"You little piece of..." Branson lunges for the young girl but is halted as Moss snatches his arm. Branson turns a vile glare toward Moss. With a leap, Sara vaults off of the bed, heading toward the cell door. Celia gives chase and snags a handful of her blonde hair, causing Sara to yip in pain as Emma claws and yanks at the bars holding her back, her silent screams unheard by the audience in the room.

Sara struggles wildly, flailing her arms and kicking at Celia. As one kick meets with her shin, Celia grunts, pushing Sara toward Branson. "Take the little bitch," Celia seethes through clenched teeth. Branson grabs the child, gripping her upper arms hard enough to produce a wince from her.

"Hold still," Branson snarls, giving the girl a fierce shake. Blonde hair blurs as her head snaps back and forth.

"Moss, help me," Sara mews as she continues to fight against Branson's hold. The mountain of a man will not look at her. A pained look skews his features. "You gave me the doll. I thought you were my friend." Her tiny frame shakes from the heartbreaking treachery.

"I am sorry, little one. I can't help you," he replies in a whispered croak.

Celia's laughter fills the space as it floats gleefully in the air.

"How cute," she mocks with a cloying pout, her intense gaze boring into Moss. Slowly she meanders toward him, her hips swaying seductively as she presses her body against his, her lips barely touching his skin as she speaks. The tips of her fingers trace softly across his chest and arms. "Is that true, Moss? Are you her friend? Should we let her know why she is going to die?"

Moss is rigid and unmoving, his gaze cemented solidly straight ahead of him. She playfully nips his chin, making him recoil from her.

"Get away from me, Celia." His stoic words only manage to invoke another high-pitched giggle from Celia. Turning her back to him, she again focuses her attention to Sara. Striding in front of her, Celia bends to meet her at eye level. An ominous smirk graces her lips as she studies the girl.

"You see, we need you, Child. You hold within yourself the last of many parts we require to create a powerful tool. The human soul possesses great potency, and the souls of innocent children have vastly more. Your soul and that of countless others will aid in forging a whole new world. And our lord, Thanatos has charged us with the collection of all these pieces. While he can be a hard master, he can also be generous to those who serve him well. And I have served him well. Together he and I will rule this world. He is a god, and I will be his goddess. Wouldn't you like to help us make the world a better place?"

"No," Sara spits.

"Stupid, ignorant, little spoiled brat," Celia swears scornfully, her lovely features contorted into a mask of rage. Turning back to Moss, she unsheathes a long copper blade. The ornate dagger of solid copper is etched with several runes and symbols. "That's the problem with children. They ruin your body, your marriage, and your life. They take away your freedom then have the audacity to act as though you owe them something. My children were nothing but a plague, and I was finally at peace when they died. There was no one clinging to me, no one asking stupid questions, no more snotty noses, nor being labeled as used goods."

She coldly meets Moss's gaze as she stands in front of him. Glancing back over her shoulder at Sara, her look is wholly crazed.

"Do you know my husband was actually mad when they died? That ungrateful bastard beat me to death, and all I did was what we both wanted. From now on it's about what I want and what I need." She offers the handle of the blade to Moss. "Go ahead, friend. Take care of this." Her voice is rich with condescension.

Moss glances back and forth from Celia to the dagger. "No." The single word cuts crisply through the air.

"I gave you an order." Her mouth purses in a deep-set frown. "You will do this or I will inform Thanatos of your lack of devotion." Lips upturned as a sneer once again appears on her face.

"Tell him whatever the fuck you want. I'll destroy any man alive or dead, but I don't kill little girls." His tone is detached as his dead gaze meets hers.

"Fine. Pathetic pussy," she snaps as she strides over to the small girl. "Useless, lazy man," she mutters more to herself. Sara weeps sheepishly, her cheeks stained with dirt and tears. Her little form weak from struggling continues to shift and pull against Branson's strong hold.

With a quick strike, Celia plunges the blade into Sara's chest. Sliding the dagger between two ribs, the heart is pierced. Sara's eyes widen as she gasps several times, fighting for breath. Celia draws out the blade, and a large red plume forms on the girl's shirt. She slumps forward, and Branson lets go as she collapses to the floor.

Celia hunches over the dying girl as an eerie blue light emanates from the body, flooding the room. The light becomes impossibly white, obscuring everything inside the space. The blue and white light swirls and flows into Celia. Emma sobs as she numbly clutches the bars, a black void threatening to swallow her from the inside out. Wrecked with loss and despair, Emma mindlessly weeps for the child she loved as her own. The interior light from the room fades as the darkness draws in, pushing out all of the remaining light. Emma releases herself to the cold darkness sucking her under.

Chapter 18

Emma's eyes flash open, soaking in the dark solitude of the cell. It takes her a few seconds to register her surroundings, but slowly the fog begins to clear and she recognizes her location. Her night clothes are still neatly folded in the corner where she left them. Her reflection stares back at her from a filthy mirror mounted to the wall above the sink. Even the sink and musty cot are the same—untouched by the horrific vision that still leaves her feeling unsettled. The side effects of the hallucination play havoc on her senses. Perhaps it was simply a nightmare brought on by the stress of her imprisonment. She tries to reason with herself, but the experience seemed so eerily real. She is left feeling more bewildered than reassured.

Her gut squeezes as she catches sight of her own hands. The skin is broken and welted. Her index finger and the joint are angrily swollen as the bone underneath has already started to mend itself. As her body starts the healing process, it draws on Emma's energy to fuel the regeneration. The copper collar lashed around her neck sizzles painfully. As her body battles against the constraints of the copper, Emma knows that when her body is fully healed the pain will eventually subside. She regulates the beat of her breath and steadies her hands.

Through the endless void of vast caverns, a high-pitched scream pierces the air. Emma's breath seizes in her throat, knowing instantly that it is Sara's voice. She violently hurls herself against the bars of the cell door, yelling and slapping the metal, trying to get one of the guards to come. Her heart shudders against the looming panic as it presses in from all sides. From down the darkened hall, the sway of a faint light and the solid clop of footsteps approach her.

A lanky man comes up to her cell carrying a single lantern. Jasper is taller than most, and his frame is lean, bordering on skinny. His hair is black as pitch, his eyes even darker. He is an extremely gruff man with a tendency toward stoicism. Despite his youthful appearance, there is an underlying hardness about him. A thick beard and mustache hide the majority of his features. Under the dim light Emma can see he is wielding a solid metal pipe in his free hand.

"What the hell is your problem?" he shouts, holding the lantern higher to see into her prison.

"I heard a scream. I think it was Sara. You have to go and help her." Her words are rapid and volatile. Fighting the extreme distress makes normal speech precarious. She clutches the bars hard enough to make her knuckles ache. Jasper stares coldly at her, barely blinking an eye.

"You didn't hear nothing." His voice is a graveled growl. "Now sit back down and shut it."

"At least send someone to check on her," Emma pleads. "She can't be too far from here."

His stern features momentarily soften as he slowly meets her gaze.

"Look. There ain't any noises, and I ain't wasting my time checking on some kid." He lowers the lantern and begins to leave.

"But you have to…" Emma jumps, the words halted in her throat as he slams the iron rod against the metal bars of her cell.

"I ain't gotta to do shit. Sit down and shut up or I'll shut you the hell up." Briskly, he turns and stalks away.

"Hey, wait," Emma calls out to him, but he ignores her cries. Emma inhales a ragged breath as she tamps down the urge to scream and wail. Unbridled fear and rage push at her insides, a rampant beast trying to crawl its way out.

Save the girl. The words ring crisply in her ears. Swiveling around, Emma realizes that somehow the disembodied voice originates from within her. She paces nervously as the voice booms again in her mind. *Save the girl.* Her mind works feverishly, ticking away all of her escape options.

Breathing deeply, Emma calms her body, focusing on her dingy reflection in the mirror. With several quick strides, Emma closes the gap between herself and the sink. She punches the mirror solidly, raining large shards of glass fragments into the basin and scattering about the floor. With a swift kick, she separates the copper piping under the sink from the hand basin. Grabbing a larger shard of mirror, Emma slices into the meat of her left arm. Blood wells and flows immediately, large droplets splattering onto the ground. She tosses the glass into the sink and clutches the wound, applying just enough pressure to keep the cut open.

"Jasper," Emma yowls. "Please, come quick. I'm hurt." For several seconds only the silence surrounds her, and Emma fears that no one will come. "Jasper, help me," she calls out in desperation. At last she hears the angry plod of Jasper's footsteps and his quiet mutterings to himself.

"Someone better be fucking dying in there." His tone is sharp.

"I fell, Jasper. I fell and cut myself on the copper pipe. I need you to help me." Emma allows the panic she is feeling to slither its way into her voice as she holds her gashed arm toward him. His eyes sweep from her to the cut on her arm and then to the broken pipes under the sink. She waits anxiously as his mind digests the design of her constructed scene.

261

"Ah, shit. Ok, I'll get help," he huffs, and starts to back away.

"No, wait," Emma stammers. "There's no time for that. By the time you get back I'll be dead. I need you to take my restraints off and bring me some water to clean the wound." Seeing the hesitation on his face, Emma approaches the cell door. Manipulating the cut, more blood plops to the ground. "I can't heal myself with the collar on. It's copper, Jasper, it'll kill me if we don't act fast. Ambrose said that you would keep me safe." A twinge of guilt slashes through Emma at the lie, but desperate times…

"For fuck's sake," he mutters, dropping the iron bar and fishing his key ring out. As he enters the room Emma releases the force she is using to keep the wound open. Jasper gruffly grabs her unharmed arm and drags her toward the sink. Emma feigns a winced cry as they move forward. When they are within arm's reach of the sink Emma pushes Jasper toward the basin, tripping his legs at the same time. Sent careening forward, his face smacks the rim of the sink with a solid thud.

Breath raging, Emma studies his motionless form to make certain he is unconscious. His chest slowly rises and falls with his breathing. She wraps an empty pillowcase around her arm to quell the residual bleeding. Carefully approaching him, she snatches his keys and throws a blanket over him. She steps out into the hall, allowing the cell door to click shut behind her.

Padding quietly down the hall, Emma scans each cell she comes across. To her dismay, most of them are dark and unoccupied. She takes stock of the cells that do have occupants— none of them are holding the child. Every few feet she calls out quietly, whispering for Sara, but is only met with an answer of silence. Pushing forward, she spies the unassuming glow of a lamp emanating from one of the furthest chambers. Quickening her pace, she approaches the mutely-lit cell.

Gazing through the metal bars, Emma's heart plummets. Sara's small form lies face down in a pool of slick blood. Panic nearly overwhelms her as she frantically tries different keys in the lock. Emma growls in frustration at the maddening task. Finally the key turns and the tumblers align, opening the door. Emma floods into the room, pulling the limp child into her lap. Sara's face and golden hair are coated in congealed blood. Her skin is ashen and cold, devoid of any life. Emma reaches out with her power but is unable to find any flicker within the child.

Her agony and grief become too much, and Emma is awash with them as she weeps. She howls as she clutches Sara closely, tears searing her eyes as her wails clamp down on her windpipe. Sorrow, grief, and regret sweep through Emma as she gasps for air. When the weeping subsides she gently touches Sara's cheek, and her mind is flooded with images of Celia, her emblazoned hair whipping violently as she laughs. Her clawed hands drip blood as a thousand azure stars dance around her.

Will you allow this child's death to go unpunished? The disembodied voice slices through the air around Emma, raising gooseflesh on her skin. Emma's eyes catch a vaguely shadowed figure lurking in a darkened corner of the room. A black mane flows over her bare shoulders. Her gown is a dark emerald green which strikingly matches her eyes. The woman is astoundingly beautiful, as well as terrifying. While Emma can make out the details of her features, the shadow woman's form is transparent and incorporeal.

"Who are you?" Emma croaks, her tongue thick in her mouth.

"My name is Tisiphone. But that matters not. You will seek vengeance for this child, and for all those like her."

"How? I'm not strong enough to face them all." Emma recognizes the specter's voice as the one speaking to her in her prison cell as well as the library.

"You will not need to face them all, just Celia. Her sins are most egregious." The apparition's head cocks to the side, like a falcon eyeing its prey. At that moment Emma felt as powerful as a field mouse.

"I don't understand. How? I'm chained. How can I defeat her if I'm chained?" Tears once again begin to well in Emma's eyes, blurring her vision. Blinking them away, the spirit's image falters and starts to fade.

"Copper, Child. It binds you, but it will also set you free. You must break through the barriers that constrict you. There must be more copper." The last of her words trickle off as she disappears, leaving an empty space where she had once been.

Emma studies the vacant spot for several seconds, but there is only silence in the void. It would appear the visitor has left. She briskly wipes the tears from her eyes. Carrying Sara, Emma carefully places her on the small cot. Then gathering a clean rag and water, she wipes the blood from Sara's face and body. Minding her task in silence, she prays and places a small doll in the dead girl's arms and pays a final respect to the child she loved so dearly, then exits the room.

Walking with a determined purpose, Emma navigates the maze of long corridors until she reaches her destination. At one time the Castigation Room was one of many. Varying in shape and function, each was a place for Fury and lost souls alike to seek atonement for misdeeds. The practice has fallen from favor as the Mothers preference sides more along the lines of less public forms of torture.

Though this room is not the largest, it still carries a plethora of devices meant to punish the unfortunate fools brought here. Various whips and flays are arranged along the walls. Several of the stations contain racks, cages, and large vats. Massive wooden gears are used to aid in the pulling and tearing of joints from bone. A large iron grate covers the opening to an oubliette– a deep pit where people were thrown in and forgotten. All of the macabre curiosity means very little to Emma at this point as she heads directly toward a small room against the back wall. The space is dark and dusty, but Emma knows this was once used as a makeshift infirmary. After an extensive torture session prisoners would be mended in here before they were thrown back into their cells or the pits.

A medical supply cabinet is securely mounted to the wall. The metal case is worn with a faded caduceus painted in red dye. Fumbling in the darkness, Emma manages to locate the needed items, her heart racing as she clasps the syringe and several small glass vials. Stepping over to a long wooden rack, she carefully lays out each item, the copper vials gleaming under the ambient light overhead. The bottles themselves are imbued with power and an incantation that keeps their contents in a liquid state. Even when the liquid is removed it will remain in a fluid state for several hours.

For as long as the new generation of Fury has existed, copper has been used to subdue, control, and punish. One could be bound in lengths of wire or pierced with thousands of needles forged from the metal. Once it was discovered how to keep the copper liquid, it could be injected or poured directly into the mouth and throat. The oldest practices were to simply pour the molten metal onto the victim, allowing it to bubble away the flesh from their bones.

None of those prospects seem appealing to Emma. And this course of action means that a great deal of pain is to be expected. But if Tisiphone is right, this may be the only way. This could also be nothing more than a path to a slow, agonizing death. Although, can she live with herself knowing she could have avenged Sara's murder and had done nothing? To do nothing will mean that Celia will continue to kill, because that is her nature. Emma sighs deeply as the cool air chills her lungs.

"If I die, at least I'm taking that bitch with me," Emma mutters as she fills the syringe.

The searing pain is immediate as Emma plunges the needle into her skin. Liquid fire erupts under her flesh as the copper flows into her veins, burning her throughout. By the third syringe sweat drips from her forehead and her hands begin to shake. She doesn't know how much copper is needed, or even how much she can take. A raging torrent is soon flooding through her as the massive influx of energy hits, and her knees give out, sending her to the ground.

Clutching her stomach, Emma feels as though her insides are about to burst. Her abdomen clenches as wave after wave of throbbing pain smashes her body. Searing needles bore into her muscles as they threaten to seize.

As the minutes pass, the sensation begins to ebb. Her limbs tremble, but she manages to pull herself up to her feet. Using any support available, she fights through the pain and heads back into the hall.

Several times while stumbling along, Emma must stop and battle the onslaught of agony yet again. Each time it varies in intensity, but eventually it passes and she continues on. But as she resumes her search her thoughts are becoming more frenzied. There is a constant thumping in her ears, seemingly propelling her forward. Following an unseen pull, she navigates the lengths of corridors and halls. Tisiphone's voice whispers to her, prompting her direction.

Chapter 19

A curious and unsettling realization hits Emma as she slinks through one of the main housing areas. The common living area should be teeming with all sorts of activities as the Fury come and go. But there is not a living soul within the deep recessed caverns. An eerie stillness seems to buzz throughout the passage ways. As she makes her way forward she detects a subtle hum of sound, as if fireworks are being set off in the far distance— a muffled sound in which the origins are difficult to detect. Following the spectral nudging, the noise becomes more distinct. It is the reverberation of battle.

Emma peeks around a doorframe that leads into the great hall. Mounds of bodies are strewn across the floor, the blood and gore seeping into the ground beneath them. From the mangled piles, arms and legs stick out at disjointed angles. Emma's attention is drawn to a single bloody hand, clawed in the throes of death. Near the rear entrance to the Hall, a small group is caught in the midst of a frantic melee. Some of the Fury and their men are fighting other Gyges. The Ebon Mortis seem to be involved in a coup d'état to overtake The Hallow and kill everyone. The great hulking attackers wield blades and battle axes made of copper. The odor of blood and entrails is thick in the air. Fires burn from several obliterated pieces of furniture that have become casualties of the encounter. The massacre is fierce and bloody, with the Fury and their Gyges being felled within moments by the superior numbers of the Erebus guards. Emma's guts curdle at the screams of the dying.

As a deadly black mass, the attackers rejoin each other and retreat down a long passage. Emma needles her way through the gore toward the other side of the hall. Looking left and right, Emma can detect no signs of life from those that have fallen. Seeing the dead Fury only fuels the murderous ice growing within Emma. Emotions and thoughts of mercy are swallowed by the black tar of the determined vengeance. Stepping out into the corridor, Emma halts as she spies Celia down the length of the hall. Moss is holding another Gyges up off his feet, choking the man, whose face is shifting from red to a sickly blue hue. Branson and another Ebon guard stand behind Moss, looking on. The choking man slumps and his arms dangle by his sides.

"See, I told you he could do it," Branson brags with a toothy grin. He holds out his hand as the other man slaps a few bills down onto his palm. Branson's smile fades as his eyes lock with Emma's. The stillness of his body draws the attention of the others. All four of them stare at Emma with a deadly stillness.

"Kill her. I want her dead," Celia screams as Branson and Moss begin stalking down the hall, directly for Emma. Celia and the third man scurry out of the hall to an adjoining corridor. Moss's pace is slow, methodical, but Branson is running full tilt at her. He quickly closes the gap between them and meets her with fists flying. She dodges several swings, and others she pushes aside, redirecting his momentum. As she leaps backward she clips her lower back on a small table. While Emma is momentarily thrown off guard from the pain, Branson leaps at her. His strike barely misses her, but he commits to the attack, and she counters, driving her knee into his stomach. The air whooshes out of him, and as he doubles over Emma clutches the back of his head in both hands. Interlacing her fingers, she yanks his head down and drives her knee up, breaking his nose. A sense of satisfaction flows through her as the cartilage snaps and pops and blood gushes from his broken nose with thick plops.

As he gasps and moans on the ground, Emma fumbles with the clasp keeping his blade sheathed. Branson is torn between stopping the blood pouring from his broken face and keeping her from taking his weapon. Looking, Emma catches the blur of Moss's black, polished boot rocketing toward her head. Lunging backward, the toe of his boot grazes her arm. Emma is astonished by his size and subsequent agility. Most men that size would never be that quick. Before she can scramble to her feet his long arm shoots out toward her, his hands clamping down on her throat. Attempting to push his arm away proves to be futile. He hoists her into the air and launches her backward through the air, crashing against the wall. Emma hears the sound of her own skull smacking against the stone surface, her lungs seize, and blackness spots her vision.

She is dazed as she rises on all fours, trying to find her balance. Two anaconda arms wrap around her chest, lifting her up. Emma finds her arms trapped under Moss's. He squeezes her against him, constricting the air in her lungs. She struggles, kicking her legs as his moist, ragged breath heats the back of her neck. Branson stalks toward her, a heavy copper dagger in his hand. Tacky blood drips from his nose, staining his shirt a deep crimson red.

"Are you ready to die, bitch?" Branson seethes, pointing the blade at her as he spits out a large glob of bloody phlegm. Emma's breath comes in pants as her heart pounds frantically. Her focus narrows as she keenly studies his movements. Just as he steps into range, Emma kicks her foot up into Branson's shattered nose. Another ruby flow erupts from his face, and at the same time she snaps her head back, making solid contact with Moss's eye. Moss's bellowing scream echoes in her ears, yet his hold stands firm. His back arches, lifting Emma higher into the air. Branson staggers, clutching his face, his curses muffled by a busted lip as he is blinded by blood.

Throwing her legs up, Emma scissors Branson's neck between her knees, his blood-slick hands clawing at her legs in a weakened attempt to break the hold. Moss twists and yanks at her, trying to pry her away from his counterpart. Again she jerks her head backward, slamming into his unprotected skull. Her vision blurs as his hold slackens and she starts to fall. As the ground rushes up to meet her, Emma squeezes her legs tighter and jerks her upper body. Branson is pulled down with her. They hit the floor with a jarring thud and a rewarding crack as Branson's neck snaps. His body lies at an odd angle, his head bent to the side with the broken spinal column bulging in his throat.

Air rushes into Emma's lungs as she gasps for breath. Staggering to her feet, she picks up Branson's dagger from where he dropped it. Moss's face is bloodied and swollen. His breathing is steady, though he appears to be unconscious. Watching his motionless form, Emma contemplates killing him. But she knows as the seconds tick by Celia is getting further away. Yet leaving the man alive could prove troublesome later. Internally, Emma feels the flicker of Celia's presence becoming more distant. The overwhelming compulsion to follow Celia urges her feet forward. *Can't let her get away.* Regardless of the risks, she decides that she may end up regretting it. The time lost killing him could mean losing Celia. Emma turns, heading to the far end of the hallway.

As Emma rounds a corner her senses are inundated with the heavy odor of gore and death. The narrow corridor is lined with even more of the bodies of dead Fury and their guardians. Countless dead eyes stare starkly throughout the room. As she weaves around the empty husks, her feet stick in the pools of clotting fluids.

One of the bodies behind her shifts and stirs. It rises to its feet outside of her line of sight. As Emma scans the scenery in front of her, she is unaware of the figure lurking from behind. Sensing the life-force and movement, Emma spins around. She leaps to the side as the axe blade clips her shoulder, slicing into her skin. Quickly rolling away, she avoids the second strike, which sparks as it skims across the stone floor.

The Gyges that had accompanied Celia has lagged behind to ambush Emma. With each swing of the heavy broad axe he grunts, then hefts it up again, preparing for the next attack. He is relentless in his assault. Sweat glistens from his exposed flesh, and his shoulder-length sun-burnt hair sticks out wildly. Emma stumbles over the fallen corpses but manages to stay clear of the oncoming strikes.

Possessed by a mindless determination, he wades through the bodies swinging at her with wide pendulum arcs. His eyes are crazed as spittle coats his gaping mouth. Emma tries to stay close to the wall in an effort to limit his range of motion. With a loud chink the axe hits the wall, burying itself several inches in. Seizing on the opportunity, Emma leaps at him, slashing him. As he recoils from her attack she lunges at him, pushing forward, driving the blade into his chest. Hot blood gushes over her hand as she squeezes the hilt. His eyes widen and he gasps as he struggles for breath. His steamy breath bellows over her face and skin, and Emma notes the fragrance of peppermint. Knees buckling, he falls, and the dagger's blade snaps, breaking off inside his torso. With heaving breaths Emma cleans the blood from her hands, collects her broken weapon, and continues on.

The voices are continuously murmuring in Emma's head, the volume and intensity rising and falling as she slowly makes her way forward. It appears the voices are directing her, leading her through the twisting passages toward Celia. Her hands shake uncontrollably, and her hair is damp with sweat. Blurring vision makes navigating the passageways difficult. Several times she is forced to stop as the contents of her stomach empty. The copper flowing through her veins is still potent. If she doesn't hurry she may not survive long enough to find Celia.

The muffled swearing of Celia draws Emma closer. At the end of a short hallway Celia struggles with a locked door. Straining against the handle, she tugs fruitlessly on the solid iron door. With a surreal sense of calm, Emma quietly walks down the corridor. The temperature of the air around Emma drops drastically as her breath plumes the air. There is a surge of euphoria as she opens herself to the flow of energy, allowing it to sweep over her.

Celia senses the shift and spins around to face her opponent. Emma halts as their eyes lock. With both standing still as statues, a thick energy wafts around the two women as they study each other. Their powers seem to swirl and dance around, pushing and trying to overtake its foe. The streaming flows intermingle as two giant serpents prepare for battle.

"Do you like our renovations to the old place?" Celia asks as she arches her brow and gestures to a dead Fury lying near her feet. "I think it livens up the décor. Not so drab—grey walls and ceiling all around you can be quite depressing, don't you think? Plus, red has always been my favorite color."

She kicks the corpse but never takes her gaze off of Emma. With long, graceful fingers, she taps at her lips, thoughtfully.

"I am surprised though. I had thought all this blood would've made you happy. Isn't that what they say about vampires? The sight of so much blood will send you into a feeding frenzy. Perhaps that's how you were able to defeat Moss and Branson? But we all know that at best you're just a half vampire. No, you are not even good enough to be called a vampire, and they are nothing but rotten sacks of garbage." Celia exudes the violence and hatred fueling her.

"What is going on here? What have you done?" Emma asks, struggling to rein in the rage growing within her. Gooseflesh rises on her arms as the blood courses rampantly in her veins.

"It is simply a restructuring of management. New leadership is taking the helm, and some of the less useful staff need to be let go. That's all you need to know. In a few minutes you'll be dead as well, so it won't really matter," Celia states coolly. From a leather sheath at her side, Celia produces a thin steel rapier. The handguard is a design of curved metal rods, encasing her small hand. The silver sheen flashes as it catches the light.

"You are so confident you can defeat me?" Emma taunts. The voices chant softly through her, prodding her into action.

"I know I can defeat you because I'm better than you in every way. I'm armed, and all you have is a broken dagger. The odds are most certainly in my favor." A smile touches her lips as she slowly steps toward Emma.

With prompting from the voices, Emma slowly drags the jagged blade across the flesh of her forearm, the blood welling up and flowing freely. It splatters the ground, quickly creating a small, shiny puddle. Her skin battles against the blade trying to expel it as it knits itself back together. Emma coolly watches Celia as she crouches down, dipping her fingertips into the tiny pool of blood. Deeper her hand slides into the red depths until it is submerged up to her wrist. She clasps the leather bound hilt and pulls it upward. The leather straps of the katana are stained a deep red, and its copper blade is brilliant under the torch light.

277

"Any last words before you die?" Emma asks as she takes her stance. The katana held out vertically in front of her, Emma squares her shoulders and breathes sharply through her nose.

"I am not afraid of death, nor am I afraid of the likes of you," Celia spits as she starts to circle around Emma.

"If I were you I'd be very afraid. I have seen what you have done. I have seen the wretched stains on your soul. You murdered Sara, and your own children, and for that there is no atonement. There is only your inevitable and complete destruction."

Celia's anger spikes as she releases a huge surge of energy. Emma cringes against the pain as the sensation of a thousand swarming bees sting at her skin. Celia laughs, her lips tilting to reveal the stark whiteness of her teeth.

With a savage scream, Celia launches herself at Emma, slashing at her in a barrage of arcing swings. In quick succession Emma blocks and avoids the attacks. But each time she steps forward Celia slips out of range. After several minutes each is showing signs of fatigue. Both are dripping sweat, their open mouths gulping in the available air.

Blades screech as they clash. Their swords skim together as Celia heaves Emma away, her feet sliding across the cold stone floor. Celia flies wildly at her, throwing herself into the swing. Emma sidesteps, avoiding the strike as Celia stumbles, crashing to her stomach with a grunt. Emma pivots swiftly, bringing the katana slicing to the ground as Celia rolls away. Huffing in frustration, Emma knows she needs to close the distance between them.

With the heady side effects of the copper coursing through her, Emma can't be sure about how much time she has left. Boiling rage eats away at the peripherals of her vision, eroding the tenuous grasp she holds to her self-control. If she can't maintain her focus she'll make a deadly mistake that could cost her this fight. She needs to finish this, and quickly.

Celia scurries along the floor and rises up, retaking her stance before again lunging forward, but missing with her strike as Emma brings her blade down. The metal sparks as Celia's blade shatters, breaking in half. Both of their eyes are locked on the broken steel. A serene calm envelops Emma as the realization of what she must do comes to her. Celia frantically swings the broken weapon at Emma, her coldly calculating façade begins to fray at the edges.

Emma holds her blade out flat in front of her. In a deliberate movement, she releases the katana, letting it fall to the floor. As the weapon hits the ground it liquefies back into a puddle of blood.

"I'm looking forward to killing you." Emma smirks as the color drains from Celia's already pale face. With a leap she closes the gap between them and clutches Celia's sword hand. In one swift movement Emma jerks the broken blade, plunging it into her own stomach, pulling Celia into arm's reach. Her free hand shoots up, clutching Celia by the throat. Celia's eyes widen as she tries to escape but can't.

"You are insane," Celia pants as she stares at her blade embedded in Emma's stomach.

As if releasing a valve, Emma allows all of her energy to flow into the other Fury. Celia's lovely features contort in pain. As her knees give way, Emma maintains her hold and follows her to the ground.

The power is of such a potent intensity that it nearly backlashes as Emma attempts to focus, like trying to direct the power of a tornado. Energy is sent careening and pulsing through Celia. The blocks and guards that she has in place to protect her mind are demolished by the unstoppable force. Celia's guttural scream resonates through Emma's own mind, followed by an ominous silence.

Celia's mind cracks open as an egg bare for scrutiny. Flashing images race through Emma as she glimpses into Celia's soul, where her memories unfold, playing for Emma. Through Celia's eye she sees Sara's tear-stained face as the dagger, weighty in her hand, plunges into the soft flesh of her chest. The countless souls of children being harvested, tiny orbs of brilliant blue light sucked into a vacuum.

There is a tall, striking man with rage and anguish in his eyes. The man, who can only be Celia's husband, looms over her. His hands are bruised and coated in a thick sheen of blood. Even older recollections flood in. Warm bath water laps over Celia's arms as she holds the tiny infant under the surface. This scene is repeated over and over. Emma's heart clenches in her chest as she watches Celia's memory of drowning all of her children. Hot tears stream down Emma's cheeks.

Queasiness threatens to overtake her as the images flash before her. The next scene is a more recent remembrance. She is bent over in front of Ambrose as he presses her face down. Roughly he mounts her, the smell of blood thick in the air. There is something alien about the man. Something she can't quite figure out. A voice resounds within her as Celia cries out, calling him Thanatos.

With a shudder, Emma releases her hold and Celia slumps to the ground. Her eyes are glazed and empty. Inhaling deeply, Emma hisses as she pulls the broken sword from her stomach. The wound will heal quickly, and the pain was well worth the opportunity to get her hands on Celia. Straddling her, Emma raises the sword over her head and drives it into Celia's chest. She is caught off guard when the blade makes contact with something hard inside Celia's torso. The Fury remains still, as the mortal wound causes her life blood to seep away. Her mind is broken before her body dies. Through the blade, Emma can feel the subtle clink as it continues to hit the object hidden within the body.

With a slight sawing motion, Emma opens the wound further. She withdrawals the blade, but can't see anything in the wound. Her stomach rolls as she presses her hand into the moist cavity. Several inches in her fingers brush against a cool, smooth surface. At first the slippery orb seems determined to stay just out of her reach. She gags as she pushes further into Celia's chest and manages to find a hold on the object. As Emma eases the object out, her stomach drops at the sight of it. The softball-sized orb is made of clear glass. The inside holds a suspended black fluid and thousands of neon blue smaller orbs. Emma is holding in her hands the confined souls of countless children. Removing the pillow case that she wrapped her forearm with, Emma carefully drops the ball into it. The ball seems to hum from within the sack. On weak legs, Emma pushes to her feet, stumbling toward the door.

Pushing forward, Emma knows that she must find Mei Li. She needs to warn her of the uprising, and she has to get these souls some place safe. The pain muddles her sense of direction, and she feels as though she is wandering in circles. Upon reaching the ground floor, Emma is paralyzed as the pain crushes her insides. She falls again, overturning a table, glassware shattering around her. Pulling herself forward on hands and knees, the jagged shards dig into her palms.

Black rings start to eat away at the outer rim of her vision as her breath comes in labored pants and the floor rushes up to meet her. Warm blood begins to seep from her nose. A soothing calm washes over Emma as she welcomes the darkness, a respite from the torturous pain assaulting her body. Perhaps after a few minutes of rest she can continue on. Her mind flickers to an image of David. A smile touches her lips as she thinks about him, his warm smile, noble soul, and good heart. She longs to see him one more time, to tell him how much he means to her. Sadly she doesn't think she'll get that chance. Finally the last light is sapped from her view.

The darkness of a restless sleep pulls at her. From somewhere beyond her sense of perception she feels herself being lifted. As her consciousness wanes, her last recollection is of being cradled against the warmth of a broad chest, carried away in the mist of two powerful arms.

Chapter 20

The slow, cantered walk lulls Emma in and out of a restless sleep. Two solid arms cradle her against the chill of the night air as a heartbeat thumps gently under her ear. Snow falls softly on her exposed cheeks and sticks to her eyelashes. Her lids feel painfully heavy, and as she tries to pry them open the world is skewed and blurry. Emma struggles to focus her vision. In incremental steps, the image of the man carrying her becomes clearer. Dark hair frames his sharp features. His trimmed goatee is slowly being coated in a thin layer of ice and snow. Two expansive and gnarled horns spiral from either side of his head. Finding him familiar, it still takes Emma several moments to recognize Aidan.

Working her mouth, Emma tries to form words that only emerge as a pitiful squeaking. Her throat is an arid dryness and feels as though she has swallowed a sack full of broken glass shards. She fruitlessly rubs at her neck trying to get it to clear.

"Don't try to speak." Aidan's voice is low as his gaze scans the tree line ahead of them, searching. "We will be there shortly, and we can get you warmed up and something to drink."

Emma whispers hoarsely asking where. Thick, wooded areas flank them on either side as the heavy cloud cover and the darkness of the winter night make it nearly impossible to see. Aidan readjusts Emma's weight as he continues down a snowy back road, his boots crunching as they break through the freezing snow.

Aidan turns off of the sled trail, wading into thigh-deep snow. As he moves, only the sound of the falling snow can be heard. Large snow drifts mound up at the bases of several trees. His pace slows, but he plods on, heading silently into a copse of massive oak trees. Their bows dip heavily under the weight of repeated snowfalls. He approaches an impressive and aged oak, the tree spanning over six feet in diameter, its gnarled bark etched and weathered from its vast number of seasons. While holding Emma, Aidan gestures his hand, and a seam running the length of the tree grows wider. Within seconds a darkened passage has appeared within the heart of the trunk.

Stepping into the abyss, they enter what appears to be the simple living space of a country cottage house. A single window peers out into the snowy night. A cold fireplace sits against the far wall. Cobwebs cluster in the corners, and a thin layer of dust clings to all of the surfaces.

Gingerly, Aidan carries Emma over to the darkened fireplace, resting her in a small wooden chair as he starts to build a fire. Within a few minutes the small living space is drastically warmer. In a pot suspended over the raging fire, Aidan heats a golden-brown liquid. He ladles some out into a wooden cup and passes it to Emma. The rich brew has an aromatic fragrance of clove, cinnamon, and star anise. Tentatively, Emma sips the warm fluid, and it coats her throat and lessens the ache in her body. Her pain has weakened, yet is still there, rumbling just beneath the surface. Helping her stand, Aidan leads her to sit on the bed. Once he is satisfied that she is stable he returns to the simmering pot and ladles himself a cup.

"Where are we?" Emma croaks, drinking more of the wine.

"It is a safe haven for the forest folk. The satyr have used these dwellings for millennia. No one will be able to find us here." Aidan sits on a small stool and props his feet up on the bed next to Emma while he somberly sips his own drink.

"What happened back there?" she asks as she stares into the amber liquid of her cup.

"I'm not exactly sure. Quiet and normal one minute, then the next all hell is breaking loose. A bunch of the men started attacking everyone. It would appear that Ambrose was leading them. I helped where I could, but there were just too many of them," Aidan states with a shake of his head.

"Survivors?" Emma asks as her stomach clenches, recalling all of the dead bodies. "What about the Mothers and Olivia?" Emma tries to stand, but the room spins and she has to sit back down. Aidan stands and takes the cup from her, placing it on the counter nearest to the sink.

"You need to rest, at least for a little while. I don't know what happened to you, but you're not looking that good. I'm not a doctor." He stokes the fire before retaking his seat adjacent to her. "As far as I know, both of the Mothers left before the fighting broke out, and I don't know where Olivia is. But from what I've been able to gather, she is tough enough and smart enough to make it out of there. She'll be alright," he states, trying to calm Emma. "Right now my concern is figuring out what to do with you."

"I could just stay here, I feel better here." Emma drops her head into her hands, wanting nothing more than to pull the musty blankets over her and sleep. Her wounds have stopped bleeding, but she desperately needs sleep to heal.

"I don't think that's an option. This place is good for hiding because it mutes the flow of energy, but it won't work long term. We can stay here while we figure out where to go and get you warmed. But we need to get you some help." Concern knits his eyebrows as he feels her forehead.

"I need to find Mother Mei Li." Emma shivers as sweat trickles down her back. She can taste blood, and she fists her hands to keep them from shaking as she instinctively pulls her knees up into her chest.

"How are we supposed to do that?" he asks in frustration, scratching at the back of his head.

"Mother Mei Li told me about a vampire named Bastian. If we find him maybe he will know how to find the Mothers." With heavy eyelids, Emma's head lists from side to side. "Do you know where we can find him?" The words are slow to form. Her skin flushes as a bolt of searing pain crashes through her. She hugs her knees and screams as the glass in the window implodes. Emma is struggling to keep the flow of energy under control, Aidan is knocked to the ground from the sheer force of the wave. He wraps her in a blanket, cradling her against him as gusts of wind whip violently around them.

"Unfortunately I know exactly where to find him." As they venture out, the passageway is once again swallowed up by the great oak tree.

Once they are back on the trail Aidan breaks out into a galloping run. Faster and faster they move until the world around them fades into a blurred movement of muted colors and lights. Streets and signs zip by them at such a dizzying rate Emma has to clench her eyes closed against the nausea rising to envelop her. A stimulating white noise pulses around them, but starts to ebb as his pace slows. In the distance cars ramble along their way and dogs bark in the night.

Once again as the falling snowflakes kiss her cheeks she dares to open her eyes. The street is sparsely inhabited, though the few homes are divided by hedge rows, wrought-iron fences or thick brick walls. The seemingly expansive yards are well maintained even under the paleness of the moonlight. Snowy walkways wind around frozen bird baths and fountains. Bushes and tree limbs sag under the snow.

As they reach the end of the road all of the remaining houses slip away. A long driveway curves away from the main street. Emma squints as she is barely able to make out the house hidden within the scenery. Aidan weighs each of his steps as he cautiously follows the path. A few times his footing fails and they slide on the ice concealed under the snow.

Amid the white of snow and the encompassing darkness of the woods, the vast structure emerges. The three-story building surpasses her tiny apartment in girth by at least six times. It seems to be more of a small hotel rather than a home. Shaggy hedges trim the driveway leading up to the main entrance, where a highly-pitched roof with several gables juts above the tree line. The grey brick of the outer façade leeches the glow from the surrounding light posts. Many of the vast windows are darkened, but a few show the faintest of glows coming from within. As they approach the front walkway Emma asks Aidan to stop.

Apprehension creases his brow as he watches her, silently questioning her.

"Aidan, you have aided me greatly this evening, and that is not something I am likely to forget. But I want you to leave me here. My body can't metabolize enough of the copper before it kills me. So leave and go back to your Fey and keep her safe." Mustering her strength, Emma tries to wiggle free from his hold.

"No. If I leave you now and Mother Mei Li found out she'd have my horns– and probably other parts– mounted to the nearest wall. Plus, you can barely stand on your own. I'm not leaving you until you are safe." His jaw locks stubbornly, an unyielding determination staring back at her.

"At some point and time I will be overcome and people will die. I do not want to see you die. Not at my hands."

Climbing the steps, he places her feet on the ground, but has her lean against him.

"I don't want to die either. That's why we are going to get you help." With fisted hands he bangs loudly against the wooden door.

The carved oaken door swings open slowly. The young female vampire studies them coldly, her icy, violet eyes chill them more than the wintry weather outside, her pale skin seeming to glow under the low ambient light. A cascading drape of black and dark-blue ombre hair swirls about her tapered shoulders.

"We are here to see the master." Aidan's tone is curt and formal.

"The master isn't receiving anyone this evening. You'll have to come back another night." The tips of her fangs peek out from underneath full blood-red lips as she speaks. Her voice has a less than subtle purr. Emma shakes her head, trying to clear the mired cobwebs from her thoughts. Structured thoughts seem to be harder for her to grasp onto.

"We need to speak with the master now, not tomorrow." Aidan readjusts Emma's weight, leaning against him for support. Even through the blanket she can feel him shivering.

"What you need is not my concern. My concern is seeing that my master is not disturbed. Come back tomorrow or leave and not come back. Those are your choices." The young woman crosses her arms over her chest as she leans against the doorframe. Emma's focus wavers as a rush of white noise overtakes the sound of Aidan and the vampire's argument. Her blood boils and steam rises from her skin. Breathing deeply, Emma struggles as she is inundated by the growing wave of energy. Her eyes once again focus to the vampire, staring at her with an alarmed expression.

"What is wrong with her?" the vampire asks, her voice straining under her apparent uneasiness. With eyes incredibly wide, the vampire steps back, trying to shove the door closed. Emma kicks her foot out, blocking the door and pushing it open. In a stalemate, the door remains wedged halfway open. The blue-haired female strains against the door as the wood moans in response.

"Now here are our options," Emma slurs around her swollen tongue. "You can let us speak with the master, we ask our questions and we will be on our merry way, or you can keep pissing me off, in which case I'll level this fucking house and everyone inside it. I'll get my answers from the master, and whatever remains of you will be staked outside to greet the morning sun. So what's your decision?"

Emma allows the smallest amount of power out to envelop the vampire. Not enough to kill– or even to hurt her– just enough to get her attention. The female vampire stands rigid as the heaviness weighs down on her. Emma cringes, fighting with the energy surging within. *Don't kill her, don't kill her, just enough to scare her. Please, God, don't kill her,* Emma silently prays.

A large hand clasps the door from inside, opening it further. The second vampire is much taller than the first, a full head taller as he watches them. "Is there an issue here?" the man asks. The hulking man fills the space behind the female. His onyx hair is clipped short and black as pitch eyes stare impassively back at them. An intricate lattice work of scars crisscrosses his face and neck. Some scarring peaks out from the sleeves of his shirt, and part of his left ear is missing, melted away. Just a small flap, unrecognizable as an ear, remains. Emma realizes the scars are various impressions shaped like crosses, all overlapping each other.

"Poe, they are trying to get in to see the master. I told them he was not to be disturbed." Her chin lifts as her cold demeanor returns. He scrutinizes them both from head to toe, the thick lines surrounding his eyes deepening as the edges pucker and pull against his scars.

"I've never known a Fury to keep company with a satyr." A smirk lifts and creases his marred skin. Looking past them, he observes the winter scenery. "Well, it's just going to get colder out, so you'd better come on in."

"You can't let them in, Poe. She's dangerous." The younger vampire clutches at his arm, her expression of disdain quite evident. Without looking away he pulls himself free of her grasp. Gently he pats her hand as he speaks.

"Of course she's dangerous, Jillian, she's a Fury. Do not worry, the master has been expecting her. Go back to your duties and I will accompany them from here." Jillian eyes them dubiously but nods and disappears down one of the halls. Poe closes the door behind them and heads toward a long adjacent hallway. "If you will follow me I will bring you to my father."

"Your father?" Aidan asks as they follow cautiously behind him.

"Not my biological father. Very few vampires can breed through traditional means." He perks half of an eyebrow toward Emma. "Bastian sired me, so yes, he is my father. I have been in his service for nearly two hundred years now." Poe speaks yet never turns in their direction.

Walking together, they cross the threshold into a stylish parlor. Thick drapes are drawn closed, barring the chill from the cold night. The room is painted a rich burgundy, and the warm flicker of light dances from a fireplace against the wall.

The air surrounding them seems to thicken with an eerie hum. Emma's mind is muddled as a growing siege of sensations begins to batter at her. Lights and sounds coalesce, swarming around her in a torrent, causing her knees to buckle under the strain. Both men turn to quickly grab her, Aidan catching her before she hits the ground, Poe stopping himself mere inches from her.

Glancing upward, Emma meets his gaze. His stare holds hers. Eyes black as midnight, black as death itself, but within lies a great sadness and turmoil. Emma tries to pull her eyes away but is paralyzed as the vision overtakes her.

A beautiful woman, her long blonde locks whipping about wildly as she laughs. Her laughter transforms to shrieks of pain as a blazing fire envelops her. The hot sunlight bubbles her skin, dissolving flesh and bone alike. The screams are snuffed out, replaced by the subtle creaking of overhead lights as they swing back and forth. Distorted faces cloud her vision with their bloodshot eyes and blood-filled mouths. Emma feels her own skin scorch as the metal relics are pressed into her flesh. The smell of burning meat rises, curdling her stomach.

"Emma." Aidan's voice pierces the vision. He is shaking her as her eyes snap back into focus. A chandelier sways wildly overhead, streams of light dance back and forth across the room. Poe watches her, his demeanor guarded and dubious. Without further mention he turns, leading them away.

The long corridor is modestly lit with several fine works of art framed along the walls. A well-worn rug runs the length of the hall leading to a backroom. At the end of the hall they stop in front of two massive doors which are etched with intricate scroll work.

"Wait here. I will tell the master of your arrival." Stepping through the doorway he turns, shutting the doors and leaving them alone in the hall.

"Are you certain this is where we should be?" Aidan glances cautiously around. "This could be a deception."

"Mother Mei Li told me to come and find Bastian."

Di Angelo is a clan chief, a knight among his people. Bastian's power surpasses his by nearly twenty-fold. In a vampire society, Bastian is equivalent to that of a duke, one step below royalty.

"If we are looking for a powerful ally, then this is the place to come." Emma's knees shake as she claws at Aidan for support. Warm air blows up and around her from floor ducts, but does little to abate the rising chill within her.

"Yeah, but can we trust them?" Emma rests her head against him as the scenery spins wildly about her. Vaguely she is aware of the doors swinging open again.

Poe holds the doors as he ushers them in. "The master will see you now."

With Aidan's help, he and Emma enter the small parlor.

The office is small yet elegant, the floor a highly-polished hardwood covered with an intricately woven rug. Bookshelves are filled to capacity along the far walls. Lining the walls, several display cases and curio cabinets showcase statues and trophies from ancient cultures. In one case, from behind the thick, tempered glass, overhead light shines down on a tribal mask, two ceremonial daggers, and a small stone-carved figurine. Each of the items are laid out with a museum-like precision on the velvet padding.

From behind a large desk a man of his early forties rises to greet them. His brown hair is peppered with grey collecting predominately by his temples and the soft lines of his manicured beard. Rising up, his six-foot frame is lean, yet fills the lines of his finely tailored suit. He rounds the desk to stand before them. Glacier-blue eyes study them solemnly, judging them with a glance.

"I am Bastian. I am the master, and this is my home. Mother Mei Li had hinted that I could be expecting you. What is it that you seek?" he asks, folding his arms across his chest.

Emma tries to speak, but her throat clenches tightly. The taste of blood sours her mouth, and her vision blurs and twitches. The wound on her stomach has reopened, and blood seeps through her shirt. She clutches and presses on the gash to ebb the flow. Her whole body is trembling, shivering as the temperature of the room plummets.

Over the roaring in her ears, Emma can barely make out Aidan's voice. "We just need to find the Mothers. That's all," he explains.

"If she is a danger then you both need to leave here now," Bastian booms with an air of authority. His voice hitches slightly with concern.

"I need to leave now," Emma groans through clamped teeth. The room sways around her as her insides feel as they are being torn in half. She is frozen in a silent, wretched scream. The glass in the nearest cabinet explodes, spraying the room with powdered silicate. Cold sweat streams from her face and down her back. As the thunderbolt of pain rockets through her body she collapses.

Mother Mei Li rushes to her side from a hidden room. Her black dress blends into the darkness that is pulling at the fraying corners of Emma's vision. Blood trickles from her nose, cutting a wet line toward her ear. Mei Li pulls Emma up, cradling her in her arms. Emma's lungs seize as she is severed from the source. Her heart fights to beat, and her lungs scream for much needed air. Mei Li's touch deadens the surge of energy flooding into Emma. As the great tidal force collapses in, it yanks her into the inky abyss of unconsciousness.

Chapter 21

Emma is afloat in a sea of empty nothingness. In the tidal darkness she is removed from the agonizing torment of pain. Suspended weightlessly, the world around her slows. Everything is nonexistent aside from the bubbling ooze which engulfs her like an inky crude oil. The dark brew laps at her skin, sending alternating currents through her as it continually burns then freezes her. From somewhere in the distance, beyond the fluid, noises wash her ears and she can make out a clinking sound. It seems incredibly familiar, but she can't figure out what it is. Her mind is clouded and as befuddled as the soupy miasma surrounding her. Struggling against the dense fog, she claws her way up, out of her dream-like state. Her eyes burn as the dim light peeks in.

A sudden clamor of sharp cracks echoes in her ears, jerking her fully from her slumber, the weight of her own body crashing into her awareness. Pain and sensations ricochet through her as her jumbled brain starts to clear. She pries her heavy lids open just as another bucket of ice rains down over her. Ice cubes swirl around her as she is half submerged in the large claw-footed bathtub. The ice quickly melts into the near scalding water, and wisps of steam languorously rise from the surface. Emma's mind stumbles trying to take in her current setting. The denim of her jeans constricts her legs tightly under the hot water.

Her shoes and shirt have been removed, but she is modestly thankful that they left her bra on. The wound on her stomach has closed again, though it is still raw. Her feet and torso have a bright red hue to them, taking on the color of a sun-burn from the extreme heat. Around her the small bathroom is open and simply decorated. The dim light is enhanced by the soft shades of taupe and tan. A brighter overhead lamp funnels light directly over the tub, which obscures all that is beyond its reach.

David's arm is snaked under her, holding her above the surface. As she meets his gaze she can see the concern welling in his eyes, thick lines worry at his face. "Hey, I know you." He breathes slowly, carefully watching her face for a sign of recognition.

"David," Emma rasps. Her throat is dry and thick, but she manages a weak smile.

"There you are. Rest, we're taking care of you." His somber eyes are pained as he stares into hers. "Aidan told us what happened. When I saw all that blood on you I nearly died. If something would have happened to you…" His words trail off as Poe enters the small bathroom carrying a bright blue bucket which clinks as it shifts.

"This is the last of the ice in the house. If we need more we'll have to get snow from outside." Hoisting the heavy bucket up, he adds more ice to the bathwater. Emma groans as another rippling wave over takes her. Biting down on her tongue, she tries to ride it out as her body convulses. David lifts her, pulling her head away from the side of the tub. Energy arcs and pulses through the water as millions of tiny bubbles line the inside of the tub. David's voice is peacefully quiet as he attempts to soothe her. Mei Li enters through a small, white-paneled door. Her black hair is pulled up into a tight bun, her eyes darkly circled and drained. Standing over the tub, she silently studies Emma.

"I don't think it is working," Mei Li huffs in frustration as she wrings her hands.

"You said it would work," David bites, his features tightening.

"It should work. The cold bath method has been used successfully for generations. But I told you we don't know how much copper is still in her system."

"What if we brought her outside and put her in the snow?" David asks, exasperation bellowing from him. Emma studies his face, trying to memorize each line and shadow. His shirt and the tips of his hair are damp from the bathwater. A sheen layer of steam settles on his cheeks, highlighting the bone and rough lines.

"No, it won't work." She holds up a hand to silence David's oncoming questions. "It must be water. The Fury has to be submerged so that it can wick away the energy.

The ice water will lower the body temperature, and in response she will need to burn off more power to warm it up. You repeat this until the copper levels reach a manageable state. The snow would melt too quickly, and the water would run off. Even if we buried her, her body would simply create a snow cave."

"There has to be a way. Can't you help her? You can disconnect her from the source," he pleads. "I won't let her die."

"Yes, but I can only stop the flow of energy. Whatever copper is in her system will remain there until it is dissipated. There might be one more option. I cannot be certain it will work either." Mei Li thoughtfully fingers at her lips, biting the tips of her thumb. "The problem is I don't know if Emma will allow it. If we can't release the escalating energy, then Emma will die and she could take all of us with her."

Emma's stomach drops as both of their gazes fall upon her.

"Well there are actually two other options," Tatiana interrupts from a blackened doorway, her voice echoing through the small, tiled area, her silver hair glinting under the fluorescent lighting. The deep burgundy of her gown glimmers and softly swooshes as she enters the now seemingly crowded washroom. With an arched brow,

Tatiana sternly eyes Emma. Shame and guilt flood through her as she shifts uncomfortably in the tub.

"So what are our options?" David asks, leveling his glare toward Tatiana. Emma can feel the tension radiating from him. His muscles tighten and shake against the small of her back where his arm is pressed firmly.

"Mei Li has suggested asking the vampires to drain Emma dry of blood. This will effectively remove all of the copper from her system. The element will not harm the vampires, and bleeding out will not kill a Fury, but there is an issue with this plan."

Before Tatiana is finished speaking Emma is violently shaking her head.

"No, no, no. I will not let them feed from me." Emma gasps for air that won't come. David clutches her tightly to him, causing hot water to splash from the tub. Panic seizes her as tears blur her vision, washing down her cheeks into the bathwater. Her limbs tremble as heaving sobs overwhelm her body.

"What is the other option?" David barks as he hugs Emma against him.

"We kill her," Tatiana states callously, her face plain and apathetic. "It may be our best course of action. She is refusing to let them drain her, and even if she did there is a great risk that she will use her power to kill one or all of them. The death of these vampires will be quite problematic, and will make our situation worse, as we currently need their help." Tatiana steeples her hands to her lips as if gathering her thoughts. "Plus, it would be far less cruel than allowing her to suffer. It is a great kindness to end the poor dear's suffering. You must kill her, David," she states blankly.

"No, I won't do that. There has to be another way," David growls at them. A small nerve ticks in his cheek. His gaze shifts rapidly back and forth, watching the two women. "What if we could drain her blood without the vampires?"

"No, I'm afraid that won't work either." Tatiana shakes her head softly. "Her wounds would close too quickly, and there is no way for us to draw out enough of the contaminated blood."

Mei Li brushes past Tatiana, kneeling by the rim of the tub, careful not to touch Emma.

"I do understand that this is difficult for you. I would never suggest this if I did not think it was our only option." Her gaze flickers over to Tatiana. "But I know that my plan will work. Right now we are in a dire situation, and I refuse to lose you." The genuineness in Mei Li's eyes claw at Emma's chest, pulling more anguished tears from her.

"No," David echoes. "After what Aidan said about the attack on The Hallow, how can we trust any of you? I won't let you or anyone harm her. From where I sit, you Mothers are either keeping secrets or just plain lying. I don't trust the lot of you." He skeptically eyes Tatiana.

"I highly doubt the credibility of the satyr. He is not a reliable source as to all of the events," Tatiana interrupts as she scowls at them. Mei Li raises a hand to silence the other Mother, and addresses David.

"I know that you care for Emma. As of right now we have no idea what prompted the attack. But the truth is that we can either try this or let Emma die. And we have very little time left." Mei Li turns her questioning gaze back to Emma. "The choice is yours. I will not force your hand."

Silent tears stream down Emma's face. Her whole being shrieks for the pain to end. Death could bring a welcomed respite from the agony that is consuming her. Allowing them to feed off of her seems impossible to contemplate. But the thought of never seeing David or Olivia again fills her with an unbearable sorrow. Searching around the room to all three of them, she numbly allows her head to dip in compliance.

David frowns at them as he lifts Emma from the nearly bubbling water. Emma gasps as the seemingly frigid air cloaks her wet skin. Feeling the warmth radiating from David, she presses into him fiercely.

"If anything happens to Emma I am holding you both responsible." His hard stare is leveled on the two Mothers. Mei Li nods in a silent understanding, while Tatiana returns his glare in kind, her nostrils flaring as she lifts her chin stubbornly.

Emma is vaguely aware as Mei Li helps her remove her wet clothes. She is given clean, dry undergarments and a large white t-shirt that falls well below the middle of her thighs. Her skin prickles with goosebumps as a current of cold air wraps around her. With a warm terry cloth towel, Mei Li methodically dries the excess water dripping from Emma's hair. In a brief moment of clarity, Emma realizes that Mei Li is speaking to her. Her tone is soothing, but the words are muffled, still blocked by a dense fog. The ancient ancestor of the Mandarin tongue lulls Emma, pushing away the remnants of her recent hysteria.

They travel down several flights of narrow stairways into an area of the basement. The compact space is bare except for an expansive area rug that covers the majority of the floor. Electric wall sconces provide a dim level of light, leaving much of the room hidden in shadows.

With David supporting her weight they walk to stand before Bastian, Poe, and another man in the center of the room. The third man is unknown to Emma. His fiery hair flows like lava down his back, and his emerald green eyes observe her thoughtfully. A dubious energy seems to flitter about in the confined space.

"All the arrangements have been made." Bastian's voice echoes around them. "My people have been evacuated to the safety of a shelter. Should something go amiss it should be contained within this area." Straightening his back, his blue-eyed gaze falls directly on Mei Li. "Once this is completed I will consider my debt to you paid in full." Mei Li nods and steps alongside Emma, clasping her under the arm. As contact is made the energy raging through Emma is instantly snuffed out. The vacuum created by the loss jolts her knees, and she grabs Mei Li to steady her feet. Gently Mei Li supports Emma as she leads her toward the center of the room.

"I will be with you. I will not allow them to destroy you, but I cannot allow you to destroy them either." With sluggish feet Emma is directed forward. Her eyes stare blankly, refusing of their own free will to meet anyone's gaze. Bastian's presence looms over her. She can sense the power rolling off of him, but there is no heat. His is an icy energy that wicks away heat from all others.

"I will not tell you that this will be painless. A Fury cannot be enthralled, so we are unable to deaden the pain for you. We will try to do this as quickly as possible, but that too will cause some discomfort."

Finally forcing her eyes upward, Emma sees the excruciating remorse in his placid blue eyes.

"I know what this will be like." Even to Emma her own voice sounds cold and distant. Silently, she withdraws into the smallest, darkest place within herself.

Gingerly, Bastian touches her shoulders while Mei Li shifts her hold, moving her hand to the center of Emma's back. Emma focuses her thoughts on the feel of the Mother's hand, trying to block out all other sensations. The vampire stands before her, watching her stoically, his movements slow and deliberate, even cautious. Sliding his hand up to the back of her neck, he angles her head, exposing the right side. The flicker of his breath flows over the age-old scars.

"Not that side," Emma entreats as she forces her dry throat to swallow.

"Very well." Bastian shifts, his hand moving to the right side of her throat. Her pulse pounds relentlessly through her veins as her heart hammers within her chest. Poe and the third vampire step forward but make no attempt to touch her. In one swift movement, Bastian's mouth makes contact with her skin, his fangs plunging into her flesh. Searing pain erupts from the wound as Bastian draws hard, gulping down her flowing blood. As Emma's legs fail, Bastian wraps an arm around her, supporting her weight.

Two more sets of teeth rip into the soft flesh of her forearms. Emma strives to center her attention on the impression of Mei Li's small hand still on her back, but the onslaught of sensations is overwhelming. Her eyes clench tightly, and a rush of white noise floods her ears. Even through the blinding haze of panic, Emma can feel her pulse weakening. Time around her begins to slow. Her fingers are growing cold as they rest weakly on the marred surface of Poe's face. The lines and creases etched within his skin push and pull as he greedily feeds.

The room fades as it is enveloped in a murky fog. Emma shivers violently as a bone-jarring chill settles in. As her body wilts against the blood loss her mind ebbs and lulls. An insidious memory of the last time she was this cold lurches into the forefront of her mind. Slashing with gnarled claws, it peels its way out from the darkness where she had securely locked it away. Her vision blurs as falling snow obscures the diminishing landscape before her. In a far-off distance she hears the soft crackling of a fire.

The heavy murkiness engulfing Emma lifts slowly, and she finds herself standing in a long-forgotten living space. Piece by piece, the recollection of a home she once knew fall, into place. The thatched roof which was often leaky would render the living quarters damp with a perpetual coldness in the air. Even in this memory she can feel the weightiness of chill that permeates the atmosphere. Smoke from the fireplace plumes and clouds the small common area. But this had been her home for many years. A place she wanted to raise her children and grow old with James.

Lacking a physical form, she drifts listlessly as the scene plays out before her. Emma watches as the echoed version of herself clears the table after their meager dinner. Nestling her two children into the communal bed, she and James prepare to retire for the night. The longer winter months always seemed to aggravate her unexplainable fear of the night. It was the warmth and protection from her family that kept the demons at bay.

Emma still can't recall why she awoke early that evening. Perhaps it was a mouse in the rafters or an errant dish clattering to the smooth dirt floor. The interior is cloaked in a malignant play of shadows, the only light emanating is that from the dying fire. A chill rattles through her as the realization dawns that she is alone in the bed.

Wrapping herself in a thick, woolen shawl, Emma lights a tallow candle. The small cottage is deathly silent and absolutely vacant. A sudden gust of wind flings open the door, swallowing Emma in a painful blanket of frigid air. The flames of the candle and fireplace dance wildly, the blustery deluge whipping through the living area. Emma rushes to the door, pressing her body against the wood to force it closed.

Outside, a frozen maelstrom rages as lightning flashes, filling the tiny house with intense light. In an instance, the light is gone, leaving Emma blind in the darkness. Under the dim surrounding light Emma catches the sight of several black pools dotting the floor of her home, small puddles splattered in a circle around the door. Squinting and fumbling against the darkness that surrounds her,

Emma searches the hidden recesses within the room. Cautiously she creeps forward.

In a small nook her flame light falls on two crumpled and motionless forms, their details obscured by the hazy darkness encompassing them. The first body is vastly larger than the second. For a moment Emma muses as if the smaller shape is just a bundle of clothing dropped errantly on the floor. But as she creeps closer she discerns a tiny foot peeking out amid the folds of cloth. Horror and dread claw at her throat as she lifts Robert's lifeless body into her arms. His soft, white skin is icy to the touch. A ragged wound at his tiny neck oozes what remains of his lifeblood. Clutching her dead child, Emma scurries toward James. Struggling, she pushes him over onto his back. As he flops over, his dead eyes stare out blankly. Her breaths come in ragged pants as she jostles her husband, trying to stir him. Tears sting her eyes as she gasps for air that won't come. James's neck is also torn away, and the ribbed white bone of his trachea is visible through the gaping hole. Silently, Emma prays and pleas to be woken from the catastrophic nightmare surrounding her.

Probing around the bodies, Emma desperately searches for Anna. Hoarsely she calls out for her daughter. She is overwhelmed by the rampant terror, and in a frenzy she searches the small cottage. Strangled whimpers slide from her as her search builds toward a delirious hysteria. Her voice cracks as she screams over and again for Anna.

Supporting herself against the table, her mind races as her wits tatter and fray. Over the howling wind outside, a high-pitched shriek pierces the night, sending a prickling sting down Emma's spine.

Without thought, Emma launches herself out the door into the snow-covered woods. Her feet break through the hard, frozen snow as she careens into the brush, screaming for Anna. By the time she reaches the clearing her ankles and calves are slashed and bloodied. But even as her feet are completely numb and icy tears freeze on her cheek, she continues to run. A thick blanket of snow covers the field as the lonely elm stands guard against the bitter cold. Huddled in the contours of the graceful tree, a murky shadow moves, drawing her attention.

As the figure stirs, Emma can distinguish its human form. Tall and lithe, yet completely cloaked in darkness. In his arms he clutches a small blanket-wrapped bundle. Emma's heart seizes as a small pale arm flops out from in between the folds of fabric, the miniature limb illuminated in the dim moonlight. The crimson eyes glow as they study her from behind the child's limp body. With a deliberate callousness he tosses his parcel to the ground. Lightning pierces the sky, filling the pasture with blinding light and forcing Emma to shield her eyes.

In a burst of movement the darkened figure closes the distance between them, an iron vise-like grip closing around her neck. Her heart shudders in her chest, pulse pounding in her ears. His cold breath cascades over her face, reeking of fresh blood and rotten flesh. A scream clogs Emma's throat as she thrashes against him, pulling at the clawed hand encircling her throat, her arms shaking against the strain and the cold. Reaching upward, Emma claws and gouges at his exposed eyes and face. Fragments of skin and blood gel under her nails. Pushing with all of her weight, Emma tries to bury her thumb deep in his eye socket. With an anguished howl, he shoves her away, sending her careening backward into the snow. He bellows and curses as he holds a hand against the gaping hole where his eye once was.

On all fours, Emma scuttles past him toward the motionless body of her daughter. Yet with her child within arm's reach she is halted by a hand entangling her loose hair. A constrictor arm snakes around her, pinning her arms against her body. The hand entwined in her hair wrenches her head back, forcing her to look at his marred face and seeping socket. A low, unearthly growl brews in his throat, and Emma's heart seizes as horror paralyzes her. In a swift movement of blinding speed he buries his fangs into the soft curve of her throat. Skin rips and shreds as he sucks at the wound with avarice. Emma shrieks, but the bubbling sound is devoured by the whipping winds and endless night.

Silently she screams for her limbs to move, to fight against this overwhelming force, but her hands grow steadily numb as they flop uselessly at her sides. The white noise of blood rushing through her ears blocks any outside sounds.

The cold snow threatens to swallow her up as his larger form presses down. A swirling eddy of darkness engulfs her peripheral vision. Blackness looms as it erodes her sight. Frozen tears trace her cheeks as the pinpoints of her vision fall upon her dead child. She knows that this will be her last haunting vision– her beautiful child that she was unable to protect. Her beating heart painfully slows as the image is branded into her mind. Snowflakes fall, kissing her skin softly as the brutal darkness devours her.

Her heart fails and dies as the snowfall buries her body.

Chapter 22

David steadies his breathing as he walks down the long, expansive corridor. *How many hallways can one house have?* he mused to himself. An itch of tension twinges through his back as he keeps a safe distance between himself and the female vampire leading him. When Jillian had offered to show him the way outside for some fresh air he had been hesitant at first to trust her. The undead could, in his opinion, be seldom trusted.

It becomes quickly apparent to him that her intentions, while not dangerous, are not completely innocent either. Her ample hips sway seductively in a rather obvious way as she glides in front of him. Several times she turns to face him as they walk. Toying with her hair, she playfully licks and bites at her lower lip, laughing quietly to herself as she watches him. David has to hand it to her, she is bold, confident, and she knows what she wants. Unfortunately, David doesn't want her. Her face is pretty enough, and something about her eyes is somehow familiar. He's not dead, nor is he a eunuch, but he just doesn't want her.

Through a kitchen door they enter an enormous conservatory. Potted plants encircle miniature trees as a stone-paved walkway weaves throughout the greenery. The room is engulfed in an overcast darkness that is intermittently broken up as the moonlight shimmers through the glass-paned ceiling. At the far end they reach an exterior door where Jillian hands him a single cigarette and a book of matches. Her cold fingers graze the skin of his arm, causing the hairs to stand on end.

"When you're done you can come and find me to return the matches. We could get some coffee, maybe keep each other company for the night," she purrs softly in his ear. Her voice has a hypnotic effect, holding the promise of many wicked things.

"I appreciate the offer," David chokes. "But I shouldn't indulge in…social interactions. But thanks for the tour and the smoke."

"Suit yourself," she says with a slight shrug of her small shoulders. "If you change your mind come find me." She winks, turning and walking away.

"Yep, definitely not dead," he whispers to himself as he watches her leave.

The plume of arctic wind passes through the small exterior garden. David flips up the collar of his jacket as a meager barrier against the icy current. The snow has ceased its skittering descent to the earth as it leaves the scenery coated in an eerie frozen silence. Bushes and shrubs are masked as dips and hills under the thick blanket of snow. Standing just outside the closed conservatory doors, the building shields him from the brunt force of the wind.

Still, his toes start to tingle as the cold seeps in despite the high quality lining of his boots. A small patch of ground has been shoveled by the exit, allowing a person a place to stand. As he shifts his weight his shoes softly crunch over the frozen gravel, emitting a crisp echo through the empty night. Moonlight washes over the exposed areas of yard. The glass-encased room behind him sits quietly, painted in a murky blend of shadow and moonglow. On his passage through the conservatory he notes the deep and heavy fragrance of roses and herbs. Outside smells of snow and cigarette smoke.

The cherry tip of his cigarette glows brightly, cascading the surrounding area in a soft, red hue. Instinctively he cups his hand over the cigarette, hiding the burning ember from being seen. It has been over seventy years since the last time he smoked a cigarette. His system didn't crave the nicotine anymore, but it seemed the best option right now for settling his nerves.

In Europe, 1944, every foxhole from Normandy to Dresden was teeming with soldiers and wafting puffs of rising smoke. Smokers and nonsmokers alike understood the value of your cigarette rations. A man could buy a Sherman tank as long as he had enough smokes. David chuckles to himself, bracing against a gust of cold wind. When you are slowly dying in a frozen trench or some burnt-out building, your soul longs for some semblance of normality. A tremor rolls through him as he gruffly shakes the memories away. It always seemed like a smoke was a simple reminder of better times– away from the frigid, bone-chilling cold, dirt-clogged wounds and ever-present looming threat of death. After a while your longing for home becomes a distant memory belonging to someone else as a frigid numbness erodes away the person you once believed yourself to be. He had thought joining up was the right thing to do. He was more than willing to perform his patriotic duty, to offer his life in service to his country and her allies. It seemed at the time it was the only thing he could offer. Maybe if he fought bravely enough, he could atone for his prior weaknesses and failures.

Like how he failed Carolyn? The noxious thoughts coiled through his mind– a serpentine personal demon who is always there to highlight his missteps. He pushes away the bubbling rise of dark recollections and attempts to coax and steer his thoughts toward more pleasant memories. But each time, his winding stream of thoughts would careen him back to Carolyn.

The warm summer nights on the shore with close friends and the prettiest girl he had ever seen. Warm and kind with soft, violet eyes that swept him away like a tidal current. Eyes that sparkled and danced as they swept through an impossible range of bluish hues. Her hair catches the brightly colored lights from the carnival at night. An unexplainable need to see her smile urged and prompted him to push himself even harder. She was his reason for wanting to be a better man. The first woman he had ever loved. He recalled soft kisses stolen by the pier that had sent his heart racing.

His mother believed that he was simply a flight of fancy for Carolyn. She was an affluent doctor's daughter slumming with a low-life punk before packing it up to go off to her prestigious college. He'd never allowed himself to believe that. Naïve as he was, he believed that they loved each other and they could make it work. He would get promoted and they'd get married. Simple as that. Even when the draft letter came he still believed they'd be together.

A deluge of rain poured down over him as he weaved his way through the traffic. By the time he reached the diner where Carolyn worked his clothes were drenched and cold. He shivered despite the humid summer heat. His mouth was dry and his heart raced as he clutched the ring tightly in his pocketed hand. The soles of his boots squeaked on the tiled floor of the diner. The overcast skies cloaked the space in a dreary gray tone. His heart leaped as he spotted her. Carolyn was seated in a booth toward the back. Walking toward her, he practiced what he would say. *Tell her what she means to you, tell her you love her. Ask her. Ask her to wait for you, ask her to marry you.*

His footsteps stutter under him as he spies a young, well-dressed man seated across from her. His pace slows and his heart stops as Carolyn leans forward, taking the man's

319

face in her hands, bringing her lips to his. A shiny diamond ring twinkles on her left hand. David remembers wanting to run, but his legs refused to move. He watched in dumb horror as she smiles brightly at the man. Some movement behind David draws her attention and she sees him. In that moment he felt so exposed and naked– in front of her and everyone else. He had been so stupid. Just some low life that would be nothing more than a dirty secret she'd giggle about with her rich friends as they play tennis or some shit.

He turns, heading toward the exit as she calls his name. Mindlessly he pushes his way past people, blocking out all sound until he can feel the cold wash of rain on his face.

Carolyn clutches his arm. He jerks away from her as she pleads with him, her large, beautiful eyes glossy with tears.

"David, please stop." He turns rigidly to face her, hands fisted tightly at his sides. "I didn't want you to find out this way." David watches her pained expression as an icy numbness slithers through him. "I do love you, but I could never be with you. My family will never agree to us being together, us getting married. We would have no money and no prospects. We'd be destitute. Doug comes from a good family, and my father wants to me to marry Doug."

David eyes the prim man standing shielded on the other side of the glass doors of the diner.

"I love you, Carolyn. With everything I have in me, all I want is to be with you. I could've been what you needed, and I would protect you from anything and everything if only you'd let me."

"You can't protect me, David, and you can't give me what I need." A sheen of hardness flashes in her eyes. "Please, David, I need you to understand."

"Understand what?" David spits as his blood boils, the agony ripping at his chest threatening to overtake him. "Understand that you are a disgusting shallow whore who enjoys destroying people. You can take your rich life with your rich husband and shove it up your rich ass for all I care. Better yet, why don't you get out of my face and fucking die? If I never see you again it will be too soon."

The color drains from her appalled expression as he turns, darting across the road. Her voice rings out as he dodges the oncoming cars. Angry motorist blare their horns at him, but he doesn't care. She calls his name but he ignores her. As he steps onto the sidewalk the loud squeal of brakes stops him in his tracks.

He didn't need to turn around to know what happened. The empty hole growing in the pit of his stomach was enough. Enough to tell him how badly he'd messed everything up. A thin crowd encircles Carolyn as she lies on the pavement in front of the bus.

As he silently approaches she is whispering his name. A long gash on her head spills blood onto the road, and her breaths come in wheezing gasps, her beautiful violet eyes staring upward into the falling rain. He tries to go to her but is roughly pushed back. A man claiming to be a doctor kneels by her side. When the ambulance arrives she is gently moved to a gurney and lifted into the waiting transport. He calls out to her but she does not hear him. She dies before making it to the hospital. His last words to her had been cruel and said out of anger, and he can never take them back. Over a thousand times he has asked himself why he just didn't keep walking, why had he said anything at all? If he had ignored her maybe she wouldn't have followed him. Maybe she'd still be alive.

The burning embers of the cigarette singe his skin, making him wince. The pain brings him back to the present and back into the conservatory garden. Snuffing out the cigarette, he fieldstrips it, tearing the paper from the filter and placing the filter in his pocket. Stepping back through the conservatory door, David is wrapped in the organic warmth. He pauses briefly, inhaling the rich, earthy scent. Quietly he follows the path leading back into the house.

"Why do you feel responsible for the girl's death? Cancer would have killed her in three years." The soft voice echoes through the open area.

David halts rigidly as he scans the room. The exit door is still yards away. Encompassing darkness hides much of the space as the hairs on his arms rise against the humid air, the atmosphere humming with a soft current around him. Catching movement, his eyes are drawn toward a white upholstered daybed nestled amid the dense foliage of some potted azaleas.

Reclining casually on the plush material is a woman, her one arm draped lazily over her stomach while her head rests thoughtfully on her other palm. Rich waves of black hair fall around her slim shoulders. Despite the low light, the brilliant sheen of her green dress appears to glow around her. Unearthly eyes of the same emerald hue study him with a hardened intensity.

"Who are you?" David asks, struggling to keep his tone unwavering. A pulsing agitation snakes through him as his guts scream at him to run like hell.

"Over the millennia we have had many names: Erinyes, Semnai, Fury." A cold trickle of sweat drips down his spine as she rises from the seat. Her head tilts to the side as she seems to gauge his response. "I am Tisiphone, the eldest of the Fury."

"What do you mean? I've never met you before," he asks, racking his mind, but he knows he has never seen this woman before in The Hallow.

"Of course you've never met us before." A second woman emerges from the darkness. She seems similar to the first, but her deep brown hair is halved into two braids which fall together down the middle of her back. Like her partner, the vivid azure blue of her gown matches her eyes. Unlike the smooth calmness of her partner, this woman appears to be a subtly bundled mass of ticking nerves. As she approaches, her gaze flickers sporadically about. "We are the original three," she states almost petulantly. "I am Alecto, second born of the Fury."

"What do you want?" Involuntarily, David steps back from the two women.

"You ask too many questions," Alecto spits. Spontaneously, a frigid wash of air sweeps through the garden as frost blooms across exposed leaves and branches. As Alecto steps forward, advancing on David, she is abruptly halted by the outstretched arm of her sister.

"We have simply come to offer a few words of advice, nothing more." As Tisiphone speaks, the chilled air recedes.

"Well, that and we are curious too," a third voice calls out to him. David turns his head, glancing over his shoulder. The bloody crimson of her dress surprises him. How could he have missed her approach? She leans lightly against a low rock wall, and in her hand twirls the stem of a freshly cut red rose. Her hair flows softly around her, stirred by an unseen breeze. It's the color of sun-kissed honey, almost like Emma's. Silver eyes stare at him as she inhales the fragrant bloom in her hand. "I am Megaera, last born of the three."

"What are you curious about, and why offer your help?" His stomach pitches and rolls, trying to leap out of his throat, past the thunderous pounding of his heart. Alecto hisses, lunging forward toward him again. Tisiphone snatches a cord of her sister's braided hair, yanking and sending her reeling backward on the rough rubble walkway. As Alecto glares at him from the ground, several thin vipers writhe in and out of her tightly woven braids. Thin wisps of green vapor rise from the serpent's nostrils.

"Alecto, stop. We haven't time for your foolishness," Megaera snaps. "Our sister hates being questioned," she tells David. "Why curious, you ask." Her tone purrs to him in rhythmically mesmerizing pulses. "I, unlike my dear sisters, have always been intrigued by your human nature. You are intrinsically of both light and darkness. You create as well as destroy. You are capable of such intense love and vehement hatred. So rarely are we strong enough to shatter the bonds of death and cross back into this world."

Stepping forward, she stops inches from David, her body nearly grazing his. The soft touch of her breath flows over his skin as she seems to scent him.

"The brutal power of life and death is absolutely intoxicating. So often they are entwined so closely, as two mating vipers." She reaches up, the tips of her fingers a breath away from his cheek. He is powerless to move away from her, as if unseen shackles hold him in place. The air that separates them is alit with the subtle hum of electricity. Her hands gently sweep over the lapels of his coat. The tympanic beat of his heart swells in his chest as a cold sweat coats his skin. "We tread the ground between the living and the dead. Our power reaches and spreads deeply into both domains. Tell me, is that why you love her? How alluring that ultimate power must be?"

"Who? What are you talking about?"

Her small hand clamps over his mouth.

"Don't bother denying it," she snaps. The skin underneath her thumb starts to burn. His adrenaline spikes, and he struggles against his frozen body. "I can't stand a liar, and you will not lie to me." Her eyes glow as she glares at him with contempt. "It doesn't matter though. In the end you will still lose her and she will lose you. The ribbons are woven and cannot be undone. Struggle as you might, you will be separated from one another."

"Megaera, behave yourself as well. As you have said, we have little time for this," her eldest sister, Tisiphone, chides. Megaera's features transform into a rigid icy mask as she steps away from David.

Both Megaera and Alecto return to their sister's side as the eldest eyes him coolly.

"We have a vested interest in the lives and prosperity of our descendants. With the recent calamity that has befallen our children, the severity of the situation has become apparent. A Herculean task has been laid before you to ensure the safety of the remaining Fury. A great darkness grows and slithers within the shadows. It will try to seize control over our strength. This cannot be allowed to happen."

A nervous energy trembles through David's limbs as the three statuesque women glare staunchly back at him.

"If you know what or who we are up against, tell me." His muscles ache as they cramp painfully under his skin.

"Telling you changes nothing. Fate's thread is already spun. You must stop this. If you should fail, then a cataclysmic judgment will cast its shadow across this world, and none shall be spared. To gain control of the Fury with no sense of balance would mean the destruction of all mankind. Without equilibrium all will be deemed as lacking and be pulled down into Hades, where an eternity of torment awaits them." In unison the bodies of the three sisters flicker, their images fading, becoming transparent for a brief second before becoming solid once again. "Our time has drawn to a close. We must return to the dead. Do not fail, David." Their forms shift and fade until they are wisped away as an emerald green vapor.

The hold gripping his body relents, and his knees buckle under his own weight. Gasping sharply, David steadies his breath. With heavy limbs he stands, searching the room for anyone else who may be in hiding. Moving cautiously, he makes his way out of the conservatory, closing the door behind him.

Chapter 23

Emma's eyes open slowly, her mind clasped in a lethargic fog. Sorting through her jumbled thoughts, she tries to recall where she is. The warm, quilted comforter is pulled up around her, and the thickly padded mattress blocks the view of her surroundings. Lying on her side, she can only see a small nightstand and lamp. Anything beyond the lamp glow is swallowed in a haze of darkness. Her only conclusion is that she is in a bed, but where she is and whether she is alone eludes her. Shifting her feet slightly, she realizes that her legs are bare underneath the fluffy blankets.

Chancing a glance downward, she can see that she is wearing a simple white t-shirt. The events of the last several days flood back through her mind– The Hallow being attacked, Aidan bringing her to find the Mothers and the vampires. Flicking off the covers, Emma sits up and surveys the area. She is in a small, modestly furnished bedroom. Aside from the nightstand and lamp, the only other furniture in the room is a wooden chest sitting at the foot of the bed and a plain wardrobe against the far wall. Instinctively, her hand glides up to her neck where she expects to find a nasty wound, but she feels nothing. She inspects her arms only to find two sets of faint marks on each.

Standing up, her legs are unsteady, but she seems to be without pain. Emma walks gingerly across the plush carpet to a small attached bathroom. Clicking on the overhead light, it flares to life with a hum. She stares at her reflection in the mirror mounted above the sink. While her skin is paler than normal, the left side of her neck is unmarred. She touches the skin, confirming that it is intact. Her hands tremble as she turns on the faucet, washing her face, neck, and arms with the icy cold water. Grabbing a hand towel, she dries off her skin and reenters the bedroom to look for her clothes.

She opens the wardrobe doors and peeks inside as a timid knock sounds from the other door. Emma stares in silence at the wooden exit, her glance flickering about the room. There seems to be no other exits or weapons available. Again, a tiny tapping echoes from the door. Inhaling deeply, Emma steadies her nerves and cautiously opens the door.

She squints against the brighter light filling the hallway. A young female vampire with black and blue dyed hair stands in front of her, holding a silver tray with a glass of ice water on it. The outside of the tumbler glistens from the condensation. Emma's parched throat clenches as she watches a single bead of water race down the side of the glass.

"Bastian thought you may be thirsty. My name is Jillian, may I come in?"

Emma's attention is drawn back to the girl.

"Yes." Backing into the room, Emma holds the door open, allowing her guest to come in. Jillian calmly brushes by her, setting the tray on the nightstand. "Where am I? Where are Mother Mei Li and David?" Emma asks, her hand still lightly resting on the door knob. Turning to face Emma, Jillian patiently studies her.

"You are in one of the guest rooms in Bastian's home. He and your Mothers are waiting for you upstairs in his office. I have been asked to collect you and bring you up there." Jillian placidly strides toward the door, her gaze unwavering from Emma. "Take a few minutes and get ready. I'll be waiting for you outside. Should you need something, let me know."

"Where are my clothes? I would prefer not going up there like this." Jillian's gaze flickers down Emma's body and back up.

"No, I guess you wouldn't. Your belongings and clothes are in the chest by the bed." Jillian tilts her head, indicating the direction. "Unless you need assistance, I'll be outside."

Emma steps to the side, allowing Jillian to leave.

As the door softly clicks closed she cautiously opens the chest. Inside she finds her clothing washed and folded. The blood-stained pillowcase she brought from The Hallow is wrapped within her sweat jacket at the bottom of

the container. She can feel the cold resistance of the glass
orb through the sheen cotton material. Quickly, she gets
dressed and gulps down the glass of cold water. Emma
tucks the pillowcase into her sweat jacket and zips it closed
and opens the door to find Jillian waiting for her.

They walk in silence down several halls and up flights of
stairs, finally stopping in front of two doors that seem
familiar to Emma. Nervous energy claws at her. The
unknown outcome of this meeting seems overwhelming.
How much do they know? Will they blame her? Did she
make the right choices? All of these questions gnaw and
pluck at her guts. But there is no use in delaying the
inevitable. Steadying her hands, Emma pushes open the
doors.

Jillian glides silently beside her as they enter the spacious
office. Glancing around the room, the recollections from
the previous night flood in. Bastian sits behind his desk
emanating confidence and an air of old power. His blue
eyes study her dubiously, but there also seems to be a slight
hint of something akin to sympathy.

David stands against the far wall, his features softening
slightly as his gaze meets hers. Tatiana and Mei Li stand
next to him. Both Mothers study her apprehensively,
almost as if she were a feral beast. Carefully, Mei Li rounds
the desk.

"How are you feeling, Child?" Her tone is guarded as she weighs Emma's response.

"Better. Thank you, Mother." Emma's own apprehension spikes as she battles the impulse to flee.

"Aidan told us of what happened in The Hallow. But we as yet still don't know why. It seems very much out of character for Ambrose to do such a thing." Mei Li thoughtfully rubs her chin, tapping her lower lip with a long, graceful finger. Several thick strands of long black hair have loosened from her bun. Darkness rims her eyes that are heavy with burden.

"That's if the satyr can be trusted," Tatiana adds, following Mei Li out to the center of the room.

She is ever a woman of classical beauty, who always appears with never a hair out of place. With cold, silvery eyes she surveys everyone around her.

"Is it not possible that the satyr was purposely planted within The Hallow to disseminate false information? Or even the fact that he may have simply misidentified the culprits involved?"

Mei Li stares at her with a look of frustration.

"Glare at me if you want, but you know I am right. We cannot jump to conclusions until we have all of the facts."

With a self-satisfied look, she turns her eyes back to Emma.

"I am not sure if what I found will clear anything up or just add more questions." Emma's voice cracks under the piercing scrutiny of the Mothers.

"Tell us what you know, Child." Mei Li speaks softly as she clasps her hands in front of her.

"I don't believe Ambrose is who he claims to be. I do believe that he is in some part involved in this collusion. I heard someone referring to him as Thanatos." The color instantly drains from Tatiana's already pale skin. "Plus, I found something down in The Hallow." Emma's voice shrinks to a whisper.

"What did you find?" Mei Li asks, wetting her parched lips. Emma glances swiftly about the room to all of the vampires standing audience to the conversation, then back to the Mothers. "It is alright. Whatever is going on here involves them too. Tell us, Child."

Silently, Emma unzips her jacket, withdrawing the stained pillowcase. A heavy air seems to settle over the room. Her hands tremble as she reaches into the sack and pulls out the glass artifact. "I found this," Emma rasps, holding the orb closely to her chest.

The expression from both of the Mothers gives nothing away as they look on stoically.

"Do you know what this is?" Emma asks as all eyes seem transfixed on the dancing lights held within it.

"It's a soul stone. I have never seen one except for drawings in some ancient tomes." Mei Li steps closer, but maintains a safe distance, as if weary of the object.

"What is its purpose? Is it a weapon of some sort?" David asks, drawing everyone's attention to him.

"Yes and no," Mei Li answers, turning her focus back to Emma as she gingerly takes the glass ball from Emma. "From what I gathered the soul stone is simply a container. Its purpose is to hold souls or spirits."

"Why would Ambrose, or whoever is behind this, want souls?" Emma queries as Tatiana glares fiercely at her.

"As you know, some of the Mothers died trying to bridge the gap between our humanity and Fury nature. They dabbled in a black art, which was ill-advised, and they paid with their lives. But what they discovered was an ancient ritual which could reawaken the Fury. They believed that ultimately there should only be three Fury. The three Fury that would be the living embodiment of their predecessors. And with the death of a Fury their power will be funneled down to the rest until only three remain. But they would still need souls to act as a catalyst to lend energy to the ritual– blood and souls. Of course, the idea of such a ritual is simply depraved and was forbidden." Mei Li's voice shudders as she finishes.

"So what would someone gain from doing this, reawakening the Fury?" Emma asks, her own gaze pulled toward the orb.

"Control." Tatiana's voice hums around them. "If you control the ones that judge, you control everything."

"But they would still have free will. The Fury I mean. They could just turn against whoever was trying to control them." David walks next to Emma as he speaks, folding his arms over his chest. Emma's nerves calm slightly at his proximity.

"That would be the case, yes." Tatiana huffs at David in contempt. "But if you would allow me to finish... The free will can be bypassed. A complex incantation of control can bind the will of one to another."

"Making them slaves? What would one need for this incantation?" David asks pointedly.

"If I remember correctly, an animal pelt, blood from an undead, and the blood of whomever you are trying to control." Tatiana's eyebrow arches as she continues.

"So a werewolf skin, blood of a vampire." David's look turns toward Bastian as he speaks. "And Fury blood. We have to find Olivia."

"Bastian, can you store this?" Mei Li asks, still holding the orb in her hands. "We must secure it some place safe."

"The wall safe here in my office is the most secure container I have. It is near impenetrable," Bastian answers as he moves a painting on the wall. Once the orb is sealed away they all turn to the exit, staring straight at Tatiana.

"Stop," Tatiana commands, and everyone freezes. "There are still some questions that I want answered before we leave." Her gaze slices through the room, landing on Emma. "Where exactly did you find the soul stone?"

Emma shifts nervously as all eyes turn to her.

"Celia had it," Emma answers as calmly as she can, tiny tremors rolling through her body.

"Why would Celia have something like this?" Tatiana snaps.

Emma inhales deeply, then blows out a single, long breath.

"I believe Celia was working with Ambrose. She was charged with collecting the souls for him," Emma replies.

Mei Li's gasp can be heard over the silence permeating the room.

"That's impossible. You're lying. Celia may be a lot of things, but she would never betray the Fury." Tatiana's skin burns red as her growing outrage becomes apparent.

She lengthens and straightens her back, an air of righteous indignation exuding from her.

"It's the truth. She told me as much herself," Emma counters as she battles to find her voice.

"Where is Celia now? I will speak to Celia first before I believe anything you say. Where is she?"

"Celia is dead." The whisper rushes out before Emma can contain it.

Tatiana freezes mid rant, her incensed anger melting away into a cold, stoic mask.

"And how did she die?" Her cool demeanor belied by the unchecked emotion in her voice. In a fluid motion she glides forward, standing before Emma.

"She killed Sara, so I killed her. I hunted her down and judged her." Tears glaze Emma's eyes as she recalls the dead children. "I saw the evil, wicked, cruel things that she had done, and I killed her. The orb was buried inside of her, in her chest." Tatiana tilts her head back, breathing deeply. Her eyes close against the surrounding light as she methodically breathes in then out.

The strike from Tatiana comes with a blinding speed. The slap nearly buckling Emma's knees, but she remains standing. Her cheek burns under the cool air.

"Why must you continually lie to me? I have tried to be fair with you, but I will no longer tolerate this deceit."

Mei Li rushes forward, trying to calm Tatiana, but is roughly pushed away by the other Mother.

"Enough. You have always coddled her," Tatiana screams at Mei Li. "Celia would never have harmed the child. Sara was one of our own. She lies to pull eyes away from her own guilt. For all we know she could have killed Sara and then Celia to cover it up."

Numbly, Emma shakes her head.

"No." Her voice rattles. "I saw her do it." Emma's eyes flash between the two Mothers.

"You watched her kill Sara and you did nothing?" Tatiana rages, wrenching her arm free of Mei Li again.

"I tried but I couldn't get to her." Emma's vision blurs as weighty tears cling to her lashes, blinding her as the second slap comes. The third slap is harder, ringing her ears. Emma presses her arms to her sides.

Tatiana's face blooms red as she bellows at Emma. "Everyone knows that you and Celia had no love for each other. She outranked you, and you have the gull to stand there and lie, disparaging her name to save your own skin. Well, I'll have no more of it." An open palm meets

Emma's face again. She can taste the warm trickle of blood coming from her nose.

"No," Emma sobs. Her glance catches Mei Li pressing a hand to David's chest, anger and a pained expression etched on his face.

"Don't look to them." Tatiana roughly yanks on Emma's chin. "No one will save you from your atonement. You betrayed your sisters in their time of need. You let them die, and worse. You claimed the life of one of your own." Yet another strike punctuates the sentence. Strike after strike now follows– so many that Emma loses count. Emma tries to pull out of her body, hiding from the pain and the shame. It's not the first time she has been punished by Tatiana, but she wishes the others weren't here to see her shame.

Closing her eyes her vision flashes white-hot, in sync with each hit. Tatiana's railing dies away into clamorous background noise. Unfortunately, sterile silence is not awaiting her within the depths of her own mind. A chorus of murmuring voices chants for her to make it stop, to stop her. The growing crescendo of sound escalates, wiping away all other sensations.

In an instant, Emma's eyes flash open and she is clutching Tatiana's forearm. The Mother's eyes are wide as she stares mouth agape, panting at her.

"No more," Emma states coldly

"How dare you. I'll have you…" Tatiana is cut off as Emma yanks her forward by the arm, their noses almost touching. Tatiana starts to shake as Emma's irises flood with a liquid copper color. Emma presses her thumb into the soft flesh of Tatiana's arm. With the slightest pressure, the thumb pops through, puncturing the skin, and blood oozes from the wound. Tatiana wails, tears flowing down staining her cheeks.

"If you ever strike me again I will kill you." Emma stares apathetically at her for a second before releasing her. As Tatiana stumbles to the floor, Emma barely registers David and Mei Li taking hold of her, trying to pull her away. She stands rigidly against their prompting.

"David, go and help Tatiana," Mei Li urges him.

"You've got to be kidding me. After what she just did? No flippin way," he snarls at her.

"Well, I need to stay with Emma. If she's at all unstable then I need to help her. Please," Mei Li pleads, and David's face softens.

With a reluctant sigh he heads over toward Tatiana. Taking off his t-shirt, he wraps her wounded arm tightly.

Mei Li clutches Emma's arms, restraining her and trying to soothe her. A cold numbness continues to spread throughout Emma as she watches Tatiana being bandaged. Emma laments, praying that she could feel nothing for the wounded woman, who is a crying heap on the floor. But an unbearable sadness settles within her. Her gaze lulls from Tatiana to Mei Li, shifting between the two women. Emma concentrates on the warmth of Mei Li's hand resting on her arms.

The vision erupts through her mind as flashing still-shot images flutter by faster and faster, until they become a living, moving scene. The great hall is vacant aside from three obscured figures. At first their forms and words are amorphous, meaningless. But as they approach their lines sharpen, coming into focus, and their speech takes shape.

Emma can clearly recognize Mei Li, Agnes, and Tatiana. Their appearance is unchanged, but Emma knows this is an event from a long time ago. As a vigilant seeker, she observes their secret interaction.

"She is returned now, barely half a day. We should collect her before it is too late," Mei Li murmurs, shaking her head.

"And what if you are wrong?" Tatiana's arched brow lifts. "We don't know what she is. And I will not risk the lives of many to possibly save one."

"But if we abandon even one of our own, then our cause and purpose are meaningless," Agnes chides, her familiar eyes bright and serene.

"What good will our cause be if we are all destroyed by this creature? A creature that may not be strong enough to even pass the admission

tests. I say, if we bring her back to The Hallow it should be only to end her suffering. A painless death will be the only mercy the gods will show her." Tatiana studies each woman, her chin hitched high.

"I cannot agree to kill this... Emma. And I know that she will pass the initiation. I have seen that she is strong enough to do so. But to leave her alone in the world seems cruel as well." Agnes firmly counters.

"The world in which we survive is, by its very nature, cruel. What is cruel is the fact that she should have died in that field with her daughter. but the gods chose to bring her back. Her blood is tainted by the foul beast that devastated her family. And I will not allow such a wicked insidiousness to befoul our sanctuary. It is best that we allow nature to take its course." Sternly, Tatiana folds her arms across her chest as the two other women nod in assent.

"Emma," Mei Li shouts, shaking Emma by her shoulders. "What did you see, Child? Speak to me."

"You left me." Emma chokes out a gasp, freeing her arms from Mei Li as she backs away. "You knew I was out there and you left me."

Mei Li turns ashen as her head shakes ever so slightly. "Emma, please listen to me." She lifts her hand as if to stop her.

"Don't touch me," Emma grits through clenched teeth. "For two hundred years. Two hundred years of rotting in a hole, starving and dying every day. And the whole time

343

thinking I'm a monster, the whole time thinking I am completely alone." Emma pivots, making her way out the door, slamming it behind her.

Chapter 24

Careening at a full-out run, Emma propels herself down the halls, blindly searching for some avenue of escape. Her vision is blurred by sopping wet tears that sting her eyes. Her throat and lungs ache from the torrent of emotions coursing through her body. An ominous silence permeates the halls, causing her hasty footfalls to ring out loudly. Through some small miracle, she stumbles back to the door of her temporary room.

With a heavy thud she shuts the door behind her, leaning against the cool, timbered surface, the deep, harsh pants of her breathing the only sounds in this quiet, desolate place. The room is still dimly lit by the incandescent light of the bedside lamp. This is the last place she wanted to end up, but her options are limited. The Hallow is a no go, and who knows if she has enough strength to open a portal to her apartment. She wages a silent battle with herself, whether she should stay or go. Despite the questionable loyalty of the Mothers, she still can't bring herself to abandon them. Random snippets of Mei Li's memories keep flashing through Emma's mind, each time rekindling her anguish and seething anger. Heatedly, she paces the room, a bubbling cauldron of leashed rage from the betrayal.

A small tap at the door sends her nerves rattling, bouncing down her spine as she nearly jumps from her skin. Glancing around the room, she is yet again reminded that there is no way to escape from this room. A gentle knocking sounds softly from the door again.

"Emma. It's David. May I come in?" The worry radiates from his voice even through the solid mass of the wooden barrier. Emma cringes at the thought of seeing anyone right now, but she also knows that she wants and needs to see David. Her stomach twists into tightly woven knots as she wonders if he'll think poorly of her after all that has happened. They've been partners for a while now, but she has never allowed someone, let alone David, see her fall apart like this. To make matters worse, she attacked a Mother. Would he be disappointed in her because of her weaknesses? Again a patient but determined knocking persists. The air within the room is flooded with the sounds of knocking.

"Come in, David." Her voice is barely more than a whisper, her heart thudding passionately in her chest as she struggles to catch her breath. Slowly the door opens, and David cranes his head into the room. He studies her silently for several seconds as he enters and shuts the door behind him.

"Is everything ok?" he asks, folding his arms over his chest. He seems cautious, a tense hesitation flowing out from him.

"I don't know," she responds numbly, all the while trying to gauge his reactions. The soft, warm glow of light dances through his coffee hair. His very presence is often soothing, giving her something solid and concrete to cling to. But right now she is terrified– terrified that he'll be as disgusted as everyone else seems to be, and that he'll desert her.

"Do you mind telling me what exactly happened back there?" he asks, an undercurrent of extreme emotion wrapping around him. It is so intense that Emma nearly loses what little nerve she has remaining. She battles to stave off the urge to bolt for the door.

"I'm sorry. I know that I crossed a line. I shouldn't have touched Tatiana, and I bear the full responsibility for my actions." She can't arrest the tremors shaking her hands.

"Damn it, Emma. I'm not talking about that. I don't give a crap about Tatiana and her wounded pride." He racks his hair in frustration as he looks down, his hands resting on his hips. "What happened with Mei Li?"

"Oh. I received a vision," she whispers, as each word needs to be pushed out with a measured pause in between. "It just came on so quickly. Just a strobe light sequence of images. It was of the three Mothers. They were discussing me. I had just died, and they debated on if they should go and get me. They decided to leave me there."

Again Emma can feel the heaviness of tears weighing down her lashes. She squeezes her eyes closed tightly, wishing the unwanted emotions away. Before her eyes open, David moves forward, pulling her into his arms and holding her gently. His warmth enfolds her, wrapping her in the solidity of his being. And for the briefest of moments everything else melts away. She simply focuses on the sound of his thunderous heart beating under her ear and feeling the safety of his arms.

The subtle intrusive sound of knocking emanates from the door. Emma nestles her head further into the unyielding shelter of David's chest. The trepidation from the night's previous events needles at the fringes of her mind, and it threatens to shred her remaining nerves.

"I don't think I'm ready to see the Mothers again. Not yet." Emma's breath shakes, her eyes refusing to look toward the sound.

"I'll tell them to come back later." David squeezes her shoulders tightly before releasing her. Emma's body is chilled by his sudden absence. He walks to the door, opening it only slightly as to allow the visitor no line of sight into the room. She cannot see who is there, but realizes quickly that it is not either of the Mothers. The male voice from the other side of the door is muffled, obscuring his words.

"She is not seeing anyone," David answers firmly. Emma strains to make out the conversation, but her body stubbornly refuses to advance closer. "About what?" David asks gruffly, a sour look gracing his features. "Wait here. I'll ask if she wants to see you." Without waiting for a response, David quietly shuts the door and turns to Emma.

"It's Bastian. He wants to speak with you." David's panhandle expression reveals nothing.

"What does he want?" Emma asks guardedly.

"He refused to say." David's annoyance with the vampire is apparent. "He just said he needs to talk to you before you leave. Do you want me to get rid of him? I could send him bouncing down the halls." David nods his head toward the door as a mischievous grin spreads across his cheeks. Emma can't help but smile at his wicked glee. But her smile slips away as she sighs deeply.

"As much as I don't want to, I should probably see him. As soon as I get through this I want to leave." Emma steels her nerves as David opens the door, admitting Bastian.

Bastian saunters into the room wearing an expensive-looking charcoal-grey suit with a deep aqua-blue tie that complements his eyes exquisitely. The man's charisma and stunning good looks are enthralling. Yet there is a subtle darkness that makes Emma leery to trust him completely.

"I wanted to personally come by and see as to your wellbeing. I know the last twenty four hours have been difficult." Bastian measures his words carefully, methodically.

"I am feeling well. I am certain that Mother Mei Li is grateful for your assistance and considers your debt to her repaid." Tension wells within Emma, but she keeps her voice calm and formal.

"Most certainly my debt to her is paid." He agrees with a small nod. "If I may be so bold as to ask, what are your plans?" His expression takes on a tone of serious determination. Emma senses an underlying motive brewing.

"I have not conferred with the Mothers as to their plans. And while your hospitality has been truly gracious, I myself intend to leave as soon as possible. Tarrying here would only serve to risk you and your kin."

"That is quite interesting," he muses, his long, graceful fingers stroking his chin.

"What is interesting?" Emma asks.

"So you would leave here with a debt still to be paid to me?" His expression doesn't change, but there is small glint in his eyes, making Emma feel as though she has walked into a trap.

"Correct me if I'm mistaken, but I was under the impression that in exchange for your aid the debt with Mei Li would be remunerated?" Emma guards her tone as the rising apprehension builds around them.

"True, very true." He smiles widely at them, his fangs catching the light.

"I think maybe you should explain yourself a little bit better," David warns, glaring at Bastian.

"There is the matter of the risk involved in cleansing you of your affliction. As you recall, we aided you in removing the copper from your system. Therefore there is now a debt between you and myself."

"So you fed off of me and still believe that I owe you a favor?" Emma asks bitterly with a lift of her eyebrow.

"I take my duty to protect my children very seriously. We had no way of knowing the possible dangers to ourselves, yet we still helped you." His expression is deathly grim.

"And what exactly are you asking in exchange for this favor?" Emma asks dubiously.

"Oh, it's nothing too dramatic or exceptionally painful," he reassures them with a wave of his hand. "For one of your skill set it should be quite simple, in fact."

Emma's patience is waning as she folds her arms over her chest.

"Spit it out, troll, or I'll throw you out,"

David barks as his own frustration rises to the surface.

"Very well." He feigns an insulted look that is nearly laughable. An oddly seductive smirk turns his lips. "Your guard is impressive in his loyalty even if he does lack something in the art of the social graces." Bastian's smile fades as he pins Emma with an intense stare. "I have heard from Mei Li that you have an extraordinary ability to heal. I want you to heal Poe. If you heal my son then your debt to me will be forgiven."

"What if I try and fail?" Emma asks as her pulse quickens.

"Over the last two centuries I have paid more than a small fortune bringing in every sort of Shaman, voodoo priest, healer, doctor and necromancer I could find. I even called in psychologists and therapists. No one has been able to heal his scars. Most can't even make a dent in them. Those that do find the scars growing anew as the skin repairs itself. I am confident that you can restore him. But if you make a valid attempt and still cannot help, I will be open to discussing the debt further."

"What happened to him?" David inquires, leaning a hip against the nightstand. Bastian walks over to the wardrobe, lightly running his fingers over the wood, carefully inspecting the natural imperfections in the grain.

"I was called overseas to be a guest to the new king's coronation. Every master vampire was to be in attendance. While I was gone my home was attacked by a rival clan." A deep sense of loss etches his handsome features, making his eyes seem even more blue. "During the attack my wife, Grace, was murdered, and several of our children were taken hostage. Poe was one of those taken." Bastian steadily stares at the wood before him. As he speaks his gaze is fixed upon some far distant place.

"What did they use to scar him like that? After two centuries most of the wounds should have healed on their own," Emma asks. A morbid fascination begins to grow as Emma tries to ascertain the cause.

"We think it was some kind of molten silver that was poured into molds placed against his skin. It channeled and held the burning liquid there as it cooled. Poe was the only one to survive, and even then, at that point, he was so weakened that I feared he would still perish. It took months for him to rebuild his strength so that he could even speak or eat. Some have suggested that he cannot heal because he blames himself for the deaths of his kin, for the death of Grace. I never blamed him for their deaths, but I think he feels responsible." Bastian finally looks back to Emma and David.

"What happened to the other clan?" David asks solemnly.

"I salted the earth with their ashes." Bastian's lips curl slightly as he recollects on his revenge.

"I still don't understand why you think I can help him." Emma's tone is cautious and guarded.

"Because when we were cleansing you, your hand must have rested on his face." Bastian's eyes wander down to Emma's tightly clenched hands. Emma fights the urge to hide her hands from his curious gaze. "Where your hand touched him, the scar flaked off, and underneath was his unmarred skin."

Emma and David's eyes meet as they each weigh their own options.

"If it will alleviate my debt I will try my best, though I cannot make any promises. I will also need a few things." Emma gathers her sweat jacket and heads toward the door, David already at her side.

"I will make sure you have everything you require." Bastian snaps at a waiting vampire as all three of them enter the hall.

After about twenty minutes everything that Emma had requested is assembled and waiting for her. They have once again filtered into the dark corridors of the basement, navigating several stone-walled hallways. Emma quickly assesses that the underground chambers encompass far more area than the upstairs house.

They walk by the open door to where her cleansing occurred. Emma refuses to look into the room. A few doors down they break off the main hallway and enter into a small side chamber. This location is bare as well, a mirror image of the other rooms, yet this space lacks the large area rug and the lighting sconces on the walls. The center of the room is well lit from above by a recessed light. Its dramatic ribbon of illumination showcases a simple wooden table and stool. A few wooden chairs stand against the walls. A vampire sorts and tidies items on the table. When he seems pleased with the set up he turns to address Bastian.

"Everything you have requested has been prepared, Father," he says with a formal bow.

"Thank you, Jonathan." Bastian dips his head in response to his servant-child.

"I will let you know when it is completed," Emma addresses Bastian.

"I would prefer to stay if you don't mind," he states with an unyielding resolve.

"Very well." Emma gestures to a seat along the wall. "We can begin when you are ready." Bastian turns, taking his seat. Emma walks over to the table inspecting each item. Everything that she will need is here: several towels, a basin of hot water, a glass tumbler, and a sharp dagger.

"Are you sure about this?" David whispers to her as she finishes her inventory.

"No, but all I want to do is leave this place behind, and if that means healing this vampire, then so be it." His concerned look is not eased by her words. Thick lines crease his forehead. "There is one thing that I can do very well, and that is to heal. If I can't heal him, then he cannot be healed."

David nods slowly and starts to back away.

"Please don't leave me, David." Emma's voice is barely a whisper. A powerful emotion claws at her chest as she watches him, a pained expression flashing in his eyes.

"Never," he replies softly as he stands with his back leaning against the wall.

Through the open door Poe enters the room. His black t-shirt appears almost a deep navy blue under the lights. His feet are bare, and even the denim of his jeans makes no sound. He stops just before Emma, his gaze cast downward. Emma can sense the tension rolling off of him.

"Are you ready?" she asks softly. His eyes stay glued to the floor as he nods. "Poe, please look at me."

Emma waits patiently as he slowly pries his stare from the floor to meet hers. His expression is impassive and unyielding. Emma can see beneath the façade there is a primal emotion hiding there just below the surface. Reflecting back at her from the deep black wells of his eyes is fear. Perhaps it is fear that this attempt will be yet another failure, or even fear that they may actually succeed.

"Do you want me to try to heal you?"

A brief look of confusion flashes over his face, but he squares his shoulders, watching her with a sense of determination.

"Yes." He simply nods to her. As the light hits his face, Emma can make out five fingerprint marks on his cheek. Underneath, perfect skin peeks through.

"Ok." Emma examines his exposed arms and face. The skin appears to have been burnt then healed, then burnt then healed again. Progressive scarring, which gives the tissue a melted look in some areas. Several long bands of scars run up his arms, hiding under the sleeves of the shirt. The scarring may very well crisscross his entire body.

Emma's mouth is arid as she tries to clear her throat. For some unknown reason she is more nervous than she expected.

"First, I need to know the extent of the damage and its location."

Poe must have picked up on her nervousness, as he flashes her a seductive smile. In a swift single motion he pulls his shirt over his head. Despite the massive scarring, his physique is well toned. The realization, that this brutally attractive man could very well strip down to nothing in front of her hits her like a punch to the stomach. Her peculiar nervousness seems well justified now. Emma's eyes lock on his as he unbuttons his jeans, letting them drop to the floor. The smooth lines of his body are uninterrupted. The lack of any contrasting color lets her know, without looking, that he isn't wearing any underwear.

Cautiously, Emma begins to circle Poe, and with a concerted effort she keeps her gaze from trickling too low. The damage seems to be primarily localized to his face, torso, and arms. A small splatter of raised scars dances across his upper thighs. Chancing a scant look south, she quickly determines that his manhood is thankfully unmarred. Her cheeks burn as her eyes rise and catch Poe watching her smugly.

"Please, sit." Emma coughs as she motions to the stool. An irritating skitter of nerves causes the slightest of tremors to ramble through her. As Poe sits, Emma stands at the table next to him. Breathing slowly, she concentrates on the rising wisps of steam coming from the large bowl of water.

"Do you know why all the other methods to heal you have failed?" she asked Poe from over her shoulder.

"No." His voice echoes through the silent room.

"They failed because they were trying to heal a dead body."

Her tone is smooth and soothing as she plucks the blade from the table, testing its sharpness.

"To successfully heal you, we must first bring your body back to life." Glancing again over her shoulder, Emma nearly laughs at his dumbfounded look of disbelief. "Now bear in mind that the results will not be permanent. As of yet I know no cure for vampirism. But I tell you this because the old sensations of life flowing back into your body can be a little disorienting. Just remember, you will need to breathe."

Turning back to the table, she makes a small slice down the palm of her hand. As the blood wells she drips it into the short glass. When it is roughly half full she dips her hands into the hot water and the wound seals shut. A red plume of blood blooms in the basin as it is dispersed in the water.

Pivoting, she offers the glass to Poe, which he takes with a steady hand. "Drink all of it," she prompts him softly.

Closing his eyes, he downs the glass of viscous red fluid in several throaty gulps. Within seconds his skin flushes and his lungs expel an anguished gasp. His wide eyes stare into her as his pants for breath become erratic. Emma kneels next to him, laying a hand on his arm.

"Breathe, breathe. Remember, in then out. Stay calm and it will be alright." Emma continues her comforting chant as his breathing slows to a normal rhythm.

Once she is certain his respiration is under control she returns to the table. Dipping the hand towel in the basin, the material quickly becomes saturated. She squeezes out the excess water and returns to Poe's side, towel in hand. With the lightest touch she begins to wipe down the scarred skin of his arms and chest. Slowly she releases a small amount of energy, allowing it to flow gently from her to him. After each area of his body has been wetted she submerges the towel then wrings it out again. Approaching Poe, she now focuses on the skin of his face and neck. Around each line and curve she covers the affected areas several times. When she is done the skin is glossy with a thin layer of water.

Grabbing a dry, soft towel, Emma pats the skin dry, dabbing at the skin until there is no water left. Under the stark lighting of the basement room his skin appears to grow paler, thinner. The flaking layers of dead skin start to pull away from his body as it dries. Touching a bit of scaly skin on his shoulder, the exterior tissue crumbles, falling away and exposing underneath, intact skin that is free of any scars. She repeats the process all over his body, blowing softly on some stubborn places. Her breath gliding over his skin sends slivers of shed skin dancing into the air. His face and neck are a little more work, as there are many more crevasses and creases. After several minutes Emma steps back to study Poe.

Glancing over to Bastian she nods as he stands and steps forward with trepidation. The elder vampire cautiously circles his child, searching for any defect. As he seems to be satisfied, he bends over looking directly into Poe's eyes and placing a soft hand on his shoulder.

"You're good, Poe. It's all gone," Bastian stammers through a well of emotions. Glancing at Poe, Emma can see the light reflecting from his unshed tears. Poe stands as Bastian helps him. The two men embrace as old friends sharing the simple joy of becoming whole again. Emma, feeling excessively drained, makes her way back to her room and falls into a deep, restless sleep.

Chapter 25

After a few fretfully restless hours of sleep Emma awakens, exhausted and irritable. She is so drained from a constant lack of quality rest that she is in a quite ill-tempered mood. She is keenly aware that the sun has finally set, and hears a growing bustle of activity throughout the house. Errant voices and footfalls echo into her room. Despite her grouchy feelings she can see that this lair seems remarkably different from any of the others that she has experienced. While other clans thrive on opportunistic manipulations, these vampires appear to be a very close-knit group of individuals, highly relying on one another. Unfortunately, as interesting as they are, she really doesn't want to stay any longer then she must.

She knows that some distance and time away from the Mothers should help her to process everything that has transpired over the last several days. Yet, deep down, Emma also knows that now is the worst time to abandon them. Her issues with Mei Li and Tatiana will have to wait for another day. Especially when there is still so much that needs to be done. They still have to find Olivia and determine what can be done about Thanatos. And as much as she wants to be selfish and leave all this mess behind, she can't. Not now. A nervous agitation bubbles in her blood, prompting a need to bolt for the door. She breathes deeply as she reins in the emotions that are playing havoc with her, reminding herself that she had promised David she would wait for him. Upon arriving back to the safety of this room, word was sent that the Mothers needed to see David. Emma recalled the look of dread that flashed in his eyes, but he left reluctantly. He asked that she wait here, and when she agreed he told her he would return as quickly as he could. That was nearly a half an hour ago. Firmly, she has decided to bide her time a little while longer before she goes to find him.

Emma loads her empty plate on a brass tray. The serving dish is intricate with an etched hunting scene on it. Emma hadn't cared about the filigree when Jillian had arrived with her food. The hunger pangs were intense and immediate. The turkey sandwich, while simple, tasted wonderful. Emma sarcastically laughs to herself as she muses that having food in her belly must mean the night is looking up for her.

A small knock sounds from the frame of her open door. Looking up, Emma stares at Mei Li, who is standing ever proper in the archway. While dark circles ring Mei Li's eyes, her silken black tresses are pinned in an elaborately interwoven bun at the nape of her neck. Emma's smile fades as she watches the Mother cautiously.

"May I enter?" Mei Li asks softly.

Emma nods.

The fatigue from the night is suddenly weighing heavily on Mei Li as her arms hang weakly by her sides. "Bastian wishes to convey his gratitude for your help." Mei Li's gaze is unflinching as she walks. Her countenance is regal and majestic as always, but there is a subtle hint of a cautious hesitation as she glides into the room.

"Are you his messenger now?" Emma asks coldly, making no attempt to hide the bitterness flowing through her as she sits down on the bed with a flop.

"No," Mei Li snaps in response. Her anger flares as she looks fiercely at Emma. "I just thought that you would like to know." She nervously rubs the knuckles of her right hand.

"I would very much like to explain what you saw back there. Our decisions... My decisions." Mei Li corrects herself.

"Maybe I don't much care to hear your excuses." The bite of Emma's tone cuts cleanly through the air.

"I understand that you are a little hurt, but now is not the time for this." Mei Li's tone turns stern with impatience.

"You think I'm a little hurt, huh? Is that what you think this is all about?" Emma spits, her volume louder than normal, but she doesn't really care.

"What is this about then?" Mei Li shoots back with her own venom.

"For all these years I have endured the shame, the guilt, and the cruel judgments. I have been ostracized and made out to be this shameful monster that you all must endure. And I allowed all of this because I fooled myself into believing that no matter what, there was somehow a small hope that I could belong. But that will never happen, will it?" Emma chokes on the words as they rip through her. "From the very start you decided that I would never be one of you."

"I have always tried my best to be fair, to put the interests of the Fury and justice before everything else, even my own needs. You have no idea about the amount of pressure we are all under. Do you understand how much is riding on my shoulders?" Mei Li seethes as her voice pitches to a hushed scream.

"Do you want to know what I understand?" Emma hisses as an intolerable aching rage slithers its way through her chest. "I understand that I have dedicated my existence to the Fury and everything we fight for. I also understand the inevitable excruciating truth that the Fury can so easily throw me into the river as it suits them. Yet for how many years have I heard you expound about never letting one Fury fall or be left behind? But you did. You chose to abandon me. You left me to suffer, for centuries, in the arms of that monster, and the whole time you could have saved me. When I needed you the most, you weren't there. Do you even understand what I went through?" Emma huffs loudly as she staves off the urge to either run or hit Mei Li. Hugging her knees, Emma stares at Mei Li's feet and prays that she could just disappear. She breathes deeply, pushing down the part of herself that wants to draw on her power.

Mei Li exhales a deep sigh of exhaustion as she sits on the bed next to Emma. Mei Li suddenly seems ages older than she is. She rubs vigorously at her face as if that could banish the rigorous responsibilities cast upon her shoulders. "As I walked down here to speak with you I tried to determine the precise words to make things right between you and I. I thought about the inspiring principles of honor and the greater good. I thought about the unknown and how we can be so easily swayed by fear. The problem is that every thought, every well-meaning speech that came to my mind seemed like a ridiculous excuse, a shallow and meaningless ploy to shield the fact of the matter."

Emma stares wordlessly as Mei Li's eyes glisten under the soft lights. "A Mother has a great deal of responsibilities and one of the most important duties we have is to protect our children. In this respect I have failed you. We allowed ourselves to be convinced that leaving you would be the best course to take, as we didn't know what you were. I have had to make many difficult decisions as a Mother. I regret none of them save this one." Mei Li stares at Emma as a bleak and consigned sorrow spans the distance between them. The Mother's eyes are mournful, yet fervent with desperation.

"What made you change your mind…, About coming for me?" Emma asks, her head tilting to the side as she studies Mei Li's face.

"At some point you started giving off a great deal of energy. We sensed it growing and that's when we realized our mistake. That is when we set out to find you." Mei Li touches the copper band encircling Emma's upper arm. It catches the light, shimmering back with a warm glow. "I knew that because I had wronged you and we needed to make every endeavor to keep you safe, to make sure he never found you again. I know that it will take a lot to gain your forgiveness. Just know that at the time I truly thought I made the correct decision."

Emma clasps Mei Li's hand, which is still resting on her arm. Several seconds of silence pass between them as Emma weighs the words of Mei Li's admission. "For myself, I am trying to work through everything that has happened. Understanding the reality of your decision will take time. I may not be able to completely trust you as I did before, but I will do my duty," Emma tells Mei Li firmly.

"Good," Mei Li says with a soft nod of her head. "I hope after time that we can work to repair the damage that has been done."

"Perhaps," Emma answers as she battles back the flood of emotions. The overwhelming desire to escape is still there as it pushes to the forefront of her mind. She tamps it down as Mei Li rises from the bed.

"We should head to Bastian's office now, if that's alright?" Mei Li asks cautiously as uncertainty washes through her lovely dark brown eyes.

"Why are we going there?" Emma asks, standing.

"We need to figure out what is going on with Ambrose... I mean Thanatos." Mei Li shakes her head. "We also need to save Olivia and potentially the world, and hopefully we can do this without anyone else dying."

"Sounds simple enough, let's go." Emma nods and gestures toward the door as they both head out.

They walk wordlessly through the halls until reaching Bastian's door. Everyone turns to stare at them as they enter Bastian's office. David is quietly talking with Poe as they stand by a large bay window. Outside, the silent, deathly-cold winter bears down on the thick panes of glass as crystals of frost gather in the corners of each window. A large fire roars, pushing warmth throughout the room. Bastian stares blankly at papers strewn about his desk.

Tatiana looms over him, a sour scowl creasing her noble features. Standing from his chair, Bastian rushes over to greet them as if he is relieved to see them. Tatiana's overbearing nature is wearing thin on the vampire's nerves.

"Ah, you are here." He sweeps over to them. "My gratitude is yours, Emma. Consider your debt paid in full. You have healed my child and brought him peace." He nods his head, his eyes brimming with wondered amazement. Emma gapes silently at him until Mei Li gently elbows her in the side.

"You're most welcome," Emma stammers, and is jolted out of her uncertainty. As she has never encountered an admiring vampire before, the appropriate response eluded her. Mei Li ushers Emma farther into the office as Bastian returns to his seat. Tatiana lasers Emma with a spiteful glare, her disgust apparent, yet she says nothing.

"After some discussion we have decided that the best course of action is to first rescue Olivia," Mei Li tells them calmly. Her emotional flare from earlier neatly stowed away. "I believe that David and I should sneak back into The Hallow and search for her. When we locate her we will bring her back here."

"You are not serious, are you?" Emma looks at them aghast. "Just the two of you would be suicide."

"Not suicide. Fewer people will draw less attention. And David can handle the stragglers we do encounter. And I am not totally defenseless when it comes to protecting myself," Mei Li counters with a determined set to her chin.

"I'll go with you then. One more shouldn't draw that much more attention," Emma blurts out. Her stomach begins to knot as she glances between Mei Li and David.

"No, because we need someone here to guard Bastian and Tatiana. It's his blood that they are after as well," Mei Li says, shaking her head.

"Then maybe I should go with you, and David stay here and protect them?" Emma's mind starts to spin as she frantically searches for a solution that doesn't involve David being at risk.

"No," Both Mei Li and David say in unison.

"David is impressive, but we need a strong Fury here at the mansion." Mei Li's expression and voice are stern and calculating. Emma's gaze glides of its own will to Tatiana, who instantly fluffs her feathers in indignation.

"Strength is not always measured by one's ability to fight. Knowledge and cunning are my weapons, and they work quite well," she huffs as she folds her arms across her chest.

"I could always go." Poe's voice is deep as it draws everyone's attention.

"No," Bastian barks.

"But they are threatening you." Poe shakes his head aghast at Bastian's quick denial.

"Yes, they do threaten me. They threaten my life and the lives of my family." Bastian's tone and energy bellows throughout the room. "I will not stand by cowering while others charge into the fray. Not if I want to remain your father." His eyes soften as he looks at Poe.

"If you are killed trying to rescue this other Fury then what will stop them from coming here in force anyway?" Poe questions coolly.

"We are trying to keep you alive, not throw you into the lion's den," Mei Li warns, placing her hands flat on Bastian's desk to meet his stare.

"I will go with you," Bastian commands stubbornly, his gaze swinging to Emma. "I trust she will do her best to ensure the safety of my children." Mei Li shifts uncomfortably, searching for a response. Tatiana's hand falls lightly on Mei Li's shoulder.

"He is right, unfortunately. This would appear to make the most sense. A clandestine assault, or at least a preemptive strike might be the most advantageous. And Bastian has more power and experience than Poe." She simply smirks with a shrug of her shoulders at Poe's sour face. "David is strong, but with him alone you are sure to fail. Emma should stay here so that the lair is not left unguarded." She frowns at Emma again. "Between Emma and Poe we should be adequately safe here." Mei Li scans the room, looking at everyone directly, stopping on David.

"What do you think, David?" she asks with a tired voice.

"Any way you slice this, I don't like it. And I've got a bad feeling about this. But it doesn't seem like we have any other options." He scrubs his beard hairs in frustration.

"I guess that's that then." Mei Li heaves a heavy sigh. "Pack light, we leave within the hour." Clutching her hands tightly together, Mei Li heads toward the exit with Tatiana trailing closely behind her. As they reach the door Tatiana grabs at Mei Li's arm. Though she cannot make out the words, Emma can see the heated expression on Tatiana's face and hear the sharpness of her tone.

Poe and Bastian stalk over to a set of weapon display cases. Producing a small brass ring of keys, Bastian unlocks several of the cases, lifting the solid glass lids and propping them up. He withdraws a machete, four jeweled daggers, a Luger pistol, a Taser, a shot gun, and several boxes of ammo.

"Quite an arsenal you have there," David says with a whistle.

"When facing overwhelming odds, two things in life are certain– you can never have too much knowledge or too much ammo." His eyebrow raises high. Both vampires laugh as they exit the room carrying their weapons store.

"He may not be all that far off," Emma muses as she rubs her arms, trying to abate the growing chill in her bones.

"Our goal is simple– sneak in and sneak out. The best-case scenario is that we avoid detection. Worst-case scenario is that it may get a little messy. But we will be prepared for either outcome." He casually studies the contents of several display cases.

"It'll be alright as long as all of those outcomes bring you all back safely. What if you are captured, or worse?" Her voice quakes as she struggles to meet his gaze. A vise-like ache seizes her chest, stealing her breath. He picks up on the concern that is resonating from her and closes the distance between them, pulling her in close.

"Emma, I'm not going anywhere. If I had my way I'd stay here with you. Or better yet, we'd leave this place right now." Softly he presses his lips to her forehead. "I know that you are worried. Believe me, I know you. But also know that not even death will stop me from being at your side, keeping you safe."

"But that's what worries me the most. We are fighting death. Can death even be killed? How do we face something like this and survive? I lost Sara. I've lost so many, and you've become so important to me. I may not survive if I lose you as well." His expression is pained as he holds her tightly, pressing her further into his chest. Both of their hearts race, the beats syncopated into a crazed tempo. "Just promise that you'll make it back here in one piece. If the situation turns bad, just get out of there," Emma whispers. She can feel her eyes are heavy with suspended tears. Leaning back, David lifts her chin so that she has to look into his eyes. The strength and softness reflecting back in his gaze warms her throughout.

"I promise you that I will try my best." The warmth of his breath dances along her skin, raising gooseflesh.

"Try not. Do," she says with a weak smile, wiping away the unruly wetness.

"Well, I worry about you being here alone" His look is intense with a deep well of emotion brimming just below the surface. Softly, he touches her face. A skitter of nervous energy flows through her. She raises her own hand, placing it over his as it rests on her cheek.

"I'm not really alone. And my biggest concern here is getting bored." Emma laughs anxiously, trying and failing to break the building tension. But her breath hitches as

David's stare lowers to her mouth, an unusual smirk curling his lips.

"I've always loved your laugh, even when you're nervous." Her voice catches in her throat. Even if she could speak, the words are failing her. Leaning his head down his lips graze hers with a feather-soft kiss. The kiss is chaste, and he quickly pulls back, watching her silently. He sighs deeply before releasing her. "I should prepare myself as well." He lingers for a few seconds before turning and leaves the room. Once alone, Emma touches her lips, silently praying for the man who has become her world.

Chapter 26

❧

Emma wanders aimlessly through the numerous halls of
the mansion. It has been several hours since Mei Li,
David, and Bastian left to go on their rescue mission of
Olivia. With her insides churning in a tangled web of
knots, Emma knows that sleep will not easily come tonight.
After a hot shower and some food, she finds herself
succumbing to concurrent boredom and nervous energy.
All the inhabitants of the house are elsewhere, leaving
Emma alone and free to roam. Much of the house is
shrouded in darkness– unlit corridors and empty rooms.
An unnerving agitation needles at her mind. There is a
foreboding sense of something dark and dangerous
lingering just outside the walls. The hair on her arms
stands on edge, and she desperately searches for some kind
of distraction from the growing tension. Making her way
through the many hallways, she checks and secures all of
the points of entry. The house has only one main entrance
and a service door in the kitchen out to the conservatory.
The back door is a viable escape route, but is also a passage
that needs to be secured.

Pushing open a heavy wooden door, Emma enters an
impressive library. The two-story room is completely filled
from floor to ceiling with shelves of books. Softly, the
door closes behind her with a tiny click. Several
chandeliers and recessed lights illuminate the space in soft

incandescent light. A long conference table lined with straight-backed chairs on each side spans the length of the floor. A ladder for accessing higher books rests in its rail. A thin layer of dust coats the books, shelves, and flat surfaces. Everything in the library appears undisturbed. Like an ancient ruin left undiscovered for centuries.

Emma walks along one of the nearest bookshelves noting the varied titles. The section of classic fiction includes the complete works of Shakespeare, Shelley, Chaucer, and poems by Alfred Noyes, Emerson, and Dylan Thomas. Each book seems to be in very good condition despite its apparent age. The worn yellowing pages smell of earth and ink.

Emma pauses as she comes across another selection of books. These seem to be relating to Greek and Roman mythology. Scanning the titles, Emma pulls out a book and thumbs through the index and chapters. Inwardly she prays that she can find something to help them with Thanatos. As she flops down in an overstuffed chair, a plume of dust puffs into the air. Turning page after page, she searches for answers. Emma huffs in frustration as she places the book on an end table next to her. None of the information seems useful, or at the very least it just reiterates everything they already know.

Catching some movement in her peripheral vision, Emma glances up to see Poe standing in the open doorway watching her. She is a little unnerved that she didn't hear the door opening. His skin is flawless and Emma notes that his scars make him appear much older than he really is. Now Emma can distinguish his age at around thirty or so.

"Grace, our mother, loved this library," Poe observes solemnly as his gaze sweeps around the long-forgotten room. "She loved to read and believed that knowledge is one's greatest weapon. Anyone who came to live here needed to at least know how to read. If you couldn't read, she would teach you." His lips lift lightly at the memory.

"Her passing must have been very difficult for you," Emma murmurs softly. Poe slowly enters the room, cautiously taking an adjacent seat from Emma.

"Yes. She was like a mother to me… to us all. She was hard when she needed to be and soft when she needed to be. We loved and respected her. When she came to live with us this place became a home, and we a family." He stares silently at a long row of books next to him. "My family life when I was a child was cold and structured. My parents methodically planned every aspect of my life. I was simply a pawn to use as they vied for more money and power. So when I could, I ran away. I signed on as a powder monkey on a pirate galleon and spent the remainder of my childhood sailing on the open seas. I was my own man. I was part of a brotherhood. But unfortunately, I had no family. Not until Bastian found me."

"If you don't mind me asking, why did the other clan attack you?" Emma asks, keeping her tone soft and nonthreatening.

"It depends on who you ask," Poe says flatly. His monotone voice is devoid of even a hint of emotion. "Some say it was because Bastian was growing in strength and prestige. You see, Bastian is a lot smarter than most. He found he could gain more of an advantage through diplomacy and trade than he could through sheer violence alone. He chose his battles and his friends wisely, and he advanced, moving his way up the court. But others say they attacked us simply because they could."

"Which do you think it was?" Emma asks.

"I don't think it was either." Poe grins derisively. He sighs deeply, all emotion slipping away again. His emotions flare and fade in rapid succession.

"What was it then?" she poses, slowly peeling back the layers of the mystery.

"The Master of the other clan desired Grace, wanted her for his own. He thought that Grace was the key to Bastian's success. In a way she was, but not how he thought she was. But she rejected him," Poe answered coldly.

"So he killed her," Emma whispers as Poe battles his long buried memories. The memories of her own loss surge forward and stir some troublesome emotions.

"Eventually he did kill her, but not until after he forced her to witness our methodical torture." Poe looks away, unable to meet her gaze. Trying to calm his nerves, he breathes in deeply.

"It is very difficult to watch your family being hurt." Emma senses an unusual bond with this woman whom she has never met, Grace, who had been a mother to them.

"She was pierced by the Blade of Saint Michael and staked to a wall overlooking us. We were meant to watch her die as she watched us dying as well." Poe's voice shakes in sync with the small tremors skittering through his hands.

"I am not familiar with the Blade of Saint Michael. What is it?" she inquires, having no memory of such a relic.

"A dagger carved from a yew tree and said to be dipped in the blood of Saint Michael." Emma shakes her head as she tries to piece together his meaning. Poe, sensing her confusion, continues. "To be pierced by the dagger coated in an archangel's blood is a death sentence. No magic can save you or heal the wound. But the catch is that you will live as long as the dagger remains buried within your flesh. As soon as it is removed, you will die."

"So you were powerless to help her and you blame yourself for her death?" She speaks demurely and gauges Poe's response.

"Of course I do." His expression is aghast. "Bastian left me in charge. Who else would the responsibility fall upon but me?" A heavy silence falls between them. "I understand why you may not trust vampires," he whispers sheepishly. "But just to let you know, not all vampires are like the monster that hurt you and your family."

"How do you know about that?" Emma asks, her voice trembling and her mouth suddenly dry.

"During the cleansing," he confesses despondently, "your memories flowed out from you, washing over me. The vision was so vivid it was like being there." He studies the floor, shaking his head.

"And you still let me try and heal you. Weren't you afraid I would take out some misplaced sense of revenge on you?" she questions with a lift of an eyebrow.

"I knew it could be a possibility," he answers with a light shrug. "But Bastian had faith in you, and that was good enough for me. Plus sometimes to build trust you must be the one to give your trust."

Glass shatters and disrupts the tranquil silence of the library. It is followed by a terrifying shriek that reverberates down the hall. Emma and Poe shoot up to their feet and dash down the corridor toward the sound of screams, which seem to be coming from Bastian's office. Emma pauses briefly as she becomes keenly aware of a distant yet familiar presence, someone she knows and is unsettles by is dangerously close. It is akin to a fragrance that is unrecognizable as it dances along her skin.

Pushing open the heavy oaken doors, they rush into the devastated office, the debris of fractured glass crackling and breaking under their feet. A pane of glass in the bay window has been broken, and the opening channels sub-zero air into the room. The seemingly impervious wall-safe is a mangled wreck. The thick iron door swings precariously from a single bolt. The enclosed area within is empty, the contents gone. As Emma rounds the writing table to look out the window, she spots two long legs splattered in thick blood on the floor behind the desk.

Jillian's throat has been slashed open, but the stream of blood that courses from it is already starting to slow. As Emma approaches she can see that the wound, while bloody, is stitching itself closed. Her eyes are wild with fear and rising panic. Poe kneels, scooping up Jillian in his arms. He carries her out of the office, into the hall where there is a small open area for sitting. Poe gently places Jillian on a chaise and pulls a blanket over her. Jillian begins to calm. The wound will not kill her, but she is noticeably weakened.

"What is going on?" Poe asks, his eyes a pair of shimmering onyx.

"It seems that we've been attacked. I have to find Tatiana." Emma spins as her mind races. She has no idea where Tatiana is, but she has to find her.

Before Emma can cross over the threshold into the hallway she hears a muffled scream resonating from outside. Dashing across the room, Emma crouches, pressing against the wall next to the shattered window. Craning her neck, Emma chances a glance outside.

A jet-black SUV sits in the cleared driveway. Several outside lights illuminate the road and walkways, bathing them in a stark white light. Its blacked-out windows offer no view of the inhabitants. The scene around the vehicle is an utterly desolate snowy landscape. Emma watches as the driver's side door opens as a blustery wind swirls around the vehicle. Moss steps around the front of the truck, his black hair whipping furiously about in the wind. From across the yard Emma can make out the deep purple-black bruise nestled in the inner corners of his eyes. She recalls breaking his nose earlier.

"Emma, come on out. We know you're in there," Moss's voice bellows over the howling winds.

A rush of panic washes over Emma. Poe stares at her, a questioning look in his eyes.

"Don't worry, I'll take care of this. I just have to figure out a plan," Emma whispers as she scans the room. Twisting her neck, Emma checks on the SUV again. Moss hasn't moved, but five more Gyges exit the vehicle. One of them is struggling with a darkened figure. As they step out under the lights, Emma instantly recognizes Tatiana. Her screams carry over the gusting wind as an incoherent rambling.

"Let Tatiana go," Emma shouts through the window. Moss's gaze pinpoints onto the window where Emma is hiding.

"No way, not gonna happen. Can you imagine my luck? Having a Mother is worth their weight in gold, and Thanatos is gonna be happier than a pig." Moss walks over, grabbing Tatiana roughly by the arm, an evil smile creasing his face. "But I am willing to make a trade. Thanatos wants to talk to you, so if you come out I may let her go. If you don't come out, then Tatiana dies and we're still coming in. And if you push the issue, we will kill everything and everyone in that house."

"If I come out, you'll let Tatiana go? Why would I trust you?" Emma yells. Poe grabs her arm, glaring at her.

"Are you insane? You can't be thinking of going out there," he rasps through clenched teeth.

"Just trust me. I may have a plan. I'm not going to let anyone get hurt," Emma whispers quietly to Poe. She knows that Mei Li and Bastian are counting on her to keep these people safe.

"That woman out there hates you. Why risk everything to save her?" Poe asks incredulously. The soft snowfall that blows through the broken window settles and begins to melt in his hair.

"She may hate me, but she is still a Mother. Her rank and title mean that she holds a great deal of significance. My life is worth nothing compared to hers. If I let her die to save myself, what will that say about me? I promised to protect her." Emma's words are cool and determined.

"No, I imagine you can't trust me. But the alternative is death for you all. Dawn will be coming soon, and your vampire friends won't be able to help you," Moss's voice calls out from the night, echoing across the trees.

"Ok, I'm coming out. You release Tatiana," Emma shouts into a large, frigid gust.

"No," Moss barks back at her. "I'll walk Tatiana halfway up the driveway. You come out, and when I see you walking I'll release her. Try to take off with her, and I've some copper filled buck shot with her name on it," he shouts as he drags Tatiana about with one massive hand. His other hand holds a double-barrel shotgun.

"Ok, I'm going to the front door," Emma shouts. Quickly she turns to Poe. "Take your shirt off," she calmly orders.

"What?!" Poe's shocked expression stares back at her. "Emma, you don't have to go out there. We can fight them. We certainly outnumber them. I can't let this happen, not like this." Something that is akin to frustration and panic flashes across his features. His eyes soften under the dim light.

"The Gyges have trained for years to kill. There are too many of them for me to take on and win. If I stay in here they will kill Tatiana, then come in and kill everyone else. It will be a slaughter. I don't see another way out of this, and we are running out of time. I will not risk anyone in this house. Just listen to me and take it off, please," Emma pleads. Poe studies her in silence for several seconds before pulling his shirt off. Emma grabs a shard of broken glass as they leave the office heading toward the front door.

"Before I go I need you to do something for me." Emma breathes as she looks from Poe to the door, then makes a thin slice into the palm of her hand, wincing from the stinging sensation. The blood oozes slowly from the small cut. Using the shirt, she sops up some of the blood. Closing her eyes, she allows a trickling of power into the blood-laden cloth and whispers the sealing words. An old incantation Mother Agnes taught her. The sealing spell will remain active as long as she redirects her strength to maintaining it. Even when she does release it, the effects will take some time to dissipate. Unfortunately, while it is up she won't be able to access that power to defend herself, but there is no point in telling Poe that. Emma pushes the bloody cloth into Poe's hands. "Once I leave and Tatiana is safely inside the house, I want you to take this and touch it to all the openings in the house— windows and doors. It will bar the entrances so that only a Fury may cross the threshold. They won't be able to enter the house, and it will keep you protected until Mei Li and David return."

Emma steps out onto the landing, where an arctic gust of wind steals her breath away. The fierce gales push against her, threatening her footing. Flecks of ice and snow fall silently to the ground as they shimmer under the lights. Emma's heart pounds in her throat. She watches as Moss makes his way up the drive, dragging Tatiana with him.

"Do we have an understanding, Moss? A fair trade, me for Tatiana," Emma shouts into the blustery weather. The bitter cold starts to seep in, making her teeth chatter as she speaks.

"Of course, little cat." Moss nods to her.

After a brief pause Moss releases his hold and Tatiana starts the slow walk toward the house. Emma shakes uncontrollably as she forces her legs to move. Her vision focuses on Tatiana, and despite her impulse to run, she walks at a steady pace forward. As the distance closes, a tiny whisper hums in Emma's ear telling her to flee. But with a deep breath she pushes the sound away. Emma and Tatiana meet at the midway point. Tatiana's hair and clothes are disheveled, and there is a bruise fading from her cheek. A billowing blanket flutters around her, which she pinches closed with one hand as she glides along.

"Hurry up and get inside. You'll be safe in there," Emma whispers as they stand abreast. Tatiana's arm flies outward, clasping Emma's forearm. Emma's skin tingles as an old power skitters along her flesh. It causes no real pain, but her limbs feel numb and heavier than before. Her mind and body seem slow to react, and even the rise of panic moves at a languorous pace.

"I think I misjudged you. I had my doubts that you would actually come out to save me. It is truly refreshing to know that my wellbeing is of such importance to you. It is a pity though, that there is no one to look out for you." Tatiana's face hardens as her voice turns icy cold. Her hand claws painfully hard at Emma's. Tatiana swings the hidden club with lightning speed and deadly accuracy. Emma tries to pull away, but her body is paralyzed. The club makes contact with her temple with a sickening thud. Emma's legs give out as the world spins around. Lying on the ground, the snow underneath her is a distant and cloudy sensation. Warm blood seeps down her neck and inky blackness flows into her vision. Tatiana stands over her with a fiercely wild and triumphant look in her eyes. She and Moss stand side-by-side as a blanket of darkness engulfs Emma.

Chapter 27

As the world trickles back into Emma's awareness, the throbbing of her head sends her stomach into somersaults. Nausea skitters through her, closing her throat. She is being pulled by her arms as her bare feet skim along the cold stone floor. After several seconds she manages to lift her eyes and squint against the harsh light around her. Her gaze morphs rapidly between blurry and focused as the world around her pushes forward and then recedes. Looking up at the two men dragging her, she can tell that they are Gyges and can sense their underlying power, but she cannot recall their names.

A ring of iron keys jingle and reverberate against the metal lock of a cell. Two sets of strong hands brutishly shove her into the small, barred prison. She stumbles into the room but manages to catch herself before falling. As the door clangs shut behind her she cautiously makes her way over to a small cot. She tries shaking the cobwebs from her mind, but the jarring movement induces bolts of white hot pain to crack through her skull. It seems more and more that as she wakes from these befuddled states her mind and body are slower to recover.

Breathing deeply, she slowly opens her eyes and they begin to focus on her surroundings. The first thing she notes is that her clothes have been changed. She is wearing a simple white Stola which leaves the majority of her upper arms exposed. The soft fabric flows around her in a series of soft layers. Emma's hands flutter upward, touching lightly her throat, where she finds the thick bands of the copper collar. She grimaces as the metal scrapes along the raw skin of her neck. It hums and pulses as it deflects energy out and away from her.

Her scope of awareness pushes past her immediate area. Her cell is barred on three sides and is one in a line of many similar holding units. The shared back wall is carved out of solid stone. Two long rows of cells run parallel down the length of the underground prison. The cells across the way and to her left are occupied by a few Gyges, none of them seeming familiar. Her stomach plummets as her gaze sweeps to the containment area next to her. Bastian sits against the far wall, his face bloodied and dirt-smeared. His one arm is shackled to the wall, the silver handcuffs eating away and searing his flesh. A larger, bewildering form lies prone on the ground next to him. Even through dirt that cakes the figure Emma can make out the soft coffee-colored hair that catches the light despite the gloominess of the dungeon. Rushing to the bars, Emma reaches through, but only her fingertips graze the cloth of David's blood-stained shoulder.

"David," she harshly whispers, her throat compressing shut. "Bastian!" She forces the words out in a shrieking cry. Bastian's eyes flutter open and settle on her. As he recognizes her, his crystal blue eyes are awash with an untold wretchedness. "Bastian, what happened to David?" She tries to work moisture back into her parched mouth. Stretching, she tries to reach for him. The bars dig painfully into her shoulders, but she pushes forward.

"They knew we were coming. There were too many of them. They took Mei Li." His voice is rough and graveled. "David will be fine, you just need to give him time."

"Time for what? I need to help him, Bastian, please," Emma pleads as a growing hysteria builds within her, her arms starting to tremble under the strain.

"I'm sorry, Emma. They cut him so deeply and there was no way to stop the bleeding. There was only one way to save him. Emma, you need to get away from him." His voice cracks as he cautions her.

David's hand launches out toward her, clamping down around her wrist and yanking her against the bars, her fingers going numb against the pain. Slowly he rolls over and Emma must quell the urge to scream. The front of his shirt is saturated in wet, oozing blood. But it is the change in his eyes that nearly stops her heart. They glow with the uncanny aura that she has seen too many times– a look that can only be that of a vampire. Even with her muted strength she can detect the undead presence wafting off of him.

"What have you done to him?" Emma screams at Bastian, though her eyes remain planted on David.

"They had killed him. All I could do to help was to turn him," Bastian pleads, desperately trying to make her see.

"Why would you do this to him?" The cold numbness of loss settles over Emma as she tries to digest what has happened.

"He kept saying he couldn't leave you," Bastian mutters softly, his voice thick with a fluid emotion.

"David," Emma whispers, meeting his stark, lifeless gaze. "David, can you hear me?"

"He doesn't recognize you. He's just been turned, and it will take a bit of time for him to regain his memories. The hunger will set in soon and he'll need to feed," Bastian warns. Emma stares down to where David's now cool flesh touches hers. A low guttural growl rumbles in David's chest as sharp fangs glint under the weak light. Emma's lungs constrict with a ragged pain, not knowing if she will have to kill him. Will it come down to her ending his life as she has done with so many others? She isn't sure she has it in her to kill him. Deep within him there must be something left of the man that she has grown to cherish.

"David, it's me, Emma." Her mouth is arid, and she searches his eyes for any hint of recognition. "You know me, David, come back to me." Her free hand clasps his over her arm. She knows that David must be somewhere in there. Her stomach clenches, and there is a painful tightening in her throat at the thought that he could be gone.

For several minutes they remain this way, locked together, silently watching and waiting. Emma is pulled up against the bars as she whispers gently to David, holding his hand. While his grasp stays firmly planted, his body seems to slacken and his head lists from side to side. His eyelids lower, and Emma can't be certain if he has fallen asleep. Emma tries to gingerly remove her arm from his vise-like grip, but his fingers won't give way. Seconds away from yanking at her arm, David's head lifts and his eyes flutter open. His gaze lingers on her face as he studies her features. He is trying to recall her as his soft eyes and brow crinkle around the edges.

"Emma, are you ok? What are you doing here?" His voice is distant and groggy. Emma is awash from the wave of relief flowing through her. His hand releases her as it moves to his chest, feeling the tacky blood. His shirt has a small tear just above his heart. He looks around in dark confusion, his glance shifting from Emma to Bastian and back again. "I think I died."

"You did." Emma's voice flutters in her throat. "Bastian turned you to save your life." David turns to stare at Bastian.

"Well that's…interesting." His tone is resolute, his breath deep and rhythmic. Emma can only imagine that his feelings are mirroring her own. She is heartbroken at what he has been turned into, but overjoyed that he is still here.

"It'll be alright," Emma says, to herself as much as anyone else. "We'll figure it out once we get out of here. Where is Mei Li? Any sign of Olivia?"

"They took Mei Li away before locking us in here. We never found Olivia," Bastian answers as he struggles against his bonds.

"I have to warn her about Tatiana. She's working with Thanatos." Emma's visions spin as she tries to stand. She closes her eyes, leaning her head against the cool bars, endeavoring to stop the sensation.

"We know that she is." David's tenor is bitterly harsh, a deathly cold look of malice glinting in his eyes. "I remember she's the one that stabbed me." Again his hand touches the torn fabric of his shirt.

"We need to find Mei Li and Olivia and get out of this place," Emma mutters in frustration as she leans against the bars. Her mind works feverously against the problem, but no solutions are available.

Two solid metal doors swing open at the end of the long corridor. A pair of Gyges enter the hall, and Emma must squint her eyes to see if she recognizes them. She cannot place their faces, but from behind them there is no mistaking Moss's lumbering height and Tatiana's silver hair and crimson gown. The unlikely couple walks leisurely, side-by-side down the aisle of cells as they are flanked by the two escorts. The rattle of keys and clapping of boots precedes them, echoing the terrified thrum of Emma's heart.

As they near, Emma can see the deep bruising of Moss's face has healed to a swirling mass of purples and brown. Tatiana's dress is clean, her face and hair immaculate once again. She glares at them with an odd mixture of contempt and arrogance.

"Thanatos wishes to speak with you," Tatiana announces formally. The two guards open the door to Emma's cell. "Your cooperation is appreciated, so let's not make this any harder than it need be."

The two henchmen roughly grab Emma by the arms, hauling her away toward the door. David lurches upward to stand, his own legs wobbly beneath him. He clasps the crossbars that separate the two cells, supporting his weight as he fruitlessly yanks on the unyielding metal. A low snarl rumbles from him as he lasers the invading group with his eyes. Spittle marks the corners of his mouth.

"Shut the hell up," Moss bellows at David. "I have no problem coming over there and staking both of your asses." He glares at them in return. David slams against the walls of his enclosure, reaching out wildly in an attempt to grab his tormentor. Moss slowly approaches the barrier, yet remains outside of David's grasp. Emma's eyes lock with David's as she is ushered out of the room. "I wouldn't worry too much," Moss taunts. "You'll follow her to the grave soon enough."

Emma's stomach churns, and she struggles to keep eye contact with David as long as she can. The closing iron doors block out her last vision of David. With sluggish legs, Emma is pulled along as they follow Tatiana down the winding hallways. Moss shadows them as they all walk in a silent procession. Tatiana slows her pace so that she strides alongside Emma. The guard in between them releases his hold of Emma's arm and takes up a point position ahead of them.

"I must say that I am a little disappointed that Bastian chose to infect David with his sickness. It would have been far more merciful to allow death to claim him. My goal was for that stupid wretch of a man to die, but even I lack the cruelty of turning him into such. Though to be honest I had not foreseen that the vampire would try and turn him." Tatiana picks at some dried blood still clinging to the sleeve of her dress. "I guess perhaps it is for the best. In a short time both of you will be dead, and I don't believe that your partnership could survive his affliction anyway," Tatiana purrs with an arched eyebrow. "But could you imagine it? How ironic it would have been? If your Gyges became a vampire, the one thing you cannot tolerate in this world."

"There are things in the world that I find less tolerable than a vampire," Emma states bitterly.

"And what are those?" Tatiana chuckles softly as her pearly white teeth gleam under the muted lights of the hall.

"What I find more distasteful is when someone's soul reeks from deception and betrayal." Emma keeps her tone calm even as the smile slips from Tatiana's countenance.

"You think I have deceived and betrayed you? Perhaps in your narrowed view it would look that way. But what you do not see is that what I have done is to save millions of lives and their souls," Tatiana states coldly, the chill of her voice vibrating through the air.

"I highly doubt that you have done all of this for the betterment of others," Emma mocks, keeping her gaze forward, unwilling to look at Tatiana as her rich laughter echoes around them.

"Believe what you will, Emma, but it's true. Once Thanatos and I take the throne of Hades we will be able to, with the aid of the Fury, bring order to a world ripe with chaos."

"And you think that you can trust Thanatos?" Emma asks as she laughs cynically. "He will use you just as he uses everyone. And when he no longer has a need for you, he'll discard you as well. You are simply a tool for him."

Tatiana halts them as she clasps Emma's free arm.

"I trust him implicitly. He is my king, and I am his queen, and we will rule the world together," she snaps at Emma through clenched teeth. Emma notes a look of uncertainty that flashes through Tatiana's eyes.

"Celia said the same thing. He will betray you as he has betrayed others," Emma counters coolly. Tatiana releases Emma's arm and smoothes her gown.

"I understand betrayal as well as anyone. I was the youngest of six daughters, and my family, while wealthy and noble, refused to pay a sufficient dowry for my hand. For several years I was shuffled from one cloistered nunnery to another. Thankfully there was nothing within my nature that would allow me to subjugate myself to the three monastic vows of chastity, poverty, and obedience. While at the convent I became with child and was given an herbal tea made from pennyroyal leaves to alleviate my malady. The Abbess felt it was better to avoid a salacious scandal." Tatiana's eyes glisten as her unwavering stare petrifies Emma.

"They gave you the tea to induce a miscarriage?" Emma whispers hoarsely, her throat compressing sharply."

"Yes. And afterward I was sent to live with my great aunt, who was a countess in Hungary. Little did I know that my distant relative was a vile sadist. She kept evil and unnatural pacts with the cruelest of monsters. It was there in that isolated castle, after weeks of torture, that the countess and a bloodsucking leech took my life," Tatiana spits as her body trembles with unchecked rage.

"You were killed by a vampire?" Emma asks as she puzzles the meaning together. The hairs on the back of her neck tingle rigidly at attention.

"It matters not now. But when we are done there will be no more monsters left." Tatiana brushes the memories away as she breaks her gaze from Emma and peers down the long corridor. "We have dallied far too long. Come, Thanatos is waiting for us." On cue, the guard tugs on Emma's arm as they continue to follow Tatiana. They stop at the last door in the hallway, and Emma fights a rise of claustrophobic panic.

Chapter 28

Moss strides past them as the others wait for him to open the solid timbered door. Tentatively he knocks against the smooth surface and lingers, listening for an unseen response. With a low creak Moss opens the door, peeking his head into the room. The two voices are low and muddled, making it impossible for Emma to make out the words. After a curt bow, Moss steps back from the doorway, his large hand pushing it open, granting them admittance.

A perplexingly unsettled feeling washes over Emma as she is gently escorted into the chamber. The men surrounding her glance cautiously amongst themselves. They appear unwilling to look about the room itself. Perhaps it is the inhabitant of the room that they are afraid to catch sight of? Emma takes in her surroundings in a series of rapidly darting glances, never allowing her gaze to settle on one area for too long. The room is simple in nature. A soft but worn looking bed sits against the far wall, draped in a plain cotton quilt. A bureau stands silently next to it, several small knickknacks cluttering the top. Few things in the tiny space seem to be of any value save for an intricately carved liquor cabinet. A host of memories come flooding in as Emma realizes that this was Mother Agnes's living quarters.

Thanatos sits behind a basic writing desk as he absentmindedly thumbs through a ragged, dusty tome. When they enter the room his gaze lifts, and he watches them grimly. Silently the two Gyges leave, shutting the door behind them with a soft and unsettling click.

"Emma, would you care to sit?" he asks, motioning to a chair just on the other side of his desk.

"Thank you, but I would prefer to stand." Emma struggles to calm her nerves. She inhales deeply. Keeping her senses alert, Emma scans the room again for anything to aid her.

"Mother Agnes was an interesting woman, wouldn't you say?" Emma's gaze snaps back to Thanatos at his mention of the deceased Mother. "She kept all that bric-a-brac from her past." He motions toward her bureau. "Such a poor soul, she was haunted by the past and tormented by the future. Perhaps that's why she drank so much." He falls silent as he swirls the glass of brandy in his hand and watches the warm amber liquid churn within the crystal.

"Is that why you killed her?" Emma poses cautiously. "An act of mercy? Or were you looking to raid her liquor cabinet?" Thanatos sets down his glass and closes the book before him with a loud, jarring thwack. A soft sigh escapes him as he studies her.

"In part, perhaps, yes to both. Agnes's gift was a blessing and a curse, but it could have proven troublesome to my objectives." Leaning against the writing table with nonchalance, he holds the snifter of brandy loosely.

"And what goals are those?" Emma inquires, suddenly jerking as he launches the snifter against the wall in one fluid motion. She recalls watching him spar with Moss and how deadly he can be.

"For eons I have been forced to sit by and watch as Hades ruled what is rightfully mine. He polluted the Underworld with his perversions, undermining its true intent. I am the Lord of Death, and I have been relegated to a ghost under the bed and a fool. But no more. With the Fury by my side I will retake my birthright. The people will once again have a fear and awe for death. My judgment will sway their lives, sculpting them into better beings. There will be peace on Earth, or there will be a fierce atonement." His body shakes with a harsh rage. Looking downward and closing his eyes, he breathes deeply, centering himself. Within seconds his whole character is once again one of tranquil calm. His head quizzically cocks at an angle as he scrutinizes her.

"Interesting. One would never know, would they?" he muses to himself. Upon seeing Emma's confused expression, he continues. "You have no energy signature. No power that radiates from you. It's as if you are nothing more than a mere human."

"Take this collar off and I'll show you a mere human," Emma snaps, her own anger spiking. The metal heats against her skin, searing a path along her neck as it works to restrain her. Thanatos chuckles at her in response.

"The question is, how did you do it?" he asks as he folds his arms over his chest, the shoulders of his t-shirt straining against the flex of sinewy muscles.

"Do what?" Emma asks, her pulse beating at a frenzied pace.

"How, with your apparent lack of strength, did you manage to best Celia and two of her guards? How did you do it?" he asks pointedly. His unwavering stare is quite intimidating, and Emma finds herself shifting anxiously.

"Well, the practical mechanics are quite simple. I had a number of years on Celia, and I practiced my swordplay quite regularly. Celia did not." Thanatos takes several steps forward, closing the gap between them. Only Emma's resolve to stand firm and the closed door behind her keep her from bolting.

"The Fury have lacked the ability to judge one another for millennia. Yet, Tatiana says that you judged her. Is this true?" The play of fascination and apprehension roam across his features. Emma can sense the intent behind his questions, what he really wants to know. But she is determined to withhold what really happened with Celia.

Her only option is to stall for as long as possible. But she also knows that short of being saved by divine intervention, her luck will eventually run out. Until then she will need to choose her words carefully.

"Tatiana has no love for me. This is known by everyone. But I am not sure why she would tell you that." Emma's insides roar, yet she keeps her tone impassive. Thanatos reaches out with blinding speed as his open palm collides with Emma's cheek, the hard impact slamming her back into the door as blood coats her tongue. His breathing is tattered as a searing anger bubbles to the surface.

"Do not for a second believe that you can lie to me," Thanatos barks as he jabs his finger at her. Emma's mind whirls and races, knowing that once the first blow is delivered it becomes a physical game. With the collar clamped on her she can only rely on her own bodily strength. And against Thanatos it wouldn't be enough. He would probably beat her until she told him what he wanted, or until there was nothing left of her. Either way she would still end up dying. Although, there is a small part of her that wants to tell him that she knows. She may be able to gain some leverage over the situation. She is someone who knows, if not for a short time, what he and Celia have done. Thanatos's nostrils flare as he battles to regain control. He inhales sharply and focuses his stare at her once again. "Did you judge her?" His tone is almost parental and lecturing.

"Yes," Emma says coldly through a partially numb mouth.

"And what did you see?" he asks, taking another step forward. This time she tries to step away but is stymied by the door. The brandy-perfumed aroma of his breath dances along her skin.

"After she killed Sara I saw everything that she had done. I saw her killing her own children for her own desires, and I saw her death." A rise of emotion chokes Emma as the vivid memories return.

"What else did you see?" There is a lilt to his deep voice as if his interest is piqued. Something dark and troubling pulses within his eyes. His gaze wonders to her mouth as his fingers gently touch her swollen cheek. "Did you see me?" he asks in a rich whisper. Emma jerks her head away from his hand as a wicked smile lifts at his lips.

"What do you want?" Emma asks.

"I need your blood." he states plainly. His demeanor appears more at ease, but he still blocks her against the door with his body. "I do not know how much I will need, though, and unfortunately, I may even need your life."

"To control the Fury, to what end?" she questions, hugging her chest against the chill racing through her.

"I need your blood to awaken the Three. They will be the living embodiment of the original three goddesses.

Unfortunately, with all of the other Fury dead, your blood must be used. I have a strong suspicion, though, that I may not need to kill you," he says with a confusingly optimistic look in his eyes.

"Why kill all of the others then?" Emma starts to ask but is shocked into silence as a realization washes over her. "You were behind the succubus and me being sent to Erebus." She is appalled, her voice catching in her throat.

"Yes. I needed to keep you and Sara safe while the remaining Fury were cleared out. You both are important elements in Olivia's life, keeping her grounded. Controlling the two of you would provide leverage for making her more malleable. With Tatiana and Olivia on board there will be no difficulty getting Mei Li to toe the line," he states matter-of-factly.

"So you knew from the beginning that Mei Li, Tatiana, and Olivia are the Fury to be reborn? What part did Celia play in all of this? At some point she would have realized that she was not equal to the rest, that she would never be one of your goddesses," Emma asks as she presses her back sharply into the door, wishing she could pass right through it and escape.

"Celia had a useful talent for collecting souls, and she was a mildly interesting distraction for a time. What she thought our arrangement was beyond that was no concern of mine." He shrugs his shoulders apathetically.

"And what if you are wrong about the identity of one of the three? With all the other Fury dead, you could have killed one of them in error." A moment of uncertain hesitation flashes through his eyes. But he shakes his head slowly at her.

"As soon as the first three sisters fell I went to an oracle deep within the mountains. I was shown in a vision who these women would be. The first would be an Asian flower drowned in the arms of a river spirit, the second would be an untouchable force falling from the sky in a new world, and finally, the third is a dark wood vestal, rich in purity, slain by an offspring of Empusa, the mother of vampires. Mei Li and Olivia are obvious," he finishes resolutely.

"You seem less certain about Tatiana. Those clues are ambiguous at best, and your murder squad could very well have killed the real one." Emma's voice is a squeaking whisper.

"I guess we will see after the awakening," Thanatos notes as he inches forward.

"So is this the part where you kill me and fill a jar with my blood? Are you going to kill me in the same room you killed Mother Agnes?" She shifts, trying to strafe away to the right. But he plants his hand against the wall, halting her escape.

"No, I need you to be there. I need you to see." Pinning her body against the door, he cups her face with his free hand, his thumb grazing her skin. Emma pushes against the weight of him, but he doesn't budge. "It's amazing you don't look like her, but you remind me of her –my Megaera." His voice vibrates through her as the solid length of his form pushes her into the door. In a flash of movement his mouth is on hers. Panic, terror, and rage roll through her as she claws against his grasp. Kicking and pushing are fruitless within her confined space. The copper bands encircling her arms and neck sizzle as she unsuccessfully attempts to draw on some of her power. Snatching his bottom lip, Emma bites down hard until she tastes his blood. He jerks his head back, yet still pins her with his body, running his tongue across the bloody wound as a devious smile etches his face. He launches himself forward again, burying his face in her neck, licking and biting her skin with a bruising force. Pulling her roughly into him, he paws and palms at her breasts. Emma cringes at the pain as tears burn her eyes. She strikes at him, but with no effect. The sound of ripping fabric skyrockets the adrenaline surging through her.

A loud rapping at the door breaks through the silence and her hysteria. By the third set of knocks, Thanatos pulls his head away from Emma, his lips swollen and smeared with his own blood. With a hand clasping her throat, he holds her against the door.

"What is it?" he barks, his breath coming in deep pants. From the other side of the door, Moss's voice rings out. "All is prepared My Lord. We should hurry if we are to catch the moon at its highest." Thanatos sighs as he sucks on his raw lip.

"One moment," he shouts to Moss. Turning his gaze back to Emma, he studies her again for several seconds. Capturing her face in his hands, he leans in again. Although this time the kiss is chaste and brief. "Perhaps if you survive this evening we can revisit our conversation."

Pulling Emma away from the door, Thanatos swings it open. Moss stares wordlessly at them, awaiting direction. Thanatos pushes Emma quickly into Moss's hands. "Have her prepared, I will join you shortly," he orders, and shuts the door, leaving her alone in the hallway with Moss.

Chapter 29

Without a sound, Moss leads Emma through the far-reaching and interwoven network of tunnels inside The Hallow. He is a granite colossus ferrying her to her impending death. Intermittent tremors still wrack her body as they walk. The truly dismal outlook of her situation has sapped her will to fight. The weight of her circumstances seems enormous as it presses down on her from all sides. Every purpose and principal that she has fought for seems meaningless in the end. The small spark of hope she has remaining is overcome by the dark clouds of despair.

Traversing an underground cavern, they exit the cave into a narrow valley. The gorge spans no more than eight feet across as the solid stone walls reach perilously upward. A clear starlit sky shimmers overhead. Despite the picturesque view of snow-draped trees, the area within the crevasse is temperate. Silence permeates the passage, giving their journey an eerily surreal feeling. Toward the opposite end, the mouth of the gorge opens into a cleared circular space which is still enclosed by a granite barricade.

The interior circumference of the ring is well lit by torches and braziers. The ground is hard-packed dirt with no signs of vegetation. The snow-kissed top of trees peek out over the wall, but all life within has been scourged away. A smaller ring of torches, inside the first, encloses a marbled area. A rust-colored terra cotta pillar in the center is displayed as it holds a deep basin of the same material. A stone altar stands next to the pillar. Flickering candles illuminate the blood-stained, rough surface. An impossibly white moon hangs low, stealing the vastness of the night sky.

Moss clutches Emma's arm tightly as he drags her further into the area through two mammoth wooden doors. Emma realizes that this area is not a physical earth bound location. It lies between the worlds, both outside and within at the same time. Only ones with a capacity for traversing dimensions or from within The Hallow could get here. Emma's stomach falls as she catches sight of Mei Li and Olivia chained to adjacent walls, the copper of their restraints gleaming under the torch light. Their features are marred by numerous fading bruises as they lean weakly against the walls. Stoically the two Fury scan their surroundings as they struggle against their bonds. Two guards are partnered as they stand on either side of each Fury. A third set of guards stand near Bastian, who is shackled to the stone wall as well. His head lists forward, his freshly blood-spattered hair shielding his face. She searches the area, but David is nowhere to be seen. Silently, she counts the guards. Seven including Moss.

Emma is led over to the pedestal. The thick slab of marble is surprisingly warm under her bare feet. A long chain of copper is snaked through a metal loop embedded into the stone, and the ends are shackled to her wrists and ankles. The chain is left short, as to make it nearly impossible for her to stand erect. The additional layer of banded copper pressing against her skin heats as it draws power away from her. Exhaustion coupled with the additional copper tries to steal her consciousness. Emma leans against the basin to support herself as her knees threaten to give way, a cyclone of blackness swirling around the edge of her vision. The loud thrum of her pounding heart and a growing pressure in her head deafens her ears. Moss clasps onto her more tightly, holding her up and in place.

The already hushed group fall into utter silence as Thanatos enters. He walks at a brisk pace as Tatiana struggles to keep up with him. She bunches the hem of her dark blue satin gown as she avoids the open flames dancing around her. A small sack dangles from a rope on her hip. The steady jaunt of her movement sends the sack swaying back and forth. Tatiana halts outside the central circle of torches as Thanatos continues forward until he stops next to Moss. Thanatos motions with his hand, and two Gyges close the heavy doors. They lift and place a thick, timbered beam into slats, securely barring the exit. For several seconds Thanatos surveys the gathering, his cool, unyielding gaze noting every detail.

"For far too long the Fury have been mere shadows of their former selves, their truest potential lost and unrecognized. They wandered without purpose, without meaning. Unjustly, they cower in their damp, dark caves, relegated to punishing only the lowest of monstrosities in this world. From this night forward, the righteous justice of the Fury will be far reaching under their ever-watchful eyes. Both human and nonhuman alike will once again understand that their sins come at a price. After tonight, even the heavens will tremble for fear of the Fury's wrath. After tonight, rivers of blood will flow as every wretched living thing on Earth is judged." Thanatos's voice resonates through the open space.

Tatiana crosses the small gap between them, coming up to stand next to Thanatos. Her hands tremble slightly as she retrieves a blood-stained muslin bundle. Inside the wrap is a large section of flesh with small tufts of fur sprouting from it. She gently places the werewolf pelt and a small vial of blood on the masonry altar behind her. Twisting, she retrieves the shimmering blue sphere from her bag, clasping it tightly to her breast. A scratching sound tickles at Emma's ears. The frail whisper of voices emanates from within the globe as their lights dance excitedly about the container. Emma struggles fruitlessly against her bonds and Moss's talon-like grip as she tries to swing and kick at Tatiana. The silver-haired woman stands outside of her reach, a wickedly self-righteous smile gracing her face.

Moss tightens his grasp on Emma's arms as he pushes them over the basin. Thanatos brandishes a thin copper dagger, the warmth of its golden hue reflecting outward.

Emma tries to pull her arms away from the bowl and from Moss, but her muscles scream at her, protesting their lack of strength. Mei Li and Olivia can be heard screaming wordlessly. All sound gets blotted out as the cool metal slices through the skin of Emma's arm. Her face blazes with heat as the blood flows freely down her arms and into the offering plate. Thanatos has cut a major vein, as thick splatters of blood fill the bowl. Emma continues to fight, hoping that the blood will make her skin slick and harder to grasp. Though the blood loss is draining her strength, she shrieks in anger and frustration.

When the bowl is several inches deep, filled with Emma's blood, Thanatos motions to Tatiana as Moss steps away with Emma. While the wounds ache, the blood flow has already started to clot and wane. Thanatos takes the orb from Tatiana and begins reciting an ancient incantation. It is a thick, guttural language that Emma has never heard before and can't understand. All eyes are trained intensely on him as he lowers the sphere into the pool of blood. Thanatos peers sternly into the murky blood for several seconds and watches for any sort of alteration.

Nothing changes. There are neither loud noises nor lightning. Emma glances around, seeing nothing new. As her eyes fall back onto Thanatos she realizes he is watching her. Panic flares in her chest at the miserable and poignant look in his eyes. It seems to herald a darkly ominous warning. His gaze shifts to Moss, and the larger man pulls

Emma back over to the pedestal, pushing her over and yanking her hair so that her neck is held directly over the bowl. Emma's breath comes in deep ragged pants. Right now she wants to be brave and say that she doesn't fear death, but she knows that is a lie. Thanatos begins his incantation again as he angles the blade against Emma's throat. His words are more incensed and vehement in their tone, every syllable a punctuated bark. A power flows through his voice, filling the confined space with a crackle of energy. A once small ache in Emma's chest starts to intensify at an alarming rate— so much so that she has a thought that her heart may burst. Waves of agony pulse from her chest.

From her vantage point, Emma watches as the blood in the bowl begins to bubble. As the fluid moves more rapidly it laps up and over the sides of the orb, slowly covering it. The bubbling concoction itself roils and stews as bursts of light manifest within it. Moss backs away from the cauldron, allowing Emma to retreat. She manages a step backward before she collapses, her legs trapped underneath her. The dagger in Thanatos's hand falls to the ground with a brash clatter. Emma is certain they should all run, as the vigorous energy jumbling around can only result in an explosion. As soon as the thought of running enters her mind, the blast shoots up and outward. Like a volcano erupting, the bowl spews forth a glowing serpentine mass of lights. The white illumination flies and shimmers about the sky as it dances around and throughout the lit torches.

Slowing, it begins to coil around and within itself. The cluster of iridescent souls has amassed into a thunderous cloud, hovering just above them all.

The swirling collection shifts and moves, thinning in some areas while others grow in size until it has transformed into three separate portions. Each cloud writhes and pulses with its own life, dipping and diving about the area. Emma can only watch in terror as the first mass spins and careens into Mei Li. As it contacts her, it melts into her as it is absorbed into her flesh, her body becoming rigid against the impact. The second cloud darts straight toward Olivia. She screams just as the ball of light smashes into her. As with the first, it is absorbed into Olivia's torso. The last and remaining entity darts and zips wildly around the enclosure. Then like an illuminated weight of a pendulum, it swings in long arcs, bisecting the open space. *Perhaps the third Fury is dead?* Emma ponders to herself. Then turning sharply, it swerves violently toward Emma, engulfing her field of vision as it slams into her, pushing her to the ground. Her wind is chased away as the sensation of a nuclear blast incinerates every cell in her body. Her throat seizes from the feeling as a soundless scream rips from her. Something deep within her bursts as the shattering energy pulses.

From somewhere in the distance, Emma vaguely notes two other screams chorusing along with hers. Acid-like blood boils in her veins. A pressure builds from within as her heart hammers toward catastrophic failure. In a unified shriek, their three bodies expel the collection of souls into the night sky. Beams of light fling from their chests, aimed directly upward. The train of spirits is not hindered by the barrier of this world as it pushes past the rim of the stone wall and continues on. She is almost vaguely aware of its departure, but the fluid spark of it still remains inside of her.

Emma's head lists weakly as she looks around and tries to gather herself. Tatiana sneers at her aghast as pure hatred etches into her refined features. Screaming wordlessly, she snatches the dagger from the ground next to Thanatos. The overhead swing is aimed directly for Emma's heart, but she manages to weakly roll out of the way. Tatiana rears back to strike again as Thanatos quickly catches her wrist. She looks up meekly, staring at Thanatos as she begins to sob.

"But you said I was the third," she blubbers as she clutches his hand.

"I know. At first I thought you were as well," he coos softly to her. There is something almost liken to a real emotion lingering behind his eyes.

"My Lord," she stammers, and gasps as the knife slides in between her ribs. She looks in shock from the blade lodged in her chest back to Thanatos. "I loved you," she wheezes, coughing up bubbling blood.

"I know you thought you did," he soothes sympathetically. Twisting the buried dagger, Tatiana falls in a heap to the ground. As Emma stares at the dead Mother she becomes aware of the etched surface of the marble slab. Tatiana's body partially covers a series of interlocking triangles that have been carved into the stone. The whole area is a ritual site, and the aura of death floods around them.

Thanatos looms over the dead body. Wide ribbons of blood flow and channel into the scored marks engraved in the stone. Thanatos's movements are hurried as he gathers the pelt and blood. On the most central triangle he places the pelt and pours the vial of blood over it. From his back pocket he retrieves a small string-tied bag. The black powder contained inside is sprinkled over the heap. Emma detects the odor of sulfur, and when Thanatos touches a match to the mound it ignites, giving off a pale blue glow. Taking the dagger, he slices into his thumb, allowing the drops to fall into the flame. In a soft, low whisper he begins the rhythmic canter of his chant.

A sudden crack of splintering wood fills the air. The heavy doors shake and bow as a large force acts on it from the other side. Again, an eminent pressure hits and the wood warps and creaks. The sturdy timber barring the doors cracks and falls away as a rush of bodies funnel into the area.

Monstrously huge wolves vault in as they are followed by Poe and several vampires. Aidan trails them as well. He brandishes a baseball bat, and running across the threshold swings it wildly as he charges a Gyges. A collective cry rings out as the two groups meet head on. Teeth and claws rip and tear flesh. Others are skewered and hacked with blades. As the guards fall the liberators begin releasing prisoners. First Bastian, then Mei Li, then Olivia. All of them seem to shake off their fatigue rapidly and jump into the melee. Emma's heart leaps as she spies David amid the fray. His eyes meet hers and he turns sharply, heading past several others to reach her.

Her heart soars at his approach, elated as hope reawakens from deep within. His very real form kneels before her as he tries to make quick work of the copper chain holding her. David mutters and swears to himself as the links of chain entangling her right foot seem especially stubborn. Tears gloss her eyes while she watches him. The moment is surreal and joyous.

A metallic copper clink rings out as the chain falls away, and David stares intensely at her. As his mouth opens to speak, a black boot connects squarely with his chin. His body lurches backward, sliding over the blood and marble. Thanatos follows. His machete slices the air at a frenzied pace, and David scrambles to stay out of the way. Emma stands slowly, her traitorous legs wobbling beneath her as she wills them to move. She focuses her mind, watching for an opening to help David.

The right hook of Moss comes out of nowhere, crashing into Emma's temple. The world turns black for a moment, and then she is sprawled on the ground as Moss stalks toward her, a copper blade in his hand. Emma fights with a length of her gown as she scurries backward trying to get to her feet. With pure malice and rage, Moss tracks her movements, closing the distance between them. Her heart races as the havoc plays out around her. She catches brief glimpses of the others slowly cutting down Thanatos's guards. David smashes Thanatos's wrist on the ground, forcing him to drop the machete. Both men are battered and bruised as they wrestle for position.

Emma rolls out of the way just as Moss reaches out, trying to snatch her. He arcs the blade toward her roll and catches the skin of her shoulder. Blood streams from the gash. Moss moves quickly, standing on a bunched-up portion of her skirt. Not enough to trap her, but it slows her movement. Emma kicks upward violently, catching Moss's wrist and sending the knife flying from his grasp. The fabric rips as she pushes to her feet. Before she can gain her footing; Moss lunges at her, his sheer weight pushing her back down. The impact knocks the wind out of her as his hands tighten around her throat. He pins her to the ground as she claws at his wrists and face. The evil glint in his eyes is unbearable, and the peripheral of her vision morphs into a grey fog. Instantly, Moss's body goes rigid as the loud thwack of something wooden makes contact with his skull. Limply he teeters and falls away from Emma. Olivia stares fiercely at the disoriented man, a blood-soaked baseball bat in her hands.

Moss groggily lurches to his feet, blood trickling from his hair and down his temple. From a sheath on his hip he pulls out a long bowie knife. It is not made of copper, but its steel edge is razor sharp.

"I'll peel you like an orange," Moss taunts as spittle flies from his mouth.

"Bring it, dumbass," Olivia barks as she motions him forward. Moss lunges in and out, striking at her several times. Olivia dodges or deflects each hit with her bat in hand. He rushes at her, attempting to bypass her defense, but she steps to the side and brings the bat down fiercely across his back. Moss howls as he whips around, eyes burning with hatred. "You can't win this one, Moss, just give up," Olivia informs him calmly. With a steadfast determination he runs straight at her, swinging violently. One slice gets through, nicking her cheek. Spotting her opening, Olivia thrusts the bat straight forward, driving it into Moss's solar plexus. With a whoosh the air rushes out of him, doubling him over. Olivia steps to his side and strikes the bat hard against his head. His knees sag and he falls to the ground. She swings again, bouncing the weapon off his thick cranium. Olivia watches him breathe weakly for several seconds before allowing herself to look away.

Olivia rushes to Emma, checking her for any significant wounds.

"Are you all right?" Olivia asks as she tears off the bottom of her dress and applies pressure to a deep cut on Emma's arm.

"I think I'll be alright," Emma replies as Olivia helps her to stand, her gaze feverishly scanning for David.

She finds that he is still battling Thanatos. Both men appear exhausted. David clutches his ribs as blood trickles from his nose, and he inhales deeply trying to catch his breath. Mei Li launches herself at Thanatos, landing a kick squarely in his back. Thanatos stumbles but keeps his footing as he spins around. He strides towards her, covered in sweat and blood, a cold malevolence burning brightly in his eyes. Thanatos unleashes a barrage of strikes at her, several of which she deftly dodges, but a few connect, sending her staggering back.

Bastian jumps in and attacks, his assault sending Thanatos reeling backwards. Mei Li assails in unison, leaping onto Thanatos's back. Her legs interlock around his waist as she uses her forearms to squeeze his neck. Thanatos jerks and bucks, trying to dislodge Mei Li.

"Do it now, Bastian," Mei Li screams at him. Bastian hesitates for a moment, looking uncertain. "Now!" Mei Li bellows.

Bastian retrieves a small plastic pistol-like device and carefully approaches Thanatos, who is still trying to free himself. He grunts and rages as Bastian takes aim and fires, sending two metal probes shooting out which embed into Thanatos's skin. A current of electricity is sent coursing through him. Thanatos howls violently as his body constricts and he and Mei Li collapse to the ground.

Bastian and Olivia sprint over to Mei Li. Emma's body is still slow to respond, but she makes her way to the group. When she arrives, Mei Li is being helped to her feet and she appears unharmed. Emma sighs in relief as David wraps his arms around her.

"Thank God, Emma, you are alright," David's voice quivers. Aidan, Bray, and the wolves shackle the Gyges that are still alive, as well as Thanatos.

"Where did you get a Tazer?" Olivia asks, her eyebrows crinkling in awe.

"I always have one on me. You can never be too careful. They didn't search me well enough to find it, and that was their mistake." Bastian's eyes gleam as he answers, a sly and bloodied grin lifting at his lips.

"What do you want done with them?" Bray asks, motioning to their captives. Thanatos is disheveled and coated in sweat and dirt. He laughs to himself as he is pulled from the ground and his hands are bound in front of him.

"What's so funny?" Olivia asks, her anger tightly leashed as she steps closer.

"I just find it amusing that I could be bested by the lot of you." He chuckles again.

"We defeated you," Olivia corrects him with a smile of her own.

"Only a fool believes that he or she can truly defeat death." His own face takes on a stern expression.

"Brave talk from someone in shackles," Olivia bites back.

"Yes and ten minutes ago you were wearing the shackles, and you may be again in the near future." The corners of his lips lift as he studies them. "But nonetheless I did succeed in awakening the complete Fury strength within you. From this day forward your powers will be vastly stronger, and it is all thanks to me," he notes smugly.

"Yes, you increased our power, but it gains you nothing," Emma points out.

"But that is far from the truth. I have gained knowledge. I know your strengths and weaknesses. I know what your greatest fears are. Your power may come from the Fury, but you still are very much human. I also know that as

425

much as you may want to, you can't kill me. Not without risking the whole race of humans. So go ahead and lock me up for now, but Tartarus will not hold me forever. I'll get out, and one day it is you who will be coming to me for help. The original Fury were the puppets of Hades. They could not survive on their own without being directed and controlled. And how well do you think the three of you will fair?" Thanatos asks as his gaze shifts between each of the Fury. "How will you survive with no one there to lead you? Who will pilot you? Will it be Mei Li, the ancient hermit who never leaves The Hallow unless it is absolutely necessary? Surely it can't be Emma, as you and Mei Li will always view her as your lesser. So that only leaves you, Olivia. Can you garner enough courage to lead the other two? Or is it possible that your death has crippled you beyond repair. How long can you maintain the charade that you have it all under control?" His eyes burn as he taunts Olivia. Olivia launches herself toward Thanatos but is held back by Mei Li.

"You slimy, weasel-faced bastard!" Olivia screams over Mei Li's shoulder. "You have no idea what we are capable of, and you will rot in Tartarus forever," she spits. Olivia struggles to ease her frantic breathing.

"Who knows what the future may bring," Thanatos muses whimsically as he gazes up at the night sky. "It will be interesting to find out, and there are many things left to do."

His gaze flashes to Emma. "My dear, sweet, sweet Emma, who tastes sweeter than strawberries. Perhaps in the future we can finish the conversation we started." His confident smile returns as he winks at Emma. She closes the distance between them, swinging at him mid-stride, the knuckles of her hand making solid contact with his nose. Thanatos grunts as he staggers, the strike rocking him backward. A fountain of blood surges from his broken nose. Emma hovers over him, her fists clenched tightly.

"You'll never control me," she spits at him while several werewolves gather him up.

"Take them to Tartarus, the lowest level in Erebus. They should be secure there. We can figure out what to do with them later. Right now we just need to heal," Olivia tells them coolly. Bray studies her quietly for several seconds before nodding and walking away. Emma glimpses an uncommon display of nervousness from Olivia. Her eyes shift about, and she keeps touching the back of her neck as she watches the wolves leave.

Severe exhaustion overwhelms Emma. She can barely recall the long trek out of the ritual grounds. Few words are spoken, and even if they were Emma doubts she would hear them. With heavily burdened eyes, David helps her to her apartment door. A deep dreamless sleep claims her even before David places her in the bed.

Chapter 30

The few days that follow the events in The Hallow seemed to go by in a foggy haze. Emma recalls David bringing her home and helping her into bed. The passing time is a surreal blend of awake and dreaming. For nearly two days she slept, awoken only by David who'd come in to rouse her so that she could eat or drink. Sleep allows time for her body to heal. Bleeding stops, and wounds turn to thin scars. There is this constant and soothing thought that as long as David is with her she can rest without worry.

On the third day, her eyes open as the sun is low on the horizon. The apartment is empty with only a note from David saying that he will return tonight. After a long shower and some food, she sits by her bay window, watching as the night swallows the bright red hues of the fading sun. The tea is warm in her hands as the cold dusk presses at her window.

So much has changed in such a short period of time. The Fury have been whittled down to just three. Emma wonders what her position will be amongst them- does she even have a place? David's turning also brings on a whole host of other worries. Never in all of her experience has a vampire been allowed to be the guardian of a Fury. Then again, both Mei Li and Olivia lack a Gyges completely. Would they allow David to stay with her? If she is going to be honest with herself, she knows she will not survive long without David. She can't deny her feelings for him any longer, and he has become a vital part of her life.

A flash of movement catches her eye, and as she jumps up she spills some of her hot tea on her arms. In the growing darkness of the room, an elegant woman sits at the dining room table, watching her. Her crimson gown and dark blonde hair seem to shimmer under the fluorescent lighting. Even her eyes dance with a curious silver sparkle.

"Who are you and what do you want?" Emma asks, her burns forgotten. She scans the room, searching for any additional intruders. Emma can sense that the woman is ancient, but something about her feels vaguely familiar.

"You know, there was a time when I needed no introduction. Humans were wise enough to steer clear of a Fury, yet they always paid their proper respects. But alas times do change. My name is Megaera. You had counsel from my sister, Tisiphone. To be honest, I am here out of simple curiosity." Megaera stands, smoothing her dress as Emma steps backward. "Don't be silly. If I wanted you dead you would already be so," she snaps. She meanders about the room, looking at various items. But it is her nonchalant nature that unnerves Emma.

"What are you curious about?" Emma asks, her voice trembling as she fiercely clutches her tea cup.

"I had heard that you look like me. I wanted to see for myself if it was true." Megaera's tone is critical as she inspects Emma, her head tilting from side to side, her soft golden locks swooshing about her shoulders. "No, I don't see it. I can understand why Thanatos would be confused, but Tisiphone should know better. She's not blind after all." She clicks her tongue to herself. A frown creases her face sharply and she continues to study Emma. She recalls meeting one of the sisters while she was imprisoned in The Hallow, but this one seems nothing like her kin.

"You know Thanatos?" Emma poses, her pulse quickening as she skirts the outer wall of her living room, trying to keep a distance between them.

"Yes. I knew him quite well. Though it has been quite some time since we shared the pleasure of each other's company." A wicked smile touches her lips. Emma is confused, and her mind races. She tries to piece together Megaera's meaning. Megaera huffs in annoyance as she spies Emma's puzzled expression. "We were lovers, dear. But why they're called that I'll never know."

"Called what?" Emma guards her words, afraid to say much in front of her visitor. Megaera simply looks at her with derision.

"Why they call them lovers." Megaera emphasizes the last word before she continues. "Thanatos and I could never share love. I know that he fell victim to the emotion, but for myself it was simply a pleasurable way to pass the time. I don't think that he ever understood that I could never love him. Even if his little scheme had worked and he managed to revive us, I still won't love him. I do often wonder what it feels like," Megaera whispers, leaning her head toward Emma, a heady excitement in her voice.

"What feels like what?" Emma is starting to get frustrated with herself now. But complex thoughts escape her at this moment. She inhales deeply, calming down her pounding heart. Reason tells her to be patient, but her insides tell her to run.

"Why love, of course." Her silver eyes glitter as she speaks. "It is one of the few human emotions that we are unable to experience. Alecto said it is the greatest and worst of all human emotions. Perhaps that is why she is insane? At first being incapable of the emotion and now cursed to suffer from it for eternity." Megaera stares out the window silently for several seconds. Her gaze drifts back over to Emma. "I must leave you now. But don't worry, we will see each other again." Before Emma can form a response Megaera walks directly into and through the wall. Only green wisps of smoke remain, spiraling along the surface.

Emma stares dumbstruck at the wall for several seconds before registering the knock at her door. Quietly crossing the living room, Emma opens her front door. The security chain only allows limited visibility, but she clearly sees that Mei Li, Olivia, and David are by themselves.

"One moment," Emma says as she closes the door and slides the chain out of the way before reopening it. "Please come in." She addresses them all as she steps back to allow them entrance. The three enter, and David stands in the kitchen as Mei Li and Olivia take seats in the living room. Emma notes how well the two of them look, their cuts and bruises have healed completely. David leans against the counter his arms folded tightly over his chest. Emma can almost see the rage rolling off of him. Emma studies him briefly, but his expression gives nothing away. "Would you care for something to drink?" Emma asks nervously. Both Olivia and Mei Li shake their heads.

"No thanks. We only stopped by for a bit to see how you are doing." Olivia's tone is warm, yet her words seem rushed. A miniscule level of nervous energy flows from her.

"Thanatos has been sealed in Tartarus. The prison that holds the Titans should be able to secure him," Mei Li announces, her demeanor still structured, but less formal. "The remaining Gyges have been offered the position of guardians to ensure that no one escapes. We are really unsure as how to deal with Thanatos beyond that."

"My vote was to kill him," Olivia adds with a sideways glance to Mei Li.

"Killing him may be the worst thing to do. Because he is the Lord of Death we don't know what kind of ripple effect his death would have on the human world. For right now we have ordered that no harm come to him," Mei Li continues, brushing Olivia's comment off with a wave of her hand. "But that also brings into question of what our lives will be now. With it only being the three of us now, the initial guidelines and edicts that structured our existence may no longer apply."

"What do you mean?" Emma watches them suspiciously.

"It means we'll all have to shoulder the responsibility together. So some of the rules have to stay, and some have to go," Olivia interrupts.

"Our aim is still unchanged. We are to maintain order and balance, seeking justice for those who cannot gain it themselves". Mei Li glares at Olivia now, and Emma almost laughs.

"So where do we go from here?" Emma asks as she glances at both women.

"I think that going forward our duties should be impartial. I see no reason why we can't maintain order and keep our humanity intact. But as for right now, I say we address each issue as it is presented."

"So she's basically saying wait and see, take it as it comes," Olivia mocks with a lift of her eyebrow.

"Will you stop that?" Mei snaps in mild frustration as Olivia smiles widely in return. Obviously the Mother is still getting used to a democracy. Olivia and Mei Li's demeanor shift to somber as they return their attention to Emma.

"After some discussion we have come to the conclusion that the edict banning emotional attachments should stay intact. We are not sure what drove the original sisters insane, but we should do our best to avoid making the same mistakes. Keeping to the rules for now will hopefully allow us to stay focused and rational." Emma can only stare at them mouth a gap as they stand. "We should be heading out and let you rest." Emma follows them, finding her voice as her feet begin to move.

"I would think discussions involving the Fury should include all of us." Emma scrambles to catch up to them at the door. As Mei Li opens the door, Emma shoves it closed firmly with her hand. "For too long I was a simple puppet doing as you commanded me. Without a thought or care about my life or fate, time and again you threw me to the dogs because that was my duty. Well those days are gone. I have earned my say." Emma's hand cramps as she pushes firmly against the door. Both women watch her stoically, their features blank and steadfast.

"I do understand your dissatisfaction, Child. I think it would be unwise to make rash decisions. We will have many things to discuss once we are ready. But for now we will continue as we have, and you should rest." Mei Li tries to soothe her.

"No I really think that we should talk about this now," Emma urges as she battles the feeling of being locked out of the group.

"We'll discuss this later!" Mei Li barks at her. Her irritation quickly replaced by a cool serenity. Memories float into Emma's mind of the beatings and tortures that followed when a Fury disobeyed a Mother. Mei Li maybe a Fury, but she will always be a Mother.

Emma's hand falls away from the door. They step out into the hall, closing the door behind them. She knows this conversation is far from over, but she has a feeling that winning them to her side will be difficult.

Frustration eats away at her until she wants to rant and scream. She stomps back into the living room muttering to herself. *"If that woman calls me child again... I am a grown mother of two..."* She halts mid-sentence when she sees David standing casually in the kitchen. Emma's face warms as she stands silently watching him.

"So what will you do?" Emma asks timidly, afraid of what he will say.

"I will be staying with Bastian for the time being," he says with a long sigh as he briskly rubs his face in his hands.

"Why? How long will you stay with him?" She speaks softly as her throat squeezes shut painfully.

"Bastian saved my life, I owe him a blood debt which must be repaid. I also know nothing about what I am now. So I will stay with him as long as needed I guess. Hopefully I can learn what I need to from him. But that shouldn't matter, the Fury no longer have a need for Gyges," he states as he watches her with intense eyes, as if a thousand emotions lie trapped in their depths.

"But what if I still need you? Who will train with me?" Her voice is barely a whisper. She wishes she could summon the words to make him understand, to make him stay.

"Olivia can always spar with you. She'd make an exceptional partner- she's strong, well versed in combat styles, and patient." He stares out the window, his voice thick and low.

"I don't want Olivia, I want…you." Her voice cracks under the strain, and his eyes flash toward her.

They watch each other wordlessly for several seconds before David crosses the living space, collecting Emma in his arms. Emma breathes softly as he holds her. She can detect a slight shiver of nervous energy rumbling through him.

"I don't care what they say." His voice is a ragged breeze in her hair. She cranes her neck to look up at him, seeing his face so close to hers.

"What?" Is all that she can manage with a trembling voice. The look in his eyes sends her heartbeat racing. He leans forward, his mouth hovering millimeters from her ear.

"I refuse to lose you because I'm afraid of what you'll say. And my feelings scare the hell out of me, I love you." He breathes the words against her skin and her knees nearly buckle. She can feel the shaking travel through his limbs. Running her hands along his arms, Emma gently touches his cheeks. She can see the strange and unyielding fear in his eyes.

Lifting up on her toes, she can only manage the lightest touch as her lips meet his. With the smallest contact his whole body relaxes. He pulls her up to him, his mouth on hers. Her heart pounds as she tastes him. There is a sense of being whole with him as his hands and arms hold her tightly. He slowly pulls away from her, setting her feet back on the ground. They both are breathless, holding onto one another.

"I love you too," Emma murmurs through deliciously numb lips. He kisses her forehead softly as he pulls away, drifting into the living room. Emma's stomach drops as she realizes he is leaving.

"Don't worry, you're not getting rid of me that easily." He smiles arrogantly as he pulls on his jacket.

"Getting a little overconfident there aren't you?" Emma teases.

"Hell yeah. In fact, I knew you were going to tell me that you love me tonight." He laughs, an overtly certain look is in his eyes with one hand on the door knob.

"Oh really? And how is that?" Emma smiles and crosses her arms over her chest.

"Because you are the most interesting, irritating, kind, and beautiful woman I have ever met, but most importantly, I know you." His smile is powerful and contagious. Emma is warmed as she laughs.

Without another word he winks at her and closes the door, leaving her. Emma stares at her door quietly for several seconds, a hopeful ember glowing in her eyes and a smile on her face.

The End

Thank you for reading "Emma's Fury". If you enjoyed this book (or even if you didn't) please visit the site where you purchased it and write a brief review. Your feedback is important to me and will help other readers decide whether to read the book too.

CPSIA information can be obtained
at www.ICGtesting.com
Printed in the USA
BVHW031824150721
612065BV00011B/29